the manny

the manny

(man-ee) n: 1. a nanny of the male persuasion.

Holly Peterson

the dial press

THE MANNY

A Dial Press Book / June 2007

Published by The Dial Press
A Division of Random House, Inc.
New York, New York

Library of Congress Cataloging-in-Publication Data
Peterson, Holly.
The manny / Holly Peterson.
p. cm.
ISBN 978-0-385-34040-3 (hardcover)
1. Nannies—Fiction. 2. Male child care workers—Fiction. 3. Rich
people—Fiction. 4. Manhattan (New York, N.Y.)—Fiction.
I. Title.
PS3616.E8428M36 2007
813'.6—dc22
2006102945

Printed in the United States of America
Published simultaneously in Canada

www.dialpress.com

10 9 8 7 6 5 4 3 2 1
BVG

For Rick
My life source

the manny

1

Wheels Up!

If you want to see rich people act really rich, go to St. Henry's School for Boys at three p.m. on any weekday. *Nothing* makes rich people crazier than being around other rich people who might be richer than they are. Private school drop-off and pickup really gets them going. It's an opportunity to stake their claim, show their wares, and let the other parents know where they rank in the top .001 percent of the top .0001 percent.

A cavalcade of black SUVs, minivans, and chauffeured cars snaked its way up the block beside me as I ran to my son's after-school game. I'd skipped another meeting at work, but nothing was going to keep me that day. Gingko trees and limestone mansions lined the street where a crowd gathered in front of the school. I steeled myself and waded into a sea of parents: the dads in banker suits barking into their phones, the moms with their glamorous sunglasses and toned upper arms—many with dressed-up little darlings by their sides. These children play an important role in their parents' never-ending game of one-upmanship as they are trotted out in smocked dresses, shuttled from French tutor to cello class, and discussed like prize livestock at a 4-H fair.

Idling in front of the school, with his tinted rear window half open, a cosmetics giant read about himself in the gossip columns. By his side, his four-year-old little girl watched a *Barbie Fairytopia* DVD on the small screen that dropped down from the ceiling of the vehicle while he finished the article. The nanny, in a starched white uniform, waited patiently in the front seat for him to inform her it was time to go inside and pick up his son.

A few yards down the block, a three-and-a-half-inch green lizard heel was reaching for the sidewalk from the back of a fat silver Mercedes S600. The chauffeur flashed its yellow headlights at me. Next I saw a brown tweed skirt jacked up on a shapely thigh, ultimately revealing a thirty-something woman shaking out her honey-colored hair while her driver sprinted like a madman to get her arm.

"Jamie! Jamie!" called Ingrid Harris, waving her manicured hand. Dozens of chunky gold bangles jangled as they slid down her arm.

I tried to shield my eyes from the glare. "Ingrid. Please. I love you, but no. I've got to get to Dylan's game."

"I've been trying to reach you!"

I ducked into the crowd, knowing she would come after me.

"Jamie! Please! Wait!" Ingrid caught up to me, leaving her driver behind to contend with her two boys wailing in their car seats. She let out a huge breath as if the fifteen-foot walk from the Mercedes had taxed her. "Hooo!" Remember, this is a crowd that touches down on actual pavement as seldom as possible. "Thank God you were home last night."

"No problem. Anytime."

"Henry is so in debt to you," said Ingrid.

The burly chauffeur carried each of her younger boys in one graceful arc from their car seats to the curb, as if he were placing eggs in a basket.

"The four Ambien. Henry was going hunting with some clients for five days, it was wheels-up at ten p.m. to Argentina, and he was crazed!"

"Jamie." Next, a voice I loved. My friend Kathryn Fitzgerald. She commuted from Tribeca and she was wearing jeans and French sneakers. Like me, she wasn't one of those people who grew up on the Upper East Side and never touched a doorknob in their entire life. "Hurry. Let's plow up front."

As we started up the marble stairs, a white Cadillac Escalade pulled up to the curb. You could tell a hundred feet away that there were children of a major CEO inside. It came to a stop and the aristocratic driver, wearing a bowler hat like Oddjob, got out and walked around to open the door, and the four McAllister kids piled out of their SUV with four Philippina nannies—each holding a child's hand.

All four of the nannies were wearing white pants, white rubber-soled shoes, and matching Dora the Explorer nurse's shirts with little Band-Aids all over them. There were so many little children and nurses in their tight little pack that they looked like a centipede making its way up the steps.

At five minutes after three, the school opened and the parents politely but forcefully pushed each other to get in. Up four flights of stairs to the gym, I could hear echoes of young male voices and the screech of sneakers. St. Henry's fourth-grade team was already out practicing in their royal-blue and white uniforms. I quickly scanned the court for my Dylan, but didn't see him. The moms and dads from Dylan's school were beginning to gather on one side of the bleachers. Scattered among them were the team's siblings with their nannies, representing almost every country in the United Nations. No Dylan. I finally spotted him huddled on a bench near the locker room door. He was still dressed in his khakis and white button-down shirt with the collar undone. His blue blazer was draped on the bench beside him. When he saw me, he squinted and looked away. My husband, Phillip, summoned the exact same expression when he was angry and feeling put upon.

"Dylan! I'm here!"

"You're late, Mom."

"Sweetheart, I'm not late."

"Well, some of the moms got here before you."

"You know what? There's a line outside, four moms deep, and I can't cut the line. There's a lot of moms still coming up behind me."

"Whatever." He looked away.

"Honey. Where's your uniform?"

"In my backpack."

I could feel the waves of stubborn tension emanating from my son. I sat down next to him. "It's time to put it on."

"I don't want to wear my uniform."

Coach Robertson came over. "You know what?" He put his arms in the air, signaling his exasperation. "I'm not gonna force him into it every time. I told him he would miss the game, but I can't make him put the uniform on. If you wanna know the reality of the situation here, he's being ridiculous . . ."

"It's really not being ridiculous. Okay?" This guy was never in tune with Dylan. I brought the coach to the side. "We've all discussed this—Dylan's unease before a game. He's nine years old. It's his first year on a team." The coach didn't seem to be moved, and he took off. Then I put my arm around Dylan. "Honey. Coach Robertson isn't my favorite person, but he's right. It's time to put on the uniform."

"He's doesn't even like me."

"He likes all the boys the same, and even if he's tough, he just wants you to play."

"Well, I'm not gonna."

"Even for me?"

Dylan shook his head. He had big brown eyes and strong features, with thick dark hair that never fell just right. Dylan's mouth smiled more than his eyes ever did.

"Dylan! Hurry!" Douglas Wood, an obnoxious little kid with freckles, a crew cut, and a pudgy bottom, waddled over. "What's wrong with you, Dylan?"

"Nothing."

"Well, then how come you're not playing?"

"I am playing."

"Well, how come you don't have your uniform on?"

"Because my mom had to talk to me. It's her fault."

Coach Robertson, angry with Douglas for leaving the warm-up and with my son for his refusal to play at all, marched toward us, pumping his elbows. "Come on, kid. Time's up. Let's go." He picked up Dylan's backpack and pulled him by his hand toward the locker room. Dylan rolled his eyes back at me and lumbered along, dragging his uniform behind him on the floor. I headed for the bleachers with an ache in my heart.

Kathryn, who'd gone ahead to save me a seat in the bleachers, was now waving to me from the fifth row on the St. Henry's side. She had twin boys in Dylan's grade, as well as a daughter at our nursery school. Her twins, Louis and Nicky, were fighting over a ball, and Coach Robertson leaned down to whistle loudly into their ears to break it up. I watched Kathryn stand up to get a better look at their arguing, her long blond ponytail cascading down the back of her worn suede jacket. As I edged by twenty people to slip in next to her, she sat down and squeezed my knee.

"We made it just in time," she said, smiling.

"Tell me about it." I placed my tired head in the palms of my hands.

A few seconds later, the Wilmington Boys' School team burst through the gym doors like an invading army. I watched my tentative son hang back beside the other players. His sweaty teammates ran back and forth, all in their last fleeting years of boyhood before the gawky ravages of adolescence took hold. They rarely threw the ball to Dylan, mostly because he never made eye contact and always jogged along the periphery of the team, safe outside any commotion. His lanky build and knobby knees made his movements less than graceful, like a giraffe making short stops.

"Dylan's not playing well."

Kathryn looked at me. "None of them play well. Look at them; they can barely get the ball up into the hoop. They're not strong enough yet."

"Yeah, I guess. But he's down."

"Not *always* down. It's just sometimes," Kathryn answered.

Barbara Fisher turned around from the row in front of me. She was wearing tight jeans, a starched white blouse with the collar turned up against gravity, and an expensive-looking fuchsia cable-knit sweater. She was too tan and as thin as a Giacometti statue.

"Ohhh, here's the busy-bee-worky-worky-mom at a game."

I jerked back. "It means a lot to me to see my son." I looked over her head toward the boys.

Barbara moved over five inches to block my view and make another point. "We were talking at the school benefit meeting about how hard it must be for you, never being able to get involved in Dylan's activities."

She was so annoying.

"I like to work. But if you choose not to work outside the home, I can certainly understand. It's probably a more enjoyable lifestyle."

"You're not doing it for the money. *Obviously.* Phillip's such a heavy-hitter lawyer these days." She was whispering (she thought), but everyone around us could hear her. "I mean, you can't possibly be contributing much financially on a scale that *matters*."

I rolled my eyes at Kathryn. "I actually make a pretty good salary, Barbara. But, no, I'm not really working for the money. It's just something I like to do. Call it a competitive streak. And right now I need to concentrate on Dylan's game because he can be competitive too, and I'm sure he'd like me to watch him play."

"You do that."

Kathryn pinched my arm too hard because she hated Barbara more than I did. I jumped at the pain and smacked her on the shoulder.

She whispered into my ear, "Amazing Barbara didn't find a way to bring up the new plane. In case you missed the billboard, Aaron's Falcon 2000 jet finally got delivered this weekend."

"I'm sure I'll hear about it soon," I answered, staring out at the court. Dylan was now attempting to block a shot, but the player ran right around him toward the basket and scored. The whistle blew. Warm-up over. All the kids retreated to their sides in a huddle.

"You know what's so obnoxious?" Kathryn whispered to me.

"So many things."

"They can't just say, 'We're leaving at three for the weekend,' which would actually mean they are leaving at three in the afternoon by car or train or some commercial flight or whatever." She leaned in closer to me. "No, they want you to know one thing: they're flying private. So suddenly they start talking like their pilots—'Oh, we're leaving for the weekend, and it's *wheels-up* at three p.m.'" She shook her head and grinned. "Like I give a shit what they're doing in the first place."

When I first married into this crowd, coming from middle-class, Middle American roots, these Manhattan Upper East Side families naturally intimidated me. My parents, always donning sensible Mephistos on their feet and fanny packs around their waists, reminded me all too often that I should keep a distance from the people in this newfound neighborhood—that back home in Minneapolis, it was easier to be haaaapy. Though I've tried to adjust for the sake of my husband, I'll never get used to people throwing out their pilot's name in conversation as if he were the cleaning lady. "I thought we'd take a jaunt to the Cape for a dinner, so I asked Richard to please be ready at three."

Dylan was on the bench with about ten other teammates as Coach Robertson threw the ball in the air for the jump ball. Thankfully, Dylan was excited by the game. He was talking to the kid next to him and pointing to the court. I relaxed a bit and let out a breath.

Two minutes later, a sippy cup ricocheted off my shoulder and landed in Kathryn's lap. We both looked behind us. "So sorry!" said a heavily accented Philippina nurse. The McAllister centipede was trying to maneuver into a row of bleachers behind me. Two of the younger children were braying like donkeys. This was the kind of thing that really got Kathryn going. She was no stranger to poor behavior from her own children, but she couldn't stomach the lack of respect the bratty Park Avenue kids spewed at their nannies.

She looked at them and turned to me. "Those poor women. What they must put up with. I'm going to do it. Right now. I'm going to ask them if there is a set schedule for matching uniforms and see what they say. You know, like Sponge Bob on Mondays, Dora on Tuesdays."

"Stop. Kathryn. Please. Who cares?"

"Hello? Like you, the obsessive list keeper, wouldn't want to know?" Kathryn smiled. "Next time you're at Sherrie's house for a birthday party, sneak into the kitchen and go to the desk next to the phone. There's a bound color-coded house manual that she had Roger's secretary type up. Instructions for everything—I mean every single thing you could imagine."

"Like what?"

"I thought you weren't interested."

"Okay, maybe I am a little."

"Timetables for the overlapping staff: first shift, six a.m. to two p.m., second, nine to five, and third, four to midnight. Schedules for the pets, for the dogs' walkers and groomers. Directives on which of the children's clothes should be folded or hung. How to organize their mittens and scarves for fall, for winter dress, for winter sports. Where to hang all the princess costumes in the walk-in cedar closet once they're ironed—yes, you heard me—after they are *ironed*. Which china for breakfast, lunch, dinner, and season: seashells for summer, leaves for Thanksgiving, wreaths for the Christmas holidays. I can't even remember half of it." Kathryn pressed on. "It's priceless."

"You know what's even sicker?" I added. "I'd want to get cozy under my sheets with a mug of hot tea and read every goddamn word of that insane manual before bedtime."

Thirty minutes later, the game was going strong. Suddenly Wilmington scored and the crowd jumped to their feet and roared. I stepped on top of the bleacher to get a better look, almost falling onto Barbara Fisher. Then Wilmington stole the ball again from St. Henry's. My Dylan, in sync with them for once, wildly trying to block the ball while his opponents threw the ball back and forth around the key. Time was running out before halftime. Wilmington was up one point. One of their players made a bold move to score again, but the ball bounced off the rim. They grabbed the ball and tried again. This time, the ball bounced off the bottom corner of the backboard at a hundred miles an hour. Right at Dylan. Miraculously he caught it, and was completely stunned. Looking petrified, he surveyed the distance to his basket on the other side of the court, miles and miles to go before he scored. Then came an opening between two opposing guards and Dylan sprinted. The crowd cheered him on. I looked at the timer . . . :07, :06, :05, :04. We all counted the seconds before the buzzer rang. Dylan was directly under the basket. Oh please, God; scoring this shot would rock his world.

The shot was clear. He looked at me. He looked at his teammates rushing toward him. He looked back at the basket. "Shoot, Dylan, shoot!!!" they screamed.

"C'mon, baby. C'mon, baby. Right up there, you can do it." I dug my nails into Kathryn's arm. Dylan took the ball, grasped it in both his arms like a baby, and fell to the floor sobbing. He just could not shoot. The halftime buzzer honked. Silence on the court. All eyes on my little mess of a boy.

2

Morning Sickness

"So what'd he say this morning?" My husband, Phillip, was leaning over his sink naked, wiping a dab of shaving cream off his ear with a thick white towel.

"He says he's fine, but I know he isn't." I stood half-dressed at my own sink three feet from him, jamming the mascara wand back into the tube. "I just know he isn't. It was really bad."

"We're going to work together to get him through this, darling," he answered calmly. I knew he thought I was overreacting.

"He doesn't want to talk about it. He always talks to me. *Always.* Especially at night, when he's going to bed." I crinkled the crow's-feet around my eyes.

"By the way, I know what you're thinking right now and you look thin and very young for thirty-six, and, secondly, I don't blame Dylan for not wanting to relive it. Give him a few days. Don't worry, he's gonna make it."

"That was a big moment, Phillip, I told you that last night."

"Fourth grade is tough. He's going to move on, I promise, and I'm going to make sure to get him there."

"You're so good to try to reassure me. But still. You just don't understand."

"I do too! There was a lot of pressure on the kid," Phillip continued. "And he freaked out. Let it rest or you'll make it worse." He patted my bottom and walked toward his dressing room. At the door, he turned around and winked at me, his expression full of his easy confidence. "Enough with Dylan. I have a surprise for you!"

I knew. The shirts. I tried very, very hard to switch gears.

Phillip disappeared again into the bedroom and yelled, "You're going to faint when you see what finally arrived!"

The shirts lay nestled in a large navy felt box on the bed. Phillip had been waiting for them with more anticipation than a child on Christmas Eve. When I returned to the bedroom, he had pulled the first two-hundred-and-fifty-dollar custom-made shirt from the box and was carefully peeling off a sticker that held the red tissue paper wrapping together. The tissue was thick and expensive, soft like a chalkboard on one side and shiny and slick on the other. The paper made a loud crackling noise as he tore it open to reveal a shirt with wide yellow and white candy stripes. Very British aristocracy and very every other lawyer we knew.

I had no patience for shirts that morning. I walked down the hall toward the kitchen.

"Jamie! Come back here. You didn't even . . ."

"Give me a minute!"

I came back stirring my coffee and clutching the newspaper under my elbow. "The kids are getting up. You have two minutes for your little shirt show."

"I'm not ready yet."

I sat in the corner armchair and started reading the headlines.

"Just look at this!" Phillip, delighted with himself, slipped the yellow shirt on his broad six-foot-two frame. A few wet brown curls covered the top of the back collar, and he combed his wavy hair back and then slicked it down with the palm of his hand. He chuckled to himself and hummed a happy little tune as he buttoned himself in.

"Very nice, Phillip. Nice cloth. Good job on that choice."

I went back to my papers, and out of the corner of my eye I saw him head with an ever-so-light skip toward his mahogany dressing room, where he rummaged through a silver bowl that he had won at a sailing regatta in high school. His picked out three sets of cuff links and placed them on top of his bureau—a little ritual that had only developed once Phillip began making good money and could afford to have more than one set of decent cuff links. He chose his favorite Tiffany gold barbells with navy-blue lapis marbles on either end.

"Okay, honey." I threw my papers down and headed for the door. "We done here? Mind if I . . ."

A dark storm cloud appeared out of nowhere. "Shit!"

There was clearly a very big problem with his new shirt. Phillip was trying to jam the cuff links into holes that were sewn too small. This made him what one might call angry.

He took off the yellow striped shirt and squinted.

Our five-year-old, Gracie, walked in rubbing her eyes. She grabbed him around his slender thigh.

"Pumpkin. Not now. Daddy loves you very much, but not now." He shooed her over to me and I picked her up.

Phillip returned to the bed, no skip in his gait now, and took out another custom-made shirt; lavender and white stripes this time. He paused and breathed rather deeply, kind of like a bull in a Madrid ring before he charges. He held the starched shirt in front of him and cocked his head sideways as if to help him remain positive. Standing there in his blue oxford cloth boxers, white T-shirt, and charcoal socks, he put on a brand-new shirt and again attempted to stuff his lapis barbell cuff links into the holes. Again they didn't fit. Our Wheaten terrier, Gussie, loped in, sat on his hind legs, and cocked his head sideways as Phillip had just done.

"Not. Now. Gussie. Out!" The dog cocked his head in the other direction, but his body, rigid and firm, remained in place.

I leaned against our bedroom doorway biting my lip, with Gracie in my arms.

Third-generation Exeter, Harvard, Harvard Law attorneys do not possess tremendous psychological apparatus for dealing with life's little disappointments. Especially the ones like Phillip who were born and bred on Park Avenue. Nannies have raised them, cooks have served their meals, and doormen have silently opened their doors. These guys can win and lose three hundred million of their clients' dollars in the blink of an eye and retain their cool, but God forbid their driver isn't where he's supposed to be after a dinner party. When a glitch discomforts my own husband, his reaction is not, in any scenario in the history of the world, commensurate with the problem at hand. As a rule, it's the most insignificant events that unleash the most seismic explosions.

This morning was one of those times. This was also one of those times when Daddy's strict rules about swearwords didn't apply.

"Fucking Mr. Ho, obsequious fucking midget, comes here from Hong Kong, charges me a goddamn fortune for ten fucking custom-made shirts, in two separate goddamn fittings, and the guy can't sew a goddamn buttonhole? Two hundred and fifty dollars can't get me the right goddamn fucking buttonhole?" He stormed back into his dressing room.

I placed Gracie under the covers of our bed, where she lay with tightened lips and big saucer eyes. Even at five, she knew Daddy was being a big fat baby. She also knew if she said anything right now, Daddy would not react favorably. Michael, our two-year-old, toddled in and reached his hands in the air next to the bed, signaling he wanted help getting up. I placed him next to Gracie and kissed his head.

I waited while I struggled with the zipper on the back of my blouse, knowing . . .

"Jamieeeeeeeeee!"

When Phillip proposed to me, he told me he wanted a woman with a career, a woman who first and foremost had interests outside the home. He declared himself a modern man, one who didn't care to have his mundane needs serviced by a wife. A decade later, I beg to differ.

I put on the *Pinky Dinky Doo* tape for the kids and calmly walked toward the voice now in the study, wondering, at that exact moment, how many women across America were dealing with early-morning husband tantrums over absolute nonsense.

"How many times do I have to tell Carolina *NOT* to touch the contents on my desk? Would you please remind her that she will lose her job if she once again takes the scissors off my desk?"

"Honey, let's try to remember we're just dealing with a cuff link problem here. I'm sure she didn't take them, you must have put them—"

"I'm sorry, honey." He kissed my forehead and squeezed my hand. "I *always* put them in this leather cup right here so I know where to go when I need them. Fucking little idiots. Fucking Mr. Ho."

"Phillip, cool it. Do not call Chinese people little idiots. I know you don't mean that. Stop that, please. It's extremely offensive. I'll get you another shirt."

"I do not want another shirt, Jamie. I want to find some small scissors, preferably some nail scissors, so that I can cut a little bit out of the hole."

"Phillip, you will ruin your shirt if you do that." I retrieved a perfectly fine laundered shirt from his closet. At the sight of it, he closed his eyes and took some long deep breaths through his nose.

"I'm sick and tired of my old shirts."

He jerked open the drawers of his desk and rummaged through each one until he found a pair of small silver nail scissors. Then for the next two minutes I watched my husband—a man who was a partner in a prestigious law firm—try to operate on the expensive Egyptian cotton.

The cuff link went through the hole and fell to the floor. "Fuck, now the goddamn cuff link hole's too big."

Dylan picked this unfortunate moment to enter the scene. He had no idea what was going on and didn't care.

"Dad, I heard that. You said the F-word, so you owe me a dollar. Mom can't do my math. She can't even do percentages." He thrust a fourth-grade math book at his father. "I need you to help me do it."

Dylan was dressed for school in a blue blazer, striped tie, khakis, and rubber-soled loafers. Even though he'd tried to smooth the top of his head down with water, there was still a clump of messy hair sticking out the back of this head. I reached out to give my son a hug, but he shrugged me off.

"Not right now, Dylan." Phillip studied the enlarged holes and kept poking at them with the nail scissors. "I've got a major problem here."

"Phillip, I told you, you're just going to ruin your new—"

"Let . . . me . . . do . . . what . . . I . . . need . . . to . . . do . . . to . . . get . . . to . . . my . . . client . . . meeting . . . on . . . time . . . so . . . that . . . I . . . can . . . make . . . a . . . living . . . here."

"Mom says she forgets how to multiply fractions."

"Dylan, now is not the time to be asking for help with work you should have done yesterday." Phillip was trying to be gentle, but his voice came out high-pitched and strained. Then he softened a bit, remembering. He sat down in his desk chair so he could be eye level with his son. "Dylan. I know you had a really really bad experience on your basketball team yesterday and—"

"Did not."

Phillip looked at me for guidance; he hadn't gotten home last night in time to even talk with Dylan. "You didn't have a, uh, rough time at the game?"

"Nope."

"Okay, Dylan. Let's forget the game for now and talk about the math. . . ."

"Just so you know, I don't ever want to talk about that game. Because it's not important. My homework is important and it's too hard." Dylan crossed his arms and, with a wounded look on his face, stared at the floor.

"I understand." Phillip was really trying to reason here. "That's why I want to discuss the math situation as well. How come you didn't finish it last night? Is it because you were upset after the game?"

"I told you! I wasn't upset! The game doesn't matter! We're supposed to be talking about why you can't help with my math. Alexander's dad *always* does his math homework with him *and* picks him up on his tandem bicycle after school."

"Alexander's daddy is a violinist and Alexander lives in a hovel."

"Phillip, *please*! Grown-up time-out. Come with me." I grabbed his hand and pulled him back into his dressing room and closed the door.

He winked at me. I crossed my arms. He clenched his hands like two big suction cups on my bottom and pulled me into him. Then he kissed me up and down my neck.

"You smell so good. So clean. I love your shampoo," he whispered.

I wasn't having any. "You have got to listen to yourself this morning."

"I'm sorry. It's the client meeting. It's gotten me nervous. And now you've gotten me hot."

I slapped his hand. "You can't say Chinese people are little idiots within earshot of the kids. It's so offensive to me, first of all, and if they ever heard you . . ."

"You're right."

"And if Alexander lives in a small apartment, you don't need to use that as a criticism against his father, who happens to be a world-class musician. What the hell kind of message do you think that sends?"

"That was bad."

"So what are you thinking? You're driving me crazy."

He tried to unzip my shirt. "You're driving *me* crazy." He tickled the back of my rib cage.

Gracie banged on the door. "Mommy!"

"Stop." I laughed, despite myself. "I can't take it. I've already got three children. I don't need a fourth. It's a cuff link hole, okay? Can you try to get a grip?"

"I love you. I'm sorry. You're right. But those shirts cost me a lot of money and you would think . . ."

"Please."

"Fine. Let's start again." He opened the door for me, gallantly motioned for me to go through it, and carried Gracie back into his study like a bundle of wood under his arm.

Dylan was staring out the window, still furious. Phillip sat down at his desk chair and concentrated once again on his son. "Dylan, I know the homework's hard. I suppose if you can give me some time and not ask when I'm rushing to the office . . ."

"You weren't here yesterday, or I would have asked you to help then."

"I'm sorry." Phillip grabbed Dylan's hands and tried to look him in the eye. But Dylan pulled away. "You're a big boy now and you're old enough to do your own homework without your mother or father. If you need a tutor, then we can discuss it, but it is almost seven-thirty and I have my car waiting and you have to get to school on time."

Dylan flew onto the sofa in abject frustration. "Oh maaaaaan." He lay spread-eagle on his back, his eyes buried in the crook of his elbow. He was too old to cry easily, but I know he wanted to. I also knew that if I went to hug him, his fragile composure would crumble and he would lose it. I kept a safe distance.

"All the moms can't do the math homework, and all the dads in my class have to do it for everyone. It's not fair that you won't help me."

"Were you spending too much time on your Xbox?" Phillip looked at me. "Jamie, we've got to start monitoring his time with those screens, it's just too—"

"Dad, you're the one who bought me Madden '07!"

"He doesn't play video games until he's finished with his home-work. He knows the rules," I answered. "You know, today'd be a good day to ease up on the rules around—"

"Dylan," he said tenderly, now sitting on the edge of the couch. "It's just that Daddy has a hard time understanding sometimes. I love you very much and I am so proud of you and I will figure out some time tonight to get this done." He tapped Dylan on the nose. "You got it?"

"Yeah." Dylan stifled a smile.

Gracie appeared at the doorway of Phillip's office with a small pink pair of plastic Barbie scissors and raised them in silent offering.

Phillip looked at her. Then at me. Then he laughed out loud. "Thank you, honey." He pulled Gracie over and ruffled her hair. Then he picked up Dylan and gave him a huge bear hug. Just when I was convinced Phillip was a real monster, he would do something that would make me think that maybe I could still love him. In my moments of deep honesty, I tell my friend Kathryn I might leave Phillip at some point down the road. We drift, he's impossible, but then he acts responsible and fatherly and I think I'm going to try to make this work after all.

"Dylan, we're going to get through this together. As a family." Then he turned to me. "Give me the old shirt. I'm late. Call Mr. Ho for me and tell him he's got twenty-four hours to fix all ten shirts. If I have to deal with him, I'll call in a hit squad."

We rode down in the elevator together with backpacks and cell phones and jackets flying everywhere: my husband, Dylan, Gracie, and baby Michael, Carolina the housekeeper with our Wheaten terrier Gussie, and our nanny Yvette. The fact that Phillip had moved beyond his buttonhole tantrum didn't mean he was going to actually engage with the rest of us. Dressed in his lawyer suit and shiny black shoes, he was readying himself for a client meeting and successfully ignoring the chaos around him. Jamming his cell phone earpiece into his ear, he started dialing his voicemail with his thumb while he pressed a thick bunch of folded newspapers into his side with his upper arm.

I picked up Gracie with one hand and put a clip in my hair with the other. Yvette, filled with pride over her well-kept charges, dressed my two little kids like every day was a Sunday going-to-church day in Jamaica. And because she'd been with us since Dylan was born, I didn't interfere. Gracie was wearing a red gingham dress with matching red Mary Janes and a huge white bow the size of a 767 on the side of her head.

"Mommy, are you going to pick me up or is Yvette?" Gracie started whimpering. "You never pick me up."

"Not today because, you know, Tuesday is a workday, sweetheart. I have to go to work all day. But remember I try to pick you up on Mondays and Fridays."

"Try" being the operative word there; though I worked at the network part time, my hours were erratic and increased to full time when a story broke. This lack of consistency wasn't easy on the kids. Her delicate face began to curl up in that look I knew so well. I brushed her hair down with the palm of my hand and kissed her forehead. I whispered, "I love you."

Dylan's backpack was bigger than he was. He pulled it around to find the Tamagotchi on his keychain and began poking at it like a mad scientist. Just like Daddy with his BlackBerry.

"I can't do a conference call at three p.m." Even if we're in an elevator, Phillip insists on returning voicemail messages the second he hears them. "Call my secretary, Hank, she'll work it out. Now let me give you a full report on the Tysis Logic transaction. . . ."

"Phillip, please, can't that wait? It's just so rude."

Phillip closed his eyes and patted me on the head and then put his finger up to my lips. I wanted to bite it off. ". . . It's just going to be a hell of a crapshoot for the following three reasons—let's start with the stock split; we don't even have enough shares authorized. . . ."

Michael grabbed at my skirt from his stroller and dug his nails into the inside seam, tearing a few stitches out.

Carolina pulled tighter on Gussie's leash as the elevator stopped on the fourth floor. Phillip shot her a scary look; apparently he hadn't recovered from the missing nail scissors.

The elevator door slid open for a white-haired, seventy-eight-year-old man wearing a striped bow tie and a beige suit. Mr. Greeley, a stuffy Nantucket old-timer from apartment 4B, had recently retired, but still wore his suit every morning to get his coffee and papers. Somehow he mustered the courage to step into the packed elevator, only to have Gussie begin feverishly scratching and sniffing at his groin as if he'd found a rabbit hole. Carolina yanked at the leash and now the dog was standing on his hind legs with his front paws on the door. Phillip was still barking into his cell phone about battle plans. I nodded at Mr. Greeley with an apologetic smile and a pleading look in my eyes. He, meanwhile, focused on the elevator's descending numbers, pointedly ignoring us all. In the two years we had lived in this building, he had never once smiled back at me—all I ever got was a discreet nod.

The door slid open again and we poured into the marble lobby. Clutching his overflowing Dunhill briefcase, Phillip waved good-bye and rushed ahead, jamming his earpiece farther into his ear. In his distracted mind, his meeting had started five minutes ago. "Love you!" he yelled without looking back. The doorman, Eddie, offered to carry something, but Phillip paid no attention and bolted into his waiting car. As his Lexus peeled away, I could see the *Wall Street Journal* snap open in front of him.

Yasser Arafat's motorcade had nothing on ours. With Phillip's car out of the way, my driver, Luis, pulled up in front of the awning in our monstrous navy-blue Suburban. Luis is a sweet, forty-year-old Ecuadorian man who works at our garage and speaks about four words of English. All I really know about him is that he has two kids and a wife at home in Queens. For fifty dollars a day—all cash—he helps me drop off Dylan at eight and Gracie at eight-thirty. Three days a week he also waits while I come home, change, and play with Michael, then he takes me to work at the television network by ten. It doesn't escape me that for two hundred and fifty dollars a week in Minneapolis, my mother could feed us, pay all the utility bills, and still have some left over.

Eddie helped me place Gracie into the car seat as Dylan climbed clumsily over her, brushing her face with his backpack. "Dylan! Stop it!" she yelled. I kissed Michael in his stroller, and he reached out for me and tried desperately to yank off the shoulder straps binding him to his seat. In an instant, Yvette put a tiny Elmo doll in front of his face and he smiled.

In the rearview mirror, I watched Gussie's doggy daycare van take our place. On the side of the van it read "The Pampered Pooch." The doors slid open magically for Gussie, and Carolina managed to get in a big kiss on his head before he disappeared inside to greet his slobbering pals.

I closed my eyes as we drove the twenty blocks up Park Avenue to Dylan's school, grateful to be out of eye-contact range with everyone. Luis never spoke at all, just smiled his warm Latin grin and concentrated on dodging the taxis and delivery trucks around us.

Gracie was young enough that the motion of the car made her sleepy, so she stuck her thumb in her mouth, her eyes fluttering like butterflies as she resisted slumber. Dylan's thumbs sped over the keys of his Game Boy; he knew I'd let him continue if he put the sound on mute.

"Gracie, stop! Mooooooooom!"

My head ached. "What is going on?!"

"Gracie kicked my hand on purpose so I missed the last few seconds and now I'm back at level three!"

"Did not!" Gracie screamed, suddenly very alert.

"Dylan, please," I pleaded.

"Why are you taking her side?" he screamed.

"I'm not taking sides, it's just that she's five and I think you can move on. We've talked about this."

"But it's so wrong what she did, Mooooom. She made me lose my game." He threw the Game Boy on the floor and stared out his window, his eyes welling with tears. Maybe it wasn't such a good idea for him to take a break from Dr. Bernstein. He hated going to the psychiatrist and said that all they did was play Monopoly and build model airplanes. I felt forcing him to go was stigmatizing him, as he didn't even have a formal diagnosis such as the ubiquitous Attention Deficit Disorder. And I didn't want to pathologize a situation that seemed to be primarily about sadness and loss of self-esteem more than likely due to an absent dad, and, yes, maybe a harried, distracted mom too—though it pains me to say that.

I looked back at my son and his Game Boy on the car floor. Dr. Bernstein said it was important to show empathy with Dylan, to acknowledge his feelings. "I'm sorry, Dylan. That must be really frustrating. Especially when you were about to win."

He didn't answer.

3

The Waffle

"Hurry, we gotta talk." My Korean colleague, Abby Chong, had spotted me across the crowded newsroom as our colleagues completed a live newsbreak of a space shuttle landing. I passed the rows of cubicles and said hello to some of the twenty-something P.A.'s inside, most of them looking like they hadn't slept in days. I navigated the portable screening machines lined outside the cubicles, tapes piled precariously on top. In my ears, I heard the familiar cacophony of ringing phones, the tapping of computer keyboards, and the audio of dozens of televisions and radios going at once. Abby grabbed my elbow and pulled me toward my door. I managed to pick up three newspapers from the pile.

"You almost knocked my coffee on the floor!" I looked down at a few drops on my new blouse.

"Sorry," Abby answered. "I'm tired. I'm frazzled. But you've got bigger problems now."

"Really big? Like your Pope problems?"

"No. Crazy Anchorman's off that. Now Goodman wants a Madonna interview."

"How do you get from an exclusive with the Pope to an exclusive with Madonna?"

"The cross thing. The crucifixion stunt at her concert from a while ago. He went to a dinner party last night. Sat next to someone who convinced him she would appeal to the eighteen-to-forty-nine demo. He decided she was edgier than the Pope. But only after we were here till four a.m. doing research. He used the 'fresh' word. Everything had to be *fresh*. He wanted Pope references from the Bible so he could write a letter to the Pope and quote them. I told him there weren't any. He said, 'He's the Pope, for Christ's sake—find them!'"

"Well, I won't be working on Madonna either. I don't produce celebrity profiles. It's in my contract."

"You're not going to get another contract when you hear what shit you're in."

I figured she was overreacting. Abby was always calm when we were live and rolling, and a nervous wreck the rest of the time—like now. Her black hair was clipped on the top of her head like a witch doctor, and she was wearing a bright violet suit that looked simply awful on her. She pushed me into my office and closed the door behind her.

"Sit down," she said, while she paced around the room.

"You mind if I take my coat off?"

"Fine. But hurry up."

"Just give me two minutes, please?" I hung my coat on the hanger behind my door, sat down, and took my cranberry scone out of the bag. "Okay, Abby. What's got you so wound up this time?"

She leaned over the top of my desk with her arms straight out. She didn't hesitate, no niceties, just delivered the fatal news.

"Theresa Boudreaux granted the interview to Kathy Seebright. They taped it on Monday in an undisclosed location. It's airing this Thursday on the *News Hour*. Drudge already has it on his website." She sat down and her left knee bounced uncontrollably.

I laid my head facedown on the desk with a thunk.

"You're screwed. No other word for it. I'm sorry. Goodman's not in yet, but apparently our fearless leader called him fifteen minutes ago to give him the news. So the two big cheeses already know."

I struggled to look up. "Is Goodman trying to reach me?"

"I don't know. I tried your cell, but it went straight to voicemail."

I fished my cell phone out of my purse by pulling the cord for my earpiece. The ringer had been in the "off" position since last night and I had forgotten to switch it back. Six messages. I plugged the phone into the charger on my desk. Nausea roiled up inside me. It didn't help that I'd swallowed a bunch of vitamins on an empty stomach. I ripped apart the cranberry scone, picked out a few berries, and lined them up while I thought about my next move. "Give me a sec to figure out how to handle this disaster."

"I'm here waiting." She leaned back in her chair with her arms crossing her chest. Abby was a very pretty woman who, at forty-two, looked young for her age, with her straight hair and creamy Asian skin. She was head researcher on the show, and during live broadcasts always sat off-camera five feet from our anchor, Joe Goodman. On the console in front of her were thousands of index cards with any fact and figure a pompous newsman could want in an instant: type of armored tank most commonly used in the Iraq War, number of passengers killed on Pan Am Flight 103, and biographies of important historical figures like Kato Kaelin and Robert Kardashian.

I rattled off some options. "I could just apologize to Goodman right now before he comes charging in here. Preemptive action is always good." Deep breath. "I could listen to my messages to see if that Boudreaux lawyer bothered to give me a heads-up that his client was talking to another network. He only promised me the interview on Friday. No wonder he didn't return my calls over the weekend." I moved the piles of broadcast tapes to create some space on my desk, and they slid to the floor like a mudslide.

"I thought the interview was yours." Abby was trying to help. "Really I did, especially after your charm-offensive trip last week—I thought you'd nailed it down. Goodman'll be here in fifteen minutes. Check your messages first so you sound on the ball, even though . . ."

"Even though what?" Even though I had lost the biggest "get" of the year to a perky blonde: Kathy Seebright, America's official cutie-pie? As insiders, we knew her as the woman with the sugary smile who would chomp a man's testicles off and spit them in his face. "Why did I tell Goodman on Friday that we had a done deal? I should have known it doesn't count till the tape is rolling."

Abby shrugged. Even she didn't know I'd left work early on Friday to take my daughter to her ballet class. They'd probably assumed I was out greasing the wheels for the interview.

Sometimes sexy women like to act stupid because it helps them get exactly what they want. Theresa Boudreaux was one of those types: a bodacious waffle house waitress with a devilish streak. Unfortunately for a certain high-ranking elected leader, she had the wits to go to Radio Shack and buy herself a nine-dollar phone-recording device. She then used it to tape her dirty phone calls with U.S. Congressman Huey Hartley, a powerful, sanctimonious, married-for-thirty-years politician from the solidly Red State of Mississippi. When network news anchors lose interviews like this one, they get mean and scary. That's why producers call them anchor monsters whether they just lost an interview or not. They're scary people even when they're trying to be nice. But no one was being nice to me that day.

For a moment, I thought I'd be fired. In my defense, I really thought we had it. I grabbed my cell phone.

Message number four was in fact Theresa Boudreaux's lawyer calling at ten last night. What a sleazebag. Just after the Seebright interview was in the can, he thought he should tell me that things had changed.

"Jamie, it's Leon Rosenberg. Thank you again for the flowers on Friday. My wife thought they were beautiful. Uh, we need to discuss some changes in the plan. Theresa Boudreaux has had some concerns. Call me at home tonight. You have all my numbers."

I dialed Leon at work, fury raging inside. His irritating assistant, Sunny, answered. She never knew where he was, didn't know how to reach him, but always put me on hold to "see." I waited two full minutes.

"I'm sorry, Ms. Whitfield. I'm not sure where he is right now, so I can't connect you. Is there a message?"

"Yes. Could you please write this down verbatim: 'I heard about Seebright. Fuck you very much. From Jamie Whitfield.'"

"I don't think it's appropriate to write that down."

"Mr. Rosenberg won't be surprised. He'll think it's appropriate given the situation. Please pass it along." I hung up.

"That'll get his attention." Charles Worthington gave a nod of approval as he strode into my office, found a place on my couch, and grabbed a newspaper. Charles was a fellow producer who did all the investigative work on the show. A thirty-five-year-old fair-skinned African-American who would have easily passed the brown paper bag test, he had grown up as part of the black Creole elite in Louisiana. He was short, thin, and always immaculately dressed. Charles spoke in a soothing voice, with a discreet Southern drawl. We'd worked together for ten years, growing up in the business side by side. I often referred to him as my office husband, even though he was gay.

The phone rang thirty seconds later.

"Yes, Leon."

"Jamie, really. That's so rude, she's just my secretary, and she's all shook up now. And very embarrassed."

"*Rude? Rude?* Why don't you try unethical? Unprofessional? Fraudulent?" Charles leapt from the couch with two fists clenched, giving me the rah-rah sign. "You said we had a done deal. How many letters did I write that little sex vixen client of yours? How many times did I bring big Anchorman Goodman to try out her soggy pancakes? What'd you do, grant the interview to Kathy Seebright at ABS and shoot the Theresa Boudreaux No Excuses jeans ad the same day? And why did she go with a woman anchor anyway? Doesn't fit the bill." Vixens like Theresa always go for the male anchors who can't concentrate on the proper follow-up question because they're discreetly rearranging the bulge in their pants.

"Jamie, try to calm down. It's just television. At the last minute, Theresa decided that Kathy would lob easier questions in the interview. She got scared about your guy. He does have a reputation for going for the jugular."

"And I'm sure it was *all* her decision, Leon. You had no input whatsoever." I rolled my eyes at Abby and Charles.

"Now, look," said Leon. "I promise I'm going to make this up to you. I've got some O. J. Simpson sealed court documents that would blow the roof off that little network of yours, and I can sure . . ."

I hung up on him.

"What was his excuse?" asked Charles.

"Same thing every time we lose one to her: 'Seebright seems so much sweeter than Joe Goodman.'"

How had I let this interview slip through my fingers when we had it solidly in the bag? Why hadn't I taken extra steps to secure her? And why were we doing this interview in the first place? Just because Hartley was a controversial, pro-family politician with four children? Did his prurient behavior deserve all this media coverage? Absolutely.

Hartley wasn't a deeply entrenched Christian conservative, but his ferocious anti-homosexual, pro-family oratory singled him out as one of the most outspoken Southern politicians. About eighty pounds overweight and six feet four inches tall, he usually walked around the lectern to speak so he could tower over the audience, rattling his fist in the air as his jowls jiggled. His gray mustache and goatee high-lighted his enormous mouth and protruding lower lip. He had crystal-blue eyes and a perpetually sweaty bald spot that reflected the camera lights. He helped win the 2004 elections for Mississippi and the White House by supporting the drive to put the anti–gay marriage referendums on ballots in twenty-four states. That White House strat-egy brought all the mega-church crowds out in their Greyhounds and was a major factor in the triumph of the Republican Party. Now he'd already jumped on the anti-gay bandwagon again for 2008, lobbying to put the ancient anti-sodomy laws on the ballots in the thirty-odd states where they weren't already on the books.

I tried to accept the magnitude of my screwup before I walked into executive producer Erik James's office. That way, I wouldn't argue. Arguing was never a good idea when Erik was angry. He was behind his desk finishing up a call when his assistant showed me in. I stared at the dozens of Emmy Awards lining his top shelf. He had worked for NBS for almost twenty years, at first executive-producing the Sunday news shows and then launching the multi-award-winning ratings bonanza *Newsnight with Joe Goodman*.

He hung up the phone and stared me down. Then the diatribe began.

"You talk a big game."

"I don't mean to."

"And your follow-through is lacking." He pushed his chair back, walked around to the front of his desk, and took off his gloves. At five foot six, Erik had a potbelly like a pregnant woman two weeks past her due date. Even though he was standing a safe distance away, his stomach was almost touching me. *"You! Suck!"*

"I do not!"

"Do too!" He waved his hands in the air like King Kong. One of his suspenders popped and he furiously clawed at his back trying to reach it. Now he was really pissed off.

"Erik, Leon Rosenberg assured me—"

"I don't care what he assured you! How many times did you go down there? What were you doing, shopping?" That was low. No question I was the only *Newsnight* producer with a rich husband, but I'd worked my behind off for over ten years for this guy and I'd broken more stories than any producer on his staff.

"That's really unfair. You know I've killed myself to get this story."

He flared his nostrils. "Last I checked, you didn't get me *any* story, F.-fuckin'-Y.I."

"I, I . . ."

He sneered at me. Then he reached into a huge glass jar on his desk and gobbled a fistful of jelly beans. "Get out o' here," he mumbled, and some of his kelly-green spit landed on my shirt, next to a coffee stain.

The battle was over for now. We'd start fighting for another angle on the Theresa Boudreaux story together as a team again the next morning. This wasn't the first time I'd gone through this. Not that my defeat didn't depress me, but I refused to let it derail me. The pressure was intense to break some news and advance the story. Every tabloid in the country had published cover photos of Theresa, many with a question mark, "Hartley's Heartthrob?" Right-wing radio talk shows chimed in with their unwavering support of Hartley while they trashed the bloodthirsty members of the liberal media elite.

Ultimately, as the story played out, Theresa gave nothing away to Kathy Seebright; she'd merely confirmed that she knew him, that they were "close." So, at that moment, my bosses and I were having a cow over nonsense. But histrionics over nothing is the price of entry in the network news business.

Back in my office, I applied some lipstick very carefully as I tried to take control of my day. I stopped for a moment with the compact in my hand and stared out the window at the Hudson River. The anxieties piled on: a major professional screwup, my insufferable husband, Dylan and his troubles. My watch read eleven o'clock—Dylan had gym before lunch: perhaps the exercise had already cheered him up. He had asked me to cancel his playdates that week. Obviously the humiliation at the game made him want to hide behind his door after school and get lost in a Lego robotics trance, but I told him I wouldn't cancel anything, believing that interaction with his friends was curative. I felt bewildered about what else to do with him except follow the routine and make sure he didn't close in on himself. When I get very depressed, I eat Kit Kats. As I tore the wrapper off with my teeth, my cell phone rang.

"Honey, it's me." I heard honking and car brakes screeching in the background.

"Yes?"

"I want to apologize."

"All right. Let's hear it."

"I'm sorry about this morning. I'm sorry I was difficult." A siren whizzed by.

"Difficult?"

"Sorry I was impossible."

"You were." I took a bite of chocolate.

"I know. That's why I'm calling. I love you."

"Fine." Maybe I could forgive him.

"And you're going to love me more than ever."

"Oh, really? And why would that be?"

"Well, you know my success with the Hadlow Holdings deal has had some ripple effects."

"They owe you big."

"And they're giving me something big."

"Okay. And what might that be?"

"The question is, what are they giving my wife?"

"Phillip, I have no idea. It's not cash, so what is it? How can they repay you?"

"They asked me that very question."

"And . . . ?"

"How does pro bono work for Sanctuary for the Young sound?"

My charity. It supported foster children, and I had served on the board for a decade. The organization was broke, almost going under; they could barely serve the desperate kids. My eyes welled. "You didn't."

"I did."

"How much help?"

"Lots."

"Like how much?"

"Like they're going to treat it like a regular account."

"I can't believe you did this. It's going to change everything."

"I know. That's why I did it."

"I don't even know what to say."

"You don't need to say anything."

"Thank you, Phillip. It's totally amazing. You didn't even tell me you were considering this."

"You give them a lot of your money, and a lot of your time, but I wanted you to give them something even more substantial. I know what they mean to you."

"So much."

"I know."

"I love you back."

"Item two: there is something you need to do for me before my flight to Cleveland."

"Where are you, anyway?" I asked. "I can barely hear you with all those horns honking. Are you in Times Square?"

"I'm actually rushed as all hell. Are you going to pick up the kids?"

"Just Gracie. I couldn't deal with her expression this morning. I'm going to pick her up in her classroom, but ask Yvette to meet me outside to take her home. Then I'm hightailing it back to the office."

"Perfect. I need you to stop at home first before you get Gracie."

"I won't have time."

"This is critical." Phillip suddenly sounded like a British boarding school headmaster. "I need you to go home. Go into my office. Turn on my computer. Get the code for my new safe. The screen will automatically ask for my password."

"Phillip, can't this wait?"

"Please do as I say, for God's sake!"

"No. I'm not doing as you say. I've had a shitty day so far and I've got more work to do. I'm telling you, this is most definitely *not* a day I am going to be leaving the office for a long time. I can't tell you how much the pro bono thing means to me. You know that. But I still can't do this right now."

"Honey, this isn't an ask. This is a 'you gotta do this for me now.' I'm traveling for three days and before I take off I need to know that this is handled."

"This is really so important?"

"Yes, beautiful." He laid on the charm with a soft voice. "It is. I love you. Please. I'm going to owe you huge."

I decided I would make a quick stop at home after picking Gracie up, perhaps without anyone even noticing I'd left the office. "Hurry up. What is the password?"

No answer.

"Phillip, I will do this for you, but I am very rushed too. What is the password for your home computer? Couldn't you have thought of this this morning?"

"I was distracted this morning. By Dylan, of course."

Tapping my pen on the pad, I sighed. "You were telling me the password . . ."

"Uh . . ."

"Phillip! *What* is the password?"

"The password is 'Beaver.'"

"You're kidding."

No answer.

"Phillip, your password is 'Beaver'? That is so lame. Is this on your work computers too? In a stuffy law firm like yours? What happens if your I.T. guy has to get into your account?"

"Why should I care about an I.T. guy?"

"Phillip, I can't believe you want me to type in B-E-A-V-E-R."

"Yes. I'm sorry. It's a private password. I'm the only person who knows it, and now, unfortunately for me, you do too. I'm a horn-dog, so shoot me. Now go into my office when you get home and type B-E-A-V-E-R into my computer. Get the new safe code; it's hidden in a document titled 'kids activities.' It's 48-62-something . . ."

"And then what?"

"On my desk, in the in-box, under some bank stuff, or just on a pile on the right on the top of the desk, you'll see a folder marked 'Ridgefield.' I need you to put it in the safe."

"Why?"

"Carolina."

"Carolina what?"

"First it's the nail scissors. Then she puts a pile of newspapers to be thrown out on top of my desk as she's dusting, then by accident she grabs important folders and throws everything out. I lose everything. And I can't risk losing this."

"Phillip, please. You're being crazy neurotic. I'll call her up and tell her not to touch your desk."

"Every day, I tell her not to touch my nail scissors or my collar stays or my favorite Mont Blanc pen, and every day, I can't find any of them. She doesn't listen."

"You know that husbands are more work than children, don't you?" My body was now splayed over my desk like a banana peel.

"I never would be asking you this, but in this age, you never know."

"You never know what?"

"Never know anything! It's the information age! Everything is stolen from people's trash, their mailboxes, their computers." Phillip was now in calm, lawyerly I-know-everything-there-is-to-know-on-the-planet mode. "I come from three generations of lawyers, and I am trained and versed in making prudent decisions. This is a prudent precaution and I'm going to Newark Airport, no way to stop on the East Side. I want to leave knowing this is taken care of."

"Why can't I just do it tonight when I get home?"

He'd lost his patience. "For the last time, I beg you, please stop questioning me. It'd be so much easier for me today if, for once, just this once, you could just do as you are told."

I harrumphed and went straight home, where I didn't exactly do as I was told.

4

Everyone Knows That

It was pouring in New York at noon the next day.

"Oui?" The maitre d' stuck his enormous French nose through a crack in the thick, chocolate-brown lacquered doors.

"I, uh, came for lunch?"

"Avec?"

"I'm getting wet here. Susannah, she's—"

"Qui?"

"Susannah Briarcliff, surely you—"

The door opened. Jean-François Perrier looked right through me. I pointed to him that I was with my friend Susannah over there, smiled foolishly, and stared plaintively into his deep blue eyes. He waved his hands to motion for the busboy to take me there. No-contact rule in play. Francesca the check girl sized me up and concluded that I wasn't really "one of them." So she decided to sip her Diet Coke at the bar rather than bother with my raincoat. I shook the raindrops off my umbrella in disgust.

La Pierre Noire has no sign on the awning, no published phone number. It is the executive watering hole of one of the world's most peculiar tribes: a breed of very rich humans inhabiting a specific grid that stretches from Seventieth to Seventy-ninth streets to the north and south, bordered by Park Avenue and Fifth Avenue to the east and west.

Pity the poor West Sider who strolls by and mistakenly believes this is a restaurant operating by normal procedures, one that actually caters to the public. Soon enough they will learn that they are not welcome, even though many tables are free. From the window, one can see rich tangerine velvet banquettes that surround the small, café-style mahogany tables. Handsome thirty-something French waiters dressed in blue jeans and starched yellow oxford cloth shirts squeeze between the tight tables.

My closest girlfriends don't have lunch for a living like Susannah Briarcliff. Most of them have actual jobs, but Susannah is one of the few inhabitants of the Grid whom I go out of my way to see. It's easy to forget that beneath Susannah's fabulous wealth and stunning genes, there's a fun girl that lurks inside. You can basically look for her in any column with party pictures—*Harper's Bazaar, Vogue,* the *New York Times* Styles section—and it's kind of like finding Waldo. Susannah has two kids, three dogs, seven on staff, and one of the largest apartments in the city. All this courtesy of her family ties to one of America's great real-estate dynasties. She's five foot ten, has a thin athletic build and a shortish blond Meg Ryan haircut. She is also married to a top editor for the *New York Times,* which sets her apart from most of the East Side socialites married to deadwood bankers. Although she doesn't reach the best-friend category—Kathryn from downtown and Abby and Charles from work all hold that title—she's a close second.

I slipped into the plush banquette beside her.

"Jamie. You look *good. Really good.*"

"I'm not sure I'm properly dressed. . . ."

"Stop."

Twelve of the fifteen tables were taken, many of them filled with New York's young socialites in fur-collared sweaters and their gay party-planners, most of them charlatans who charge three hundred and fifty dollars an hour to pick out just the right fuchsia water goblet to go with a Rajasthan-themed dinner for twelve. Or just the right cheetah print heel for a plain black suit. If any of these women purchase a recognizable piece of a certain season, they have to burn it before the following year. And once a blouse or shirt appears in *Vogue,* it's already passé for them. I studied my khaki trousers, white blouse, and plain black silk sweater. When I'd tell my mother about these women around me—and how sometimes I felt that I didn't measure up—she'd chastise me for getting sucked into their nonsense. "How do you expect to get where you want to go if you're rubbernecking at everyone else along the way? Don't focus on what you wrongly perceive as your shortcomings."

Ingrid Harris blasted through the door with her nanny and four-year-old daughter, Vanessa. Jean-François stumbled on his thick French loafers as he ran to greet her. *"Chérie!"* Kiss kiss.

He snapped his fingers and Francesca eagerly swept the tan shawl off Ingrid's shoulders. She then unbuckled the fireman hooks from Vanessa's rain jacket, revealing a pink tutu underneath. The nanny stood back and held her own coat, used to this drill.

Ingrid looked perfectly gorgeous: she had far-apart brown doe eyes and long layered hair pulled back with a Jackie O.–sized pair of black sunglasses. Better than anyone, Ingrid knew that serious style is all about attitude. She had on ratty jeans and was wearing a four-thousand-dollar lime-green Chanel jacket as if she'd just grabbed if off the closet floor. It's not what you're wearing, it's *how* you wear it; you can't act like you're all excited about an expensive fancy new jacket. You wouldn't be "one of them" if you did that.

"Jamie, nice to see you," Ingrid said. "Hello, Susannah."

Susannah mustered a smile but didn't speak or even look up. She concentrated on dipping bread into her rosemary-scented olive oil and twisting a straw in her Pellegrino.

An uncomfortable silence ensued. I broke it. "Ingrid, I still can't believe you had a baby just a month ago. Your body—you look fabulous!"

Ingrid threw back her silky caramel mane. "Well, I told them what path to take to get me back to normal quickly, and I was right, even though they *all* objected."

Susannah chortled. "What you did wasn't normal. I'm sorry, but most doctors would object."

Ingrid, not at all intimidated, put her hands on her hips. "It may have sounded abnormal to you with your two perfect children delivered naturally. But I don't come from the same Pilgrim stock as you do. My people don't believe in voluntary discomfort."

"That doesn't mean—"

"And that means *nothing* was going to make me push. I told that to my doctor the second he told me I was pregnant. I said, 'Dr. Shecter, that's wonderful news, but just so you know: I don't push.'"

I thought Susannah was going to kill her.

Ingrid went on. "Too sweaty. Told him my motto: 'If I can't do it in heels, I'm not interested.' I just told him I wouldn't do it. And I wanted a C-section."

"And what did he say?" asked Susannah.

"He said, 'Sweetheart, I got news for you. Your body's gonna push whether you like it or not.' And I said, 'No, buddy, I got news for you which you are clearly not understanding: I *do not* push.'"

"So what did you do?"

"I went to another doctor, who understood that I meant what I said, so he basically agreed to the C-section and told me we'd do it in the thirty-ninth week."

Susannah rolled her eyes.

"But then *that* doctor wouldn't promise to give me general anesthesia." Ingrid tapped her boot and crossed her arms impatiently. "Well, I told them at East Side Presbyterian that they were bringing it back for *me!*"

"And they agreed?" Susannah asked incredulously. "Without a medical reason?"

"Well, my dear, they sure didn't want to, but I made Henry give the chief of obstetrics a membership at the Atlantic Golf Club, so they really had no choice."

Susannah coughed into her napkin like she might throw up. Despite Ingrid's crazy behavior, I admired her for always getting what she wanted, and never being scared to ask.

"Which is why I came over here, Jamie," Ingrid continued. "Did you get my e-mail about the auction?"

"I did."

"This year they aren't holding it in that hideous gallery space in the West Village. I told them if they did, I wouldn't chair the event. I said to the organizing committee, 'Hello? Look at the crowd that's coming. Rich people don't like to leave the Upper East Side!' We also don't like to pretend we're poor and hip. Okay? Because we're not. So they're doing it at Doubles. Nice and close for you."

"I'm not sure I can come."

"Even if you can't, we want your anchor to let us auction off a visit to a taping of *Newsnight with Joe Goodman*. You're close to him, right? I mean, you've worked at his show for as long as I've known you."

"Well, he is my boss—I, I, I'm not sure I really feel comfortable . . ."

"Oh, puh-leese, Jamie. What's more important to you, a few awkward moments with your boss or a cure for Alzheimer's? So I can count on you?"

"Well, I, I, have to check with his—"

"Tell you what. How 'bout I just send him a nice note on my personal stationery saying you and I are the dearest of friends and couldn't he please . . ."

"Ingrid, I don't think he'd respond well to that. I think I should ask him."

"Okay fine, that's what I said in the first place. You ask him." She had outfoxed me and she knew it. I had to smile.

"And by the way," she whispered as she raised her newly waxed eyebrows and glared down at my feet.

I looked down at my strappy black sandals, thinking I had stepped in something unsavory on the sidewalk.

"Those shoes," she instructed with grave concern. "*Soooo* nighttime. It's noon, for God's sakes."

As the main courses arrived, chicken paillard with braised endives for Susannah and tricolore salad with grilled shrimp for me, I broached the one topic that had been on the forefront of my mind.

"I'm worried about Dylan. He kind of lost it at a basketball game."

"I heard."

"You did?"

"Yeah. Fetal position instead of scoring a basket?"

"Oh no, do you think all the kids are talking about it?"

"Yes."

"They are? Oh God." I buried my head in my napkin.

Susannah pulled it away. "Sounds like it was a scary moment in the game."

"He just heaved sobs into my arms. He was so ashamed."

She rubbed my shoulder. "Performance anxiety, that's all."

"Well, that and a little more. Whether it's normal or not, I don't know—but I think Phillip's hours are creating serious self-esteem issues for him. He doesn't want me to do his homework, he wants Phillip to help. He was completely devastated last week when Phillip didn't take him to the baseball birthday party on Saturday. He was crying like a four-year-old, throwing his toys all over his room and dumping his baseball cards on the floor. And then the whole basketball moment too."

"Is he still seeing that shrink?"

"We stopped. He begged me not to make him go. And honestly that guy didn't seem to be helping. He made him feel like something was wrong with him. And you know, he's fine, there's nothing wrong with Dylan. I don't want to paint him as this hyperdepressed kid. He's still my wonderful boy who gets enthusiastic about his Legos, and he's a great reader and so school is fine, but there's still something not right."

"And what does that darling Phillip have to say about all this?" Susannah adored my husband; they had so much in common, both coming from the same little inbred, Waspy fantasia land.

"Who knows?" I shrugged my shoulders.

"What does that mean?"

"He is concerned about Dylan. Of course he is. He's just . . . you know, we don't have a lot of time to talk these days."

Susannah shook her finger at me. "Remember what I told you?"

I bobbed my head.

She leaned in close to me. "And are you doing it?"

I put my hands in the air, like maybe I wasn't.

She tapped the table. "I've told you this a hundred times. Always blow your husband. *Always* blow your husband."

Even though I loved Susannah, it was sometimes hard to bond with her because there was so much about her that made me feel inferior. Starting with the fact that she *always* blew her husband first thing in the morning.

She tapped my hand this time. "Don't *ever* forget what I said."

"You know what? I don't always *want* to blow my husband."

"Neither do I! But it takes, like, ten minutes and you're done and he's so happy he's bouncing around the room. It'll save any marriage. I promise you. I wish I could go on *Oprah* and say this; it would prevent a lot of divorce. It'd be a good episode: 'Always Blow Your Husband.'"

"So how often, really, are you doing this now? Don't exaggerate."

She looked up and hesitated for a moment. "Four times a week."

"That's a lot."

"And *I* initiate, that's the key. You have to act *really* into it. That's the other key."

"Really into it? Like what?"

"Like you have to act all horny, that's what they love."

"Well, even if I wanted to, even if I felt all horny first thing on a weekday morning, which I certainly don't, Phillip is never around."

"Is Phillip traveling more now than he used to?"

"He's gone three nights a week now. And has a lot of client dinners when he's in town."

Susannah stepped off her blowjob soapbox and sighed. "That's a lot for a nine-year-old. They didn't sign up for the absent father thing."

So true. "When I first moved into our neighborhood, I met all the East Side mothers who hired huge full-time staffs. Nothing against you, Susannah, I'd just never seen that. Separate nannies for each child, housekeepers to clean, chefs to cook, drivers to drive, *house* managers to run the whole *house*hold." Susannah nodded. She had all of those, and then some. "I even heard that they hired 'guys' to rough-house with the boys while the absentee investment banker fathers were kneading the dough. That one stuck out for me, hiring a 'guy' to parent your child. I swore I'd never be one of those women who hired a substitute father in the afternoons."

Susannah smiled. "And?"

"And then I started thinking, here I am now, living this obscenely fortunate life, and I, well, maybe I should hire a 'guy' for Dylan. You know, some male college kid who could pick Dylan up, kick the soccer ball around the park, talk about cars, whatever. But have I turned into one of these horrible women who can't even deal with their own son? This is crazy." This conversation was making me anxious. I speared a huge shrimp and stuffed it in my mouth.

"It's not a 'guy,' you fool," said Susannah.

"Well, it is. That's exactly what it is. I've surrendered. I'm like *you*. God help me."

"It's not a guy," she interrupted. "It's a manny. M for *male nanny*. *Everyone knows that*."

Everyone but me. "Mannies? That's what you call them? Are you kidding me?"

"Forget the shrink. I'm telling you, get a manny! They give the sons male attention while the daddies are out sucking up to clients in Pittsburgh."

"So my city kid could go to the park and catch bugs and do all kinds of suburban boy stuff with his manny?"

"Hell yes! Jessica Baker's manny takes her three sons to the ESPN Zone in Times Square every Tuesday. Do *you* want to go to the ESPN Zone in Times Square? *No.* Your housekeeper and nanny wouldn't ever go there, or if they did, they'd sit in the corner and sulk. You know who else had mannies every summer?"

"Who?"

"The Kennedys. All those Kennedy cousins had mannies taking care of them up in Hyannis. Sailing mannies. Football mannies. Only they didn't call them that. They called them governors." I laughed.

Susannah continued. "Yes, dear, a manny is the answer to your prayers. Don't fire the nanny or the housekeeper, because I can assure you he won't do windows or cook dinner. But start hunting for one this afternoon. And your little pouty Dylan will be over the moon. Consider him the older cousin we all dreamed of, but with the patience only money can procure."

5

Is There a Manny in the House?

The receptionist at work buzzed my phone. "Nathaniel Clarkson is here for you."

I was hopeful. "Send him back, I'll meet him halfway. Thanks, Deborah."

I charged out my office door and almost knocked Charles over in the hallway.

"Hey! It's eleven in the morning," he said. "Nothing's going on the air for hours. Slow down, baby."

"Sorry. I have to meet someone. Don't want him to get lost coming back here. I'll call you."

"Who you meeting?" he aked.

"Not meeting. *Interviewing*." Then I whispered, with my hands cupping my mouth, "Mannies."

"Real professional thing to be doing in the office," he said over his shoulder as he walked back down the hall.

I didn't care if it was professional or not. Who would notice exactly what I was doing anyway? They were all so crazed around the show. I had decided to do the manny interviews in the safety of the office because the first two guys I'd interviewed at home had good resumés but looked a little off-kilter: one had greasy hair with his warm-up suit hiked up too high on his crotch and the other never smiled once.

Through a domestic help agency, with a thorough vetting process over the past week, I'd already met about a half dozen young men who were interested in the afternoon job with Dylan: out-of-work actors or waiters, concert musicians looking for extra money, trainers hoping to get in a few extra hours. All wrong. They were either too talkative or too quiet, and all of them lacked the experience to handle a kid like Dylan. I was looking for someone who wouldn't let Dylan manipulate them and wouldn't let him fade into outer space.

Nathaniel seemed like a fine candidate on paper, his resumé impressive: he'd graduated from a reputable public school uptown with a 3.0 average. He hadn't taken any college courses yet, but at twenty had spent most of his time coaching at a small charter school in Harlem. I'd called the principal, and he seemed to be well liked and a hard worker.

A black kid in an oversized hooded sweatshirt with a Tupac logo that covered his hands and hid part of his face waited for me in the reception area. Under the hood, he was wearing a do-rag, one of those stocking caps with a little knot on the top. "You must be . . ."

He stuck his hand out. "Nathaniel."

"Come on back," I said, trying to be as friendly as possible.

We walked into my office. He didn't take his hood off and I could barely see his eyes.

I opened my manny folder and tried to keep an open mind: maybe this was the perfect antidote to Dylan's malaise, maybe he needed a cool homeboy manny to contrast his sheltered Grid life, maybe *I* needed a cool homeboy manny to help me chill out. His references told me this guy had hidden talents, a gift for bringing kids out. What the hell did I know about mannies? I had never hired one before. I looked over his resumé again.

"So you coach a team in Harlem?"

He kept his head down. "Yeah."

"And is it just basketball or multiple sports?"

"Both."

"Both? You mean basketball and a lot else?"

"Yeah."

"Sorry, both what? Basketball and one other or lots of others?"

"Just basketball, some baseball sometimes." He still didn't look up.

Charles stopped in my doorway, checked out Nathaniel, and looked at me like he thought I was insane. Then he walked in just to bug me and put the pressure on.

"Oh, hi. Didn't know you were doing some reporting here in the office." He sat down on my couch.

I sighed and gave him a look. "Charles, this is Nathaniel. Nathaniel, Charles is a colleague, he was just stopping by for a second." I turned to Charles. "But now, Charles, I'm going to ask you to leave because this is a confidential meeting." I gave him a fake, screw-you smile. He gave me one back and left.

Twenty minutes later, after I had walked Nathaniel out of the office, Charles appeared again. When he didn't have a story, he liked to come in my office and annoy me. I ignored him and kept typing, staring at the screen.

He sat down in front of me and put his elbows on my desk to get me to look at him. "You're nuts, Jamie."

"What?" I snapped.

"Like Phillip's really gonna go for you hiring a kid who looks like a badass dealer?"

"Charles! You're so racist. He's a good kid, he works really hard, his mentor—"

"Bullshit." He leaned back with his arms crossed in the back of his head. "You cannot hire a tough kid from the 'hood for your manny job."

"How can you talk like that?"

"Hey. He's a brother. I'd like him to get the job. But I'm telling you, you're out of your mind. This isn't going to fly in your fancy-ass apartment with your uptight husband and the whole—"

"It'd be good for Dylan. He was a good kid, smart, not that he actually said that much, but I could tell anyway he was. It'd bring Dylan down to earth," I answered, but not with great conviction.

"You are the one stereotyping here, Jamie. Hiring a black kid who's poor to help your kid be less spoiled? Like only a black kid knows or something?"

I buried my head in my hands. Maybe Charles was right—Nathaniel was monosyllabic and had barely looked me in the eye. Clearly I was getting a little desperate. Most of the coaches I had contacted on my own and really wanted to hire had full-time jobs and were busy in the afternoons with their teams. Nathaniel was the one coach who was available.

I looked up at Charles. "But I need a man."

"You sure do." Charles was not a big Phillip fan.

"Charles, I'm serious. I need an older, responsible male in the house, in the afternoons at least, taking Dylan to the park. Not a heavyset Jamaican woman like Yvette who doesn't know how to kick a soccer ball." I put my hands over my face. "The school called this morning. Again."

"Stomachache?"

"Yeah. Came on five minutes before phys ed. He goes to the school nurse, it's not just basketball, it's dodgeball, and now it's soccer. At least before that basketball game, he was still doing gym."

"Make him go! I'm not a parent, but I watch you guys coddling your kids and, I'm telling you, it's screwing them up. My momma was such an ass kicker. And we weren't poor, so don't tell me it was some black thing to get out of the ghetto. She sure didn't put up with any bullshit like this."

"I'm trying."

"So what's the problem? Why is he still in the nurse's office? Why is that allowed?"

"Charles, it all looks simpler when you're not a parent. You can't force kids to—"

"Hell, yes you can!"

"But he won't leave the nurse's office! The school shrink has to go in, with the gym teacher's assistant, who can't stay, because it's the middle of class. But he won't engage, just looks at them and says, 'Hey,

I said I'm not feeling well enough to play.' Then the teachers talk to him after school. They call me. Phillip and I go in to meet with them—of course. Phillip, always wanting to present a united front to school authorities, clears his schedule to come to these meetings, but can't make it to a basketball game. What else do you want me to do?"

"You need to be tougher. That's exactly what's fucked up. You should be tougher on him, then he'll have no place to go and he will start coping."

"I am tough, but you have to remember that he's sometimes depressed, and I just feel he needs to be loved by me and feel safe to cry with me. He still does, and if I play a military commander role, he's not going to come to me anymore. Phillip doesn't connect enough; tries to handle his little rough spots, but can't seem to break through. And though he tells me not to worry, I know he's secretly disappointed his son is so complicated."

"What happens with the basketball team?"

"We make him go because I'm strict about it, like you say I'm supposed to be, but the coach says he won't shoot, he'll dribble and run around a bit. Kind of. Not really. But now it's spread to just regular gym. Look. I know my kid. I know what he needs. I want to find a great guy every afternoon to kick his ass, just like your momma did, but in Central Park."

Charles grabbed my wrist across the desk, converted. "You're going to find the right guy. But it's not any of the ones you just met. You know that."

On an Indian summer day a week later and no further in my search, I walked across the park to my office after a business lunch on the East Side. I was in the middle of a call with Abby, who was mortified by Goodman's latest request.

"I'm going to kill Goodman!" She was screaming into my earpiece. "Literally. I was daydreaming about it this morning on the subway."

"Oh, Abby. What now?"

"You know Ariel LaBomba? The hot Latina weather girl from *Good Morning New York*?"

"I guess. Maybe. Not sure."

"I promise you, she's nothing great. But she does these adventure-travel-type pieces and Goodman wants to close the show with them, thinks she's ready to jump from local to network."

"Okay, so that's not unusual. I'm sure she's pretty."

"No. It gets worse. Listen to this: he's meeting with her this afternoon and he wants to make sure I go down and wait for her *outside* the building."

"Not in the lobby? And his assistant can't do this?"

"Nope, he trusts me more. Then he wants me to take her down the block to the wrong entrance . . ."

I laughed. "I so know what's coming next."

"Yes! Just so we can pass the bus stop ad with him anchoring on top of World Trade Center rubble."

"Abby, wait . . ."

"I hate that ad. He thinks it looks like Iwo Jima."

Just then I happened upon a kind of Alice in Wonderland scene on the Great Lawn: about thirty kids were laying a huge chessboard piece of fabric out on the grass. They were dressed in strange outfits too: a horse's head, kings and queens, soldiers . . . was this some kind of performance piece? The director—a nice-looking guy in khakis, a Cassius Clay T-shirt, and a baseball cap—was ushering each of them into position. Maybe he was running a rehearsal for an outdoor festival. This being New York, and the heart of Central Park, where all the eccentrics come, I wasn't surprised.

And then I realized: a human chess game. I couldn't wait to get closer.

". . . Jamie, can you believe the Windex thing?" Abby's voice pierced through my headset.

"What Windex thing?"

"Are you listening? He gave an intern, of course that bitchy leggy one, five bucks and asked her to go get some Windex and clean the bus stop ad."

I couldn't keep my eyes off the kids.

"Hello?" Abby yelled. "Windexing a bus stop? Get angry with me! You're so distracted!"

"Honestly, Abby, I am. I'm going to have to call you back."

I watched the director. "I guess you should first move the pawns out," he said.

Two kids at either end took two steps forward on the chessboard.

"No, no, no!" he called through cupped hands. "You can't have two kids at once go! Didn't Charlie go over that?"

He could have been about twenty-six to thirty-two, tall and solid. He walked with his back very straight, a sense of confident poise about him. Longish dirty blond hair pulled behind his ears framed his square, open face. His blue eyes were alert and warm. I wouldn't have called him classically handsome, but he was definitely attractive.

"Didn't Charlie tell you any key strategies? Can't believe he calls himself a teacher! First the pawns in front of the queen, not the ones at the ends." The kids, laughing and joking now, moved back into their lines, and the soldiers in front of each queen took two steps forward.

Two giggly teenage girls standing nearby, but not on the chess-board, sidestepped closer to him. I noticed one of them patting her chest and secretly batting her eyes at Directorman. The other one leaned over and whispered in her ear, then pushed her toward him. This guy was radiating light and they wanted some of it.

"What's next, kids?"

A tiny boy with a huge papier-mâché horse head covering his entire upper body raised his hand. "Me, me!"

"Why?"

"I don't know."

The other horse shot up his arm.

"You! In the red hat. Alex, right?"

"I know! Because you want your knights out early to control the center and attack the other team."

"Yesssss!" the director yelled. He reached into his pocket and threw a tiny chocolate bar at the kid. "And do you only want the knights out early?"

Four kids screamed, "No!"

"Then who else?"

"Bishops!" shrieked an eager kid. "Get the knights and bishops out of the way so you can castle early and protect the king!" Mr. Director took a handful of candy from a bag and threw it in the air at that kid. The kids piled on each other trying to grab the pieces from the ground.

Okay, I thought, *this guy is obviously knowledgeable about the game. I'm not crazy about all the candy, but he's tough without being a prick, just maybe . . .*

I stepped up beside him and waited for a momentary break, when I could get his attention. Finally, he stopped issuing orders to give the kids a moment to figure out the next move on their own.

"May I ask you a question?"

"Sure." He turned to me and smiled briefly, but his eyes instantly went back to the game.

"What are you doing?"

"It's a chess game. A human chess game."

"I got that far . . ."

"Excuse me. What are you thinking, dude?"

He trotted over to a kid and picked him up by his shoulders and placed him in an adjacent square. "No candy for you!" He yanked the lolly out of the kid's mouth and threw it high over his shoulder. The others all hooted and laughed.

"Soooo . . ." I began again when he returned, "are you part of a school?"

He ignored me. "Jason, is that your name, kid? What are you doing over there?"

"I mean, are these kids—?"

"You move the bishop like that and it's game over, buddy. You're crazy! Think again."

Okay. He was preoccupied. I waited two minutes, then tried again. "So. Sorry to bother you, but I'm just so curious. Is this for a school?"

This time he looked directly at me. "You really interested?"

"I am."

"It's not a school. This is a group from a summer camp for kids with special needs or special situations."

"Serious situations?"

"Some very awful situations. Yes."

"Why chess?"

"Because it's hard, I guess. Must make 'em feel smart. Do you know anything about chess and kids?"

"I have a son who's nine."

"Does he play?"

"They do it at school, but he hasn't gotten hooked."

"Well, maybe you should get him hooked." He smiled. Major kilowatt smile.

Bingo.

"Are you also a teacher?" I was so excited. I knew this was my guy. "Are you working at a steady job in this field?"

"I'm not a teacher at all."

Shit. I thought he was a professional. Maybe he wasn't my guy.

"I'm taking a break while I figure out some plans."

He waved to the kids. "Okay. You with the goofy smile." He pinged a piece of bubble gum at the girl's head. "You're in charge of the whites and Walter is going to do the blacks. You can argue with their moves, but they get the final say!" When he saw that I wasn't leaving, he stopped and rested his arm on the park gate and looked me in the eye.

"I'm just subbing for a pal. He's my roommate who's a teacher in the public school system and a counselor in the summer. I'm not an expert with kids like him." He picked up a pile of cloth on the ground and smiled. "Excuse me, if you don't mind . . ." Still. He was really good with them.

One of the kids had stepped off the chessboard and turned his back to the game. His shoulders were hunched up around his ears. Mr. Director tried to drape the cloth on the kid's shoulders, but he shrugged it away. He stuffed some candy down the back of his shirt, but the kid didn't laugh. He threw the cloth on the ground and got down to business with the distressed kid, dragging him a few feet away to talk to him privately.

I couldn't help but notice how his worn-out khakis traced the lines of his impossibly hard ass. I put down my tote bag full of newspapers and waited.

Mr. Director flicked the kid's baseball cap up. "Darren, c'mon." He held the kid's shoulders and tried to maneuver him back into the group. Darren just slowly shook his head and then pushed the brim of his hat farther down. Mr. Director smacked the cap off the kid's head. Darren didn't think it was funny. He put it back on and pulled it down real hard. Something was wrong.

Mr. Director bent his knees and looked up under the kid's hat, and then sucked hard on a lollypop as if it helped him focus.

"Talk to me, man."

Darren shook his head.

"Russell! Take over." Russell, an older kid on the sidelines, waved back.

Mr. Director put one arm around Darren's shoulder and another on his arm and led him over to a park bench about thirty feet away. Darren, who seemed about eleven years old, wiped his cheek with the back of his hand. I was riveted. A few minutes passed and he seemed to be breaking through to the kid, gesticulating wildly. Darren started to laugh and this cute guy knocked his baseball cap off again—this time they both laughed—and Darren raced back and took his place again on the board.

All right, I thought, *he doesn't look like a psychopath. He doesn't smell like a psychopath. Obviously, the kids like him. Let's try this again.*

"Sorry . . ."

His expression was direct and polite. I was sure he wasn't a native New Yorker.

"You again?" He smiled at me.

"Yes, me again. I have a question."

"Want to get into the game?" He cocked an eyebrow.

"No . . . I mean yes. My kid might."

"I'm afraid the group is pretty tight-knit. They've been together the whole summer. . . ."

"No, no, not that. I just was wondering," I said. "Do you have a full-time job?"

"Yeah, I'm CFO of Citigroup. This is the investment banking division."

I laughed out loud. "Seriously. Is this your job?"

"No, it's not."

"Do you have a job?"

"Does it look like I have a job?"

"Do you want a job?"

"Are you hiring?"

"Well, maybe. Do you know what a manny is?"

"A what?"

"Oh God. I apologize. Let me start over. My name is Jamie Whitfield." I pulled out my business card and handed it to him. "I work at NBS News. I have three children. And I live nearby. Do you work with kids often in any capacity?"

He kept one eye on the group of kids. "Not really."

"You don't work with kids? Like ever?"

"I mean, I can fill in. They're in no danger here, maybe have a little sugar high, that's all."

He just seemed like a guy who wouldn't take any nonsense from Dylan and might turn things around. Maybe he had some free hours. Obviously, if a real teacher had asked him to control a group like this . . .

"And what's your name, and if you don't mind me asking I have another question . . ."

"It's Peter Bailey."

I didn't know how to begin, so I just blurted out, "I'm looking to fill a really good job that is high paying. Afternoons and evenings."

"Okay, so maybe I'm interested in a really good job that's high paying. What kind of job?"

I took a breath. "It's complicated." I needed a few seconds to come up with my marketing strategy.

"Okay."

"I have a son. He's nine. He's, well, he's kind of down. A bit depressed even."

"Clinically depressed?" Now I had his full attention.

"Well, no, there's no formal diagnosis, he just had some panic attacks. Can't perform at sports anymore really because of them."

"And how do you see me fitting into this?"

"Well, I don't know, maybe the chess . . ."

"I know how to play chess. But I'm not a chess tutor. Though the high-paying part might make me a good chess tutor." He grinned.

"Well, not just a chess tutor exactly, but yes, why not, some of that."

"I see."

My cell phone buzzed inside my purse. I reached to turn off the ring tone and saw Goodman was calling. Maybe he wanted more Windex.

"Look, you need to get back to them and I have somewhere I'm supposed to be. You have my card. If you wouldn't mind, please call me in the morning and I'll tell you more."

"Sure. I'll call you. Nice to meet you."

I stopped for a moment and then walked back to him. "Can I just ask you one thing?"

He nodded.

"How did one person get thirty-two kids with huge papier-mâché contraptions on their heads into the middle of Central Park?"

"Hey. I didn't do anything. I had help: *them*." Then he turned back to the kids.

And as I wandered back to the West Side, I couldn't wipe the smile off my face.

6

Time to Talk Turkey

"So!" I had no idea what to say.

Peter Bailey looked at me expectantly. He sat in a chair across from my desk at work wearing khakis and a white button-down shirt. I found his stillness strangely intimidating. I couldn't figure out why I felt so ill at ease if *I* was hiring *him*.

"So, thank you for calling me back," I said.

"Thank you for asking."

"So!"

"Yes?"

"Did you get here okay?"

"This building is on one of the biggest intersections in Manhattan. Avenue of the Americas and Fifty-seventh Street is pretty easy to find, you know."

"It is. Yes. I—"

"Cool seeing a newsroom behind the scenes."

He took in the hundreds of tapes lining my office shelves, each categorized by topic and show, with huge letters on the ribs. Two colorful posters advertising a past broadcast inside the CIA and a "groundbreaking" West Bank town meeting filled the wall space on either side of my desk.

"Yeah, it's kind of messy behind the anchor desk."

"Not in here." Next to me were four newspapers neatly piled in a descending row and my office supplies in their black wire baskets on my credenza: Sharpies and Post-its in every color, little boxes with drawers for different sizes of metallic binder clips, legal pads and reporters' notebooks in perfect bunches.

"You've worked for Joe Goodman for a long time?" he asked.

"Ten years. Since I started out here. I was twenty-six."

"What's he like?"

"Great mind, lyrical writer. He's demanding, let's just say that." I didn't want to tell a manny candidate that Goodman was cranky, crusty, and usually ungrateful.

"Yeah, seems like he's pretty full of himself." Peter pointed to the enormous portraits of Goodman lining the hallways outside my office: one of Anchor Monster standing in front of an armored personnel carrier, dressed in a Kevlar vest and a blue U.N. helmet, another next to Boris Yeltsin on a tank, and another with cameras and lights visible as he interviewed Lauren Bacall, who had thrown her head back and was laughing as if he'd asked her the most brilliant question in the world.

"You watch the show?"

"Not really."

Most people would at least pretend.

"You're at your computer a lot, I guess. I read on your resumé that you're developing this online software? So doesn't that take up a lot of time?"

"The hours are flexible. The software program—I'm calling it Homework Helper, by the way—will, I hope, change the way students in public schools communicate with their teachers. It'll help them collaborate on assignments."

I liked this guy. I had no idea if this software thing was some lofty plan or if it had legs, but he seemed focused and assured underneath his scrappy exterior.

"Sounds interesting."

"Yeah, who knows? Some people tell me it may be quite lucrative once the schools catch on."

"Well, that certainly sounds like it will be a full-time job. And if that happens, I worry you'll . . ."

"The software program isn't a job. It's an idea. And I believe it's going to be big at some point, but, truth is, I'm not there yet."

My phone rang. "So sorry. Give me a second. . . . Jamie Whitfield."

I should never have picked up the receiver.

"Oh, thank *God* you're there."

"Who is this?"

"It's me, Christina." Christina Patten. One of the great airheads of our time and the class mom at Gracie's nursery school class.

"Christina, I'm in the mid—"

"Sorry, Jamie, I just have one really really important question. I mean, on the scale of things, I guess it's not crucial, but it's just one of those things you have to get right."

Balancing the receiver between my ear and shoulder, I reached awkwardly into the fridge behind my desk and pulled out two small Evian bottles and handed one to Peter. I'd missed what Christina was saying, but I figured the world would still turn.

". . . I mean, you're a professional producer, right? So you should know. I'm sure you're soooo great at organizing. That's why I'm calling you on this."

"Christina, I really hate to rush you, but it's just not the most convenient—"

"Here's the thing. Do you think I should bring the medium-size dessert paper plates for Grandparents' Day, or do you think I should bring the larger, lunch-size plates?"

Surely she had to be kidding.

"I mean, do you think the grandparents will be putting fruit salad *and* mini muffins on their plates? Or do you think it will be fruit salad *and* mini muffins *and* a half bagel? Because if you really think it's a half bagel too, then I want to get the big ones. But if not, I don't want the plate to look empty even though they have kind of filled it with a mini muffin and some fruit."

"Christina, it's not the Normandy invasion. I know you're really trying to pick the best thing, but just trust your instincts and—"

"A big plate with just a mini muffin and fruit salad? It wouldn't work, and I think it would look really sad. That's what my instincts are telling me."

"I agree. That would be sad, Christina. But I think they'll eat a bagel and mini muffin too. Go for the big plates. That's my expert advice."

"Are you sure? Because—"

"Positive. And I really really have to go now!"

Click.

I looked at Peter. "I'm sorry, just domestic nonsense." Not the smartest thing I could say at an interview with an overqualified guy to fix the problems in my domestic life.

The digital clock on my desk blinked to the next minute. He was so still in his chair.

He leaned in closer. The leather on the chair squeaked. "And what, exactly, do you have in mind?"

I'd been vague on purpose. I'd learned from Goodman that it's best to use the phone to lure someone into a face-to-face meeting first. Then you hit him or her with what you really want in person. I didn't want to lose this guy because I'd given him some half-baked manny overview on the phone.

Okay, Jamie. Get yourself together. I took a deep breath. "Well, it's like this. I have a kid, actually three kids, like I told you. Dylan is nine, Gracie is five, and the baby, Michael, is two. And, well, Dylan's the one I mentioned to you already."

"I remember."

"He's a little out of sorts these days. His father is gone all the time, and though I work three days here, sometimes I have special projects that bleed into the rest of the week. And sometimes I have to travel. And my son needs a male figure to kind of peel him off the floor. That's the one thing I'm sure of. Little boys worship older guys who pay attention to them."

"I know."

"And so, he knows a little chess, he loves to read and draw, but the sports thing is not working and . . ."

"So you want me to work on the chess with him? You gave me an awfully high figure on the phone. That's a lot of money for just chess."

"It's really like, come in the afternoon, mostly at pickup time, which is three p.m. And work with him."

"Work with him how?"

"Well. He's nine. Not, like, work."

"Okay, then you mean homework."

"Yes. Definitely. But also much more than that. I mean, he needs someone to play with him." In my head I was thinking, *Just make him better, please just get him liking himself again.* Suddenly I felt my eyes begin to sting and quickly picked up his resumé to hide my face.

"I mean, you have a master's in computer science, and you've taught skiing. You worked in this textbook company. That's a family business?"

At this point in the interview, I learned the following: he was twenty-nine years old, turning thirty in December. He grew up in the suburbs of Denver, studied four years at Boulder before joining the workforce, mostly for his dad in his educational printing operation. He'd gotten his master's degree in computer science at nights.

When I asked for more details about his Homework Helper project, I began to see how creative the idea really was. He was so impassioned by it that I honestly got lost halfway through, but I didn't let on. He'd moved to New York because he'd made headway testing Homework Helper in the New York City public school system. And, like many Internet start-ups discover after the initial excitement, there were some major kinks in the program. He had a few more tenuous months in the red ahead of him. Plus he had graduate school loans to pay off.

I began to understand why this guy didn't have a more traditional career in place—he was entrepreneurial, a bit of a risk taker. What did the long wavy hair signify? Was this a mountain dude, a ski bum who'd enjoyed the slopes a bit too much after college, or was he just someone who didn't ruthlessly climb career ladders? I couldn't peg him, though I hung on his every word. As he spoke I studied his prominent cheekbones and large blue eyes. He looked like someone who would take command of any situation, though there wasn't a bureaucratic bone in his body. I felt he was responsible and trustworthy right away, if a little bit of a screwup on the career front.

Then I told him everything I could think of about Dylan, about the basketball meltdown, about how he'd pulled back from some of his friendships at school, and my fear that things would get worse.

"And what about his father, if you don't mind me asking? Are they close?"

"Sure they are."

"Does his father play chess with him? What do they do together?"

Phillip hadn't sat down on the floor with Dylan since he was three years old. "Well, on weekends, we all have lunch together, or my husband might take him to a movie. Phillip very much wants him to become a lifelong reader, so they lie on the couch and read about airplane engineering or something. You know, Phillip's a lawyer, he's gone most of the week. He sees the kids for breakfast and just before bedtime, maybe once or twice a week."

"Do they go to the park on weekends or anything?"

Phillip hated playgrounds. And he wasn't one to stroll around the park and enjoy the nature. "Uh, sure, they've been to the park together. I mean, it's not like a regular thing they do."

"So you live like a block from the park and you have a nine-year-old boy and it isn't a regular thing?" He smiled. "I mean, I'm not criticizing here, I'm just not getting . . ."

"No, Dylan goes to the park with his friends all the time—or, well, he used to."

"Okay, but not with . . ."

"No. Not with his father. Like ever." I wondered if he'd ever come into contact with a Grid lawyer before. I tried to imagine the loop going on in his head at that moment—something about spoiled kids and how much parents like me and Phillip were messing them up.

"And where are you living, Peter, if that isn't too personal?"

"I share a loft with two guys in Brooklyn—Red Hook actually. You know it?"

"I, I know Brooklyn, yes."

He grinned. "I can't really see you in Red Hook."

I had to grin back. His irreverence charmed me. For the first time during the interview, I felt myself relax. "Well, actually, I have a lot of friends who live in Brooklyn."

He didn't look convinced. Working-class/bohemian Red Hook and toney, yuppie Brooklyn Heights—where I really do know some people (vaguely)—are continents apart.

"So what do your roommates do?"

"One wrote a novel that got great reviews, but he had to bartend because even good books don't make any money. So he got a job working for a hot literary agent at InkWell Management. The other is the teacher in the public school system. The one I was subbing for. He's consulting on my program."

"So each of them have pretty set career paths."

"I guess so. But you're offering more than they make."

"So is the salary more important than a set career path?"

"I'm on a set career path. Listen, are you trying to convince me not to take this job?"

I put my tough-reporter hat on. "Okay, let's talk turkey." I took a sip of water. "You're living in this year's hip new Brooklyn neighborhood, even I know that. You're personable, smart, and well educated, and of course I'm not trying to scare you off. But I need to know how you feel about working in a home when your friends are becoming teachers and agents. Would that be . . ."

"Be what?"

"You're almost thirty. Do you mind taking a job like this?" I crossed my fingers under the desk. "In a household with kids?" I hated saying that out loud, reminding him he was a guy with a graduate degree on an interview for a job as a Park Avenue nanny. But I also didn't want him ditching us after a week when he realized what he'd agreed to. "I mean, not that it isn't, you know, substantive; some consider it a calling to work with kids . . . have you ever even heard of the term 'manny'?"

"No. But now that you say it, I get it right away." He laughed. "Now I'm remembering. Britney Spears has one."

"Well. I mean, for her, that's a bodyguard guy. I think the word 'manny' sounds kind of . . ."

"What?"

I was thinking *demeaning*, but I didn't say it.

He leaned in closer. "I think the word 'manny' is hilarious."

"So you don't mind it?"

"First of all, I'm never going to be a suit."

"But you have worked in offices."

"Not happily."

"Like at the Denver Educational Alliance? You didn't list a reference from there."

"I was there for fourteen months doing a study. You're not going to get a reference."

"You mind telling me why?"

"Happy to. They do great work, but the founder's a passive-aggressive guy who likes to make his colleagues miserable, and, frankly, I told him so."

"You told him he was passive-aggressive?" What will he think of *me*? A lame Park Avenue mother trying to have it all and failing miserably in the process.

"Not in those words. Well, maybe I used that term, but I was very clear and respectful when I said it. Listen, someone had to say it. My boss was a complete jerk. And one day we were in a meeting, and, as usual, he was completely undermining a colleague, a woman whose work was top-notch, and I just couldn't take it. So I just lit into him. Anyway, I said all the things I knew everyone else was thinking."

"That's, I guess, impressive."

"You know what? I didn't tell you that to impress you. Just to show you I don't like the B.S. that goes with the structure of an office. This is why I like kids. Because kids tell you what they mean. First time out. And if you just listen, they have an innate sense of fairness that I totally respond to."

"I get that."

"I also like working independently. Honestly, your job sounds good. I can't do a full-time gig right now, and the job would let me work on the computer project whenever I'm not needed during the day, with Dylan in school. I assume I'd go home after Dylan's asleep, right?"

"Yes. Carolina lives in, so she's fine to cover if we're out or something."

"And the other kids?"

"Sometimes I might need you to pitch in. It's hard in a family with three kids just to focus on one child at a time."

"Makes sense, but I'm not totally experienced with little kids."

"The regular nanny will be there all the time. I'm going to need you in the mornings sometimes too, just for drop-off mostly if I am traveling or whatever."

"If I'm available, sure. Depends on how the software's going. How often do you think that might be?"

"Like a few times a week."

"That's fine. If I can." I was getting the impression this guy wasn't meant for the service industry.

"Are you sure this position is something for you . . . ?"

"Scout's honor." He put two fingers in the air. "Listen, if all goes according to plan, my project should hit in about eighteen to twenty-four months. And when that bang happens, Dylan's going to be off and running like new."

I laughed. "Sounds like a plan. So you like New York?"

"I do. But also, my backers are here. All the technology funds are here. . . ." He looked down. "And . . . and there's a little situation at home I don't need to be around."

"A situation? Something I should know about?"

"Nah. No big deal." He looked up with a slightly crooked smile. "Sorry. It's personal."

Charles had done a thorough background check, including his criminal record, and there was nothing. Besides, I didn't want to pry. At least, not then.

"But I do have one problem," Peter said.

"This is an interview. You're not allowed to have a problem yet."

He smiled. "You told me Dylan's dad is gone all the time. You can buy someone's time and attention, but it is not the same as a dad. And for what the job pays, I don't want to disappoint you—or him—from day one. Dylan'll figure out right away I'm pinch-hitting for his father. How do you think he'll feel about that?"

I knew Dylan would do just that. But I also felt that Dylan would have such fun with this cool guy that he wouldn't focus on it.

The door banged open. A bright canary-yellow flash whooshed through. Abby, breathless, clad in a brand-new suit, looking like a car rental agent.

"You're never going to believe this. There's another fucking Theresa Boudreaux tape!"

Wow. Maybe I had a shot at career redemption. "I knew this wasn't over. I just knew it! Are you sure? How do you know?"

"Charles."

Charles appeared and leaned against the doorway. He eyed Peter, then me, reticent to talk business in front of yet another manny candidate.

Peter already had his hands on the armrests, ready to stand.

"Peter, sorry. I've got a little situation here. There's a chair right outside my office."

He gave a little wave to Abby and Charles, then closed the door behind him. Charles piped in. "That guy is a major piece of ass."

"Please. This is a professional environment."

"And it's really professional to interview your mannies here."

I ignored that. "So what do you hear?"

"I hear these tapes blow the other ones out of the water." Charles clasped his hands together. "Plus whatever tapes she gave the Seebright people were crap anyway. You couldn't really hear a thing, and I hear these new tapes are the real deal."

"Doesn't make sense. If you're going to talk, just talk the first time you give an interview."

"Maybe she liked the publicity but held back. Maybe she had some kind of scruples that have now gone."

"Oh, c'mon. Scruples nothing."

"The point is that the story is snowballing. Maybe she wants to ride a bigger wave? Get a book deal, sell her life story to the movies!"

Charles sat on the edge of my couch. "You're gonna come out on top of this one and blow ABS's doors off. It's your time to shine, baby!"

Erik and Goodman had barely spoken to me since Theresa went to the rival network, even if she hadn't broken any new news.

"Our affiliate in Jackson, Mississippi, is trying to get the new tapes; the local newspaper reporters are all over it," Charles continued. "No one's got anything yet. The station manager called Goodman to see if he could use his big network muscle with Theresa Boudreaux. I guess they knew we were close to getting the interview, even though we didn't. Or I guess *you* didn't."

"Thanks for reminding me. What do you think is on these tapes? What could be on that woman's mind?"

Abby screamed at me, "Would you please just call Leon Rosenberg and stop asking dumb questions we don't know the answer to?"

I dialed, remembering I had hung up on him during our last conversation. His impossible secretary answered once again.

"It's Jamie Whitfield from the NBS Evening News. I need to talk to Leon."

"Hello, Ms. Whitfield. I will have to—"

"Please don't tell me you're going to 'see' if he's in, Sunny, I know he's in. That's why I'm calling him. There's a breaking story with Ms. Boudreaux."

"We are aware there is a breaking story, but unfortunately about twenty reporters have called before you this morning. So I think it's only fair—"

I tried to be polite while saying "Would you please tell Leon Rosenberg I will personally throttle him if he doesn't pick up this phone?"

"No need to get overexcited once again, Ms. Whitfield. I will put your name on his call sheet in the order—"

"That's just not going to do." I stood up and talked into the phone as coldly as I could. "Our anchorman Joe Goodman and a team of NBS lawyers are standing right in front of me and will destroy your entire law firm with a story we have on the shelf about your unethical practices. I will personally see to it that we mention you by name, Sunny Wilson."

No response. Five seconds later: "Hello, Jamie," Rosenberg said. "No need to traumatize my secretary every time you call. She is doing exactly what I told her to do. You really doing a story on *us*?"

"No." I had to laugh. "Of course not."

"Jesus, you scared even me this time."

"Sorry, Leon. And I really want to apologize for hanging up on you the last time we talked. That was very rude and uncalled-for. How can I make it up to you? You know, everyone at NBS thinks you do a phenomenal job. And we know how hard you work to protect your clients."

"Cut the shit, Jamie. I know I owe you one. I always play fair, especially with the pretty ones like you."

What a pig.

"Of course it doesn't hurt you're Joe Goodman's producer."

I rolled my eyes. "Okay. What have you got for me?"

No answer. Was he playing games? Did he have anything? Were there really more tapes?

"And don't forget the handsome shot I put of you in that Brioni suit walking your client out of her waffle house. The other networks just had the shot of her alone. But not NBS. NBS not only had twelve seconds of you in that suit but also mentioned you by name." I mimicked Goodman's deep voice: " 'Boudreaux shown here with her high-powered attorney, Leon Rosenberg, leaving her café in Pearl, Mississippi.' Goodman didn't think we needed that in. I thought you might be pleased to see it. Of course, I did think that would seal the deal for the interview with her."

"I get it. I already got it. I owe you."

"That's convenient. I feel the same way."

"Why don't you just get on your knees and start puckering up?"

I made a loud kissing noise. Charles put his finger down his throat in solidarity. Pause. No answer. "I'm still waiting, Leon."

"Are we alone on this line?"

"I promise. Let me just put you on hold one sec."

I looked at Abby and Charles and scrunched my eyes closed and crossed my fingers on both hands and then my legs. Charles turned around and picked up the extra receiver and pushed mute while keeping the phone on hold. Abby was so jittery she could have stuck to the ceiling like Spider-Man.

I motioned 3-2-1 with Charles so that he could surreptitiously hear the conversation. It wasn't the first time I needed him to listen on a call—we'd done this a hundred times.

Leon finally spoke in a low voice. "There are more tapes."

"More tapes? Between Theresa Boudreaux and Huey Hartley?"

"Hmm-mmm."

I gave the thumbs-up sign to Abby. Charles's eyebrows danced up and down like Groucho Marx's.

Leon continued, "And no one's heard them but me."

Abby passed me one of her index cards. ASK HIM TO CONFIRM HOW GOOD THEY ARE.

"How good?"

"Makes the ones that aired on Seebright's show sound like the Teletubbies having a tea party."

Another card. ASK HIM EXACTLY WHAT IS ON THE TAPES.

"I need *details*, Leon. This is a serious news organization. I can't go to Goodman with innuendo."

"Okay. But you're not a serious news organization if you care so much about Theresa Boudreaux. Get over yourself, cutie-pie."

"I'm waiting, Leon."

Still nothing.

"Leon?"

He answered, "How about the fact that Congressman Hartley likes to go in the back door?"

"The back door of the waffle house?" I asked. Charles shook his head and put one hand on his forehead and then lay down on the sofa.

Abby kept mouthing, "What? What?"

"Maybe I didn't give you the original tapes because you are so very dumb, like all those pretty girls. Maybe you should do the weather instead of producing? Ever think of that?"

"The back door of her house?" I didn't get what he was referring to. Charles sat up and started waving his arms in the air, shaking his head wildly *no!*

Leon answered slowly. "No. Doggy-style. From behind. Literally behind, if you get my meaning here."

"Doggy-style," I repeated, in a surprisingly businesslike manner. I had to pace around in little circles to help myself take this in.

Abby bulged her eyes open; the tension and electricity were visible in the clenched veins in her neck.

"Leon, give me a few seconds." I looked at Charles. He nodded his head and motioned for me to remain calm. On one of my trips to visit with Theresa, I had gone to a prayer breakfast attended by Huey Hartley. I remembered how he always spoke like a preacher delivering an outdoor sermon in a thunderstorm. *"Fornicators will no longer be put on a pedestal by the elites of this country. God created Adam and Eve, not Adam and Steve! While the liberal media focuses on securing the rights of homosexuals to marry, while they make their assault on families, unborn children, the Ten Commandments, and even Christmas nativity scenes, I, and you, the good people of Mississippi, are going to change the conversation of this great nation of ours!"*

I recovered my equilibrium. "Mr. Married Former Minister. Former owner of the PBTG Christian television network. Current Red-State U.S. House of Representatives Congressman Huey Hartley, with four children, says on a tape to his waitress girlfriend that he prefers the doggy-style position?"

I looked up at Abby, who was no longer in her chair. I assumed she was now prostrate on the floor. I leaned over the front of my desk. I had assumed correctly.

"Jamie. Not just doggy-style. Hold on to your hat while I illustrate what we have here a bit more graphically for the mentally impaired folks like yourself. The poor son of a bitch literally says on tape that he likes it up the behind. Preferably up Theresa's sweet little Southern behind. He talks about the next time she'll take it up the behind. He talks about how much he loved it the last time she took it up the behind."

"Leon, you can't be serious."

"Nope."

"You're screwing with me, right? Literally he says 'up her behind'?"

Abby moaned orgasmically from the floor.

"Yep."

I scratched my head. "Hartley is the leader of the movement to get the anti-sodomy laws on the ballot for the 2008 presidential . . ."

"You got that right."

"And he's a sodomizer?"

Leon chuckled. "Yep. I'm with you."

"And he's such a family man, always with his blond wife in the fifties bouffant and his four kids . . ."

"Yep."

"What a sanctimonious blowhard. Remember when he was on that show on his network, with all the proselytizing about family this and that?"

"Yep."

"Some family man."

"Yep."

"And Boudreaux is ready to discuss all this? I mean, the nasty sex?"

"Yep."

I shook my head. "Okay, Leon." I had to laugh. "I take your point about my serious news network. I tried, but I can't keep a straight face and tell you you're mistaken."

Leon laughed. "And it goes on and on and on. It's the real thing. She's ready to sing on the record. About this. In detail. And it's all Goodman's."

I put the receiver down, fell to my knees, and closed my eyes in silent prayer because I, Jamie Whitfield, had just landed a story that was going to bring in serious Super Bowl ratings. And maybe it was going to be the most salacious crap ever broadcast on a mainstream network, but, boy, was it beautiful.

About five minutes after Charles and Abby left, there was a knock on my door.

Peter.

He put his head in. "Are you, uh, done with whatever you needed to do?"

"I am soooo sorry!" I ran around my desk and shepherded him back into my office. "I am sooo appalled by my bad manners. I just got totally preoccupied with the most unbelievable story."

He seemed to get I was kind of out of my mind at that moment. "Sounds like a good one, whatever it is."

"I don't know if 'good' is exactly the right word. More like I said: literally unbelievable. If you heard it, you'd maybe excuse my rudeness."

"Okay. So I'm very interested in this job."

Omigod. "You are?"

7

The Manny Makes His Debut

I sat on the edge of Dylan's bed, brushing the hair off his forehead. "I have some good news for you."

He looked up at me. "What is it?"

"Guess."

"You won the lotto?"

"No."

"You're going to quit your job?"

"Dylan!"

"Well?"

"Dylan, I'm with you a lot."

"Are not."

"Sweetheart, you know I need to work, but it's just a few days a week. We have dinner together all the—"

"No we don't. You're always working."

"Okay. I admit I am working a lot on my piece. And I told you it was the biggest piece I'd ever done. And I want to do it well. And I want to be proud of my work."

He rolled his eyes and turned away from me toward the wall.

"Dylan, I love you and being your mom is still the most important thing in my life."

He pulled the covers over his head.

"You know what? I'm not going to get into a debate about this. I know how hard it is to have a mommy that works hard. I know you would prefer that I were here more. But I promise it will get better in just a few weeks' time. But I have news. Something that's going to make you happy."

Intrigued, he now lay on his back, edging closer to me. I turned out the light and lay down next to him with my elbow propping up my head. I caressed his forehead with my fingers, our bedtime ritual, and pulled his hair back.

"A cell phone? My own cell phone? You said I had to wait till I was—"

"It's nothing like that. It's not a thing. It's a person." I massaged his eyebrows, outlining them down with my thumb and index finger. He closed his eyes, all dreamy, letting his anger go.

"Tell me," he whispered.

"You're going to make a new friend, someone who is going to be so much fun for you."

He sat up, appalled. "Oh, maaaan! You said I didn't have to see Dr. Bernstein anymore! I don't want to see another feelings doctor. It's so stupid."

"It's nothing like that, Dylan."

"Someone at school?"

"Nope, not—"

"At sports? At the—"

"Dylan, lie down." I pushed his shoulders down to get him to lie on his back once again. "You're never going to guess, so just let me explain."

"Okay."

"His name is Peter Bailey. You're going to have your own friend in the house all the time. I mean, from after school on until bedtime. He'll be here after school tomorrow."

"Like my own boy babysitter?"

"Better than that."

"How old is he?"

"He's about twenty-nine. He's from Colorado. He's an awesome skier, or snowboarder, I guess. He loves chess, works on chess computer games or other games making homework fun for middle school kids. And he's super cool. I mean, *really* cool. He has long hair."

My son had shifted into neutral. I thought he'd be ecstatic about the kinds of things he and Peter could do together—and relieved this wasn't another Dr. Bernstein. Of course, in retrospect, that was just my own hyped-up fairy-tale version of how Peter would glide into our lives.

I added, admittedly with forced enthusiasm, "What matters is he's fun! He's going to pick you up, take you to sports, anywhere you want! Even the batting cages at Chelsea Piers."

Still nothing.

"Honey. You're not excited about batting cages? How come?"

He kept his eyes closed and shrugged his shoulders. This was heartbreaking. I thought this would bring joy to my little Eeyore; instead, it just made him sad. I had waited for this moment to tell him because I wanted him to go to sleep happy. His lip quivered.

I tried one more time. "You only get to go to the cages for birthday parties. I'm telling you this guy is going to take you there just on a regular weekday!"

He sat up. Then he turned on the light and looked at me with those squinty eyes. "Is this all because Dad's never home?"

Kids are always smarter than you think.

"**W**hoa." Peter Bailey handed me his coat the next afternoon and I searched for a hanger. "This closet is bigger than my bedroom." He peeked around the corner to the living room.

"It still seems big to me too. We just moved in a few months ago. But you'll see, we run a very relaxed household."

I had told him to dress casually, so he showed up for duty wearing two-toned Patagonia snowboard pants with pockets and zippers up the flaps on the sides. A worn-out flannel shirt covered up a T-shirt with a Burton logo on his chest. He had brown suede Pumas on his feet.

He took off his baseball cap and I gasped.

"Oh, this." He pointed to a scab the size of a tangerine on his forehead. "That's why I wore the cap. I slipped off the skateboard last night. Stupid. And I know it's ugly. Sorry."

I shook my head. "No worry. Dylan will think it's cool."

Peter was a bigger guy than I remembered. Two minutes in, it was already strange having a full-grown man with a deep voice in my house in the middle of the day. And I hired him to be my nanny help? And with a graduate degree? He was so much taller than me. How could I boss him around—stand on my tippy-toes and order him to clean up those toys right now? I felt panicky.

"Peter, I'm just really excited about you being here."

"You don't look it."

"Really. It's going to be great. Just great!"

The early-afternoon light streamed through the yellow silk curtains in the living room and reflected off the piles of books on the coffee table and the two large Tupperware boxes on top of them. I motioned for Peter to sit in the small antique armchair while I sat next to him on the sofa.

"So! Can I get you a drink?"

Would he ask for a guy drink, like a Corona?

"Sure."

I jumped up like a jackrabbit.

"Ginger ale. If you don't have that, Coke is fine."

I got some ice out of the ice machine and started to put it in a crystal highball glass. Wait a minute, was I sending off the wrong signals? He wasn't a guest; he was an employee.

Meanwhile, Peter was considering the Tupperware boxes. One had a sticker labeled "Children's Medicine," and the other "Household Emergency Medicine." Next to the table was a cardboard box labeled "Household Emergency Supplies"—boxes I had put together that ghastly fall of 9/11. There was also a folder with two stapled copies of important phone numbers and addresses plus the daily schedules, all color-coded by child and by academic, sports, or cultural activity. My mother was a librarian at the local Cretin High School, so I grew up in a household where the Dewey decimal system was used to organize the garage. It was all her fault I was a little compulsive at times.

I could hear the clock ticking on the mantelpiece while Peter sat, an attentive, polite look on his face. "Why don't I explain to you how things work here. . . ."

"What things?"

"Well, you know, the house, for instance. How it runs."

"You mean, like a little company?"

"No. These are just schedules."

"Is there an employee handbook?"

"Very funny. No, but we do have employees. Yvette the nanny and Carolina the housekeeper. They're both wonderful women, but it's going to take a few days for them to get used to you."

"No, it's not. Where are they?" He stood up.

"Wait! Let's just . . . go over a few items . . . I mean, if that's okay. I mean, are you okay? Are you okay being here?"

"Yes. It's been, like, seven minutes. Doing just fine so far." He smiled. "Are you sure you're okay?"

Was I that transparent? I shuffled my papers nervously, still feeling like I didn't know how to talk to this grown man without talking down to him. I didn't want to sound patronizing. And then I thought how sexist it was that I could more easily boss around the women in my house (or try to), but not a man.

"Dylan goes to St. Henry's School on Eighty-eighth and Park. On Mondays he has sports on Randall's Island. It's called the Adventurers. They pick the kids up on a bus, and then bring them home, but sometimes the moms drive so they can watch the games. You could drive him. Do you know how?"

"Hmmm, driving . . ."

"You don't?"

"Maybe you could teach me?"

"Me?"

"I'm just joking. I can drive."

"You can? Okay, good." I had to start acting normal. This was ridiculous. "Okay, I deserved that . . . I think I just meant, have you, like, driven a Suburban? One of those huge ones with three rows, in the city?"

"How many guys who are thirty years old and who come from the Rockies do you think can't drive an SUV?"

"Not many. I'm sorry."

"Don't be sorry, it's cool. It's just, I've handled like thirty kids on my own so, you know, this is going to be just fine."

"It is?"

"Yeah."

"That is sooo great." I sounded like I was praising a three-year-old. I could feel my face flush. "And on Fridays he has cello, but not until five. At a great music school on Ninety-fifth Street. Did you have any idea it's been proven that kids who took music as young children do forty percent better in medical school?"

"Huh?"

"Yes. Something about integrating all the notes in their heads. The address is in the folder. On Wednesday it's woodworking—which really gives him a jump start on geometrics and is great for sharpening fine-motor skills and really focusing on seeing a project through from beginning to end. Then, on Tuesdays and Thursdays, from three-thirty to five-thirty, or even six, that's *completely* fine with me, you two—"

"Whoa." He looked concerned.

"Whoa? Excuse me?"

"Yeah. Whoa. Let's not even revisit that geometrics idea. But you've got, like, every day totally planned out?"

"Yes, I do."

"May I ask why?"

"Well, I work. We live in New York; that's just the way things are." He gave me a disapproving look, which I took as overstepping some bounds. But I forged ahead, needing to show him who was in charge after all. "So, on Tuesdays and Thursdays, you just do what you want. You could just . . . take him somewhere. Like there's a Mars place in Times Square with video—"

"I have lots of places in mind."

"You do? Like what?" I spoke as if I didn't trust him, as if he were going to take my son to a crack house.

"I'd like to take him to the park at first, maybe shoot some hoops . . ."

"He's really freaked out about the basketball."

"I know. I know."

"Well, then you'll have to tread lightly on the basketball."

"And you're going to have to trust me. I told you, I'm not good at strict hierarchy."

Oh Jesus. Not only was this guy not going to be a star in the service industry, but also he couldn't follow directions? "We're talking about my son here."

"And I'm going to do whatever you want. Just try to trust me a little. Remember, I'm good with kids *and* I drive." He smiled.

My mobile phone rang for the second time from deep inside my bag. I had ignored another call, but I had been waiting a week for this one. On the caller I.D., it signaled Leon Rosenberg's law firm.

"Peter, just give me a second."

I flipped open my cell. "Yes, Leon?"

"I've now triple-checked with her." He was yelling into the phone. I pictured him leaning back in his leather chair chomping on his omnipresent cigar. Like a Mafia don, he would be flicking some cigar ash off one of his hideous suits with a bold white stripe and too much sheen. At this point the networks were in an all-Theresa-all-the-time full-on media feeding frenzy. The talk shows dissected the ramifications for Hartley's political future, the prime-time magazine shows did profiles of her background—though they weren't able to get anywhere near her—and the syndicated entertainment news shows just tried to blow as much steam into the story as they could. However, none of them advanced the story at all because the two principal players weren't talking. "Most important, she knows you know what's on the tapes and she's going to confirm that while your cameras are rolling. Meaning the whole ass thing."

Goodman and I had been negotiating the exact parameters of the interview with Leon Rosenberg: where it would be held, how much of the telephone tapes we could use, and, most important, that she understood she would need to verbally detail the sex—which Leon had just confirmed. Goodman would be so psyched. I punched my fist in the air.

"And on the other details," said Leon, "Theresa's ready this week to go ahead..."

At this moment, Peter opened the Household Emergency Medicine Tupperware box and pulled out three huge plastic bags: a lifetime's supply of potassium iodide, Cipro, and Tamiflu. He began reading the laminated card I had put inside for Yvette and Carolina about what to do in case of a dirty bomb explosion, anthrax attack, or avian flu outbreak.

"That's great, Leon."

"Although she was hoping for a big-city extravaganza, she understands you will pay only for the hotel room and eighty-five dollars per diem for the two days she is in the city. But she needs to look good. She wants a spa day, facial, pedicure, manicure, and other stuff."

I pulled the other Tupperware box away from Peter and put them on the floor next to my feet. They were filled with EpiPens for peanut allergies and asthma inhalers and Benadryl—all for playdate guests, not my kids. It seemed like half my kids' friends had life-threatening nut allergies, and some of their moms were totally blasé about it. Sometimes they even forgot to remind us about it. I could see Peter thinking I was completely neurotic. Not that I wasn't.

"Leon, again please make clear to her this is not some syndicated entertainment show or a British tabloid. This is a top news division of a major network. We will pay for hair and makeup, period. We can't pay cash for interviews or appear as if we're delivering favors, like facials, to interview subjects. We have news policy standards to uphold."

Leon guffawed and slammed something down hard on his desk. "Get off your high horse for a second and listen to yourself, sweetheart." He laughed again. "Oooooo weeeee. All high and mighty like Walter fucking Cronkite and you and I know the only thing you're interested in is the ass-fuck thing."

I winked at Peter to let him know this call was going to take a few moments. He stood up and leaned against the windowsill, looking down on Park Avenue, then headed toward the other end of my living room, which opened up with pocket doors into Phillip's study. Reaching into one of the bookcases on either side of the doorway, he pulled out *How to Raise Children in an Affluent Environment,* a book Phillip had read while I was pregnant with Dylan. I was horrified, but he was all the way across the room, so I couldn't grab it from him.

"All right, Leon. We're talking about a guy who used to run a Christian television network, a guy with four children who's been married for thirty years to a June Cleaver look-alike, a guy who's in bed with Focus on the Family, the Christian Coalition, and even the Promise Keepers. So there's a little bit of hypocrisy here that is the main thing. But you are right, the, uh, exact sexual manifestations of this hypocrisy are quite interesting to us. Especially with the irony involving the anti-sodomy laws. That is kind of delicious. I won't deny that. But, remember, we cared a lot about this story before we had that little item."

"That's a twenty-five-million-dollar item, baby."

"It is. And let's just leave it at that."

"Okay, sweetheart, while you're leaving it at that, one more thing."

I breathed deeply and deliberately into the phone while awaiting his umpteenth request. I mouthed, *So sorry!* to Peter. He shook his head and mouthed, *Don't worry.* He closed the book and walked over to the large box next to the coffee table.

"And Goodman understands that he is to mention her lawyer . . ."

Peter was now rifling through the Household Emergency Supplies box. Out came a Department of Homeland Security pamphlet, which he glanced at and threw back in the box. Next he pulled out an Israeli gas mask, took it out of its protective plastic bag, and started reading the instructions.

"Yes, Leon, we will mention you by name and have the rolling video of you that you like, not the one on the windy day where your hair looks like Don King. . . ."

Peter put on the gas mask. Then he pulled out a full-body, orange bioterror fallout suit, checked the label, held it up against his shoulders, and anchored it down with his chin pushed into his neck.

The front door slammed. It was only two o'clock in the afternoon. I knew Carolina was in the kitchen, Yvette was still in the park with both younger children, and Dylan was in school. No one usually came through the door unannounced. I stretched my head around to the front hall while Leon began explaining exactly which video of himself he wanted us to use.

Phillip's overcoat flew across the foyer. Shit. Just after lunch and Phillip was home? I knew he wasn't traveling and he had never once come home like this in the middle of the day without calling. He walked into the living room with a man I'd never seen before, only to find Peter wearing a gas mask and holding up the orange suit.

"Jamie, what in God's name is . . . ?"

Peter pulled the gas mask off. His turn to have Don King hair. He politely put his hand out to Phillip.

"No, no!" I screamed at him.

Peter stopped dead in his tracks and gave me a What-the-hell-lady?-I'm-just-introducing-myself-here! look.

From my cell phone: "You don't have that shot, baby? The one I mean?"

"No. I mean not you, Leon. I do, Leon. I know exactly what you mean. I was just . . ." I waved my hand for Peter to come sit down right here now, young man! I pointed to his chair. "You want your hair flat like in the shot where you're wearing the trench coat and yellow silk scarf and matching silk socks—not like the one where it looks like a huge Frisbee. I remember. Is that all?"

Phillip shook his head and walked down the hall with his guest. Then the doors of his study closed behind him.

"All right, Leon. Thanks for the confirmation on Theresa. Good-bye."

I hung up the phone and took a deep breath.

"I'm sorry," Peter said. "I was just trying to be courteous . . ."

"No. I'm the one who has to apologize. It's just this big story again, and I wanted to introduce you to my husband in calmer circumstances."

"I see."

"So sorry to interrupt again, Peter." I stood up. "I just need to check on him. Excuse me just for a second." I tiptoed across the living room and put my ear against the sliding doors.

"Damn it, Alan. I left the papers here to keep them out of the office. Obviously."

"So where are they now? If you kept them here, they better be here."

Alan who? I knocked on the door and heard a lamp smash on the floor. The pocket doors slid open a notch and my normally composed husband put his face through the minimal crack he had opened.

"Yes?"

"Phillip, it's two o'clock in the afternoon on a workday. You give me no warning that you're coming home. Why are you here? Who are you with?"

"Doesn't matter."

"I heard you talking to someone named Alan."

"Oh, him."

"Yes, him. Alan." Still no acknowledgment from my husband. "Why are you being so weird, Phillip? This is our home."

"Why are *you* being so weird? What is the deal with the guy trying on the orange suit?"

"I'll explain later. Why are *you* home?"

"Some papers I need to find. In my study."

"And this Alan guy is helping you find them?"

"Yes. He's helping me. Yes. Are we done now? I'm sorry, honey, but I'm really stressed out. Would it be possible to be left alone from here on in? Actually, two Diet Cokes would be great. With limes. On the sides of the glass. Don't drench them in the Diet Coke."

"How long will you be here?"

"All day. But don't tell the kids I'm here or they'll interrupt. I should be done by around eight." Phew. Just enough time to introduce Peter to Dylan, have them spend some quality time together, and then have Peter leave before Phillip came out. He pulled his nose back in and slammed the doors. The turning of the lock creaked inside the mahogany doors. As he had predicted, he didn't reappear for hours. He also didn't get any Diet Coke.

"Even if there is an anthrax attack," I told Peter, "I promise I will not get up again or answer the phone."

"It's no problem." He grabbed the bag of Cipro. "You sure are prepared."

"Honestly, I just had a little breakdown after the World Trade Center. Living in this city with kids, your mind goes to all kinds of horrible places."

"I understand."

"Back to Dylan. He's extremely bright. He's also a smart-ass. Likes to say things that throw you off your game. Hates to give in."

"Me too."

"And that basketball game really upset him."

"You keep going back to that."

"That game was a big deal."

"To you or to him?"

I tried to act cool. Peter's forthright style charmed and unnerved me all at once. "Dylan is more tentative than he used to be, more than I would like. He's almost ten years old, but he still needs someone to hold his hand. He doesn't like to be pushed into things until he's ready."

"Do you push him?"

"His father does."

"You let him?"

Wow. This guy was serious. I was still a bit thrown, but also impressed by his willingness to aim right for the heart of the matter. "It's a self-esteem thing with his dad. Frankly, Phillip pushes him, but then he isn't around to follow up. I mean, he adores his son, he just works very, very, very hard."

"Could I talk to Mr. Whitfield? You can introduce me later when you're not on the phone. Maybe I won't be wearing a gas mask." He smiled. "Or, after a few days, you know, I could just call him. Get a sense of Dylan from his point of view."

My mind raced through the pros and cons of telling Peter that my husband had no idea I had hired him. "That's not going to work."

"I see."

"No, that definitely wouldn't work."

Peter suddenly understood. "He doesn't know about me, does he?"

I tried not to grin. "Well, he knows . . ."

"You sure?"

"Well . . ."

"I got it. You planning on telling him sometime soon?" He leaned back on the sofa with his hands crossed behind his head.

"Of course I'm going to tell him. He just needs to be eased into this. He's, um, open to the concept. Look, promise me you won't do what you did to that guy at your old job. I know I'm handling this right. Once Dylan is making progress, Phillip's going to be all over you. He's into results."

"Gotcha."

Our apartment had three bedrooms: one for Dylan, one that Gracie and Michael shared, and the master—all of them forming a corner along the back end of the apartment. Phillip's dressing room shared a wall with our bedroom on one side and his study on the other. Each bedroom was decorated with clean, neat lines: pale colors with tan rugs and curtains that had navy-blue or brown ribbon borders. Carolina slept in a tiny maid's room off the kitchen, which I intentionally didn't show him. I felt guilty that it was so small, but I'd tried to make it cheery. When we left Michael and Gracie's room, I could see Peter noticing the crisp curtains and celadon-green wallpaper.

"Reminds me of my room growing up," he said.

"Really?"

"No." He laughed and patted me on the shoulder, trying to get me to relax. "But I do like the apartment. No offense, but I thought it would be more . . ."

"More what?"

"More stuffy."

"We aren't stuffy!" I thought about that a minute. "My husband can be a little formal."

"He and I are going to get along fine."

Oh boy. He had no idea what he was talking about.

The homey smell of Carolina's tomato sauce drew us toward the kitchen, a bright apple-green room where my family seemed to spend most of our time. Fluffy striped green and yellow pillows lined the banquette in the breakfast area. I offered Peter some chips from an open bag on the counter, and he promptly scooped one into the sauce bubbling on the stove. Carolina, who had witnessed this infraction from the back hallway, looked like she might slam a frying pan on his head. The day before, I had told Carolina and Yvette that I was bringing a thirty-year-old man to work alongside them in the house. When I left the room, I caught Carolina giving Yvette a "she's muy loca" expression.

"Peter, this is Carolina Martinez. She works very hard to take care of us and the children." I searched for the correct words to address the tortilla chip and tomato sauce remnants on his chin. "Carolina cares deeply about the quality of the food she prepares" was all I could come up with. "And Carolina, this is Peter Bailey. He has worked extensively with children and is very excited about helping us out."

Peter rubbed the crumbs off his chin, wiped his hand on his snowboard pants, and reached out to Carolina. She put down her laundry basket with a thump on the counter and shook his hand with a limp, dismissive wrist. She gave him a napkin and a dirty look at the same time. He was undaunted.

"This sauce is delicious. No way could I have resisted."

She stared at him suspiciously.

"And I'm glad I didn't. The best sauce. Ever." He turned to me. "Hey, Mrs. Whitfield, is dinner included? If she's cooking, it better be." He smiled at her and squeezed her arm.

She instinctively jerked back, but couldn't help softening her glare. In twenty seconds, this guy had defused Carolina's temper, something I had never learned to do.

8

Nannies Are So Much Simpler Than Mannies

"Dylan, look Peter in the eye when you say hello, especially the first time," I told him.

"Mrs. Whitfield, may I handle this?" Peter said. "Kids don't like to have to be polite all the time." Dylan could barely speak and he just stared at the floor while Peter tried everything to make him comfortable. They finally went into Dylan's room, but Peter came out a few minutes later telling me we had to take it slow.

The next afternoon, Peter arrived early and we again found ourselves in the breakfast room. I told him, "So Dylan and I had a long talk last night and he got really angry."

"Because of me."

I tried to muster a reassuring expression. "Yes."

"I think I would have done the same thing at his age if I had his situation, which I kind of did."

"Really?"

"Hardly the same surroundings. But, yeah, tough, demanding dad who isn't around all the time. Controlling mom."

"I don't think I'm controlling. I'm trying to help him." Was I supposed to be insulted? And why couldn't I say "Listen: You work for me. I pay you. Be respectful. Get it?"

"I predicted this. Knew he'd think I was replacing old Dad and wouldn't like it one bit. Hate to say it, but I did."

Were all mannies this tiresome? Was I smoking something or had he been unbelievably charming in the park? He had been so cute to Carolina and he even understood that I didn't tell Phillip, both of which I took as a sign of his high emotional intelligence. But emotionally intelligent people can be annoying know-it-alls.

"Look, clearly he's angry about his father being gone all the time, not really about you."

"So we're going to have to tread even lighter," Peter instructed. "Do you have a computer I can use?"

"Sure. There's that small playroom at the end of the hall near Dylan's room. You can go in there."

"This is going to take some time. Just please understand that if I'm not actually on my hands and knees playing with Dylan this first week, I am, in my own way, working hard to get there." That was the first normal, appropriate comment Peter had uttered since he'd been in the apartment. Suddenly he'd morphed back into that magnetic guy in the park who was controlling thirty kids like marionettes.

Just as he promised, Peter didn't pressure Dylan. During the remainder of that first week, he came to the apartment, read the papers at the kitchen table, then went into the playroom to work on his computer program. Serendipitously—it seemed—Dylan would wander in and play video games on the floor. It wasn't like a Berlin Wall divided them—Peter might say a word or two, but basically he ignored him. And my stubborn Dylan refused to engage.

At the beginning of week two, Peter took an obvious interest in Gracie. She was far more lighthearted and porous than Dylan, and she'd talk to anyone right away. While she sat on his lap, Peter would show her all kinds of websites for kids, pointing out the games and music, then he'd help her play on the princess website she loved. After, she'd pull him back to her room to show off her princess outfits, while Dylan, of course, pretended not to care. Four days of tea parties and pink tutus would drive anyone crazy, but Peter kept his cool. All the while, Dylan remained on the periphery, with one eye furtively watching Peter's every move.

Finally that second Friday afternoon, as Peter recounted to me, he turned to Dylan, who was lying on his stomach perched on his elbows with a model car, and asked him a direct question: "Buddy, I'm bored. I can't stand another minute of Pocahontas. You wanna go to the park and kick a ball around?"

"No thanks."

"Okay. No problem."

And then Peter turned his attentions to baby Michael. He carried him out of his room, squealing and giggling, hanging by his feet down Peter's back—all in view of Dylan—screamed some macho football chants, and ran around the apartment with Yvette lumbering after him.

"You give me back that baby!" Yvette had to hit Peter with a dish-towel to get him to settle down. Dylan loved seeing Yvette get exercised, because she was usually so acquiescent. He smiled behind his model car.

Michael and Gracie began fighting over Peter. Pudgy little Michael, extremely outgoing and brutish, grabbed on to Peter's knees and pushed Gracie away.

"I called Peter first! Yvette! I called Peter first!" she screamed.

Dylan put his hands on his ears. "Arrrrgh. You guys! Shut! Up!"

Yvette smacked Dylan's knees. "Don't you go using that word!"

"Well, they won't! I have homework. And Peter was working on his computer thing! Hey, we're working in here!" Dylan yelled at his warring siblings. "He can't play with you right now."

"Can too!" screamed Gracie. Michael bit her wrist and she wailed.

"Yvette, could you just take them?" pleaded Dylan. "They are really bugging us."

Yvette, strong as an ox, carried both little kids under her arms and smiled at Peter on the way out.

Peter closed the door. "Thanks for saving me. Hey, want me to show you an awesome chess move that'll kick your opponent's ass every time?"

"Sure. I guess."

★   ★   ★

I realized I'd made the right decision in bringing Peter into our lives. It made me so happy when Dylan would subtly let on that he rather liked the idea of his own grown-up pal. At night, he'd want to confirm that Peter was picking him up, and he stopped wearing his favorite Polo T-shirt because Peter told him it wasn't cool. One day after school, he made Peter tell me how he'd done ten pull-ups in a row. I loved how engaged Peter was, how quickly he got to my son. Watching them together made me feel safe, as if I could let go just once in a while and trust someone else to step in.

And once we were on that safe ground together, Peter began to tease me regularly—which I of course adored. I would, for instance, come up with a sincere suggestion like "Dylan's got nothing on Tuesday. Why don't you guys go to that ceramic place where you can paint a clay piggy bank? They fire it and then you pick it up a week later and it's all glazed."

And Peter would look at me with immense disdain. "Paint a piggy bank? You think that's cool?"

"Well, I . . . he does it at birthday parties."

"Just because the rich moms have no imagination."

"And I assume you're grouping me in with them?"

"Never," he said sarcastically.

"You better not." I definitely liked this guy and told myself it was because I knew he'd cure my son. Period. It had *nothing* to do with how quickly he smiled when I came into the room. Or how much fun we had talking when Dylan wasn't even around. And definitely *nothing* to do with how good he looked in his army pants. "The kids actually enjoy the pottery, Peter. Don't forget, they're only nine."

"They might enjoy it, but it's not cool, and we're not doing that."

"So what are you going to do?"

"Dylan likes the Staten Island Ferry."

"He does?"

"Sure, we took the train down there. It's free. He thinks that's the best part. We go back and forth. It takes like twenty-five minutes. You want to come?"

"Don't have time."

"You'd have more fun than you think."

"What exactly do you mean by that?" I was really smiling at this point.

"Why don't you come and find out?"

"I don't think so." But I wanted to.

I could tell he could sense my hesitation and maybe even that I wanted to go, but he moved on. "I think I'll take him to LaGuardia Airport this week."

"You're going to walk around the airport and watch planes take off?"

"No, we are not going to walk around the airport. There's a field in Queens, right next to one of the runways. You lie on it and the planes fly right over your head."

"Bring some earplugs and a blanket."

"We're not bringing a blanket. That's a wussy thing to do."

"He'll get rat poop in his hair!"

"So we'll wash his hair when we get home."

One evening during Peter's third week with us, Dylan and Peter were playing chess at the kitchen table while Carolina served dinner, and without warning, Phillip appeared. His shirtsleeves were rolled up and his tie was loosened, and he looked dazed and dejected. He walked right past us all toward the fridge. Uh-oh. Peter swallowed hard.

"Honey, did your flight get in early?"

Peter wisely excused himself from the table.

"Nope. Meeting canceled," he said abruptly, then sat down at the banquette with the kids and grabbed one of Michael's chicken nuggets. "Carolina, do me a favor. Make me a ham sandwich with mustard on one side and mayonnaise on the other. I'll take it in the study on a tray with an iced tea, then I have to get back to the office."

Normally, at this hour the kids would be yelling at each other or competing over who got the cup with the curly-Q straw. But tonight they sensed their father was unnerved and wisely decided to sip their milk quietly.

Gracie eyed Phillip's rumpled tie and wrinkled shirt. "How come you look so messy?"

Phillip laughed, reached for one of her star-shaped chicken nuggets, and smothered it in the ketchup from her *Beauty and the Beast* plastic plate. "I'm tired and messy because I'm working hard so I can buy you all the chicken nuggets and ketchup you need."

He slid himself down the banquette so that he could put Michael on his lap and place both older kids on either side. He put his arms around Gracie and Dylan and held them close. "You know I love you guys more than anything in the world. I just missed you. I really came home because I wanted to sit with you at dinner!" Then Phillip pulled his BlackBerry out of his back pocket and checked it high in the air over Gracie's head, skillfully rolling the side dial up and down with one hand.

I heard the door to the back playroom quietly close and felt relieved Peter had gotten the difficult-husband message. Dylan leapt out of the banquette to show Phillip his new magnetic chess set. Once Phillip set his mind to teaching the kids a game like chess, he did it quite well. It made me sad he couldn't, or wouldn't, focus on them more.

"Will you play chess with me after dinner?" asked Dylan. "I got some new moves."

"Maybe, can't promise, need to check a few things . . ." And Phillip grabbed the BlackBerry again and began rolling and punching the side wheel.

Phillip wasn't always distracted with work or having panic attacks over cuff links, but—I had to face it—there had been warning signs I chose to ignore when I first fell in love with him.

We met in Memphis on a joint business trip. It was 1992: the coups in Eastern Europe over, the Rodney King riots starting, and Dan Quayle had just spelled P-O-T-A-T-O-E wrong. I was twenty-two and just starting the analyst program at Smith Barney—having gone to Wall Street after college in a misguided attempt to please my accountant father. I'd been a political junkie since high school and had already interned for both the Republican and Democratic parties over summers in Minnesota. I placed myself then (and now) politically down the middle, so I intentionally worked on both sides of the fence. All I really wanted to do was work in a political office in New York, for the mayor maybe. Still, I was trying to make the best of it at a bank in New York that had recruited at Georgetown.

Phillip and I were working on the same initial public offering for a large distribution company in Memphis, but before the deal could go through, a group of bankers and lawyers had to fly down there for due diligence.

I filled the lowest rung of the totem pole, crunching numbers late into the night. Phillip was a hotshot junior partner at a big law firm with three full partners above him on the trip. There were eight of us at the meeting, and I was the only woman. The second morning, while the rest of us were knee-deep in Excel documents, Phillip blasted through the door half an hour late with a pile of reports in his hands.

He didn't excuse himself, didn't ask permission to interrupt, he just boldly stated, "You guys have got it all ass backward. I was up all night fixing the reports, and I want all of you to listen very carefully to what I've discovered." He went on to explain how we'd screwed up our analysis and basically wasted our time. The fact that his boss had been guiding us on our current trajectory didn't stop him. This mutiny might have been inappropriate, but he had the advantage of being right. His alpha-dog performance captivated me. I wasn't sophisticated enough at the time to understand that his confidence was fueled by an outrageous sense of entitlement.

As he stood there shaking the reports, I studied his dark hair that fell a touch over his ears and the back of his collar. His suit was so finely tailored, his cuffs so neatly positioned at his wrists. Nerdy bankers and lawyers never had long hair. They wanted to look as professional as possible for their corporate clients—this guy clearly wasn't kowtowing to anyone. He was six feet tall at least, with a lanky build and long, slim legs. I caught a glimpse of the ropy muscles in his thighs as he moved around the table, dropping the files in front of each one of us.

He looked at my boss, Kevin Kramer, and said, "Okay, guys, change in tack. This is how we're going to work from here on in. If you look at the prospectus . . ." I remember thinking Phillip might even be a guy with food in his refrigerator. His big blue eyes and rugged cheekbones captivated me. Phillip reminded me of the long-haired preppy boys wearing cutoffs who played Frisbee on the front green at my high school in Minneapolis, the blond hair on their bare chests glistening with sweat as they dove for a catch.

We'd been working until midnight the third and last night when he suggested four of us get a drink in the Peabody Hotel bar, the oldest establishment in Memphis. Phillip sat close to me on the banquette side, mostly ignoring me and talking to my bosses, Kevin and Donald, across the table. The oak-paneled room was dark, with flickering candles in gem-toned vases set on each table. A heavy bartender in an open-collared tuxedo shirt was talking to a Memphis local in a black cowboy hat.

I was a little intimidated by Phillip but completely mesmerized by his brilliance. Sharing him with my boring, patronizing banker bosses was no fun at all. Kevin and Donald didn't care about anything other than how to make some more "dough-re-mi."

Kevin looked up at Ross Perot flickering on CNN from a television mounted high on the wall. "Can you believe this guy? In the great U. S. of A.? Trying to make a three-party system work here? Forget it!"

I hoped my face didn't reflect the disdain I felt for his naive political observations. "The three-party thing is not that unusual."

"Hello?" he said to me with widened eyes, acting like he was talking to a young child. He cupped his hands and put them on one side of the table. "In this country, you have Democrats here." Then he put his hands on the other side of the table. "And Republicans here. Two parties. Get it?"

"Yeah, Kevin, I get that. But ever heard of a little thing called the Bull Moose Party?" Of course he hadn't.

"The Bull Moose what?"

"Yeah, no biggie. Just Teddy Roosevelt's party," I answered, crunching an ice cube in my teeth.

"Okay, smarty-pants, so one time it happens. My point is still valid." He made an obnoxious grunt, grabbed a handful of cashews, and rolled them in his hand like dice.

Now it was my turn. This was fun. I tapped the top of his hand. "Oh, and just the Dixiecrats. You know, that Strom Thurmond: just another marginal politician."

Roger blinked at me. "Big whoop: two times in history."

"Actually a bit more than that." I couldn't hide my pleasure at trumping him, even though I tried hard. "George Wallace in '68 and '72 and John Anderson in '80."

The three men were stunned. Phillip burst out laughing and threw his arm around the back of our banquette. I inhaled his warm alpha-dog scent.

"Kevin, she may work *for* you, but you just got dissed."

"Yeah. And who do you think hired this one? Me! I knew she had a little something!"

Subject closed. Kevin and Donald began debating the merits of doing an IPO versus a recapitalization. Phillip swirled the ice in his Johnnie Walker Black with his finger, licked it, then put his hand under my hair. He whispered in my ear, "You're not going to be an investment banker the rest of your life."

"What?" He'd caught some errors in my work?

"It's just not your passion," he whispered. "You're far too interesting." Then he continued to ignore me the rest of the night, barely said good-bye, and went up to his room.

I was crushed. The next morning, he was on to Houston, while I flew back to my studio apartment on East Thirtieth Street in Murray Hill. I remember leaning against the flimsy accordion door of my minuscule kitchen, absolutely positive that I'd never find anyone to love. I'd spent eighteen months with a magazine editor lothario who cheated on me and got fired for being a flake. He was a real loser and still my heart was broken. This dashing Phillip guy I'd obsessed over in Memphis was way out of my league. New York is the loneliest city in the world when you are single, confused, and hate your job.

I pursued him anyway. The next two weeks, I sent Phillip three handwritten notes paper-clipped onto the front of the deal memos, trying desperately to come up with reasons he would need to call me. It didn't work. He'd call my boss instead. Sometimes, on the way home, I'd linger near the front entrance of his law firm, just two blocks from my bank. In the fog of gray suits flooding the sidewalks of Wall Street, I never saw him once.

Five weeks later, at about six o'clock on a warm fall day, I was trying to hail a taxi downtown when a silver BMW vintage convertible rolled up to the sidewalk. I've since come to learn that preppies don't own anything new.

"You want a ride, banker girl?"

My heart leapt. "I thought you said I shouldn't be a banker girl."

"You shouldn't. And you know it. Want a lift uptown?"

His tie and jacket lay on the backseat and he had opened the top two buttons of his shirt. He was wearing gold aviator Ray-Bans.

"Are you sure?" I couldn't believe this was happening to me.

"Of course I'm sure."

And four months after that, I was lying in front of the fireplace on his worn Aubusson rug with my head propped up on a thick tapestry pillow in his prewar, two-bedroom apartment in a small building on Seventy-first between Park and Madison. We had been kissing for an hour. Phillip loved to kiss; I'd never encountered a man who wasn't all about gearing up for the next stage. Not that we didn't have sex like bunnies in those days.

Phillip had jumped up to get me another glass of wine, and I watched his bare back going down the hallway. He took smooth, elegant, purposeful steps. I still couldn't believe he was falling for me, a short, middle-class suburban brunette, rather than some blond country-club goddess. I worried what would happen when my parents visited and insisted we see a Disney musical and tour the city in double-decker buses.

He sat down cross-legged next to me and pulled my hand over his knee. His tattered khakis were so worn they felt like thin flannel. "So here's what I think: I think you should quit your job."

"And do what exactly to support myself?"

"I would never suggest you not work. But you need to make a change. You've got to get into another field now, while you're young. While it's still no big deal to fill an entry-level slot."

"It's very hard to switch."

"I'm going to help you. Or at least help you get your confidence up. Look at this." He pointed to five messy newspapers strewn on the floor beside me. "You're a news girl. It's in your soul. You flow to it naturally. You know so much about politics and foreign news and you're not even in the business. What the hell are you doing crunching Excel sheets on some IPO when you could be working at something you actually care about?"

"I tried. I told you that once before. Those jobs are impossible to get. You can't just decide you want to go into news or politics just like that."

"Yes you can. You're more qualified now. You'd be great at the business section of the *New York Times*. You wrote for your college paper and now you know Wall Street."

"You have no idea what you're talking about. You have to do three years at the *South Florida Sun-Sentinel* before they even let you walk through the door of a New York paper. I'd have to move to some small town somewhere to get my reporting chops up to speed."

"Okay." He paused. "That's definitely not going to work for me. Not at all." He thought some more. "Then let's say television news. Go get a job as a researcher on CNBC or any of those new cable stations; you've got a business background now, they'll eat you up." He threw one knee over my stomach and leaned on his elbows. His face was close to mine and he caressed my hair as he said, "You're going to do this. And I'm going be there every step of the way getting you there."

"You are?"

"Do you trust me?"

And I did. That's the paradox of Phillip. It's always been the paradox of Phillip: he's a spoiled baby who has infantile tantrums over nothing, but when you need something done, there's no one better to have on your side. And that's why I was still with him after a decade of marriage. He could always close the deal. I despised his obsession with money, which had metastasized over the years. He was constantly comparing himself to our richer neighbors in the Grid, with someone or other's planes or larger apartments. He seemed unable to grasp how lucky we were, and his flamboyant self-confidence should have helped him rise above such nonsense, but it didn't. Instead, it ensnared him into believing he deserved to have more, that he should be richer.

But there were three lovely children that factored into the equation. He tried hard to be a good father to them. He still loved me. So I forced myself to try to make it work.

"**C**arolina! Where's my sandwich?"

"It's right here on the counter, Phillip," I said.

"Sorry." He opened the bread to make sure there was just enough mayonnaise and mustard on either side. "Hey, Dylan, who was that guy sitting at the table earlier?" Phillip hadn't connected Peter with the man in the orange anthrax suit a few weeks earlier.

"That's Peter," answered Dylan. "He's kind of like a coach."

Carolina slammed some pots around the sink, looking busy so she could eavesdrop.

Phillip looked at me suspiciously. "Why is the coach guy having dinner with the kids tonight? Did he drop Dylan off?"

"Sweetheart, I've already explained to the kids." I sat on the edge of the table, trying to act like this was nothing at all. "Yvette is a little taxed in the afternoons with getting everyone to their activities. Peter is going to be helping out a bit, especially with Dylan. You know, the boys can play a little before dinner."

"Well, that sounds fun, doesn't it, Dylan?" asked Phillip, a slight edge in his voice.

Dylan sensed that something about the manny wasn't sitting right with his father. Then he turned it to his advantage in a split second. "Sure. Why not? And he's real good at math."

Stab your father, then turn the knife.

Phillip looked honestly wounded, but somehow unable to fight back or reassure Dylan. Instead, he picked up the tray with his ham sandwich, a pile of Terra chips, and a Snapple bottle along with sterling silver salt and pepper shakers, a linen place mat, and matching linen napkin. Still holding his folders under his arm, he took the tray and started to leave, but stopped in midstep and spun around so quickly that the Snapple almost toppled to the floor. "Jamie, can you meet me in the study? I have a little item to discuss."

Shit.

Phillip leaned back in his desk chair, rubbing his eyes with his palms. As he stared blankly at me, he dragged his fingers down his face. At forty-two, he was still strikingly handsome, even more so than when he was in his thirties, but tonight his face looked loose and wan. He clasped his hands and laid them just above his waist.

"Believe me, Jamie, I've got bigger problems than this at work I should be focusing on. However, I am curious as to why we've now added a male coach to the payroll."

I sat down in a lush red paisley chair and put my heels up on the ottoman. Forest-green bookcases filled with leather-bound legal books lined Phillip's study. A brass sconce adorned each vertical rib of the bookcases and cast a soft glow on the worn brown leather volumes. This was the most lavish-looking room in the apartment, and not surprisingly, my husband adored it. A flat-screen television was mounted in the middle of the wall to my left. To my right, Phillip's desk stood, piled high with folders and papers that had mushroomed out onto the floor. I too started rubbing my forehead with my fingers and then dragged them down my face. I didn't want to talk about mannies.

"How come you keep coming home early?"

"I asked you about the male coach, Jamie."

"And I asked you about your work."

"Jamie, who is the coach guy?"

"Him?"

"Yes. Him."

"He's just a kid from Colorado I met who is going to help out once in a while with the kids."

"How often?"

"Ummm." Long pause. "Every day."

"What?!" Phillip pushed his palms down hard on his huge desk and glared at me. "For three years Yvette and Carolina have been working out fine and then suddenly one day you hire another full-time person and you don't even tell me? You think I'm made of money?"

"You should be very proud of what you make, that you made partner, and that we were able to buy this big new apartment."

"It's not so big."

"Yes. It is big."

"We don't even have a dining room."

"You poor boy."

He shrugged his shoulders. "I am poor."

"Oh my God. Let's just please not go there again."

He loosened the perfect Windsor knot on his tie. "Listen. I don't mean poor as opposed to people out there, in wherever-the-fuck-ville. I'm talking *here*." He pointed to the floor. "In my life. In *my* reality. Which is what I am talking about and what I care about. Okay?"

"You're doing very well, Phillip."

"No, I'm not. Twenty years at a top law firm and I'm still fucking maxed out on three credit cards at the end of every year." He rolled up his sleeves. "Fifty G's on two tuitions, hundred and eighty G's a year on monthly maintenance and mortgage, a hundred G's on the country mortgage and repairs, another hundred G's on Yvette and

Carolina, and now you want to add someone to the payroll." As he left his study and walked into our bedroom, he yelled back, "Food and clothes and two vacations, and I'm down to zero. Below zero. No savings. It sucks."

Phillip grew up in a time when his White Anglo-Saxon Protestant pedigree alone had purchasing power. When he was a kid, he charged snacks at his country club. He went to the same boarding school and Ivy League college as his father and grandfather. He joined a white-shoe law firm. He did everything right. And yes, his blue-chip background still counts for something on Park Avenue, but in this post-go-go-nineties, post-Internet-boom, post-9/11 world, the social measurements have become more crude. And now, in our neck of the woods, money trumps breeding. Phillip now makes one point five million dollars a year. In the Grid, he says, that's a rock-bottom salary. And the completely sick thing is he's correct.

Most every banker in the Grid is pulling in multiple millions, some in the tens of millions. He sees guys his age running corporations, building third houses in ski resorts, and renting jets, some even purchasing them. And he wonders what he did wrong. Why do they have all that? How come he's busting his butt and he's still so "poor" at the end of the year? The rich don't get richer because of tax windfalls; they get richer because they never feel rich in the first place.

I found him obsessively lining up the creases in his suit pants before hanging them up. "You know money's not the problem, Phillip. I've hired and fired plenty of people without ever asking you."

"All right, so what exactly is the problem, Jamie? Or are you implying this is *my* problem?"

"You know . . ." I shook my head. "Never mind. Look, he's just going to try it out for a little while."

"No. Really. I want to know. What is *my* problem, or, better said, what are you getting at? What do *you* think my problem is? Really. I'm very curious. Very curious as to what my problem is."

"I just don't think you like the fact that he is a man in your house when you are not here."

"Because of you and *him*?"

"God, no!" I had to laugh. "Not because of me and him." I wasn't completely 100 percent positive I meant that last line. "But because he's a guy playing with your kids when you're not there, and you prefer it be a woman. It makes you feel less guilty if it's a woman. You're not being displaced that way."

He put his hands on his hips. "Damned right I don't like some ski bum, Coach Whatever-the-fuck-he-is, pothead-looking dude teaching my kids to do football spirals in Central Park while I'm slaving away to pay for his salary. You're right, Jamie." Now he was pointing a finger at my face. "I don't want a Rent-a-Dad in this household. We don't need it and I won't have it. Bad idea all around."

I swatted Phillip's finger away. "I know this isn't ideal. The reality is that you work like a dog all week. And therefore you can't do school pickup, or afternoons, or dinner. And I work very hard too. And this conversation isn't supposed to be about you anyway. It's supposed to be about our precious, sweet, befuddled Dylan. Our boy who craves more attention than he's getting—from both of us, frankly."

"So stop working so hard and sign Dylan up for some more after-school sports stuff—he'll be fine with that. And what about your time? You can't keep up this pace with three kids; two maybe, but not three. Even part-time has you taxed to the limit. I keep telling you: switch your job to a consultant gig for five years. *Then* you can go back." He exhaled loudly. "We can't keep hiring people to parent the kids."

"Phillip, I'm not the kind of woman who can just quit her job— having a job makes me a better mother when I am at home. You know that."

"I don't buy that overused line about a woman's job making her a better mother. The children need more time. Everything in our home needs more time." He walked toward the windows. "For example: my office shades stuck at half-mast. How long has it been? You know I'd appreciate actually seeing the sun in the mornings. How many times do I have to ask to get the pulley system—"

"Let's stick to one topic: the kids, Dylan in particular. I'm home with them two days and I take afternoons off when I can. My job is not taking over my parenting." I paused for a moment to consider how to express that we were hiring someone to replace *him,* not me. "Dylan needs his self-esteem boosted by a man. It's just something Yvette and I can't do during the week. This isn't about you or me. It's about Dylan's confidence."

"It's very simple. I'm not comfortable with a coach working alongside Yvette and Carolina in my home. On the sports field: fine. But not in my home. It's peculiar. As long as I'm paying the big bills around here, that's the way it's going to be."

"Cool it. I pay for the car lease, the garage, clothes, household petty cash . . ."

"You know what? I don't give a shit what you pay for. Coach boy is not receiving payment in this house from *anyone.*"

My husband was gone again. Here for a fleeting moment, then back into lawyer world. In his mind, the coach problem had been properly disposed of. However, there was a little catch: no way I could dispose of my coach problem, which was starting to become a real problem. I was beginning to care way too much what Peter thought of me, how he reacted to my jokes, and even what I wore around him.

Phillip, in the meantime, had moved on. He started punching his thumbs on his BlackBerry with the ferocity of Beethoven and didn't even look up when I quietly left the room.

9

Exposed!

My friend Kathryn was one of those people who could throw an old scarf over a wooden box and make it look like some countess's bohemian Paris pied-à-terre.

We'd just finished looking at a series of enormous paintings in her studio on Laight Street in Tribeca—all of them one or another shade of blue—and had returned to her loft across the hall. A trestle table at the far end of the open kitchen was laden with a spread of cheese and ham from the Italian grocery around the corner. The meal formed a perfect tableau: bread, meat, and cheese on an old breadboard, iced tea in a green glazed pitcher, plush hemstitched linen bistro napkins. There were old chairs and couches strewn around the place along with odd-looking lamps and tables that Kathryn and her husband, Miles, had picked up at flea markets and antique shows over the years. Three little scooters lay on the floor next to the front door. Dark, high-gloss wood floors stretched the length of the room, and floor-to-ceiling factory windows framed a view of Battery Park and the Hudson River.

"I get the existential, Woody Allen, 'we're all ultimately alone' thing. But how exactly do blue splashes represent that? Why blue? Is blue the sky poking through and some sort of hope symbol, or is it meant to be depressing like Picasso blue?" I asked Kathryn. Her paintings were certainly bold, and moody, but I hadn't a clue as to what they were about.

Kathryn just shrugged and patted my head on her way to the refrigerator. She didn't care that I never seemed to understand her paintings. Miles, who was also her art dealer, did. And apparently so did the hip downtown people who paid a lot of money to display her work all over the walls of their lofts.

"I was sick of the self-absorbed self-portrait," she explained. "And then sick of the porno-meets-innocence thing. So I'm over portraiture and back to abstraction. This is my late de Kooning stage—just a little early!"

She was making fun of herself and the whole weird art world she traveled in, but I was still totally lost.

"Don't you see it?" she reproved. "It's a whole being spilled onto the canvas. Each mark is meant to be migratory. The artist is visually cataloguing the steps an individual takes in her isolated journey through life."

"What is 'migratory'?"

She laughed. "Relax. That's what they wrote in the catalogue!"

Miles poured himself a glass of tea and took a huge bite of bread with a chunk of aged Parmesan on top. "In that blue, she is seeking an understanding of our oneness, with ourselves, with our universe. And in that quest for oneness, we move together—that's where 'migratory' fits in." He threw a piece of bread at me. "It's just art talk. You gotta do it, baby."

We'd come downtown expressly for Kathryn to unveil to her best friend the new "format" her art was taking. It was always a joke between us that we had opposing sensibilities: she was the loose, messy-haired creative type, and I was the cut-and-dried rigid one. She was always telling me I was too focused on being a "producer" and didn't take time to contemplate the cosmic music of the spheres.

Miles broke off a piece of Parmesan and handed it to me. "By the way, Jamie. Nice to see you below Fifty-seventh Street. Did your nose bleed?"

"Stop it, Miles." Kathryn smacked him.

"Oh, I know she's cool." He grabbed a slice of prosciutto. "Kind of."

He, who'd just come home for lunch with us, slipped off his

tattered suede baseball jacket and threw it on the brown corduroy sofa. Obnoxious as he was, Miles was fireman hot: a big, bulky, six-packed guy with short brown hair and a perfect toothy grin. He always wore a black T-shirt with the sleeves rolled up just enough for the ladies to check out his biceps. Kathryn had to have monthly threesomes with her single neighbor upstairs to keep him from straying. (Phillip would have bought me a Lamborghini if I ever consented to that.)

Kathryn and I joined Miles in the seating area of her studio; two Nina Campbell couches with mismatched Indian print pillows.

"How's Phillip?" Miles asked facetiously, placing his arm around Kathryn's shoulder. Miles couldn't stomach Phillip. That's why we never went out as couples—the one time we did, Phillip gave Miles some unwelcome advice.

"Hey, buddy," Phillip had said. "You complain about moving your merchandise. Or about not moving it, as is the case here. But the real thing is, art isn't going to take you anywhere. Sure, if you're Gagosian and representing Warhol and Rothko or whomever the fuck he represents, sure, then you're going to hit it big. But not with . . ."

"I'm not *trying* to be Gagosian," Miles had responded with a big, fat hint of disdain. "I represent emerging artists. That's my forte. Discovering them, nurturing them, finding patrons who'll support them. If rich people don't buy works by the emerging artists of this city, they won't survive."

"That's all fine and good. But in the end, on the scale of things, we're talking about nobodies. A gallery full of art by nobodies that nobody is buying. And that, my friend, is the cold, hard truth. So you have to look at your strategy." Miles shot Kathryn a look and I stomped on Phillip's foot under the table. He got the message. "Well, on the other hand, if this is your calling, there's certainly something very admirable in that. And I'm down with that."

Down with that? From my preppy attorney husband?

Miles waved his hand at the waiter. "Check, please!"

Now I said, "I wish you'd give Phillip another chance, Miles. He's

good at business, and you two might bond on some financial planning."

"You think so? Maybe we should have a Gin Transfusion at the
Racquet Club?"

"I wasn't serious."

"And I won't be taking any more advice from your husband, but
Kathryn and I did follow your lead on the manny thing. We got a
great grad student for the twins."

"I know. Glad it's working."

"So how's Phillip dealing with Mr. Fabu Manny?" Miles asked.

"Phillip thinks I fired him."

"What?" Kathryn almost spewed iced tea on the table. "It's
November, Peter's been with you, what, about two months?"

I looked anywhere but at their shocked expressions. I even tried to
focus on Kathryn's prize canvas, called *Flight of Fancy.* "And so?"

"So you're, like, *hiding* a manny from your husband?" Miles was
shocked. "How have you managed that?"

"Phillip constantly travels."

Kathryn put her head in her hands.

"That's really healthy," scoffed Miles. "Even *I* wouldn't do that to
your husband."

"I just haven't had the energy to deal with the conversation. That's
all."

"The conversation with whom?" he asked. "Your husband or
Peter?"

"My husband! I'm not firing Peter. Nooooooo way."

"So, in effect, you're choosing Peter over your husband."

"That's a ridiculous way to look at it. Peter *works* for me."

"Hey, Kathryn, isn't she choosing the manny guy over her
husband?"

"Yep. And are you leaving your husband *this* year?" Kathryn, finally
raising her head, went right for the jugular. "First it was three years
ago, then last year, what about this one? Any guesses?"

"Don't want to discuss it. As for Peter, once Phillip sees how much he's helped Dylan, and stops being threatened—he'll be glad Peter's there."

Kathryn was appalled. "How much longer are you going to be in this limbo? It's weird. Really weird. Not to mention he's got a graduate degree and he's basically working as household help all day."

"So is your manny."

"It's different. Ours is still in grad school and works just for a few hours here and there."

"Okay, okay. I know it's weird. And if you told me two months ago that I'd have a twenty-nine-year-old with a master's degree working alongside Yvette, I would have said you're on crack. But it's working and I'm not going to stop because it 'isn't done.'" I put four fingers in the air to make quotation marks around "isn't done" and gave her a snotty look. Miles stood up and walked to the kitchen to busy himself—or seem to.

"I'm not the kind of person who cares 'what's done.'" She gave me a snotty look back. "We know the guy's fantastic, there's no question. But isn't he a little bit of a fuckup if he's turning thirty and wants to be a nanny?"

"I just don't think so. I told you, he's developing an online program for city schools to help teachers and students communicate better on homework. When he explains it to me, it sounds totally smart. In the meantime, he needs a job that he doesn't take home with him, and he loves kids. Most important, he loves mine."

"And you're sure he's not a pedophile?"

"Are you sure yours isn't? I already told you, Charles did a background check! I promise you, he's not."

Phillip aside, I was getting a little annoyed that I had to justify decisions about my own children. "Dylan is less sarcastic. Less cynical. Less withdrawn. And I credit Peter with this. The kid's starting to feel some joy again. He's even liking phys ed again—the shrink was getting nowhere, and I couldn't figure it out either."

"So I take it you like this guy?"

I felt the tug of an irresistible smile. "We get along very well. He respects me, but still we talk like, well, not like equals exactly . . ." I thought about it the other morning: the kids were getting ready and I had asked Peter to come early to take them to school for me. I'd decided to go for a quick run in the park before my flight to Jackson. (I was going there to meet with Theresa Boudreaux; she needed to get more comfortable with me before the interview. These interviews can take weeks or months to set up.) When I heard Peter's voice in the kitchen, I quickly changed out of my loose sweatpants and into short leggings. And I got the reaction I was looking for: when I walked in wearing those shorts, he immediately looked me up and down and then caught himself. Suddenly it seemed prudent to try to change topics with my friends.

"Okay, so he treats you like you're his boss, but also sort of a pal?"

"Yes. A pal."

Miles returned to us and jumped back into the conversation. "So why are you smiling?"

"I'm not smiling."

"Oh, please." Kathryn laughed. "What am I picking up here? You don't relate to him like you do to Carolina and Yvette, do you?"

"Are you kidding? No! What is this, a dawn interrogation? Why do you always have to be such a hard-ass?" I asked. "No, I don't talk to him like a girlfriend, but it is a level deeper than how I relate to Yvette. There's no cultural divide, for starters. We bond on a few issues; we discuss the news."

"Well, the news thing," Kathryn said. "That's something real."

"What exactly are you getting at here?"

"Oh, I don't know. Handsome, fun, cool guy in the house all day, husband gone. Can't imagine."

Miles plunked himself back down on the couch, enjoying himself immensely. They now sat side by side, like two professors giving me a law school oral exam.

"What do *you* think I could be imagining, Jamie, in your own words?" Kathryn said.

"He lives in Red Hook. Like a college student."

"Wrong! He's turning thirty," answered Kathryn. "With a master's degree. May I remind you you're only six years older than him? You are both adults."

"It's an attitude thing I'm talking about. I'm not going to fall for someone who gets into skateboard accidents."

"I will say it one more time: he's a grown man with an advanced degree and a lot of potential."

"You're right. He's smart. He's creative. He's funny. He makes me laugh. He's helping me deal with my son. And yes, sometimes we talk. Not about my shitty marriage, for example; there are no *boundaries* broken. But he talks to me about his life back home or about this project he's developing. So I'm getting to know him and I trust him."

"Trust him how much? Respect his judgment more than your husband's, for example? I just think this Peter thing is indicative of . . ."

"Of a bad marriage. I know. It's just . . . the kids."

"Obviously."

"I'm still trying to figure out if parents who are civil to each other, but not in love, are better than a separation."

"Phillip's still in love with you." Kathryn now softened her tone. "It's more than just civil."

"I know. But not like he was."

"Fine. I'm not pushing. Regardless of whether Peter stays or goes, the bigger issue is why he seems to be sharing your life and Phillip isn't. Just make sure you're casting the situation in the right light as you move forward."

"Okay. Can we change topics now?"

"Just one more time." She put her thumb in the air. "You've got to tell Phillip that Peter is in the house with his children." And then her forefinger. "Or you've got to fire Peter as you told your husband you would do."

"I get it. I told you, I'm telling him soon."

"Let me get this straight: stand up to the husband or fire the manny," said Miles, elbows on his knees. "When you say you are telling 'him' soon, who are you telling what?"

"I haven't got that part figured out yet."

10

Wherefore Art Thou, Fabio?

I felt laughter pumping through my veins as I gunned the SUV and sped over the Triborough Bridge. The sense of freedom was almost too overwhelming, too exciting. Peter was drumming his fingers on the dashboard to the rhythm of a Rolling Stones song, and seemed totally relaxed.

The two of us, plus a happy Gussie, were headed to our house at the beach to pick up winter clothes, ski gear, and boxes of books for Phillip.

This was one of those days where every building in the city seemed to catch the sun and the glittering New York skyline made the city seem like Oz. This was the city of my imagination when I was in college. I couldn't wait to get here after graduating from Georgetown and fashion a new life outside Washington, D.C.—a town that was in some ways more provincial than Minneapolis. Goodman was on another story, the kids were in school, and for once, I allowed myself to live in the present and feel just plain haaaapy, like my parents always wanted.

There was a ton of traffic on the road for nine o'clock on a week-day. A huge semi-trailer bore down on us and I quickly maneuvered the car to a faster lane. I also wanted Peter to think I was a girl who knew how to handle a car. I wanted him to think I was macho. I wanted Peter to notice everything about me these days. Maybe even since the beginning.

"You sure know how to handle this thing."

"Word."

Peter cracked up and hit the dashboard with his fist.

I stuck my tongue out at him, but quickly brought my eyes back to the road. "What?"

"Word?"

"Yeah. Dylan taught me that."

"Do you even know what it means?" He said it like I was some toothless granny in a rocking chair on a porch.

"As a matter of fact, I do know what it means. It's like 'Right on!'"

"'Right on'?" He burst out laughing.

"Yes! That's what it means."

"'Right on' is just not an expression I've heard lately. It went out with Woodstock."

"You think I'm old and uncool or something?"

"We could have almost been in college together, so I don't think you're old. No, not old. Now, uncool? Maybe."

I hit his shoulder with the back of my hand. He smiled at me and suddenly I noticed that when he smiled he had a dimple in his left cheek. I'd never been alone like this with him—no kids, no activities—and I was liking it, thank you very much. The other day, when Peter offered to lend a hand with this chore, Yvette had given me a look over the top of Gracie's head. She was right to raise an eyebrow. So was Phillip. And Kathryn. And Miles.

Okay, Jamie. Get a grip, girl.

"If you weren't doing me a favor, I'd leave you right here at exit, uh, fifty-two." I strained to read the exit sign, but Peter pushed my torso back so it faced the windshield.

"The Long Island Expressway is dangerous. And I haven't been to the ocean since last summer, so I'd actually like to get there in one piece. Just concentrate on the concrete divider three inches to your left, please."

We drove on in silence, without the shield of words to prevent the heady tension caused by his physical presence next to me. I was tense the way I was the first day Peter came to the apartment, only worse.

"Thank God you fixed the computer in the back room," I said lamely.

"I didn't fix it, you bought a new one."

"But you installed the programs."

"You could do it yourself . . . if you wanted to. I could teach you."

"Uh, maybe. I could, but not likely. But you know what I'd really appreciate?"

"Shoot."

"Some kind of computer program to organize the kids' week so that it hot-syncs into my calendar but can also be completely separate." I was talking a hundred miles an hour. "If you could also separate it, when we print it out for the kids, it wouldn't have all my meetings on it." I kept turning toward him to make sure he understood.

"Hey, I get it! Just watch the pretty road and the semi on your right, please."

"But then my calendar'd have all the kids' whereabouts. My appointments could be in blue and the kids' in all red. Can you do that?" Him and me in the car. Going to the country together. Alone. Me having to talk to him for hours. Me wanting him to like me. Me wanting *him* now becoming a constant free-floating state. I took a deep breath.

"So . . . can you separate the kids' schedules from mine that way?"

"Can I tell you something?"

"Sure." I braced myself.

"You're whacked, lady."

"Excuse me?"

"Yeah. You are. I think you need a nice long walk on the beach."

"Just so your expectations are managed, we're not going to the beach. We're going to our house. To the basement to get all the stuff we need, which you so generously offered to help me carry. Then we're driving back in time for pickup. I don't have time to go to the beach."

★   ★   ★

Forty-five minutes later we pulled into the driveway of our weathered little gray wood house. The house sat on Parsonage Lane in Bridgehampton—the middle, "down-to-earth" hamlet between the toney, old-money, Gatsbyesque Southampton and the more megabucks East Hampton. Lace curtains framed the antique paned windows in each of the three bedrooms, and a motley assortment of old furniture covered in sun-bleached floral fabrics took up most of the space in the small central living room. Huge willow trees and untidy rosebushes surrounded the property, just an eight-minute drive to the beach.

We came to this house every summer and on the warmer weekends of fall and spring, but once the late-October chills arrived and blew through the thin walls, Phillip wanted to stay in the city. I never was able to sweep all the sand off the old creaky floors, and it crunched under my hard winter soles as we walked in. The house smelled stale and salty.

"I can't picture your husband here." I noted that Peter never, ever uttered the word "Phillip." He was opening doors, looking for a place to hang his jacket.

"Why do you say that?" I pointed to the hooks next to the front hall mirror.

"It seems too, uh, basic for him."

"You're not far off. He doesn't want to change any of the furniture because it all came from his Nana. No new anything. Keep it old, keep all of Nana's stuff intact—makes it more authentic. But you're right. Phillip's often cranky here because nothing works the way he wants."

"I thought so" was all Peter said, and he gave Gussie a rubdown and then headed for the basement.

An hour later, we'd packed up the car with the books and the kids' skis and ski clothes, and Peter was carrying a case of wine on his shoulders out to the driveway.

"Okay, that's it." He put the box in the car and slammed the door.

I took one last look at the house, not knowing when we'd next be out again. The gray wood looked milky in the winter and had lost its

oily summer sheen. It was still a lovely house in any season, but closing the door felt sad. I wondered if I'd ever be here creating those
happy summer memories again—which was a tad dramatic since we
hadn't really had fun family time anywhere since Dylan was five or so.
Still, the house was so lovely. And I liked to entertain the fantasy of
being a happy mother with her young children running around the
backyard.

"Time to go back," I said finally.

"It's barely noon. It would be a sin to miss the beach on a day like
this." Peter grabbed the keys from my hand. "Let me drive, would ya?"

"You don't know where the roads turn."

"Yes, I do. C'mon, Gussie." I knew there was no stopping him. He
opened the passenger door. "C'mon, boy!" The dog flew into the car,
panting contentedly from his morning run around the backyard.

With Gussie now straddled on the front console, we started back to
New York. Gussie was a floppy dog who asked for attention all day
long. He adored Peter, who gave him almost as much love as Dylan
did.

The noonday sun streamed through the front window. I put on
my sunglasses and handed Peter his from the dashboard, then leaned
back in the seat and let the sun warm my body. I watched Peter's
right hand on the steering wheel—he looked totally in control of
the car. He had strong, lean fingers. His elbow hung out the driver's
window. Nonchalant, one-handed, cowboy driving. I knew my
naughty musings were nothing but the Fabio fantasies of a woman in
a boring, loveless marriage—but they were real enough to make me
worry about what Phillip would do if he found out I'd slept with
"the help."

Suddenly Gussie jumped onto my lap so he could stick his nose out
the window. He only does this in two places in the country: when we
turn into the driveway of the house, or when we're close to the beach.

"Wait! Peter, c'mon! We've got to get back! Go right, go right
here!" I yelled.

"I know exactly how to get back to the city. Thing is, we're not
going back to the city right now."

"What are you talking about?"

"It's a gorgeous day. We're going to the beach. The dog needs it. And apparently so do you."

He pulled up to Coopers' Beach and drove the SUV right up to the sand so we could see the surf. Gussie was going crazy at this point, so Peter opened the door and let him out. Next to us, a guy eating a meatball hero in a Verizon truck waved and gave me a little wink. I thought, *Does that guy know me? Could he be one of the local tradespeople Phillip has abused over the years? Even if he doesn't know me, he'll think we're a couple. If I run into anyone, Tony from the vegetable market, Roscoe, the flaky handyman who never shows up, they're going to think I'm having an affair. Bridgehampton is such a tiny community. I can't walk on this beach. But Peter will think I'm an uptight loser if I can't just enjoy the beach for ten minutes with the dog.*

And I had to admit, the beach was beautiful. Even more so at this delicious time of year when the summer crowds are gone. The waves rolled lazily against the sand, barely enough to disturb the tiny sand-pipers that ran along the shore.

"It's too cold to walk on the beach," I said halfheartedly.

"No, it isn't that cold. Look at the waves. They're smooth. That means there's no wind. You're going to be okay. The dog needs it. You need it. And I'd love it."

"But we can't. We have school pickup."

"Yes. We can." Peter grabbed my phone and punched in some numbers. "Hey, Yvette." I tried to grab it from him, but he pulled away and slid out the door.

I lunged at him over the console. "Give me my phone!" I whispered.

"It's Peter. Boy, we got a lot of stuff to deal with out here. . . . Yeah, no way we're going to make it back in time for pickup. . . . Could you get Dylan for me? . . . Great . . . We'll be home late afternoon some-time." And he snapped it closed, threw it back underhand right into my purse, and trotted down the dune after Gussie.

This was ridiculous. What was I feeling guilty about? So we'd take a short stroll and then head back. Big deal. I got out of the car and walked down to the beach and stopped where the sand made a three-foot cliff drop. I slid down it on my heels. Peter was already at the water's edge, hands on his hips. Okay. He was fabulous looking. But as my mother always said, there's no harm in window-shopping. It's the actual buying that's the problem.

"Good. You made it. Not so bad, huh?" He waved his hand at the ocean, brilliant blue sky, and soft, thick, white sand.

"It's just awful." I smiled. He found a disgusting old tennis ball and played fetch with the dog along the shore. Gussie was now filthy, with wet sticky paws and sand all over his coat. I couldn't possibly go all the way back to the house and hose him off. I'd have to get the damn car cleaned before Phillip used it.

"Hey! J.W.! Get a little blood flowing! Endorphins releasing! You could use it."

I reluctantly started after Peter and the dog. About a hundred yards offshore, a lone surfer in a winter wet suit, booties, and a cap tried valiantly to catch the small waves. A tanker moved slowly across the horizon line. The majestic Hampton summer mansions shot up from behind the grassy dunes. Most of them looked like they were built by the same architect: tan weathered shingles, mullioned windows, countless bedrooms, curved verandas flowing around the main house. From time to time, a modern structure appeared—a spare two-story black rectangle, a tall, glass-walled A-frame, a simple stone prairie-style house—built as if to remind us we were in 2007 and not the turn of the last century.

"Amazing houses." Peter was beside me again. I took a step back.

"One after the other," I agreed. "And the most astonishing thing is they're the second houses."

"What do you think that one's worth, the biggie down there?" Peter pointed to a house topped with cupolas and built in three separate sections that could each shelter a family of twelve.

"I actually know what it's worth. It's Jack Avins's house. He bought it for thirty-five million dollars after a famous deal known as Hadlow Holdings. All the principals made like eight hundred million. Phillip worked on it."

Peter looked at me inquisitively.

"No, no. He just earned his usual hourly fee, and believe me, he's pissed about that."

"Yep." And he said that like he was dying to say more.

I said to him, "I think I know where you were going with that comment, but I'll just move on. But one thing: you tell your former employer he's a passive-aggressive jerk and you tell me I'm whacked. Is there a pattern here?"

"You're nothing like him."

"But you still see reason to criticize." God, he looked good in his black down jacket and jeans.

"I'm not criticizing. Maybe just a little. But really, you need to chill a little on Dylan's scheduling."

I forced myself not to look at his face, surprised by how hurt I felt. "What do you mean?"

"I mean, it's not the end of the world if Dylan doesn't make it to something on time or misses a birthday party."

"But he loves birthday parties."

"No, he doesn't."

"Yes, he does."

"I'm sorry, but he doesn't," Peter went on, unabashed. "He doesn't like crowds, that's part of the reason he won't go back to basketball: all the crowds, all the noise, he can't handle it. He's a thinker, a solitary one. Crowds unnerve him. That day when he freaked out and couldn't shoot the basket—it wasn't just performance anxiety, it was having too many people around him."

"You've been talking about this? He said this?"

"Yes, he did."

How could he think he knew my son better than I did? I didn't like that Dylan was opening up to Peter more than me, but I tried not to let on. "Well, I'm glad, Peter. I'm relieved." I folded my arms across my chest. "Dylan's not one to lay it all out on the table. He only really opens up with me at bedtime, when he's overcome with some kind of back-to-the-womb aura and feels safe in the dark."

"It wouldn't be so bad for you to chill on your own schedule too."

"You don't know anything about being a working mom in this city with three kids. You don't know lots of things about my day."

"I dare you. Just deviate from the plan."

"No problem, I'd do that."

"You sure?"

"Yes, I am, but we're not talking about me. We're talking about Dylan."

"Can I give you some advice? C'mon, let's walk."

"Sure," I said reluctantly. "Tell me what else you think. Not that I could stop you. It won't bother me at all." But I was still smarting.

"Good to hear." He was really gearing up. He took in a deep breath—as if there were a list a mile long of my errors. "You're running your house like a slick television production. Each kid already has their own, color-coded activities listed on the wipe-off calendar board (which now you want in digital format); every staff person has a clear schedule each day. And there's no deviation from the plan. Ever. And it's too much for Dylan . . ." His voice trailed off.

I followed his eyes as they locked on a couple making out in the sand on a big striped blanket. The girl had her leg slung over the man's, and it was hard not to stare because they were really going at it. This was the last thing we needed—a passionate sexual display with the two of us as the audience.

I cleared my throat and walked faster. "Well, we live in a busy city; both parents are working. Kids thrive with order."

"Only to a certain degree. Sometimes Dylan needs to blow off his entire afternoon. Hell, let him get out of school early and I'll take him to a game. He needs to live like a carefree kid if you want him to shake that cynical side of him, where he thinks it's too cool to be excited about anything. Everything feels so critical, so orchestrated. No time ever to smell the sea grass."

He inhaled the salty air and sat on a little sand cliff. A puff of wind came from behind us and made the top of the waves spray out.

"I didn't imagine ever raising kids in a city, it's not the way I grew up," I reminded him as I sat down next to him, but not too close. "I'd be totally happy to live out here—it's our jobs that keep us in the city."

"So you have to compensate for that."

"I hired you, didn't I?"

"It's just that the intensity of the city is sapping the happiness right out of all the kids there. And the mothers too."

"With all due respect, what do you know about all the moms around here?"

"Actually, I hang with the moms a lot—the park, playdates, pickup. They tell me stuff. They don't really think I'm the household 'help,' like Yvette or Carolina. They like to confide in me, which is sometimes hilarious."

"And what do they say?"

"At first, they want to kind of check out why a guy would want this job. Once they get past that, and they find out I'm working on a project with the public schools, they get very comfortable, very fast. And they start to talk. They talk about their husbands, how much they hate them, how they're never home. The whole Wall Street widow deal. I just try to listen mostly, make them feel like somebody actually cares about all the stupid shit they care about. One of them asked me—with a straight face—'because I'm a man,' if I think it's normal that the contractor wants a hundred and thirty-seven thousand dollars to redo her husband's dressing room."

"I know, it's so shocking. The numbers . . ."

"It's beyond shocking. Aren't you a little worried about having your kids around these families?" His hair blew around his face and into his mouth and I wanted to brush it aside. God. Was I like Mary Kay Letourneau, the teacher who had sex with her thirteen-year-old Samoan student, went to jail, and then married him? But then I remembered Peter was only six years younger than I was and a six-foot-tall man.

"Well, yes, but I try to have good values in our house."

"But you can't counter what *they* see. I took Dylan to a playdate the other day at the Ginsbergs' and the mother was literally having her house detailed. Like a sports car."

"What?"

"Mrs. Ginsberg had two ladies in white uniforms and one man in a shirt and tie tracing the lines of her windows with those long Q-tips! You think that's a normal environment for a playdate?"

"No. I don't think that's a normal environment for a playdate."

"And you go into the boy's room and he's got some fancy blue and white sheets with his initials in script all over these frilly pillows, his books alphabetized, his T-shirts pressed in the drawers. Who irons a T-shirt in this world?"

"I don't know. We don't," I said defensively.

"And how much are those sheets anyway? I was meaning to ask you."

"I don't know."

"Yes, you do. You have the same ones on your bed."

"I'm not telling you."

"Then I quit." He stood up to leave.

"Stop it! Sit down! They were very expensive."

"That is so deeply sick! For a kid's bed?"

"Dylan has Pottery Barn soccer ones."

"Oh wow. That makes all the difference. For all you moms it's all about maintaining this, organizing that, planning this. Like you with your digitized, color-coded schedule fantasies."

I hated that he was equating me with all the whiny playground moms. "I don't have much connection with all those women."

"Oh, reeeeeeally?"

"Yes, really, Peter. You disagree?"

"I notice small things. I'm a 'detail' guy, that's why I'm good at programming." He was really cute when he teased me.

"And what do you notice?"

"I watch how your body language changes. I notice how you don't look your normal self around them. . . ."

"Peter, they're a whole different species."

He started whistling a little tune.

"You're kidding me, right? You don't see day in and day out that I'm from Minnesota and still struggling to fit into this life?"

He pulled his sunglasses down his nose and stared at me with a poker face.

"I'm not obsessed with buying clothes, Peter, with the idiotic things these women care about. You know that, don't you?" I think I was actually pleading.

He bumped me with his shoulder. "You may be smarter. You may have a big career. But you've drunk some of the same Kool-Aid. Maybe spent a little too much time at the punch bowl. From my perspective anyway."

Jesus. Hurt me.

"So what do *you* do at the punch bowl? Go out with your Red Hook friends? Your girlfriend?"

"What?"

"I'm sick of talking about me. Let's put you in the hot seat for a while."

"I don't have a girlfriend right now. And if you must know, I left Colorado because of a really nasty breakup. I'm not looking to jump into anything. And yes, I hang out with my friends in Brooklyn, but a lot in Manhattan too. And guess what? They're a lot cooler than those moms you know." And he jumped up and ran after the dog.

I yelled back at him, "Kathryn isn't like that!" But he was already headed for the car.

We both seemed lost in our own thoughts on the ride back. Around an hour into the trip, I couldn't help asking "Okay, give me another example. Of something I actually do. Something that screams creature from the Grid."

He smiled that killer smile and scratched his chin. Then he chuckled. "Okay, I've got one."

"What?" I was dying inside.

"Your leopard pillows."

"My what?"

"Your leopard pillows. Every single friggin' apartment around here has the exact same leopard pillows, about nine inches by twelve inches, with the fancy little silk tassels, on their main couch in the living room. Two of them, on either end, on top of other very expensive-looking pillows."

I felt exposed.

He continued. "Every time someone comes over to the house, you make a beeline for those little pillows—two of them—you fluff them up just so before you go and open the door. Cracks me up every time."

Like some CIA drone that had locked on to its target, this guy had picked up the one material thing that had sucked me in years ago. And he was right: those goddamn leopard pillows *were* a symbol. A metaphor for everything. I remember going to Susannah's house for the first time, knowing she was so beyond me in her style and class, telling myself I shouldn't care, but of course on some level I did. Naturally, I wanted Phillip's friends, with their clannish, incestuous, rich-kid behavior, to accept me.

I wanted to be like her. I knew it didn't come naturally to me. I sat on her couch. I picked up the little soft pillow under me. I smoothed my fingers over the soft velvet fabric, traced the little squiggly amber and chocolate brown patterns. I pulled at the silk yellow tassels. Scratched the delicate crochet work on the borders. I wanted that pillow. That pillow screamed money and style and entrée.

Two weeks later, my own two leopard pillows arrived from Le Décor Français in a little box wrapped in pink tissue paper with a white ribbon. I put them on my own couch. And ever since, they've made me feel like a member of a club I have no business belonging to.

"Peter, I don't see what idiotic leopard pillows have to do with this discussion."

"I think you've been mingling with the natives more than you think."

I hit him in the arm with my purse, wondering what he'd say if he knew it had cost me twenty-five hundred dollars.

11

Rotten Eggs

From the rear, a woman with a long slit in the back of her skirt and high crocodile boots did a catwalk up the sidewalk, and as she did, her skirt opened ever so briefly to her panties, revealing a tanned, perfectly toned leg. A week later, after running kids' errands, Peter and I had just turned the corner toward Dylan's school entrance, and I caught him smiling to himself at the sight before him.

Ingrid Harris: the woman who was too posh to push. In addition to her gorgeous legs, she had a tiny upturned bottom and Barbie boobs. I was suddenly taken back to a moment at the Seventy-sixth Street playground, when Dylan was about six and a group of us moms were hanging out, discussing how much we hated exercise. Ingrid, as usual, was not present, but her older son, Connor, was playing with Dylan nearby in the sandbox, and he overheard our conversation.

"My mommy uses a trainer," Connor announced. "His name is Manuel. He's from Panama and he brought me a guitar from there." We all knew Manuel: the black hunk of burning flesh from the fancy gym in our neighborhood. We also knew our Ingrid and her hyperactive libido that kicked into high gear whenever she detected the scent of an attractive man nearby. She loved to watch porn when her husband left on business trips. Her favorite video? *Cuckoo for Cocoa Cock.*

Connor continued. "Do you want to know a secret?"

"Sure, sweetheart," Susannah had encouraged him.

"Mommy and Manuel do their exercises in the TV room, and when they're done, they always take a nap together."

Now I glanced again at Peter. He was still transfixed by the grapefruit-size shape of Ingrid's rear end.

I punched him in the arm. "Put your tongue back in your mouth."

Yvette was waiting in front of the school steps with Michael and Gracie in a double stroller. As I hugged them and pulled them from their seat straps, Ingrid pranced her minuscule butt up the stairs next to us.

"And who's this dashing man?"

"Hi, Ingrid. This is Peter Bailey. And you know Yvette."

"So handsome!"

"Hands off."

"Nice to meet you, Ingrid. You have a son here?" Peter put his hand out eagerly and puffed his chest out. Suddenly I was invisible and I didn't like it. She moved in closer, her fake boob now a millimeter from his arm.

"Yes. Connor. He's the same age as Dylan. Are you visiting New York?"

"He's working with our family." I took a step up the staircase, holding my two wiggly little kids.

"Mommy!" whined Gracie. "I told Yvette I wanted to stay home."

"And I told Yvette I wanted to see you and take you to the park after your brother got out of school." I brushed her cheek tenderly with the back of my index finger.

"Well, I don't want to." She gave me one of her looks. Michael, frustrated to be trapped in my arms, arched his back violently and almost flew overboard down the stairs. Peter grabbed my elbow to steady me with one hand and then supported Michael's back with the other. Ingrid watched his deft move with growing interest.

"And he has a software company."

"Smart too? Verrrry nice." She flared her nostrils slightly.

"Ingrid!" I shot her an obvious warning, which she conveniently ignored. "I bought some tickets for the DuPont benefit." I was referring to the upcoming DuPont Museum benefit with a Hermitage

White Nights theme. Talking was the only way I could think of to dampen the fire between these two. I was so right about the Fabio fantasy thing. Peter wasn't at all interested in me or even attracted to me. The dimple in his left cheek deepened as he smiled back at Ingrid. *This* is what an interested man looked like. I felt like the fat girlfriend sidekick from central casting who'd never gotten laid once in her life.

Ingrid turned to me. "Saw you bought two tickets. I've got to hand it to you, with half the Pembroke board on the committee, buying the most expensive gala-level tickets was a smart move."

"Gracie's applying next year."

"What am I doing, Mommy?"

"Nothing, dear."

"Everyone's onto that, everyone knows exactly why you bought those tickets. Do you have a good dress?"

"No, haven't had the time to think about a dress." Peter hadn't blinked an eye since she appeared. I edged my way in front of him.

"You should reconsider that one. It's all about the dress. And you won't find anything after December first. The winter collections will be looted by then."

"Clothes aren't important to Jamie," said Peter.

Ingrid put her hand on Peter's arm. "Hello? Tell me about it. She's remedial!"

He laughed hysterically as if she were the cleverest woman he'd ever met and then just stared at her with a completely stupid look on his face.

"They're doing a czarist theme because it's Fabergé eggs' last global tour before they go into private hands," Ingrid instructed. "But remember, it's not just czars, it's white czars."

"You want me to take notes?" asked Peter.

"I'm good. Time to get Dylan." I squinted at him.

He tapped his watch. "Still three minutes to go."

"And it's not just the dress—don't forget the white fur part. Not that you would. But just checking."

"Are you kidding? I don't have white fur."

"Don't be coy, Jamie. White nights, white fur! Like Julie Christie in *Doctor Zhivago!*" She leaned in and whispered, "I'm doing vanilla sable. Short capelet. Hood." She motioned with her hands exactly where the short fur cut off. "Got it from Dennis. At a *very* good price."

"Give me a ballpark," said Peter. I knew he was just stockpiling ammunition to fire at me later.

"Nineteen," she whispered.

"Nineteen hundred?" he whispered, dangerously close to her ear.

"Nineteen *thousand*! What planet are you on?"

Peter looked ill. "I'll get Dylan."

Ingrid whirled around and followed right behind him. I instinctively reached for her shoulder, hoping to stop her in her tracks, but she'd slithered away.

Someone tapped me on the shoulder. Now Christina Patten, she of the mini-muffin crisis. I felt pistol-whipped by the drop-off hens. Christina had an aquiline face with brown hair that curled under her ears and hit the top of her shoulders. She wore a cream pantsuit with a dozen very pricey-looking gold chains hanging over a cream silk button-down shirt. She also looked dangerously malnourished. "I heard you talking about the czarist gala at the museum."

"Mommy! Can we go now? I'm cold." Gracie rubbed her groggy face.

"*Everyone's* bought a table. Who's at yours?"

I had bought two tickets, not a table. Not that I could fill a table. I wouldn't dare try to push any of my really close work friends to come—they don't care about society events. Susannah, my big connection to society, was out of town that week and not going. I had to stall.

"Jamie, who are you sitting with?" Christina looked concerned now.

"Mom!" Dylan screamed at me. Peter was piggybacking him down the stairs. "One second, Christina. Honey!" I hugged Dylan, who quickly pulled away because his friends were around. I knelt down so that Gracie and I were eye to eye. "If you let me put your coat on, I'll tell you who I found this morning. Put your hand in my bag."

Gracie stared into it with eyes wide as full moons. She nestled the dirty, smelly little Beanie Baby purple giraffe into her neck. "You found Purpy?" He'd been missing for three months. She hugged me tight against my thigh and then ran to introduce Purpy to Peter.

"Jamie, *who* are you sitting with at White Nights?" Christina persisted. "You know, if you don't figure that out, they put you in the rafters near Siberia."

"Phillip has some partners." At least I think he had some partners going.

"You'd better make sure they're the right partners. Everyone has figured out their tables."

Peter would never let me live this down, and of course I didn't own a white dress and certainly not a vanilla capelet that cut off at my elbows. I imagined all the women dressed in Gucci and Valentino gowns or white satin pants worn with beaded, backless tops. I was so behind the eight ball that I gauged Christina's intentions and wondered if I could sit with *her*.

Was she fishing to invite me? She did always think I was "interesting" because I actually did something and took home a paycheck. What a concept.

"You know the Rogerses just canceled on us early this week . . ." She was testing me.

I knelt down again and tended to Gracie's scarf and mittens and tried to engage her in another mini conversation while I thought this through. Sure, we'd applied to several good schools, but I wanted Gracie to go to Pembroke. It had the best, most creative teachers, and the most diverse student body, of any private school in the city. But the competition was fierce. There were only about twenty nonsibling openings per year, and I wasn't confident that we could get her into the school without some help from these women on the board. Christina was friends with all of them. How mercenary could I be?

Christina went on. ". . . And therefore I have two seats to fill. I'd be delighted if you'd join us. I'm sure George would adore learning about the behind-the-scenes at *Newsnight*. He reads the newspaper *every* day."

I took a depraved swan dive into the socialite abyss. "Phillip and I would love to sit with you. Thank you so much for asking me."

"Well, good, then it's all done. I'll send over some information on the Fabergé exhibit so that you can get the most out of the evening." Christina waved and started up the street with her two young children, both in matching mini hunting jackets with collars pulled up so that everyone could see the recognizable Burberry tan plaid underneath.

Peter didn't need to say another word about the ladies at the punch bowl for me to know exactly what he was thinking. "You can give me all the hell you want, but it's statistically harder to get into a New York kindergarten than it is to get into Harvard."

The sidewalk was crowded with moms, nannies, and children who had just been picked up from school. As we walked down the block, Dylan wandered over to see some friends, and Gracie was now holding my hand. Yvette trailed with the baby back in the stroller. "I may have a job in the greater world, but I do come back here at the end of the day. And sometimes, unfortunately, there are compromises one makes."

"Yeah?" He wasn't having any of it. "But you seem to think that spending most of your time with people you don't like or who make you feel bad is the price of admission."

"So I bought tickets to a stupid egg benefit to help get my kid into kindergarten. Get over it. Big whoop. But that's not what my whole life is about, and you know it."

He sighed, slowing to a stop. "I do know that. But the reason I'm giving you a hard time here is that I've sort of been there."

"What?"

"I don't mean literally been here. It's like I started to tell you at the beach. I mean I left a set of relationships that didn't fit me, and a place that didn't fit me either, or that I didn't fit into. I didn't tell you this because it didn't really seem relevant, but now that we're . . . well . . . anyway, I was all set to step into my dad's business, as you know. But I was also in this relationship that was serious—everyone thought we were the perfect match: she came from a nice family, our right-wing parents were friends, she was really great in a lot of ways." I could feel him assess whether he was crossing some intimacy line, but he forged ahead. "What the hell . . . she got pregnant and we had to think about getting together for real. We even started looking at houses. And the pressure was on. And all of a sudden I realized I was heading down a nightmare suburban-dad road that just wasn't me, and it wasn't really her either. She woke up one morning and felt very strongly she wanted to have an abortion—she knew I'd support her either way. She went ahead and had one. And then I freaked."

"Because you wanted the kid?"

"Of course I wanted the kid. I'm dying for my own kids, but I knew in my heart it wasn't the time. I freaked because I realized one more step and I was going to be living a life that absolutely did not make sense for me. I was *that* close."

"What happened?"

"It was really painful. A big breakup. But she wasn't the one. And I wasn't right for her either. When my parents found out about the abortion, it was also really bad. While that might be okay in some places, it wasn't where I came from, and that was that. My dad kept saying he couldn't believe that ending the pregnancy had been so easy for us. And I kept telling him it was the hardest thing I've done, but he wouldn't hear me. We had words. He didn't understand where we were coming from or what we'd been through. So I just cut out. My dad and I have barely spoken in a year."

"Parents don't stay angry forever."

"I know. But that's really not the point. I was living in a world that didn't make sense for me, and it took a huge drama for me to figure that out."

"What are you suggesting? That I cut out on my life here? Quit my job and just move somewhere else? Pull up the family roots and move back to Minnesota?"

"Would Mr. Whitfield be in that particular picture?"

"I, I . . ."

"I don't mean to pry. It's just . . ."

"Just what?"

"Not going there, J.W." He'd begun calling me that and I liked it.

"That's probably wise."

"Yeah." And he looked up at me.

I was embarrassed that he had Phillip pegged, not that it took a genius to do so. "Anyway," I pressed on, "your situation with your father has nothing to do with my learning to cope with some silly women, and talk their talk and walk their walk just to make my family life easier. . . ."

"It's just, the similarities are there. That's all I'm saying," he answered. "You don't want to live your whole life in someone else's movie. It'll make you crazy."

It already had.

12

The Big "Get": Be Careful What You Go For

Abby threw open my door the next morning, knocking a National Press Club plaque off the wall. I looked at her and shook my head. She was wearing one of her awful Ann Taylor suits from last century—a cherry-red one.

"You look like an Avis car rental agent again."

"Cycles of abuse. You're just hurling the abuse the Park Avenue girls throw at you every morning."

"It's not abuse, I'm trying to administer some emergency relief for a walking disaster zone. You can't wear that suit anymore. It's from the eighties."

"I don't care." She sat down on the chair in front of my desk.

"Fine. Your life." I picked up the front section of the *Times* and Abby grabbed another.

After a few minutes she peered over the top of her paper. "I had originally come in here to give you a compliment, but I guess that's not necessary." She whistled a little tune.

"Tell me."

"Tell me I look good first." She crossed her hands on her chest.

"I can't do that. I would be lying."

She blew the steam from her cup of café latte, weighing whether she could be nice to me. "Where were you during the morning meeting?"

"I'm trying to study all the Theresa coverage. And there's so much going on with the kids. I got into a whole stupid deal at Dylan's school about an egg party, which just requires more time and effort that I don't have. Going from Fabergé and furs to Red-State hanky-panky is giving me whiplash."

"Fabergé and furs?"

I took a huge bite of my buttered bagel and talked with my mouth full. "I am not going into it."

"One of your bunny events? Or your seven-hundred-dollar-hat events in Central Park with all your rich friends?"

"They're not my friends."

"What is the egg event?"

"It's for the Fabergé eggs."

"Something that's always been such a passion for you."

I rolled my eyes at her. "It's for Gracie's school; actually it's to benefit the Hermitage Museum."

"St. Petersburg. One of your all-time favorite locales."

She grabbed *Madison Avenue* magazine off my shelf. Here comes the tsunami.

"Your photo going to be in here again?"

I started to grab at it, but she held it close to her chest. Flipping the pages, she added, "Look, here's the Armory Antiques Show, the Children's Storefront School of Harlem benefit, and oh, a really smart-looking person here."

"I know, Abby. I look like an idiot."

"No. You look like you ran headfirst into an enormous lampshade."

"It was an expensive lampshade."

She grabbed the photo.

"It says, 'Susannah Briarcliff and friend.' Don't they know your name?"

"They don't."

"Your nose is bright red. Why are you wearing a pink suit, and if it was Chanel for four thousand dollars, have the good grace not tell me. And this enormous pink flying saucer on your head in the middle of winter?"

"The Bunny Hop. And that's all I'm saying."

I turned on my computer and checked a few news sites for head-lines while Abby read the gossip pages of the *New York Post*. "So why should my ears be burning?"

"Nominations for new Secretary of Homeland Security." She put down the *Post* and placed three cards on my desk with neat handwriting on each one.

1. HOMELAND SECURITY HEARINGS
   JAMIE WHITFIELD, PRODUCER: NEWS DESK
2. HOMELAND SECURITY HEARINGS
   JOE GOODMAN, ANCHOR: STUDIO
3. HOMELAND SECURITY HEARINGS
   ERIK JAMES, EXECUTIVE PRODUCER: CONTROL ROOM

I shook my head. "Abby, we're having a conversation. This isn't a broadcast."

"They make me feel better."

"We've been over this once or twice, I believe. The cards really bug me."

"You're in charge of coverage on the news desk."

"I can read."

"See, it's clearer when you can read it!" she answered, pleased with herself.

"I'm honored. But I'm not happy—it's just more work than I need."

"In front of the whole staff, Erik James said they chose you because you're so good under pressure. I think they had a smaller meeting right after the morning staff meeting, which I guess you also missed."

"Amazing they don't fire me."

"You're only producing the top-secret political story of the year."

Charles sauntered in and sat down on the couch in his usual spot, crossed one of his long legs over the other, opened his ginger ale, and started in on me. "You ready to fry when this piece airs?"

"Stop."

He made little bouncy conductor movements with his toe. "Just watching out for you. Of course, I'll be doing this while I plan the boondoggle of my career."

"I can take care of myself. And don't even tell me about the boon-doggle."

My phone rang.

"It's me. Peter. Everything's fine."

"What happened?" I turned my chair around to face the window.

"Dylan's in the nurse's office. He says he has a stomachache."

"He was fine this morning . . ."

"J.W., so he didn't tell you about the soccer game?"

"What game?"

I was frustrated, and on a short wire anyway, and still not digesting well the idea that my son was confiding in Peter more than in me. "Peter, I'm busy. I know I'm always busy, but today I'm particularly . . . no. Dylan has not told me anything. What game is he upset about?"

"He told me yesterday after school. They're starting to do soccer in his regular P.E. class at school and he's scared. He says he doesn't go for the ball because he doesn't want anyone to kick his shins. And he thinks he's the worst player in his class. He says it's 'dumb.' And he doesn't have a stomachache. I mean, not a real one, like he's sick. But the nurse called me since she couldn't get through to your cell and she wants someone to come in."

"Peter, I just can't. Not right now."

"Don't sweat it. I'm sure he'll be fine with me coming." For the first time ever, I felt it might be better for another person to comfort my own son. And I trusted Peter to handle the situation.

"I appreciate it. Really. I'll talk to him about it when I come home."

"Don't do that."

"Of course I'm going to talk to him!"

"No. Let me. I'll take him home. We'll have some popcorn, and then we'll play chess in his room and talk. Just do me favor, and don't bring it up with him until you and I talk. Okay?"

"All right. I guess. Let me know how it goes. And thanks. Good-bye." I hung up and stared out the window. I was grateful that Peter was breaking through to my son, but I hated sitting on the sidelines while he did. And if he wasn't so damn charming, I'd have protested more.

"Manny to the rescue?" Charles looked at me with a despicable grin.

"What?" I shot back.

"Nothing. Just funny that your studly manny calls all the time."

"Would you please grow up? What's the boondoggle?"

"Guess."

"Paris? Rio?"

"Better. The Jane Goodall Institute. The great apes may be extinct by 2015. Going to Gombe National Park."

"Great, you're on safari and I'm trekking the backwoods of Mississippi."

"Interview still happening Thursday?"

"Yep."

"Do you have the goods?" Charles asked. "Last time we talked, you were a little short."

"Sure we do." I started counting on my fingers. "Point number one: we're going to have her on camera explaining every detail of the relationship."

"But of course, that's just her word against his and he's denying it," snapped Charles. He'd been educated at Westminster in Atlanta and Yale University, which taught him to talk in a superior tone. He always acted like he knew more than me, and unfortunately, he usually did.

"Well, the tapes. We have her saying 'You dog!' And him saying 'I want that behind of yours, that nasty . . .'"

"You can't use that."

"We're working with the lawyers on how to handle the tapes."

"And last I heard, four audio experts don't agree on whose voice is on the tape." Charles was trying to do me a favor by poking holes in my story so that I could shore it up before airtime, but I was so weary, he began to irritate me instead.

"We had three experts confirm that the male voice was our man Hartley, and one other who couldn't," I snapped back at him. "That means the majority said it was Hartley. So that's point two. You heard the tapes, you said they sounded credible!"

He shrugged. "Look, homos are meticulous and I'm just checking that you've got everything covered. Go on."

I continued, counting three on my middle finger. "We have a photo of them together with some of his aides."

"Jamie, there's no lovey-dovey stuff in that photo."

Charles was right. I would have preferred a photograph of Huey Hartley and his little lamb canoodling in the park to cement my case.

Abby put a card on my desk: WITNESS ON THE RECORD: FUNERAL HOME EMPLOYEE

I put the card against my forehead. "Point four: the undertaker at the local funeral home swore to me that they'd been together and that they looked very much in love. This he says on the record and on camera: 'When you saw 'em together you couldn't tell where one stopped and the other one started.'"

I'd been to Mississippi since the summer on a few two-day trips to check everything out, hoping to find others who actually saw Theresa and Hartley together and could double-source her story. No such luck. I tried to strengthen my case. "And the funeral home guy is the one who—"

My phone rang.

Erik James, the executive producer, on the other end of the line: "Jamie, surprise. Big fuckin' surprise. The lawyers upstairs are not happy about your piece."

"Okaaay." I looked at Abby and Charles wide-eyed.

"And they're fuckin' babies," Erik said.

I whispered to my friends with my hand on the earpiece, "Erik's pissed."

Abby leaned in and mouthed, *Why?* I shrugged my shoulders, and put up my hand to get her to be quiet for once in her life.

He continued. "They're concerned because Huey Hartley's supporters are going to town on their websites. Trashing Theresa, writing scathing editorials, marshaling their forces . . ."

"So what?"

"So, as I said, the network lawyers are bein' fuckin' babies. They'll be down here at two o'clock. Can you come to my office then?"

"Yep."

"And bring Charles with you."

I hung up. "Charles, you're getting roped in."

"What do they want now?"

"The executives are freaked out by the bloggers again. Second story this month. Amazing how much they buckle."

"They should be freaked out." Charles had become uncharacteristically serious.

"We've been around for over fifty years!" I reminded him. "There's like two thousand people who read the biggest blogs and fifteen million people who watch *Newsnight*."

Charles was aghast. "You are so wrong."

"Sorry, *you're* wrong. Not everyone's a lonely computer geek like you. My parents don't even know what blogs are."

"Have you read them at all?"

"Yeah, sure. I've read Huffington Post, Media Bistro. Just incestuous media types writing and reading each other's little editorials."

He sat down on the couch. "You have no idea what you're talking about. There're millions of blogs and literally thousands of really good ones—right on our tails. DailyKos on the left, Hugh Hewitt on the right . . ."

Abby pulled out a card and read "Fifty blogs at the end of 1999 and almost sixty million right now."

"So what? Office productivity is down because people waste time all day online," I said. "You really think the bloggers are on the tails of a big network behemoth like NBS?"

"Bloggers make us jump by a single push of a single 'send' button. Newspapers and networks are no longer the gatekeepers of information," Abby explained. "The bloggers write, 'sources are saying' and we all have to check it out. So they're speeding up the news cycles and controlling the pack."

"Hell yeah," said Charles. "They scoop us all the time."

"They do not. You're such an exaggerator."

Charles looked at me with great condescension. "Helloooo? Monica Lewinsky on Drudge? That wasn't a slightly big deal?"

Abby interrupted. "It wasn't Drudge that broke Monica. *Newsweek* did. Drudge just went first and reported that Michael Isikoff from *Newsweek* was sitting on it, but Drudge didn't have any information himself. And Chris Vlasto and Jackie Judd at ABC actually aired it first."

"Fine, Abby," said Charles. "I know there're others."

Abby started counting on her fingers. "MemoryHole.com got the first photo of American caskets leaving Iraq, something the Bush administration had been trying to prevent because of the Vietnam correlation. Instapundit.com broke the story of Trent Lott's speech at Strom Thurmond's birthday party, which made him look like he was a supporter of segregationist views, then . . ."

Charles added, "That only caused Lott to lose his position as Senate majority leader. No big deal, I guess."

"So they scooped us a couple of times. It's a big world," I argued. "And aren't so many of them right-wingers like the Swift boat guys who took John Kerry down?"

"Yeah. I have to take Charles's side here," Abby said. "Bloggers started as a right-wing phenomenon to counter the mainstream media, which they viewed as liberal. But now there's a whole universe of ideas from all sides. I promise you, there're some brilliant bloggers out there." Abby hadn't pulled out a card in at least six minutes. I was proud of her.

I looked at both of my friends and smiled. "Okay, fine. I read the *New York Times* and *Newsweek* and fifteen other magazines to keep up with everything and I'm still behind the blogger eight ball. For once I am going to actually thank you two for being so obnoxious; now I won't sound like a complete idiot in front of the bosses."

13

Backstage Jitters

"Sending the little Ivy League faggot to cover her bases," news president Bill Maguire mumbled into the telephone outside Erik's office. "He's thorough, like all of 'em. Want him on the next flight to Jackson . . . yes."

Charles was ten steps behind me and hadn't heard, but he wouldn't have been surprised. Charles was his favorite producer, despite the fact that Bill Maguire often made homophobic remarks. Maguire, a dark African-American man with a flattop crew cut and huge muscles, had been raised on Spokane Avenue in Gary, Indiana. He had joined the Marines after getting a degree in political science from DePauw University, magna cum laude. Every day, he wore the same black suit, white shirt, black tie, and shiny shoes. He wasn't one of those smooth-talking executives who schmoozed and charmed their way from the Harvard Spee Club straight to the chairman's office. Maguire ate nails for breakfast and terrified all of us with his gruff manner. Maybe it was his jarhead attitude. Maybe it was his brilliant, sharp mind that cut right through our half-baked stories. Or maybe it was the fact that he was a six-foot-four black motherfucker who scared us senseless.

Charles and I walked into Erik's office together while Maguire continued his battle plans outside.

Erik James slipped around from behind his desk, sat down in his armchair, and leaned over. His shoulder fat bulged out on either side of his suspenders. He rolled up his sleeves. "You know the drill. Geraldine and Paul are going to milk you dry with legal questions about Theresa Boudreaux's credibility and talk about the bloggers. Charles, you hang low for now. Then we're going to talk about some disturbing reports we have about backdoor strategizing, no pun intended, by the Hartley camp."

Goodman winked at me from the armchair just as the utterly humorless Geraldine Katz and Paul Larksdale walked into the room carrying identical brown legal briefcases.

Geraldine once asked me how I could prove Michael Jackson really was the King of Pop. Another time she demanded documentation to verify my claim that the Sonoma Diet would get you ready for summer. "How can you prove weight loss means *ready* for summer?" She was plump, unattractive, and wore Fendi headbands. Her sidekick Paul looked like an FBI agent with his nerdy haircut and sharp jawline. He tried to play good cop to get on our side, but we recognized it as their little party-pooper ploy. All producers hate the network lawyers, and I assume the feeling is mutual. Nevertheless, I couldn't blame them for their vigilance over Theresa's outrageous story, riddled as it was with potential for litigation.

Erik started the meeting off. "Huey Hartley's camp is gearing up for battle in this Boudreaux case, as we know. The right-wing bloggers have been given fodder to fire back on our story as soon as it airs, and Geraldine and Paul here are concerned about the ripple effect they will have among staunch Republican supporters."

Goodman interrupted. "RightIsMight.Org is on twenty-four-hour death watch." Even I'd heard of them, the anonymous and very influential website that served as a scorecard for the far right wing. The authors, anonymous political hacks, made it a daily sport to point out holes in stories aired and printed by the "liberal media elite." They held a special vendetta against NBS news, and Goodman in particular for his decades of what they considered his rough treatment of conservatives.

Geraldine Katz continued. "A congressional source told us to watch out for this Boudreaux girl and her right-wing connections. . . ."

Goodman guffawed. "I've met her. She's the real deal. She knows too much about Hartley."

"She may know a lot about Hartley, but this source is a good one."

The door slammed open. "It happens to be my source." Bill Maguire stormed in, looking like he was going to make us do four hundred jumping jacks. Charles and I shifted in our seats.

"Jamie, if my people are right, this is for real . . . the shit! The got-damn bloggers. RightIsMight.org, those people are crazy. Did you read the shit they're posting? Don't mess with them or they'll tear us apart before we get out of the blocks."

"Hey, I'm a registered Republican," said Erik. "I don't need a lecture about the right wing of this country. All of you need to calm down, we got this under control."

Maguire sat down on the couch across from me and reached his giant hands on the far end of the coffee table for a power lean that brought his face about a foot from mine. "I want Charles Worthington to go down and take another look at what you found." He turned to Charles. "Yeah . . . let's put you on those crackers for a while. They're your people. Gotdamn Southerners."

Erik grabbed a handful of Chex party mix from a thick glass bowl he'd been awarded at an advertising conference. He never bothered to finish his food before he started talking. "Let's focus on the positive. I want this to lead the show. We can't ask for people to wait. The promos have got to be top-notch, hint a little at what we've got, but not let on too much." Mini pieces of Chex mixed with spit landed on the coffee table.

Goodman looked down at the table appropriately disgusted, then answered, "I disagree. No hinting. Let's give them the craziest shit we have: the audience will be begging for more. If we're too cautious, they'll think we don't have anything. What about the part of the tape where she says, 'Sure we'll do it, but we'll do it your *special* way.'"

Erik threw his head back and laughed so hard I thought his suspenders would pop off again. Then he was silent, but his stomach was bobbing up and down like a buoy in rough surf. Goodman and I looked at each other affectionately. Nothing in the news business was more fun than having Erik James all pumped up about a big story, infecting us with his love of this crazy profession.

Once Erik stopped laughing, he grabbed another fistful of party mix and inhaled deeply to make another point. But this time he breathed a huge peanut into his lungs and started choking. Somebody had to Heimlich Erik about once a month, and this was rapidly becoming one of those times. His secretary, Hilda Hofstadter, could do it better than anyone.

Goodman stood up and started rolling up his sleeves to save Erik's life for the twentieth time in his career. *"Hilda! Get in here!"* I cried. She calmly popped her head in to see if her services were needed, used to this drill. Erik put his hand in the air to stop her and shook his head. He coughed the peanut up in his hand and threw it across the room, missing his wastebasket by five feet. He would live to see another day.

Geraldine clasped her hands on her pad like a prim schoolmarm. "I have a dozen issues to cover before we start making party plans. What words are we going to use on the air, Jamie?"

"You know what we have on the tapes; we can just use him saying 'I want that little ass of yours,' and then bleep out 'ass.' I haven't had the pleasure of discussing Hartley's anal sex proclivity directly with Theresa," I answered. "So I don't know which words she is going to use in the interview. And of course I can't coach her on anything. Her classy lawyer, Leon Rosenberg, told me she refers to it simply as 'up my behind.'"

The lawyers were now wasting Erik's time. Under normal circumstances he had the attention span of a small toddler. "And that, ladies and gentlemen, is the most fuckin' delicious tidbit I've heard in thirty fuckin' years in this biz. There's no need to even waste any more—"

His secretary knocked and came in. "Jamie, there's a call for you."

"For me, on Erik's line?"

"It's a guy named Peter. He had the receptionist locate you."

14

Kidnapped!

Ten, nine, eight . . . the numbers in the elevator slowly descended. I tried to remain calm. When I'd gotten the call interrupting the meeting, I could feel my blood pressure rise and then fall so much I felt dizzy. "Get the hell outta here," Erik had said. The big fat oaf was always so understanding about my family.

They were seated on a long dark leather bench in the lobby, Peter with his arm around Dylan. I ran toward them. "God, did he have another meltdown?"

"Mom. Just chill."

"I'm your mother, don't tell me to chill." "Chill" was a big Peter word.

"Would you like to inform me about what's going on?"

"Don't blame me," Peter said, "it was all Dylan's idea. So I said, 'What the hell, she needs to have a little adventure once in a while.' And you agreed, remember when we talked about too many logistics? So here we are. We're taking you uptown."

Dylan's pleading eyes looked up at me, breaking my heart.

"You know, guys," I said, "I love a surprise. And it was a great idea to come to the office. You've really brightened my day. But I can't just skip out in the middle of a workday."

"It's three-thirty." Peter threw his hands in the air. "You yourself said you liked to *deviate from the plan.* What's two hours?"

"Hey. I work part-time. Why don't we have this outing on a Monday or Friday when I'm home?" I was getting resentful that he'd put me in this position with no warning and in front of Dylan. "When I'm here, I have to work hard, and every hour counts."

Peter stood up from the bench. "Oh, give me a break, you're their favorite producer. They're not going to care."

"You're complicating things for me here," I whispered to Peter—but he was having none of it.

He whispered back, "Would it surprise you to know that it was entirely your kid who wanted to come here?"

I didn't answer, trying to weigh my work responsibilities with wanting to escape with these two. The combination of Dylan and now Peter was awfully potent.

Peter took a step closer to me. I inhaled sharply, trying to figure out if I could resist him. "Look, lady," he said, "do you ever just have some fun?"

Lady?

I met him halfway. "Dylan, let's go get some ice cream at the coffee shop in my building here."

"I don't want ice cream. No time. We have a surprise. You're going to die, Mom." He grabbed my hand and began yanking me toward the revolving door.

Once outside, when it became clear to them and me that I couldn't win this battle, Peter led us to the entrance of the subway on Sixtieth Street and Broadway.

"*Where* are we going?" I asked, trying to act stern.

Peter smiled. "We're going to be riding something called the subway. It's a train that goes underground that takes poor people to work."

I burst out laughing. "I actually take the subway quite often."

"Reeeeally?" He raised his eyebrows like he didn't believe me for a second.

"Yes, as a matter of fact, I do. Like when I need to go downtown and there's traffic, I take the subway."

"Then of course you won't need to borrow my Metrocard. I'm

sure you have one in your wallet, you know, real handy like, so you can pull it out all the time."

I hit him with my bag and walked down the stairs. When we got to the turnstiles, he put his card through one slot for him and then through another turnstile for me and flashed that blinding smile. Then he added, "And I won't test you on which line goes uptown from here."

Harlem: the late-afternoon sun reflected off the bright pavement and it took the three of us a moment to adjust our eyes. I looked up at 125th Street, a planet away from the corporate atmosphere of the midtown NBS block and its gigantic mirrored skyscrapers competing with each other for space. My son, who seemed to know exactly where he was going, dragged me past bodegas and gaudy department stores with cellophane-wrapped velour recliners lined on the sidewalk out front. Shining new banks, Starbucks, and a Pathmark grocery store—all part of Mayor Giuliani's 125th Street development program—dotted the block alongside older, seedier establishments. The new and the old clashed, giving the street a fantastically vibrant urban feel.

"Dylan, do you come here a lot?"

"Not telling." Bursting with happiness, he just held my hand and kept skipping and jumping next to me.

I turned to Peter. "My kid hasn't smiled like this in, I don't know, six months."

"You ain't seen nothing."

We walked one block up Adam Clayton Powell Boulevard and stopped at a basketball court with rusted hoops. Behind a tall wrought-iron gate, we watched about forty teenage kids, mostly black and Hispanic, shooting some balls in the four netless hoops that lined the court. Huge cracks splintered the concrete and a few potholes lay in the middle of the court waiting for someone to break an ankle.

Peter yelled out, "Hey, Russell, look who's here!"

A tall, skinny black kid in an over-the-top warm-up suit did an index–pinkie finger hand signal in the air. I suddenly recognized him from the chess game in Central Park. My throat felt thick.

"Yo! D. What you got today? Hope you brought your game," Russell yelled.

"Dylan, I thought you didn't play basketball anymore. That's what you told me."

"I told you I didn't want to play with the boys from St. Henry's. They're jerks. Peter's friends are funner."

"Yo! D.! Hurry up, man."

"Mom, can you, like, watch really carefully, but don't, like, cheer me on or yell or anything. Just act like you're not even watching."

"Got it."

He pulled his shoulders back and breathed in deep like he was about to pick up a five-hundred-pound barbell. Peter whispered some instructions in his ear. Dylan nodded and walked away with an unrecognizable, manly swagger. Then he turned around and ran back to me just like an overexcited puppy. "Mom, whatever you do, when I'm done, just stand back, okay? Don't hug me or anything. Don't even touch me."

"Wouldn't dream of it."

He ran toward the kids, then stopped in his tracks and started the cool-dude swagger again for the last ten feet. They high-fived each other. Darling Russell put his arm around Dylan and handed him a ball.

I asked Peter, "How old is that guy?"

"Thirteen. No, he just had a birthday, fourteen. They're in ninth grade."

"And they're taking the time? I have never heard anything so sweet."

"It's not sweet. They like him. Dylan's cool."

"Peter, they're doing this because they love you too."

"Fine, but they still think he's a cool kid."

The eight or so other guys in his group stopped playing and either high-fived Dylan, hit him on the back, or punched his shoulder.

Russell said to him, "The whole posse is down to game, so, D., you got five. Hit some fouls." Eight of the kids lined up on either side of the hoop while Dylan stood at the top of the key with the heavy basketball in his hand.

I turned to Peter. "He's never going to make it. The ball's too heavy for him."

"He will. Just not right away." Dylan threw the ball and it missed the basket by five feet at least.

"And these guys wait?"

"It's something Russell likes to do, and the other boys follow because he's cool. Russell's always here before the other guys and sometimes he and Dylan just shoot for a while. But Dylan loves to play with all of them. Of course, if we hadn't spent ten minutes in your office lobby wasting time trying to convince you . . ."

Now I understood. "How often do you bring him here?"

"Once a week or so."

"Wasn't it hard for Dylan to adjust to these kids, all the way up here on 125th Street, playing a game he'd renounced for good?"

"Let's just say it was clear he hadn't spent much time in the 'hood. We just watched the first few times. Then we started getting here early and Russell taught him some things; he wasn't holding the ball right at first. Now he's trying to teach him to use some spin. That's not really sticking. But it's helping and Russell is the man."

"I can't believe you didn't tell me."

"You don't need to know everything. The kid's got enough pressure on him."

My scrawny little boy dribbled the ball in slow motion, it seemed, after the frenzied ballet of the older kids. He was moving toward the hoop, but then someone swiped the ball from his hands and made a gorgeous basket at the opposite end a million feet away. Dylan put his head down for a second, then straightened up and ran for the ball—but Russell had caught it on the rebound.

"Hey, D.!" Russell called, then swooped by my son and slipped the ball into his hands. Dylan looked as if he would just keel over right there and die of pride overload. He took off and ran toward the hoop.

Laughing, the kids on the other team sped past Dylan, then pivoted, waving their arms back and forth, blocking his way. There was no way in hell Dylan could throw the ball over their heads. I dug my nails into Peter's arm. But then Russell knelt down and put his arms around Dylan's hips and heaved him up so he had a clear field, and my son cracked up and shot a perfect layup over everyone else's head. I thought I might actually die right then and there. All the muscles in my throat constricted with intense emotion—gratitude for Peter, and the more powerful relief of my kid feeling good about himself again. And *here* of all places. Russell high-fived Dylan. "It's your world, D.," he said.

Dylan flicked his head up once in a super-cool nod and walked toward me with an explosive smile.

I reached out for him, then pulled my hands quickly back to my sides. Peter put an arm around him. "Nice layup, man."

"That was just amazing," I told him.

"Okay, Mom. They said I could play some more. Can I?"

"Of course, sweetie."

He ran back toward the court. Without looking at Peter, I had to speak. "Thank you for bringing me here. There's no way to quantify what you've done for Dylan. And for our family. And . . . and for me."

"My pleasure."

This was ridiculous. Just standing next to him lit me up.

15

Boundaries, Boundaries

When I heard the key in the lock, my skin started to crawl, and my body tensed like a threatened animal. The heavy front door slammed shut. Phillip threw his coat on the leopard velvet settee in the foyer and yanked his rolling suitcase down the hall toward our room. But then he saw me on the couch in his study watching my favorite show and peeked his head in.

"Hello, my dear." He sat on the edge of the couch and pecked me on the forehead. "Why you still drop everything to watch *Dancing With the Stars,* I'll never comprehend." He smelled like the airplane he'd just taken back from Cincinnati: a combination of that stale airplane vinyl mixed with sweat and plastic food.

"It's the killer app of television shows."

"What are you talking about?"

"It's pushing celebrities outside their comfort zone, live on television in front of twenty-seven million people. These people are learning something they've never done before—and it's really hard. The music is so good, and you can't take your eyes off the dancing. It's perfection. All of it."

"Whatever you say." And he stood.

I felt my whole body sag with relief when he left the room. I knew he'd now be checking out the mail, which was neatly organized in the sterling silver toast holder on the front hall table.

"Goddamn car service," he muttered. "Never shows up and still they charge a fortune."

His next stop was the kitchen. A fluorescent glow beamed out of the refrigerator as he contemplated his choices, eventually grabbing a cold bottle of red Vitamin water. He guzzled it halfway down without stopping. I watched all this from the couch, hoping against hope he would soon go to bed. Anything for time alone. Alone to gauge the political impact Theresa Boudreaux would have, alone to figure out if I still loved my spouse. Alone to think, perchance to dream, about what Peter's strong back would feel like under my hands.

Loosening his tie, Phillip wandered over to the message board in the kitchen and perused the daily calendar of activities. I pictured it in my head: Dylan to Adventurers, Gracie to ballet, Michael to gym time . . . each child's activities color-coded on a washable wall calendar. Then he flipped through the phone messages on pink slips in each of our message boxes and frowned. He seemed to be reading one message over and over again. I could see his lips moving, finally reading it aloud as if that might help him make some sense of it.

"Jamieeeeeee?" he yelled.

"Phillip, what?" I half whispered, half yelled from the couch in the study. "The kids are sleeping. Did you forget you have three children under the age of ten who are usually asleep at ten on a school night?"

He continued screaming from the kitchen; it was apparently too taxing for him to take a few steps across the hall and into the next room. He enunciated every syllable with a Locust Valley lockjaw accent. "What is this piece of paper all about?"

"What piece of paper, Phillip?"

"This one, Jamie."

"Which one?"

"The one in my hand."

"I can't read it from in here! What does it say?"

"It says, 'Mrs. W., Christina Patten called to say she would drop off catalogue for egg exhibit tomorrow. She is delighted you accepted her invitation to be seated at her table. Parenthesis. I'm not going to let you get off easy on this one. End parenthesis. Peter.'"

Shit. I was supposed to have fired Peter weeks ago. I stood up tall and sauntered into the hallway, trying to appear blasé.

I had taken a bubble bath with a jasmine candle in the room and had put on fresh soft flannel pajamas. Big fluffy sheepskin slippers warmed my toes. I was squeaky clean and my husband smelled just plain bad.

"Look at me, Jamie." He treated me like a child when he got angry.

"What?" I answered, as if I didn't know why he was pissed, but also warning him that I intended to put up a fight. If this scene had played out when we first got married, we both would have cracked up by this point. Back then, he adored my down-home resilience and spunk. "Thank God I found you," he would say during our courtship, brushing my hair out of my eyes and kissing my forehead. I knew he was thanking God that he'd found someone with a fresh perspective who talked back to him, someone who wasn't familiar with every country club and restaurant he'd ever been to. After ten years of marriage, my upbeat midwestern sheen had lost its charm. More likely, he didn't want someone talking back to him after all. Life was so much easier for Phillip when people just agreed with him.

"Don't you 'what?' me," he responded, again with that "young lady" tone. "Did you or did you not fire skier-boy?"

"Who runs the domestic side of things in this family?" I countered.

"And what's this about you and Christina Patten? Why does he know about your personal life? Why does he say he's not going to let you off the hook if he is working for you? What in Christ's sake?" He put his hands on his hips and shook his head. Then he began rolling up his sleeves as if he were preparing for a fistfight. "I'm just not getting this whole situation. You talk to this kid like he's a girlfriend? He's the *help*. H-E-L-P. Got it? They work for you. They answer to you. Once again with you, it's all about the *boundaries*, Jamie. Boundaries. Boundaries. How many times do I have to tell you not to fraternize with the staff? Don't become their friend. It complicates everything. They work here, okay? We pay them. They work. Period. Only this kid isn't supposed to be working here at all."

"Phillip, he's from Colorado. He doesn't understand the rituals on Park Avenue—why I would intentionally sit with a woman I love to hate. I just mentioned how stupid she is one day at school. That doesn't mean I'm *fraternizing* with the staff. But that's besides the point. The point here is that I run the domestic side of our life and I don't need your interventions."

"Who pays skier-boy's salary, Jamie?"

"If journalists were paid like lawyers, I would happily pay Peter's salary. But you make fifteen times what I make. Don't belittle my salary all the same. Don't forget, I'm making six figures now, which, after tax, covers a lot."

He threw his head back. "Six figures? You make one dollar more than five figures, big shot."

I took a deep breath and tried to remember whether I had ever in the last fifteen years had any feelings of love and compassion toward this man. At that moment, I couldn't even believe that he was the father of my children.

"Skier-boy's going nowhere, Phillip."

"I told you I don't want a 'manny,' as you ladies call it, in my household. It's fucking absurd."

"Give me one good reason why not to have him around."

"What the hell do you know about his background, for starters? Have you checked what he does with his time when he's not here? He hardly looks like he's doing a square dance at the church."

"He has a girlfriend who is getting her master's in teaching." The last part was an exaggeration. Peter hadn't entered into any romance—as far as I knew—but he did have a few platonic girlfriends in his life back in Red Hook.

"Okaaaaay." Long pause while he ruminated some more. "I still just don't like it. One bit."

"You're still threatened by him."

"Vis-à-vis you or Dylan?"

I could feel my face flush bright red and prayed Phillip wouldn't notice. "You tell me." I quickly recovered. "You're the one who's threatened."

"'Threatened' is very, very much the wrong word. I don't want a manny throwing footballs around the house with my son. Dylan needs to know how *I* throw a spiral. Not some pothead you picked up in the park. And no, I don't think you're going to sleep with the help."

"Phillip. Your argument would hold more weight if you actually threw a football to Dylan once in a while. You want to come home tomorrow at three p.m. and take him to the Great Lawn in Central Park for a little catch?"

He ignored that. "The simple truth of the matter is that you make chickenshit for a living and I pay the bills, and I will not pay manny bills."

"Do not demean what I make for a living." Jabbing my own chest with my pointer finger, I yelled, "*I* run the child care in this household. *I* actually make some decisions here! We're in the modern era, baby, you spoiled, Jurassic, archaic, Waspy piece of petrified wood!"

I couldn't believe I said that. What a ridiculous, over-the-top thing to say. I was dying to laugh and waited for Phillip to do so, praying he'd break down first.

But his sense of humor was gone. All he could say was "You are deeply unstable."

And he calmly walked out of the room and closed the door behind him.

When I snuck into bed after watching the late local news, I had hoped to find him sleeping—but I should have known better. I crept into bed next to him and faced my side table and leaned my body as far on the edge of the bed as I could. I could sense that his eyes were open. I closed mine and tried to sleep, feeling my head melt into my soft down pillow.

"You're so hostile," he finally said.

I didn't respond. What could I say, knowing that the attraction to Peter had energized my belligerence toward Phillip? Regardless of that inappropriate sideshow, Peter was someone I knew made my husband uncomfortable, someone I knew displaced his time with his son. And somehow I couldn't give an inch on that or help him navigate it. Phillip complained about wanting more time with Dylan, but he didn't ever really know how to connect with Dylan. Dylan *needed* Peter in his life.

"I certainly don't mean to be."

"Well, you are. Keep your damn help if it'll calm you down."

"I am calm."

"Really?"

I turned over. "I'm sorry I called you that prehistoric thing."

"What the fuck was that about?"

"I just . . . I don't think you're modern."

"Modern?"

"We're just moving forward, the earth is turning, and don't hold me back. That isn't smart."

"Why is this suddenly all about you?"

Shit. He was so right. "It has *nothing* to do with me. Just with how I see things working best for our family. For Dylan."

Phillip put his arm over his eyes and lay there. I felt guilty suddenly. He hadn't done anything wrong. He just wanted things to come a little easier: the money, the success, a wife who appreciated his hard work. He wasn't a bad guy at all.

I thought about Susannah. And how she told me to blow my husband all the time just to make things go smoother. Maybe that was the problem. I didn't give enough to him. Maybe everything was my fault. I edged over to his side and started rubbing his stomach with my hand. I was so tired and not in the mood and I dreaded the sex. So I just rubbed his chest some more, hoping he'd kind of fall asleep like a baby.

I started to wonder about Peter in bed, whether he was really sensual or not—I just knew he was—and I tried to stop thinking about him and focus on the man I had married. I tried to conjure up some desire, but all I could focus on was this tired body next to me waiting for love. Just another human needing something from me. And then I remembered that I could still call on those useful lessons from my gay college roommate, and I was pretty damn good at delivering what Phillip really needed just then. So I closed my eyes and dove in.

The next morning, I woke up to find Phillip clinging to me like a baby. "I love you and I think you make buckets and buckets of money," he whispered into my ear. "So much money I could swim in it." I had to laugh.

"I'm sorry I demeaned your salary," he offered. "My salary shouldn't be your measuring rod. You're making a lot of money, especially for part-time."

"I'm sorry I called you a dinosaur, or whatever. That was a little out of nowhere."

We lay quietly in the calm before the kids awoke, orange horizontal sunlight peeking through the sides of the shades. We'd been together fifteen years, the last five of which hadn't been particularly happy. Real passion, at least on my side, had ended before I was even pregnant with Dylan. In the early days, he would wrap his legs around me after we made love. We would play around in bed until four in the morning even though Phillip would inevitably have a six a.m. flight. The next night he would vow that he would be asleep by nine, but we were always at it again. Once in a while during the workweek, we would stay at our separate apartments to catch up on sleep just so we could function at our jobs.

Phillip could act like an infant when he didn't get his way, but he was a loyal, hardworking, well-intentioned man who took care of us. For all the strides women have made, so many of us crave a husband who can take control of fearful situations, be strong in the face of adversity, and be a rock to lean on. Phillip was all that, and I still trusted him like no one else in a real crisis. Yet there I lay, trying to find an emotional connection, to grab something in him that *mattered,* fearful that I couldn't. Fearful, too, that I felt so much more of an emotional connection to Peter Bailey. Phillip wrapped his long legs around me, but it no longer felt sexy and comforting. I couldn't get it back, that feeling of oneness between us.

"I need more time with you," he said. "I want us to go away for a weekend. I need to reconnect like we did last night. There are some things I need to discuss."

I could hear the kids fighting over cereals in the breakfast room. "What kind of things?"

"Just some job stuff. Financial things."

"Give me the headlines."

"No, it's too complicated for first thing in the morning."

"Oh, come on, you can't leave me hanging like that. Is everything okay with the firm?"

"Oh yeah." He wagged his finger at me as if I should erase that silly thought from my head.

"But we still need to talk?"

"Um-hmmm." He took a tight, deep breath and nodded.

"Like about what was going on with Alan that day in the house behind closed doors?"

"Nah." He flipped back the covers and jumped out of bed suddenly. His words did not ring true.

16

Sartorial Situations

A group of hens, very concerned, circled around Barbara Fisher. One of them rubbed her back. "I'm so sorry."

"It's just awful. Just awful," said Topper Fitzgerald, the brains behind the decorating committee.

I walked up gingerly, not wanting to disturb Barbara in her moment of obvious grief. A somber scene, indeed.

"What happened?" I whispered to Ingrid, over her shoulder. "Did someone get hurt?"

"Worse. So much worse. I'd rather give up my Birkin bag than have what happened to her this morning."

"What?"

"Her live-in, legal nanny quit."

I tried to slink away before Barbara even saw me, only to bump right into Christina Patten.

"You'll never guess who called me this morning!"

"I promise you I would have no idea." I lifted Gracie out of her seat and onto the ground.

"Can I wear my Cinderella crown? Just once?"

"Darling. No superheroes or Disney characters allowed in school. You know that. We'll leave it in the stroller where we always do."

"C'mon, just guess!" Then Christina sang the following in a little tune: "La, la, la. It has to do with White Nights. La, la."

"A designer wants to dress you," I said.

"Of course, but that's old news! Designers are dressing everyone!"

Everyone except me. Designers fall over their feet to dress society women like Christina, sending over ball gowns before a benefit, pushing them to wear them as they would any Hollywood star for the Academy Awards red carpet. Frankly, at this point I'd have been happy if someone handed me the clothes. It would save me the shopping. And the money. "Okay, Christina, you've been asked to emcee the evening."

"Are you kidding, I would *die* if I had to do that. Can't you see I'm happy and excited about something?"

Samurai-sword moment here. "I'm a bit late, and Gracie is not in a good mood."

"Yes I am, Mommy. That's a lie!"

"Oh fine, you want to take all the fun out of it, Jamie. I wanted to surprise you later, but I just couldn't wait. Just try hard hard hard to guess. Think benefit. Think white. Think our table. Think eggs, big, colorful jeweled eggs. Think photos."

"I don't know about all the brouhaha that goes on backstage at these events. I just buy my ticket to support whatever cause and show up."

"That's hard to believe, you're such a brainiac. Everyone says so. 'Jamie's so smart. Jamie's so smart. La, la, la.' That's all I hear about you. My husband, George, is dying to sit next to you. He's going to read the newspaper extra carefully that day, but he told me not to tell you that, so don't tell him I told you!"

"That's nice of you to say that I'm smart, Christina, but smart people don't automatically know everything."

She cocked her head sideways, squinted, and gazed off into outer space. "I don't really get what you're saying."

This woman was retarded.

"Mommy, c'monnnnnn."

Thank you, God.

"Maybe I can take Gracie up to her classroom and you could e-mail me the surprise?" I raised my eyebrows a few times just like I do when I'm trying to sell some idea to my kids.

"John Henry Wentworth called me this morning. He lives next door."

"Who's that?"

"You're kidding, right?" She looked concerned. "He's the editor in chief of *Madison Avenue* magazine."

Uh-oh. "And?"

"He wants to photograph our table for the February issue. He's going to make models of huge, seven-foot-tall Fabergé eggs with sparkling gems all over them, some upright, some on their sides." She was gesticulating wildly to get me to picture the stage. "Then all the ladies at our table are going to stand in front of them, dressed to the nines in white."

"This Wentworth guy doesn't know me from a doorknob; you go ahead with your friends and do what you like. It's not my thing."

"Well, I did have to explain to him who you were, because you're not, you know, superactive on the social circuit." She said this apologetically because she thought she might have offended me. "I mean, that's your choice. You work. You don't have time. But he warmed up to the idea of including you in the shoot. I mean, you *are* sitting at the table, so it would be weird not to include you, even if, well, you know, you're not . . ."

"I just don't think I'd fit in."

"You're crazy. They're going to design white dresses for us, do our hair, everything. And then we'll wear those same dresses to the party. They've got Carolina Herrera on board; one of her stylists is going to dress us. Can you believe that?"

And then I wouldn't have to figure out what to wear, or spend the time and money buying it, or wade through a white fur shrug maze . . .

"And Verdura is going to loan us jewelry," she added.

Even I knew he was the greatest Italian jewelry designer of the last century.

This was getting interesting. Enticing even. "So let me get this straight. For the photo shoot now and then the benefit party in

February, Carolina Herrera is going to lend me a dress, or make me one from scratch. Then Verdura is going to lend me diamonds worth a fortune for the night."

"Like worth over twenty thousand. The only problem is their security guys trail you a bit in the room."

"Do I get shoes?"

"Yup. And a handbag from Judith Leiber."

"Are they to keep?"

"The shoes and the bag: yes. The dress and the jewels: most definitely not."

"Why would *Madison Avenue* magazine do this? They don't even know me."

"They need a cover and the DuPont is the biggest party of the year. It's good publicity for the designers."

"This is a *cover*?"

"Well, they're photographing three tables; hopefully ours will make the cover, but we'll definitely be inside."

"Okay, let me think about this, Christina. I've got to take Gracie now, we're late."

"John Henry's office will be calling you about fittings," she called out as she pushed her daughter Lucy up the stairs.

I stifled a smile.

Later that day, Peter accosted me at the front door. I said, "Give me a second to catch my breath. Is it important?" I was getting exasperated by Peter's constant curveballs. I dropped my bags and unwound my scarf and threw it in the closet. The house seemed quiet. Unusually quiet for dinnertime.

"What happened?"

"Yvette got really pissed off at the Wassermanns' birthday party."

We slid quietly into the study so as not to alert the kids I was home.

Peter sat down on a newly plumped-up armchair. "Well, it actually started at the house before the party. Yvette said you wanted them dressed in their gray outfits, you know, and Michael's with the embroidered bib thing on the chest and the suede shorts . . ."

"Lederhosen. I know."

"So now you need to go back to the time you hired me and try hard to remember our conversations. Do you recall the one about me creating some jocky male atmosphere around here during the day?"

I nodded. He was adorable. Today he had on worn-out jeans and a dark, rumpled, long-sleeve, thin T-shirt. I was having a problem looking at him now. I was also having a problem not looking at him.

"Then would you just tell me something? Why do you people dress up your kids to look like German yodelers every time they go to a party? Michael looked like a girl, and even though he's just two, he knew it and he was *furious*. And what's with the kneesocks with those little red tassels hanging off the top? You should have seen us trying to stuff Michael into those ridiculous suede shorts—with him writhing on the floor and his head doing a 360. It was like *The Sound of Music* meets *The Exorcist*."

I laughed. "Peter, you just don't understand."

"No, *you* don't understand. And then I get to the party and every kid is dressed up the same, in the same gray shorts, and they all have red eyes because *their* four matching nannies have also forced them into yodeling outfits. What *is* it with you people?"

He was right. But all the kids we knew dressed up for parties. And I learned the hard way when I took Dylan to his first nursery school birthday party wearing pants and a T-shirt. When we ran in fifteen minutes late, all the women in the room went silent on cue like an E.F. Hutton commercial.

"So what happened with Yvette?"

"I went to the party with Gracie and Michael and when they started eating chocolate cake, I changed them into jeans, and Yvette was so pissed off, like I killed somebody."

"I know it seems totally warped to you, and okay it is, but dressing is serious business for Yvette."

Peter just stood there, an incredulous expression on his face.

I tried to clarify. "Jeans just do not work with their baby-blue wool

John-John and Caroline Kennedy dress coats with the velvet-trimmed collars."

No response.

"Their bare legs have to stick out of the bottom of the coats with the anklets on. That's the *whole* point. The dress coats don't work with jeans. They're for dresses and shorts. That's why the boys wear the shorts."

His jaw fell.

"For the John-John bare-leg effect," I explained. "Remember? The salute at the coffin? That's the big payoff moment, in the elevator on the way up and on the way out."

"The salute at the coffin? Like forty years ago? Have you lost your mind? Do you really care about whether or not Michael has bare legs with anklets like John-John Kennedy?"

"Of course I don't care. I'm just trying to explain these dress codes."

"Lemme tell you something: you're cool, you work at a big-time network. You tell me the whole deal about these women, how their values are all screwy, how they've checked their brains at the front desk, how competitive they are. You go crazy when I suggest you're one of them—which makes *me* crazy because you're so much better than that! But then you play into it all—and into velvet-collared coats of all things."

"I'm not!"

"I figured you'd think Yvette was insane and that of course I did the right thing. But you're not saying that at all! You're trying to explain some bare-leg fashion rule for a two-year-old boy! I'm telling you, it makes him feel like a ballerina and he's right and you're wrong. Then, first you say Christina Patten is an idiot, which she is, believe me—she wants to be my friend and accosts me in the park—but next thing I know you can't stop talking to her. What's with *that*?"

"Hey, when you have kids and have to deal with other parents, you'll understand."

"No, I won't. And, believe me, no child of mine will be dressed like a yodeler. Ever."

I'd lost him. Totally. I'd wanted him so much to think I was cool, and had a great job, and was above all this. But he'd nailed me. As usual. I felt pathetic and angry at myself, and worse, angry at him.

I stood up. "Are we done here? I've got a little interview tomorrow, do you mind?"

"I know you've got an interview. I'm just doing my job, making sure you don't screw up your kids in the meantime." And with that, he stood up, too, and walked down the hall to hang Dylan upside down by his ankles.

17

A Job Well Done

The following day, on the other side of Manhattan, Goodman and I sat at a small table in a back room of a nondescript bar on Broadway and Sixty-fourth Street. This was the usual routine with us. We had just come from our stealth Theresa interview in a New York hotel. Theresa didn't want us Northern reporters traipsing around Pearl, Mississippi, drawing attention to ourselves. While I was still down from my altercation with Peter, I tried to savor the golden moment that was upon us. We'd been through half a dozen of these victorious moments together over the past ten years, and we both knew the post-story drill: after spending months of intense psychic energy to get Theresa Boudreaux to talk, in the single biggest interview of the year for the entire journalistic community, we'd now completed the interview, she'd walked out the door, the cameramen and crew had broken down their equipment, and we'd silently trudged through a rainstorm to get ourselves a stiff drink. We sipped our Maker's Mark on the rocks in silence. Goodman needed absolute calm to take in the scale of the story we had. In the coming days we would be obsessing over the tapes and writing and editing the story for *Newsnight*, but now I wasn't to talk until he got through this period of coming-down time. I knew how to take care of my boss like he was my child. Fifteen minutes passed. I was dying to recap. We ordered another round.

Finally, he slammed his hand hard on the small round wooden table. "Holy fucking shit, girl. You sure as hell did it this time. Whoooooooweee. Man, that was sweet." He leaned back against his chair, clasped his hands behind his head, and stared up to the heavens. He took a huge sip of whisky and sucked in through clenched teeth like a cowboy. "You know what, Jamie? She's one dumb broad, but she's got a rack on her that would stop a locomotive. Huey Boy's gotta miss that rack." He slammed the table again.

Theresa performed flawlessly. She wore her hair in a big Farrah Fawcett 1970s do, wrapped her sexy, buxom frame in a skintight, tacky-as-all-hell baby-blue suit, and spoke with a Southern accent sweet as honey. Gennifer Flowers part two. She talked about their sexual relationship, how they met in one of his supporters' homes in Pearl, Mississippi, and were together for two years before he unceremoniously dumped her. Goodman tried to get her to articulate in twenty different ways that Hartley preferred anal intercourse. Her answers on this delicate topic were squirrelly, yet for the most part, she played ball.

GOODMAN: So you will confirm that intercourse occurred between yourself and Congressman Huey Hartley.

BOUDREAUX: Well, a certain kind.

GOODMAN: I asked you a yes-or-no question.

BOUDREAUX: Well, it's just not that simple.

GOODMAN: You mean, there was sexual activity, cuddling, perhaps petting, what have you, but no actual intercourse. No penetration. Some people, a former president included, would maintain that that didn't constitute sexual relations between a man and a woman.

BOUDREAUX: I didn't mean to imply there weren't sexual relations between us, I mean in the Bill Clinton understanding of the word. There *were* sexual relations between us.

GOODMAN: So there was intercourse . . .

BOUDREAUX: Yes. *[Slightly uncomfortable, manufactured smile. Then she leaned in.]* Intercourse of a certain kind.

GOODMAN: Can you explain . . .

BOUDREAUX: No. Not traditional. *[Pause, more leaning forward.]* And not missionary either.

GOODMAN: So you're talking a question of position?

BOUDREAUX: No, I'm talking a question of location as to where the penetration occurs.

Throughout this particularly lascivious section of the interview, Leon Rosenberg was cracking up so much he had to hide his face in the minibar.

Theresa cried when she told Goodman how Hartley had dumped her. She was speaking now because God had told her to come clean. It didn't hurt that, as she put it, Hartley hadn't "treated her right" when he broke it off. The "son of a bitch" had had the state troopers on his security team break the bad news to her. She hadn't spoken to him since. He wouldn't return her calls.

"You're wrong about one thing, though—she's not dumb." I looked Goodman in the eye.

"Give me a break, I had to ask her every question twice."

"I'm just saying we're not dealing with a dumb broad—she was acting the part, flirting with you, egging you on to ask the questions she wanted asked. You're a guy. Listen to yourself, waxing on about her rack. What do you know?" I wanted to add that Theresa's wily ways made me nervous—I'd never seen her act so sly—but now was not the time. We'd dissect it later.

"I'm a pro and I've been doing this for thirty years."

"I don't deny that, but she was playing you."

"No, she wasn't."

"She was."

"I don't want to hear that. She said what we wanted her to say, she fessed up. Don't care if she was angling for certain questions. If you ask me where's the beef, we got ourselves a side of cattle." He slammed the table and ordered another round. "And I was damn good. Did I look as good as I felt?"

I stared at the ice cubes in my glass so long they started to blur.

Entr'acte I

The linen closet was hot and airless.

Is this woman for real?

She unbuckled his pants while he feigned resistance. Between the layers of falling linens, delicate, dried rose petals.

Gaining his balance and, in the process, his wits, he shook his head and pushed her away, with determination this time. "You're insane." He thought of Jamie and a wave of guilt washed over him.

"So what if I am?" As she pressed herself against his thigh, he peeked over her shoulder and saw that the slit in the back of her skirt had hiked up, revealing a delightful pair of smooth, bare legs.

He threw his head back in disbelief. "I'm serious. I can't do this." With intense melancholy, he realized he was interrupting the knock-out lay of his lifetime.

She put her tongue between his collarbone and licked under his neck in one slow line up to his mouth. "Who's going to know?" His outstretched left hand was then guided to the back of her thigh, then up between her legs.

He could feel beads of sweat down the back of his shirt. He closed his eyes. "I, I . . ."

She breathed deep into his ear as she pushed his fingers inside her. "Oops . . . forgot my panties this morning."

"Apparently so."

Minutes passed. He was her prisoner now.

Another expensive cloth fluttered below him and past the lightly bronzed shoulders of the woman. Now she was on her knees, his entire cock in her mouth. He knew from the playground she was famous for doing exactly this. Even though there existed a universe of inequity in their net worth, here she was on her knees, servicing him like every man's fantasy courtesan.

Sex—the great equalizer, he said to himself, marveling that he could form any coherent thought at this point. *The only true democracy left.*

She looked up at him while manipulating his raging dick with her mouth and manicured hand. The only sound was the jingling from her Bulgari bracelets.

He grabbed an embroidered place mat and muffled his scream as he came like a fire hose in her expensive mouth.

She laughed softly as she licked her lips, her look of triumph and arrogance saying, *I know I'm the best and now you know it.* And indeed she had a right to this title.

Sometimes a man just doesn't know what to do or say after he comes. He awkwardly started to pick up the linens.

"Marta will do that," she threw over her shoulder as she left and closed him in the closet.

And there he was, a bundle of the best dinner napkins on the East Coast in his hands, and a slowly softening cock hanging out of his Chanel-lipstick-stained boxers.

18

That Whole Style Thing

"Lights! Camera! Action! C'mon, girls, you're the belles of the ball!"

The song "We Are Family" reverberated off the steel water pipes and rafters of the Tribeca loft. Four gorgeous socialites boogied, flashbulbs exploded, and stylists ran accessories back and forth around the perimeter of the room like ants ferrying crumbs. I felt like I had landed in someone else's music video by mistake.

Chin to chest, eyes shut, Punch Parish—the world's most famous society photographer—raised a hand above his head. Suddenly the music stopped. The assistants shushed everyone into absolute silence. The maestro needed to create, so we waited. And waited. This guy must have thought he was Richard Avedon. Slowly, he raised his head and stood before us, right arm outstretched, one eye still closed, staring at his thumbnail like Picasso. Then he pulled the bandanna off his head, slicked back his stringy blond hair, and retied it again.

"Isn't he just amazing?" Christina whispered in my ear. There is no greater display of ass-kissing on earth than a New York socialite near a photographer. "He's like some Renaissance painter. Like van Gogh."

Punch moved us around like life-size dolls in front of three seven-foot-tall bejeweled Fabergé eggs. A rail-thin Italian socialite speared her heel into my pinky toe. I sucked in air, but she didn't even notice.

I was getting very annoyed at this point. Television people in the news business produce shoots very differently from fashion people. Namely, we respect people's time. We ask the interview subjects to

show up *after* we've set up. When I walked into the studio this morning, the photographer hadn't even arrived.

Punch snapped at his assistant Jeremy, who winked at the DJ, who
turned the music on full blast. Jeremy, unleashed, made big swooping
claps over his head like a seal, swaying his ass back and forth. "'I got all
my sistahs with me,'" he yelled with the music. "Uh huh huh, uh huh
huh!"

And then Punch focused his "magic" on us again.

Christina Patten's guests for the White Nights of the Hermitage
benefit, myself included, stood in front of a huge sheet of white paper,
the eggs immediately behind us, fake snow swirling around our
ankles. Heavyset Russian seamstresses were fanning the fabric of our
gowns so the bottoms billowed out perfectly. Makeup women were
patting powder on our foreheads and noses, while the hairstylist, big
sunglasses holding his hair back like a headband, circled us with the
pointy edge of his comb. Someone turned on the fans so our hair
blew from our faces. More flashes from *l'artiste* Monsieur Punch.

After five rolls of film, Punch mimed the need for a drink by
putting an imaginary glass to his mouth. Jeremy twisted around to a
young intern and did the same, glaring at her like she'd made the
biggest screwup of her life. She ran for an Evian and tripped over the
lighting cables sprinting back to Punch.

He took a gulp from the bottle, then stepped off the stage.
Christina and her three other guests followed suit, while I stood there
alone. New York society women often have terrible manners. Earlier,
when I arrived, Christina kissed my cheeks and waved dismissively.
"Oh, you all know each other." But we'd never met, I'd just seen her
guests' faces in magazines. And in person, they were supermodel
gorgeous, like so many of the drop-off hens: chiseled cheekbones;
soft, dewy skin that hadn't seen the sunlight since high school; thick
Maria Shriver hair for the brunettes and Elle Macpherson babelicious
curls for the blondes. These people don't sit like normal people sit.
Ever. They perch one hip on the very edge of the chair with their
long, lanky legs extended, like George Ballanchine positioned them.
It's a miracle of physics that they can balance there so long. With no

careers, they exercise four days a week for hours at a time with their trainers. So their muscle tone isn't due to good genes; they work hard at it, which makes it so much more unattainable to people like me.

Though I'd done news stories with countless CEOs and cabinet members who didn't scare me one bit, these women had a cliquey girl thing that jolted me right back to the seventh-grade cafeteria. They were: Leelee Sargeant from Locust Valley, whose mother ran the board of the country club for twenty years, Fenoula Wrightsman, heiress to a British telecom fortune, and Allegra d'Argento from Italy. Her much older husband was under house arrest in Florence for tax evasion, while she gaily spent his cash on this side of the Atlantic.

Barbara Fisher nudged me with her elbow as I accepted a diet ginger ale from an assistant passing around small plastic glasses. "Oooh, interesting. You covering this for television or are you attending?"

I pointed to my white sequin ball gown.

"Of course you're not covering this, I was joking. It's just . . . not a place I would expect you to be. Not really your *thing,* Jamie."

She had a point. "Yeah, it just kind of steamrolled from getting the tickets, then Christina asked us to sit . . ."

"Not dumb, given you want to get Gracie into Pembroke. Christina's friends run the entire board. I just didn't think of the two of you as pals." Barbara squinted at me like a dirty little hairy rat.

"Well, we're not really."

"You're not friends, but you're at her table?"

"I mean, we kind of are."

"Hmmm-mmm." Barbara crossed her arms and looked me straight in the eye. "You know, there's something else I've been meaning to tell you." She leaned in close and whispered, "If I were you, I would watch that delicious Peter of yours. Why don't you do yourself a favor and surprise him and Ingrid Harris in the Seventy-sixth Street playground one day?"

"Ingrid's a riot." I shook my head, negating her ridiculous implications. "I'm sure he finds her more amusing than the other moms."

"I wouldn't be so sure. Trainers, camp counselors, doormen, do you really believe she'd have any qualms about doing a *manny*?"

"I'll be real sure to look into it." I was trying to be flip—but I was completely thrown. Ingrid and Peter? Not possible! He would never do that to me. Never. Nightmarish images flew through my head: how she'd brazenly flirted with him when I introduced them and the stupid, stunned look on his face. Would he have sex with one of those moms he loves to hate? Is every single man on the planet just hopelessly horny? No. He would *never.* Though he had been a little distant since the lederhosen argument. Maybe he was sick of me. Oh God.

Punch was back, this time commanding us to stand in a straight line, shoulder to shoulder. In unison, the girls all put one leg forward and one shoulder back with Rockettes-like accuracy. Here were four mothers, all college educated, posing like professional models on the runway. Of course, I thought to myself, they get photographed all the time, they know the drill, they *are* semiprofessionals.

"C'mon, girls! More energy. Look like you want me!" Punch yelled.

"Punch! You're so bad!" Christina screamed back at him. "But we love you anyway!"

Okay. Fine. So Peter's twenty-nine years old. He can sleep with whomever he wants, right? No. That's not right. Not on the job. But is another mother "on the job" if they met, say, after work? On or off the job, the thought destroyed me.

The ceiling lights blinked on and off and John Henry Wentworth, the Prince of Palm Beach and the editor of *Madison Avenue* magazine, blew through the studio door and let it slam behind him. He wore his blond hair combed back, boldly revealing his receding hairline. He wore a starched pink oxford shirt and a purple paisley ascot, had large brown eyes and full, round red cheeks chafed by so many years at the bow of a sailboat. Clearly unhappy with the shot, he grabbed Punch's elbow and took him aside for a huddle.

The girls waved and giggled at John Henry. I was preoccupied with one thing only: how would I find out about Peter and Ingrid without asking another mom?

The two men walked back to the group. John Henry said firmly, "I think we should, uh, change the order here."

Then he walked onto the set and seized me by the shoulders, practically picking me up, and moved me from the second to the left in line all the way to the right. A pearl-encrusted comb fell off the top of my head, which momentarily jolted me out of my manny obsession stupor. A new line order: Leelee, then Fenoula, then Christina, then Allegra, and then me. Who did he think he was kidding?

I whispered into his ear, "I'm a network producer. I direct shoots all the time. Don't think I don't know what it means when someone gets placed all the way to the right." This befuddled him. I was pissed partially because he was putting me all the way to the right so he could later chop me out of the frame, but mostly because he thought I was a knucklehead socialite who didn't understand what he was trying to do.

"Uh, well, I just thought, since you, well . . ." Wentworth stammered.

"Look, all I'm saying is I know what you're doing, buddy."

"What on earth *are* you doing, John Henry?" Christina Patten graciously took my side. This surprised me—I thought she would care more about sucking up to him than protecting me. "You're going to mess up her hair! You old fool!" She had no understanding of his motives.

Wentworth shot me a devilish look. All the girls threw their heads back in laughter and flapped their wrists at him. More flashbulbs, more disco, an interminable hour of different poses, all with me on the far right.

At the end of the shoot, Christina came up to me with her fingers crossed on both her hands. She closed her eyes. "Pray, pray, pray he picks us for the cover. It will change everything for you. Overnight."

I couldn't get out of there fast enough. Posing with women who torch their closets every season was bad enough. Imagining Peter and Ingrid was far worse—I was totally obsessing over this, and actually finding it hard to breathe. I'd witnessed her spooling him into her web. And, oh shit, who could blame her? I got into the car and called

Peter on his cell phone. It rang four times before he finally picked it up, a bit out of breath.

He answered officiously. "Yes?"

"You won't forget the cello?"

"Or the violin. I'm just, uh, packing it in here." He dropped the phone, a lot of muffled noises in the background. Then he picked it up. He sounded distracted, even more distant.

"You okay, Peter?"

"Sure."

"What's going on?"

"Nothing."

"Did Gracie have a playdate after school?"

"Yeah, at, uh, Vanessa Harris's house."

"Oh, that's nice." Ingrid's daughter. I tried to stem the biggest shit fit of my life. "Yvette took her?"

"Yes. Well, yes, Yvette was with her."

"I asked . . ."

"Yeah. I think she had fun. I'm just getting the cello and music together here."

"How long have you been home?"

"I came early. Had to pick something up uptown. Yvette needed some help."

"With what?"

"Just things. Not to worry, I'll meet you downstairs."

Ten minutes later I pulled up to our awning, and Peter, with a cello, and Gracie, with a miniature violin, piled into the backseat of the car. Peter put Gracie's seat belt on in the middle seat and studied my face. I could barely look at him.

"How come you're so made up?"

"Photo shoot. Doesn't matter."

When we pulled up to the St. Henry's School for Boys, Peter said woodenly, "I'll go in and get Dylan." A horrible cold front had blown in and we were talking like automatons to each other.

I reached back from the front seat and massaged Gracie's knee. "Mommy," she said, "can I have another playdate with Vanessa soon?"

"Sure, sweetheart, did you have fun?"

She mumbled, "Hmmm-mmm" with her thumb in her mouth. Then she pulled her thumb out. "She has a play kitchen in her room. And it's bigger than mine."

"Well, you have a great one and soooo many pots and pans."

"Peter said mine was nicer too."

My heart raced. "But when did Peter see hers? Yvette took you like normal, right?"

"Umm-umm." She shook her head no with her thumb back in her mouth, then rested her head against the side of her car seat and gazed out the window.

I jumped like a rabbit out of my front seat and was kneeling on the center console.

"Gracie. Take that thumb out of your mouth right now. Who took you to that playdate at Vanessa's?"

Her eyes were as big as saucers; she thought she was in very big trouble.

"Yvette did, Mommy."

I was so relieved I felt my whole body melt back into the seat.

"But Peter came too."

Fuck. Fuck!

19

Say It Ain't So

I promised myself I would confront Peter that night after the kids were down, but the thought made me ill. If I had to fire him, Dylan would take weeks—maybe months—to recover, and his father's absences during the week would only underscore his loneliness. My myth of a strapping manny who would ride a cresting wave into our lives and wash away our troubles was on shaky ground indeed.

Studiously avoiding eye contact with Peter after dinner, I asked him to get Dylan settled with a book, while I read to Gracie and Michael.

Peter was taking forever with Dylan, while I was pretending to read the *New York Times* on the living room couch—gazing at the same short article for twenty minutes. Could he know I suspected something? How could he not? I wasn't myself. Then again, maybe he was innocent and confused by my coldness. I felt guilty, like I was some crazy, paranoid older woman. Then I wondered why I was beating myself up over something *he* might have done.

This felt so *important* suddenly, like we were over the crush stage and in a rhythm of an established relationship—like we should hash it out over drinks and a great dinner and then have make-up sex. I couldn't believe the places my mind was going. I hit my head repeatedly with the heel of my hand. When I did confront him, I had to be careful not to act like a betrayed and immature teenager. *God,* I was thinking, *this is fucked up,* and just at that moment Peter appeared in the doorway.

His baseball cap was on backward, and his jacket and disheveled gym bag were slung over one shoulder.

"Dylan was reading aloud, then asked me to read a few pages and then he was out before I finished the first paragraph." He walked into the living room and sat on the spindly arm of Phillip's favorite Louis XIV–style armchair. I kind of wished it would break underneath his weight so he'd owe me even more. He shook his hair out of his face and sat quietly, waiting. He was so damn attractive.

I shot him a frosty look.

After an awkward moment, he broke the silence. "You okay? What's up?"

"Why don't you tell *me,* Peter?"

"Huh?" His eyes widened. I thought for a delicious moment he might be innocent, that nothing could have happened between a Red Hook hipster and fancy-pants married Ingrid Harris. Of course Barbara had it wrong; he wouldn't do that to me. Now he was going to think I was out of my mind. I didn't want to accuse him and have him laugh in my face.

I slowly flipped the pages of the newspaper on my lap, pretending to search for something absolutely critical at that moment. Then I broke the weird silence. "Did Gracie have fun on her playdate?" I decided right then and there that if he lied, I would send him packing immediately, but if he came clean, he had a fighting chance. He didn't know Gracie had spilled the beans in the car.

"Yeah, well, sure, I guess."

"Well, you would know if she had fun, *wouldn't* you?"

"Yeah. In this instance I would. Just helping Yvette out today."

"When I called earlier, you did everything you could to make it seem as if you hadn't been there."

"I did not lie to you. I was rushing to get the violin and the rest of the stuff for the kids." Peter was talking to me like I was his girlfriend, understanding how betrayed I felt. I knew he was holding back so he didn't hurt me. This was crazy.

"And who was there?"

"Well, the two girls, of course. Yvette and their nanny, Lourdes. And Ingrid, Mrs. Harris, whatever, was there, I think, for just a bit." He cleared his throat and stood up, shifting his gym bag from one shoulder to the other.

"Just a bit? So you didn't spend any quality time with her?"

He didn't answer.

"I asked if you had any quality time with Ingrid, as you call her."

"Yeah. Sure."

"So? How long was Ingrid there?"

Peter looked down and took off his baseball cap, then sat again, this time in the armchair that was closest to the couch, his knee perilously close to mine. He raked his hair with his fingers. He looked guilty, defensive, and crestfallen all at once.

Barbara Fisher was right.

After a silence that seemed to last ten minutes, he sat back up straight and squinted his eyes at me. I squinted back, trying to read him, hoping against hope that I'd pegged him wrongly.

"Okay, so she throws herself at me in the linen closet and tells me she's not wearing panties. What am I gonna do?"

"She didn't," I gasped.

"Oh yes, she did."

"In her house? With the kids there?"

"Scout's honor. But don't worry, Yvette and Lourdes were with the girls. And I wasn't into it." Not an enormous amount of conviction there.

My heart sank. I stared out the large living room windows looking for guidance.

"Then what?"

"Well . . ." His face flushed. "I won't go into it. But I'm telling you, I'm not into her . . . it was just so . . ."

"What is 'it'?" I tried to sound firm and mature. Detached.

"You want actual *details*? I'll tell you if you really want, but it's a bit awkward."

I couldn't believe Ingrid Harris would tell Dylan's manny that she wasn't wearing underwear. Now I was more pissed at her than I was at him.

"I mean, we didn't . . . It was just a quick moment and then I said we can't do this. NFW." He edged back on the chair, satisfied with himself.

"So you stopped it?" God, I was relieved.

"Well, you know it's not so easy for a guy: a gorgeous woman starts coming on to you . . ."

"You think she's gorgeous looking?" I blurted out, regretting it instantly.

"Well . . . yeah. A little trampy maybe, but yeah, she's a good-looking woman, all right." He shook his head in wonder, like she was a fucking sex goddess.

"I don't know, Peter, this is really not about her."

"I am so sorry."

I couldn't speak. For all the speeches I'd rehearsed in my head, not a word could I summon.

"I promise you I didn't sleep with her." He could see how hurt I was. "And I promise you I will always be straight with you."

I'm married! I wanted to scream. *I'm not hurt! I'm not your girlfriend!* But instead I took a deep breath and said, "Do you think this was a responsible thing to do when you are supposed to be supervising children?"

"Yo. I told you Yvette and Lourdes were playing Candy Land with the girls. Gracie was not in any danger whatsoever. I mean, it's like Versailles up there, with all the handmaiden ladies scampering around. So let's not make this out to be . . ."

Something in me finally snapped. "Out to be what?" I shrieked. "Nothing? Nothing, Peter? You screw around with a married woman in the middle of the day while you're on the job and you act like it's nothing?"

"I'm not saying it wasn't totally inappropriate, but it's not like the hamburgers in the pan were burning a hole through the roof of the kitchen and your child was dangling out the window on Park

Avenue!" He got up and started pacing around the room. "Okay, so some crazy friend of yours, a *total* man-eater, by the way—and let's not forget she is *your* friend after all—shoves me into her linen closet for a little smooch. That's it. I did not have sex with her."

"Was that all it was, just a smooch? Are you sure?" Oh God.

He took a deep breath. "Well, yeah." Pause. "Basically."

20

More Than Just a Manny

It wasn't an easy week that followed. Goodman was impossible, second-guessing my every move. And I was second-guessing my manny's every move. When Peter would call to say where he was, I would always ask him who else was there. When he tried to close up the distance now between us, I'd freeze him out. And when he'd make a little joke, I wouldn't laugh. I'd just move on to the logistics. Thursday was particularly tough because he'd snapped back at me. And then I started questioning my own behavior; I didn't want him to leave. So I was especially distracted when I went to say good night to Dylan. His reading lamp pitched a triangle of bright light through his hair and onto his book in an otherwise pitch-black room. He was reading *Eragon*.

"Hi, Mom. You're home," he said. It was almost nine o'clock and I'd been working late nights with Goodman the whole week, hashing out how we wanted to write the piece. Finally, I'd gotten a moment at home to catch my son before he drifted off.

My angel. I walked over to the bed and sat beside him. "You look tired," I said. I pushed his hair off his forehead and placed his book on the bedside table. He edged down under his covers and laid his head on his pillow. I turned off his light and spoke softly to him in the dark. "Time to go to sleep."

"I had so much homework."

"Did Peter help you? Is it all done?"

"Duh."

"Okay. Good."

"When is Dad coming home?"

"I told you, he'll be mostly gone for two weeks. With a couple of short visits back home, on the red-eye. He'll be in his bed when you wake up Saturday morning."

"How come you can't be home more when he's gone so much?"

"My piece, sweetheart. A very big piece for TV. I've told you that. It'll be done very soon."

He smirked at me. I rubbed his eyebrows.

"It'll be soon. I promise."

"Peter and I laughed tonight so hard about Craig."

"What's going on with Craig?"

"It's a long story. Okay, first of all, yesterday when we got to school . . ."

This was perhaps not my Mother of the Year moment as my mind drifted again to Peter.

"So then he told Douglas Wood that he didn't want to go to his bowling party at Chelsea Piers and that it was . . ."

My life had turned into *Desperate Housewives* overnight. My neighbor was blowing my hunky lawn mower guy and I hated her for it. I couldn't shake the feeling that Peter had betrayed me.

"Are you listening, Mom? Can you believe Jonathan said Douglas's last party sucked? He used that word. Isn't that mean?"

"Yes, dear. So what did you say to him?"

"Peter taught me something to do." My little sarcastic boy couldn't help but grin. "It's not a problem anymore. That's all you need to know."

Ten minutes later, I startled Peter, who was considering his options in front of the refrigerator.

He turned around quickly. "Hey. You told me you'd be at work very late every night this week."

"I know, but Goodman had to leave early."

I threw my huge tote bag onto the banquette and began pulling tapes out and piling them onto the breakfast table.

"If you'd let me know, I could have stalled a bit, but the little ones were tired."

"Fine, Peter. Just fucking fine, okay?" I couldn't stop myself. My anger was palpable. I put both hands on my heart, as if it might explode out of my chest like some creature from *Alien*. I pulled out the interview transcripts and slammed them onto the table.

"Whoa."

"Whoa, what?"

"Just whoa." He was quiet for a moment as he poured himself some ginger ale at the counter. "I told you I was sorry."

"You know, I'm just fed up with a whole bunch of things."

"Oh, really? Like what?"

"Your attitude about this, for starters. It sure didn't bother you that Ingrid was married. We didn't even get into that."

"It's done. I have never once in my life had a thing with a married woman."

"Ingrid's married. That's once."

"Fine." He kicked the refrigerator door shut. "What I was saying was I had never done that before."

I looked at him suspiciously.

"I mean it, women just aren't so aggressive. I was shocked. Really shocked, and then totally thrown off balance. Literally thrown off balance if you want to know the truth."

"I don't need details." That was a lie. I desperately wanted to torture myself with every truthful detail. The made-up movie version had been playing in my head nonstop: Ingrid made one of her biting remarks and he started laughing in the hallway. He kind of slapped her arm, but then let it rest there. Then she pushed herself up against him in the middle of the hallway and started sucking his earlobe. He got impossibly hard and *he,* not she, dragged her into the linen closet. He was in lust with her. And not me.

"Look, I know it was a mistake—one that *she* initiated. And by the way, I have apologized. I am truly sorry. Stupid as it might have been, it wasn't meant as an act against you. This was a completely separate event. Separate from me and you."

Me and you. Him and me. While I couldn't believe he'd said it, I denied myself any pleasure his words might have given me. *Me and you.* In my more rational moments, I allowed myself to acknowledge this man had tender feelings for me, even admired me, though I never for a second imagined I could spark any real electricity in him. I also tried to convince myself that my attraction to Peter had grown out of something rotten in the house of Whitfield: my feelings for him not organic or even natural, but, rather, a symptom of the shortcomings in my own life.

"Hey, it's not like I care about her."

"You're an awfully big guy, so it's hard to imagine you being over-whelmed or anything."

"I'm telling you, it was not an easy situation to say no in. We were in her house, in her closet, with her crazy mood overtaking the whole deal."

I faced him and yelled, "Her crazy what?"

"Would you at least consider handing me a break here? You've been distant all week now. Remember what actually happened, okay? Try to imagine it from my standpoint: I was so shocked that I couldn't respond."

"I don't need to hear it again."

"Fine, I'd rather not go into it anyway."

He got another glass, filled it with spring water and handed it to me, a tepid peace offering under the circumstances. "You sound kind of hurt."

"Are you nuts?"

"So. You're not hurt."

"No, I'm not. I mean, you work here."

He hit the wall with his fist and said sarcastically, "I *work* here. I guess that's all I do. All that's going on here is that I *work* for you." He could have hollered, called a major foul on my part and stormed out the front door. But he didn't join me in the gutter. Instead, he dispersed my hostility with a snap of his finger. "Nice try, lady. But it's a no-go. I don't *just* work for you. Not letting you get away with that."

"All right, fine. You're not just . . ."

"Not just what? Tell me." He tapped his foot, smiling slightly.

"You know what, Peter."

"What? Not just the manny?"

"No."

"So say it," he challenged.

"Say what?"

"Say it: look at me. 'Peter, you're not just the manny.'" He tucked his hair behind each ear and stared me down.

"No."

"I need you to. That was bad. And you know it. It's the only way I'm letting you off the hook."

"What the hell? You're the one who needs to be let off the hook, you're the one who ended up in Ingrid's closet."

"Say it."

I felt my face flush and tried to suppress a nervous laugh. "That is so silly."

"You can say it. Please."

"Fine." I rolled my eyes. "You're not just the manny."

"Phew." He wiped his brow dramatically with the back of his hand.

We were both silent for a moment, realizing at that instant we'd moved beyond the Ingrid situation and we were . . . well, friends.

"The whole situation's just a little weird," I said.

"I know it is. It was. Believe me." His charm was hypnotic.

"She's a pal. And I like her. A lot, actually."

"You know what?" He put his palms in the air. "I like Ingrid too. She cracks me up. But I don't want that kind of . . . I never, ever hinted at anything."

I confess, there was still one bit of naughty business I had to complete. "Henry cheats on her and she cheats on Henry all the time."

"Doesn't surprise me. It certainly didn't seem like a big deal to her, like she was doing anything out of the ordinary."

"I mean *all* the time. Cheats on him *all* the time," I said.

"Well, given how aggressive she was . . ."

"You know, she's got this huge Panamanian trainer. Maybe others."

His face paled as he took that in. And he didn't have a comeback.

My discovery strategy worked. Goodman had taught me many different ways to ferret out information. You don't have to ask a direct question to find your answer. You can make a declarative statement and see how people react. And Peter's reaction in this case spoke a thousand words: nothing like the sorry look of a guy who is thinking that maybe his dick isn't as big as the next guy's.

What word had he used last week when I asked him if it was just a kiss? "Basically" is how he'd answered. Right. I believed him when he said he didn't sleep with her, but I also knew whatever happened had to be more than a kiss.

Victorious in a certain sense, and deflated in another, I threw in the towel. "How was Dylan tonight?"

"Fine. His homework's done. It's really good you were here before he went down."

I could feel the urgency in his voice, the desire to connect with me on Dylan's neediness for his parents' time. Yet the intense way he looked at me was unnerving. Maybe he was upset I'd pulled out the employer/employee card, or just wanting to express an apology once again. Or, more likely, he was trying to telegraph that his penis wasn't that small.

"What?" I blurted out.

"Just what I said: he was happy to see his mom," he answered. "Now I better get my stuff together."

"Why? Are you leaving?"

"Well, since I just *work* here." He tapped his watch. "Hours are done. Time to punch the clock."

"There's no rush, okay?" I smiled this time. Tension gone. Sort of.

He grabbed another ginger ale from the refrigerator, then sat down on the banquette. The tapes and notebooks for the interview were all over the table before him.

"So when are you interviewing her?"

"We did."

"How could you not tell me?"

"I'm not supposed to tell anyone. So keep it extremely confidential."

"Of course. Did you eat dinner? I was just going to heat up some curry here before I go home. You want some?"

"No, but I'll sit with you. I'll be back in a few minutes," I told him. I gathered up the tapes and notebooks and brought them down the hall to the study.

When I came back into the kitchen, Peter was putting two steaming plates of chicken curry on the table.

"Here's some food for you. You can't get too skinny with all this work." All right. Maybe he did think my ass was okay, even if it didn't measure up to Ingrid's.

"So!" I said.

"Yes?"

Now that I'd admitted he was "more than the manny," this felt like a blind date. "Tell me everything about your software."

He straightened in his chair, and, as he did, his knee brushed against mine. It was like an electric shock. I jerked my leg back and hit it on the support beam under the table.

"Ow!"

"Sorry. I'm not getting fresh, I promise." He grinned. "Some of my backers have pulled out. I tested the online program with every browser version and PC I could get my hands on. But when I went to do the demo at the investor's office, the anti-spyware software on the PC kept popping up warning dialogues. I ran it again while he waited, but then the whole thing crashed . . ."

I tried to stay interested in his techie land and not be so distracted by everything else going on, such as my piece and the vision of his dick in Ingrid's mouth.

Dinner was done. Lots of work ahead of me that night. I needed coffee.

"You're making coffee now?" he asked. "Don't you need some sleep?"

"I'm going to be up late watching this interview one more time. I have to watch it once more in a completely quiet environment where I won't be distracted before I write the script. I always do this at home." I pulled a notepad out of my bag.

"Shit."

"What?" Peter had followed me to the counter. I felt the heat radiating from his body. "My stopwatch. It was my grandfather's. I lost it last week, I think in a taxi or something. I hate timing the sound bites on a regular watch because the second hand doesn't actually stop. Do you have one?" I was talking a mile a minute, anxious that our relationship had turned a corner, anxious (and maybe hopeful) that he'd let his knee touch mine on purpose.

"No, not one that stops."

"Shit." I sat back down, suddenly bone weary from everything— the piece, my marriage, my kids, Peter and that sex-machine bitch Ingrid.

"You gotta give yourself some time," Peter said.

"I don't have any time."

"I'll go with you—tomorrow we can take a walk in the park or go to some galleries on Madison Avenue. Or a museum," he said. "Mark sixty minutes on any clock and step out of everything in your life. Your work will be clearer in your head that way."

I imagined taking a walk with him, just him, without my children, and I instantly thought about running into someone I might know who would jump to conclusions. This wasn't good.

"In the meantime," he said, "let me see the tapes."

"Oh, c'mon, Peter. It's really sordid, you don't want to be bothered with this."

"Hell yeah, I do. I know all about Hartley. Don't forget, my dad's a rabid right-winger. Those are my people."

"Peter, you're one of the only people who know these tapes exist. I should never have mentioned it."

"How could I not know? I practically live here, remember? As you say, I *work* for you. You can trust me. You know that. I mean, besides what happened with you-know-who, most of the time you know you can." He smiled.

I was tired. I did trust him, despite everything. "I guess you can look at the tapes with me. But I'm going to put you to work. Act like a viewer, a normal guy. Tell me what you think of her."

We went into the study and I slipped the tape in the machine and then lay on the sofa with a pad on my knees, like a college girl settling in for an all-nighter. Peter sat in an armchair across the room. I sipped my coffee as the first minutes of the interview started to roll.

"This is the boring part where we're warming her up."

That was the last thing I remember saying before I nodded off. When I awoke at three a.m, the coffee cup had disappeared and there was a blanket tucked around me. The lights were out and the television off.

After another four hours of sleep, I finally felt calm and clearheaded. I could watch the tapes later that day and gather my thoughts then. I'd seen them ten times already, anyhow. And I was charmed by Peter's care last night. He and I had officially traveled to another place and had landed safely as friends. I could stop obsessing over him and Ingrid. Of course, he was attractive and I'd gotten sucked in to some insecure, jealous abyss, but I was out of it now. Of course I was. I would either fix my marriage and learn to live with Phillip's foibles, or we would eventually separate. But I was far from ready to tackle that issue. Meanwhile, I had nailed the biggest political story of the year, and had three healthy children. I was blessed and I knew it.

At nine a.m. I walked into the kitchen and prepared some breakfast and coffee. Carolina had already taken Dylan and Gracie to school. Michael toddled in, climbed onto the banquette next to me, and picked the blueberries out of my bowl. I hugged him tight on my lap. He sucked on a piece of bagel, put his hand in my orange juice, and laughed when I tried to eat his toes.

I kissed his head and wiped the sticky juice off his fat little hands.

The front door opened and slammed shut. Peter. Wearing a dark turtleneck. He'd never worn one before. He looked fabulous. So much for my calm and clearheaded bullshit routine.

"You're hours early."

"I was hoping I'd catch you before you left."

"I guess I didn't make it through the tapes, but I'm glad I caught up on some sleep." I took a big bite of English muffin. "Sorry about that, I guess I passed out. Better that you didn't see the tapes. It's verboten to show them to anyone. Thanks for the blanket, by the way."

"I did see them."

I looked up at him, startled. "You did? While I was sleeping?"

"Yep."

Was I snoring? I wondered. Did I drool all over the pillow in front of him? "Peter, you probably shouldn't have done that."

"I tried to ask you, but you were dead. I mean D-E-A-D." He sat down next to me. He looked serious.

"Was I asleep the whole time?"

"You looked like Sleeping Beauty."

I felt a little naked, like he'd seen me in my underwear by mistake. Not that I would actually mind, provided the lighting was good.

"We gotta talk. About Theresa. You're not going to want to hear this."

"Oh yes? I can handle it. You were bored? It's not a good interview?"

"I was riveted."

I smiled. "That's great. You're a good focus group. Male eighteen to forty-nine. Big advertiser dollars. From Red-State Republican stock. I'm glad. I'm relieved." I took another huge bite of English muffin with a piece of scrambled egg on top.

"You shouldn't be relieved."

"Why not?"

"Because there's something really off about this Boudreaux woman and I can't believe you're not picking up on it."

21

Winter White-out

"It's the potential ratings. They're skewing your judgment."

Michael grabbed my spoon at the breakfast table and dribbled egg down the front of his shirt. Holding him in one hand, I reached behind me on the counter and grabbed his favorite Little People fire engine.

Peter had no idea what he was talking about, which only reminded me just how pigheaded he could be. I resented his high-handed intrusion and, frankly, the resentment brought a strange sense of relief. It was easier to focus on his arrogance than the unsettling feelings of the night before.

"Peter, I'd really like to hear your views on this, really I would, but I want to spend some time with Michael."

"Or are you letting Goodman push you around?"

"*What* are you talking about?"

"Fine. Take your time with Michael. I'll wait for you at the front door and walk you out." He wasn't taking any bit of my brush-off. "We can discuss it then."

In the front hall, I helped Michael find his favorite toy from the back of the closet, the vacuum cleaner with the annoying little colored popping balls.

He made a little *brrrrrrrr* motor noise with his lips, spitting a little as he went around in circles. I stole a glance at myself in the mirror. I was wearing white wool pants, a white turtleneck, and heels.

Yvette, standing at the door and helping Michael get all excited about the noisy popcorn so that he wouldn't scream when I left, watched me look at myself in the mirror. Then she saw Peter gallantly hold the door and stared back at me disapprovingly. Maybe I was getting paranoid. Maybe I wasn't. I leaned down and kissed the baby, held him extra tight, and looked him in the eye.

"Mommies always come home."

He nodded, but his lower lip began quivering.

"I love you, Michael. You're my baby. You're always going to be Mommy's baby."

He clenched my coat sleeve.

"Popcorn? You want to do popcorn?"

His eyes brightened and Yvette swooped him up like a little airplane and turned toward his room. Just before I left, I took off my knee-highs and threw them on the settee in the front hall. Ingrid once told me it was all about nude feet, even in the dead of winter.

"It's cold outside."

"I know."

He hummed a little "these people are totally crazy" tune and motioned for me to go through the door. When I brushed past his body, I felt a distinct uptick in my heart and tried to distract myself in the elevator by thinking about getting sued by the Republican National Committee once the Theresa story aired.

When we stepped outside, I breathed in the gorgeous December day. It hadn't snowed yet, and the day felt arid and dry. I loved New York just before the cold season, when summer still felt near and familiar. In fact, at that instant, I realized this might be the very last nice day before the frigid winter settled in, with its icy black slush melting on every street in the city.

Luis was already in the car, waiting.

"Hey, man," Peter said, knocking on his window. "She doesn't need you this morning."

"Yes, I do."

"No. You don't." He turned to Luis. "We're going to go for a walk in the park."

I could see the panic on Luis's face. He looked at me with an expression that said, *I no listen to this guy. I listen to you!*

"Peter, we're not going to the park right now." I tried to act like I was irritated, but then I studied the dark, thick wool fisherman's turtleneck he'd never worn before, how well it set off his blue eyes. He looked frighteningly attractive in his jeans, dark brown boots, and brown leather pilot jacket. I repeated to myself, *Get a grip. He's the manny, for God's sake. Stop focusing on his looks. I'm married. And it's ridiculous that I'm having to tell myself this.*

"Hey . . . I'm not sure I can keep working for you if you don't take forty-five minutes and come with me." Then he smiled. I couldn't help but think of a boyfriend I had in college, the first guy I ever slept with. He had a kind of crooked smile that could tear me away from my books in a second.

"Tell me you're kidding."

"Actually, I'm not."

It was ten-fifteen. The meeting about Theresa didn't begin until one, but I had to prepare. I put on some lipstick using the reflection in the car window. I was looking so fabulous in my winter white getup, I could hardly stand it. "You know, we hashed it out. Okay? Can we move on? I'm over it."

"This has nothing to do with Ingrid. Believe me."

Though I didn't like to, I'd had practice winging it in meetings. All working moms do. "This better be good." I put my head inside the car window. "Luis, wait here, please. I'll be back to go to work. Soon."

Peter, meanwhile, was pulling something from the trunk of the SUV. Then he came around to the curb with our auto emergency blanket in one hand and my Uggs in the other. "Take off those silly heels and slip into these, you'll be more comfortable."

"I'm not putting those on."

"For once, just go with it. You're not producing this situation."

"Fine." I slipped my feet into the warm Uggs and grabbed my cell phone.

"You don't need the phone."

"Yes, I do. I have children and a job." I plunked it in my pocket.

We entered the park through the Seventy-sixth Street gate.

"Where are we going?"

"Walk. Walk."

"Peter."

"One foot in front of the other."

"Where are we going!"

"Keep moving, you're doing good."

He watched my face out of the corner of his eye as we walked together silently. I wasn't used to being blindsided without a game plan, but it was a gorgeous day and I so liked being with him.

We stumbled down a steep meadow path toward some water. The sun burst through the oak trees and bounced off the mirrored skyscrapers that lined the perimeter of the park. The boat pond was brimming with life early in the day: nannies gossiping on the park benches while rocking babies to sleep in their prams, an elderly woman in a big sun hat and a Mexican poncho painting a foliage scene, her canvas supported by a portable wooden easel, and a group of old men wearing ratty Top-Sider sneakers, tacking their hobby sail-boats around a pin. We paid a moment's homage to the famous Alice in Wonderland statue on the pond's north end. It was impossible not to be charmed by the bronze, larger-than-life Alice seated on a giant mushroom, flanked by the March Hare and the Mad Hatter. The kids climbed all over her every time we came to the park.

"There's something I never told you."

"What? You're gay?" What a stupid thing to say. Where did that come from?

"Hardly."

"Then what?"

He put his hand lightly on my back to guide me toward the bicycle path, which curved gently up the hill ahead. I arched my shoulder blades to pull away from him. *Stop it, Jamie,* I told myself. *You're acting like a schoolgirl. Your husband, a hard worker and a basically good person, is a prestigious lawyer making over a million dollars a year. You have three children. Peter is six years younger than you, practically a child. You're a grown woman. You're feeling a little crush because he's cute and Phillip has a zero emotional barometer. But it's destructive and wrong. Like a narcotic. So stop. Now.*

"It happened in the third or fourth week I'd come to work for you. It was a chilly day, and Dylan and I rented a toy sailboat for a little race. There was no breeze. We couldn't get the boat to move. So Dylan reached over and fell headfirst into this disgusting pond."

"Oh my God. Did he land on his head? He could get hepatitis!"

"Would you just relax? It was hilarious. And it was a great moment for us. Especially the not telling you part."

"Well, I guess I'm glad you didn't tell me, then."

"Yeah, you might have had to miss a color-coded appointment or something."

"Very funny. I'm not that bad."

"No, you're not." Those words hung in the air as we walked deeper into the middle of the park. What did he mean? That I'm just not that bad or that he thought I was even better than not that bad?

We walked up a steep, shady glade on a curvy path of cracked gray pavement, past joggers and mostly older people strolling along. We passed under an arched roadway where an older black man played "Summertime" on the trumpet, his case open before him. Peter threw him a handful of change as we walked by.

We passed the boathouse with its lakeside restaurant perched on a rise. Colorful little rowboats lay stacked on each other out front, held together by huge metal chains. I realized how strange it was that my kids lived half a mile from a rowboat pond and I'd never once taken them there. I promised myself I would take them once my piece was over.

We followed the path up and through a shady glade, then emerged on the bank of a huge pond surrounded by tall grass. Children fed a family of ducks on a wooden pier in the distance. I peeked at my watch and figured Goodman would survive a little longer without me.

"God, this is beautiful. Is this pond what you wanted me to see?"

"It's not just 'this pond.' It's called Turtle Pond and it's a big stop for birds. Like a hundred and fifty species. And no, this isn't the final destination." He pointed to a large castle up a steep grade outlined with brush, elm trees, and tall pines. "We're headed up there. Belvedere Castle."

We started up steps cut into the rock that spilled over the hill like hardened lava. I stumbled just behind him and he reached his hand back for me without looking. I instinctively grabbed it, just for a second, to help balance myself up a crumbly part of the uneven walkway. His hand was warm, and just before he let go at the top, he squeezed mine. That one affectionate gesture told me everything I wanted to know about his own feelings and had resisted seeing until then.

Peter stopped in front of a huge wooden door at the front of the castle, pulled it open, and ushered me in. We passed through a room of dusty microscopes, a hallway showing foliage and bird migratory patterns, and went up three spiral flights of old stone stairs. At the top, there was a small, thick door with a large metal bolt jammed into the cement ceiling.

"Peter, it's locked."

"Would you let me handle this? This is Dylan's favorite place in the whole park. It's always locked."

With all his weight, he pulled the huge bolt down from the latch, pushed the door with his foot, then stood aside as I walked out onto the highest balcony of Belvedere Castle. Before us was a spectacular vista: the huge rectangle of Central Park that stretched up to Harlem to the north, flanked by the west and east sides of Manhattan. It looked like an opera set, with the top of the trees at our eye level and the jagged skyline of New York stretching in every direction.

"I've never been here before."

"Of course you haven't."

"What do you mean, 'Of course you haven't'? I exercise in the park, not much lately, but . . ."

"Hey, I know you occasionally march around the reservoir talking on your cell phone, but that's not *really* experiencing this amazing space. Sit down."

"I can't. I'll get my pants dirty."

"That's what I'm talking about, lady!"

We both started laughing and he laid the blanket out on the bench. I felt tense for so many reasons, but most immediately because I wasn't sure what he was going to tell me. I rested my elbows on the ledge and looked down at the Delacorte Theater, where actors like Kevin Kline and Meryl Streep performed Shakespeare. I always wanted to go, but Phillip wasn't game for traipsing halfway across the park to an outdoor theater. I searched the pond for signs of life. Along the shore, turtles sunned themselves on the rocks like barnacles stuck on the side of a ship.

"Besides, I wanted to find a place where we wouldn't be disturbed."

"What? Do you have cancer or something?" My nerves were so on edge, this ridiculous, tactless question came out of nowhere.

"Would you *please* calm down? No, I do not have cancer. And no, I'm not gay, either."

Okay, I thought, *then what the hell do you need to tell me?*

Peter seemed completely relaxed, but at this point, my heart was pounding so hard, I actually peered inside my coat to see if it was visible through my sweater.

"Dylan and I come here all the time."

"You do?"

"Sure. The poor kid didn't even know a Baltimore oriole was a bird. You see them all the time in the trees around the pond. You can rent binoculars down there."

"Is this what you guys always do in the park?"

"No. We usually go up the Harlem Meer and fish."

"You fish? In New York City? Why didn't you ever tell me?"

"Because the kid needs to do things without his mommy knowing everything. We don't tell you on purpose. But this is his real favorite spot in the whole park. The weather in Central Park that you hear announced on the radio is measured from inside the castle tower next to us. We took a ladder up there with this nice ranger guy once. Dylan thought that was cool. He likes hearing about all the animals in the park too, so we always bring binoculars."

"You're telling me my nine-year-old son is into bird-watching?"

Peter laughed. "Not really. We check out people too. But mostly we just sit for a while. We talk. Do you think we could try that?"

"Okay. I'm calm. I promise." I took a deep breath for courage. Then I turned to him. "But I do need to know why you brought me here."

And then he stared right in my eyes. For a moment, I actually thought he might kiss me. "Jamie."

Omigod. He called me by my first name. He'd never done that. He's going to kiss me. What the hell am I going to do then? Whoaa. The manny was about to kiss me!

"Jamie."

I think I even leaned closer to him.

"How certain are you that Theresa Boudreaux is telling the truth?"

"Jesus! Is that why you brought me here?"

"Well, I . . ."

"Just that?" I felt so *stupid*. "You told me that already!" I tried to stand, but he grabbed my arm.

"Please."

"What?"

"We're not done."

"Fine. What else?"

"Nothing else. Hey, I'll back off. Honestly, I brought you here because I just wanted you to enjoy this place." He pointed to a large tree next to us that nestled its far branches up against the castle's tower. This was not the moment for a nature lesson. "That is an eastern red cedar tree, that is a great blue heron on the side of the pond, that's a bird's nest, that's a big baseball field. And if you can calm down enough to see those, you might, just might, get some perspective on your . . . whole deal."

He wasn't trying to kiss me. Probably never even entered his mind. I *had* to snap out of this pathetic fairy tale I'd concocted.

"What do you mean my whole deal?"

"Everything."

"Are you talking personal or professional?"

"I was talking your job. But if you want to go right in there, I'll get personal too. Glad to have the opening, in fact. Your husband. He's not easy."

"Peter!"

"He's not. The kids love him. You married him. Just saying . . ."

"No. You're not saying anything right now about Phillip." My husband's behavior *was* embarrassing. I worried it made Peter lose respect for me. Just another ingredient to add to the pathetic stew of my emotions. "And if you think you're being helpful by reminding me, you're not."

"I was speaking in solidarity. Just want you to know I know."

"I'd rather discuss the professional."

"Fine. Theresa."

"You're not the first person who thought she was lying," I said, trying to get my distraught feelings under control. "I'm really touched by how much you want to help me." I looked at my watch again. I was now a full two hours late for work.

"I'm not trying to be touching. I'm worried for you. You sometimes fall too much in line. With the fancy weirdos outside nursery school. We talked about that."

"Yes. And I denied it."

"And you tend to appease your husband."

Now he was getting close to pissing me off and crossing a line. "When you're married, it's easier to solve problems rather than rattle things. You'll understand that someday."

"All I'm saying is maybe it's a pattern. Are you doing this story because Goodman is pushing you? What do you think?"

"Stop. Now. Sorry to say this, but you're naive." He'd hurt my feelings. "And arrogant too."

"Really? Naive *and* arrogant?"

"Of course everyone wonders if she is lying! Don't you think that we—me, Goodman, and the entire executive floor—just might have our bases covered? The justification is that the person is telling 'his truth'—and the public has an interest in hearing from them under the 'you decide' standard. What you clearly do not understand is that sometimes there is a story that garners so much heat, you just can't ignore it."

My need to disparage him was visceral. If I could successfully dismiss his opinions, then my feelings for him were given less weight, and so they were less frightening. And I wouldn't ever again be in this ridiculous situation where I had teenage romantic fantasies that he was trying to kiss me.

"Not even a serious news network like ours would stay away. It's like a perfect storm," I went on. "Given Hartley's prominence, his pro-family stance—and not just on abortion—I mean pro-family values with his four children. And of course the whole ass thing with the sodomy laws. And if the central figure of a media explosion is going to finally talk, we—with the help of lawyers—will simply present this as her side of the story."

But what I really wanted to tell him was this: that Phillip wasn't always such a prick. And that we used to have amazing sex, which was one reason I fell for him. And that he could handle scary situations better than anyone. And that Peter didn't know what it was like to be stuck in a loveless marriage and worry about divorce when you had three kids.

"You're not presenting it as just her side of the story."

"There's just so much you don't understand."

"That's funny," he fired back. "I feel the same way about you."

"You're beyond obnoxious."

"When I got home after midnight last night, I couldn't sleep. So I logged on to a bunch of trashy gossip-mongering sites and then to all my father's favorite right-wing blogs to check out more about this woman."

"You don't think the network is already all over those guys? Sure, they're trying to discredit her. They're protecting their big guy Hartley. I know you know how to surf the web, but you're forgetting I've been a journalist for a long time."

"That's so nineties. 'Surf the web'!"

"You should hear how rude you sound. What the hell do you know, sitting in your techie isolation tank in Red Hook? God! You've never met her. You don't know what you're talking about. Okay? Get it?"

"Let me tell you something," he said, gaining fervor. "These are my people. I grew up with them around my dinner table. There are military bases all over my state and my dad thinks Ronald Reagan should be put up for sainthood. Hartley is a close second in this crowd. I've now read dozens of right-wing columns on this woman—many on reputable, respected sites—and they paint a picture of a girl who has come out of nowhere and isn't telling the truth. Maybe she's one of these crazies who crave attention. Who knows and who cares?"

"All right, Mr. Internet Hipster. I'm glad you're conversant in the right-wing blogerati, but here's what you don't know."

He sighed. "Okay. What don't I know?"

"That before the interview, Theresa surprised us and pulled out souvenirs she'd kept from hotels where she'd spent the night with Huey Hartley, conferences he attended, airplanes they'd taken. She had napkins, matches, bar receipts that proved she was in the city or in the hotel from his congressional business trips; our research department verified with his public calendar that he'd been in those cities and staying in those hotels on those days. That's enormous. No one knows we have that."

"Well . . ."

"Well what, Sherlock? That's a big deal you didn't know about. And I'm sorry, but who are you to tell me how to do my job?" I was back on a roll, successfully putting the humiliation about my husband on the back burner. "You also don't know we've got an eyewitness saying he saw them together in a 'couple' kind of way. We have photos, we've got audiotapes of conversations, and even so, all we have to say is that this is her side. We're just a little place to air her side of the story."

"Just a *little* place. Give me a break! You're legitimizing what she says by putting her in prime time on a national news network in front of twenty friggin' million people!"

I tried a different approach, even though he didn't deserve it. "You know what, Peter? It's like Tonya Harding. Remember? The skater who got the guys to slug Nancy Kerrigan's—"

"Yeah. I know who Tonya Harding is. And I even know she's into boxing now."

"Okay. Fine, exactly. She was one of my first big 'gets' in the news business a dozen or so years ago. I went to her practice rink and watched her do double salchows for weeks, pleading with her to talk to NBS. And because I sat my sorry butt on those freezing metal bleachers for longer than anyone else, she went with us and talked to Goodman. Doesn't mean we legitimized her side. Doesn't mean we said she didn't know about the plan to break Kerrigan's knees. America was dying to know what she had to say—and my only job was to get her and I did. Of course, I always prefer the serious news interviews, but sometimes we just have to stoop to conquer."

"I'm not on some high horse here. That's not what this is all about. Do all the tacky TV you want, just be careful."

"I am careful!"

"Listen to me. It's amazing what you do, handling three kids and a job and being a good wife to that guy."

"Peter! Stop!"

He wisely moved on. "Here's what I'm saying: some things are going to fall through the cracks. A missed birthday party. Fine. Late for bedtime. Fine. But missing what this crazy woman is really about is different. That has you taking down one of the highest-ranking, most visible members of the U.S. Congress. The United States Congress! And being wrong about that is not fine."

"Honestly, Theresa Boudreaux is on the cover of every major gossip magazine in the country. It's like if you landed an interview with Scott Peterson talking about Laci—what are you going to do, say we're not interested? These interview subjects are already out there, the center of this humongous frenzy, it's just a matter of who's going to get them to talk. And I beat everyone, for better or for worse."

He still didn't seem impressed.

"And now I've got a meeting I can't miss."

"Yes, you can."

"No, I can't."

"You brought your cell phone. Just call and say you can't come in, and sit here with me."

"Are you out of your mind?" I asked.

"I was thinking the same thing about you."

"Why?"

"Because you know why."

"You're right, I can't do it. I have a teeny tiny interview to edit. And I have a meeting with my boss. And my boss pays me to show up for meetings."

"Just tell him you'll be late."

"I can't."

"It's really too bad. Sad, actually."

"What's too bad?"

"You just can't do it."

"Do what?"

"You can't call your office, cancel a meeting, and just sit here, maybe even enjoy the morning. It would make you nervous."

"No, it wouldn't."

"Fine. So do it." He smiled, knowing he'd caught me in his ridiculous web.

I hesitated. Then I looked out at the operatic skyline in front of me. Was there a chance Peter was coming on to me? Or was he just enjoying some time with a new friend?

"You know, I'm not dumb. I'm not falling for your ploy. I get what you're doing here."

"Stay."

God. I felt so drawn to this man, in the sanctuary of that tower, high above everyone else. "Okay, so say I did, what would we do?"

"Forget the Boudreaux topic entirely. I'm done with that, it's in your court now. We could just talk. About anything. About everything. You might even get to know what makes me tick. And me, you."

"I can't . . ."

"You can. Just stay."

And so I did.

Two hours later, I was back in the car and heading toward the office. Luis spoke English poorly and in three years we had never once had a conversation about anything, ever. But I knew, without doubt, he assumed I was having an affair with the manny.

"Peter talked to me about Dylan," I said defensively. "Long talk. Long, long talk."

Sitting under the gorgeous canopy of trees above the Belvedere tower, we did have a long, long talk. I made Peter promise he would steer clear of talking about Phillip. He could sense my sadness and the humiliation I felt over my marriage, and apologized for his flippant remarks. He told me how much he adored my kids, and I found myself telling all sorts of stupid stories about them, such as how Dylan's stomach was so fat when he was a baby, it covered his knees in the bath. We laughed about the high-priced power birthday parties he'd taken the kids to. Peter even invited me to his own birthday party.

"You sure?"

"Of course I'm sure. I'd love to have you. Bring Dylan."

"But we won't know your friends."

"I want to show you off to my friends, J.W."

That sounded funny when he said it, like I was his new girlfriend. However he meant it, it made me giddy.

"Yes, Luis. Such a long walk, too." I wiped my forehead, miming exhaustion. Luis, who had a sweet, frozen, subservient smile on his face almost every time I'd ever seen him, now gave me an all-knowing look that said, *Yeah, sure, lady.*

22

Table Talk

The floor tiles were warming and I turned on the heat lamps above to redden the bathroom that smelled of lavender. It was Saturday afternoon, four days until the piece aired, and I was trying to take care of myself. I got into the tub, laid my head up against an inflatable pillow attached to the back of the tub, and listened to *La Bohème*.

Hai sbagliato il raffronto.
Volevi dir: bella come un tramonto.
"Mi chiamano Mimì,
il perché non so . . ."

Just as I started to zone out, the bathroom door flung open, knocking two bottles of lotion off the commode and onto the floor. Phillip blasted through, with his squash outfit falling out of his Prince bag. "You have time to loll around in a bubble bath, but we can't get away for the night?"

"Phillip, please, can we take this up in an hour? You know, when you're gone, it's double duty for me with the kids. Like a single parent, so it's not like I've been at a spa. This is literally the first moment I've had to—"

"You've had plenty of time to yourself. I've been gone for days."

"And we missed you. We did, honey."

"I'm late for my game at the Racquet Club, and it's raining out." He looked at me as if I were supposed to stop the rain.

"So wear a raincoat and take an umbrella." He didn't react. I tried another tack. "Why don't you wear different sneakers, so you have fresh ones that won't slide on the courts?"

"The sneakers are not the problem."

"Then what is the problem, Phillip?"

"There are no umbrellas in the house. Can you tell Carolina to do her job, please? Can you help me find one?" Anytime one teensy-weensy item in my husband's life is out of order, he blames Carolina, the hardest-working woman in New York.

"Please just look outside the front door in the umbrella stand. There are plenty there." Nothing, not even an umbrella crisis, was going to get me out of my warm bath.

I slid my head under the water, trying to avoid the coming argument, one that we have four times a year. Phillip came over to the bath and started raising his voice so I could hear him underwater. "I mean, can't you supervise the help? Make a checklist or something? I like umbrellas with wooden handles, not the cheap plastic fold-up ones. It's a gentleman's club. I'm going to the Racquet Club. One doesn't show up with some tacky umbrella one buys on the street."

I popped my head out of the water and decided to appease him rather than further ignite his tantrum, though I'm not sure the subsequent resentment was worth it. "Can you just take a fold-up one today and then I'll make sure we get a dozen with the wooden handles, so that this doesn't happen again."

"No, I really can't, Jamie."

"Why not? You're crazy!" I slunk under the water with my hands over my eyes, trying to erase the maniacal spoiled-husband image from my personal space. He waited silently. I came up for air and looked at him. He was still standing in the doorway, with the door wide open letting cold air in. I sighed heavily. "Go into my closet; in the back you'll see a brand-new Burberry umbrella we bought as a class gift to

Dylan's homeroom teacher for his thirtieth anniversary at the school. It's wrapped. I am supposed to bring it in Monday morning, but I'll try to find something else tomorrow. Just take it and go to your game."

"You're the best!" With that, my husband smiled and slammed the door, knocking my silk robe off the back of the door.

Qui . . . amor . . . sempre con te!
Le mani . . . al caldo . . . e . . . dormire . . .

I laid my head back on the inflatable cushion and stared at the ceiling. Then I submerged my head again with my hands over my eyes. When I came up for air, tears mixed with soapy bathwater streamed down my face.

Four hours later, as we dressed for dinner, Phillip grabbed my midsection from behind, startling me. "Love the getup." He slowly reached his fingers inside my bra, pinching my nipples slightly, thinking that would turn me on. He was mistaken.

I twisted away from him, pushing a pair of large shell-encrusted earrings into my ears. I sprayed some perfume around my head.

He came after me playfully, snapping the back of my bra.

"Phillip, not now," I pleaded, and walked into my closet to put on a pair of pants. It was Saturday night and we were late for a dinner party. "This is just my underwear, not a getup." He couldn't know I was wondering what Peter would think of that "getup" if he happened to see it.

I hadn't eaten since our walk the week before.

"C'mon, baby, you're looking so hot in that lacy pink. Just a quickie . . ." He came up behind me and began squeezing my ass with one hand and gyrating his crotch up against me, humping my thigh like a dog. I had to steady myself with both hands. Could I do this? Hadn't we already had sex when he arrived at six a.m. from the red-eye? Wasn't my quota reached for the day? Could I suffer through a quickie just to tame him?

Thankfully, the door swung open and Gracie flew toward me, grabbing the same naked thigh that my husband seconds ago had been furiously humping. "Pleeeeese don't go out, I hate it when you go out. You always go out."

I knelt down to meet Gracie at eye level. "Sweetheart, I know I had to work some nights last week, but I don't really go out that much."

"You *always* go out!"

"No, that's not true. I almost *always* put you to bed."

I watched her do a face-off with me as I slipped into my clothes. She stuck out her chin, but I knew she was too tired to battle on, so I picked her up and she clung to me loosely like a rag doll. I breathed in her baby girl scent of sweet children's shampoo and body cream, then took her to her room and lay down with her as she drifted, fighting slumber, then relenting.

The white-gloved doorman slid the elevator door shut, then stared straight ahead as the little mahogany-paneled box sped up to Susannah Briarcliff and Tom Berger's penthouse apartment.

I quickly applied another coat of lip gloss, then reached into my gold rectangular evening bag and turned my mobile phone to "vibrate."

"Phillip, turn your phone off." He obliged and winked, commending me silently as if to say, *Wouldn't want to act crass in front of Susannah.* He looked me up and down, taking in my purple velvet pantsuit, my tight black-ribbed turtleneck, black high heels, and gold chain belt. The gold chain belt matched my purse. I'd thought I'd done pretty well on the clothes, considering how distracted I'd been.

"What?" I asked him, flipping over one of the links on my belt.

"Your outfit, it's just so, so . . . ordinary." Nice of him to finally look at me. He looked disappointed, as if my outfit reflected poorly on him somehow. Which, in his mind, it did. "Susannah always dresses so . . . festively. She wears sexy clothes with bright colors. I wish you'd do more of that. Ask her for help next time."

"I do, all the time. You know that." This was so defeating. Couldn't get it right in front of the drop-off hens, nor in front of my husband. "The whole damn fashion deal just doesn't work on me the same way."

This was all code for Phillip really just wishing he'd married Susannah—or someone like her—instead. Phillip and Susannah shared a tight kinship, seeing as they both had ancestors traceable to the *Mayflower*—although every hard-core WASP in the Grid claims the same thing. On the other hand, Susannah's husband, Tom, a man ten years her senior, couldn't have been more different. He wore thin Albert Einstein glasses that matched his wiry gray hair. He held the managing editor for foreign news slot at the *New York Times* and had grown up in Scarsdale, New York, the son of Jewish parents who had both been gumshoe reporters. Susannah met Tom while in her midtwenties, auditing a course in Middle Eastern politics at Columbia University. Her parents, quietly horrified that she was marrying a Jew despite his professional prominence, made her promise to keep her maiden name; it was painful enough that they would have grandchildren named Berger. Tom brushed off their anti-Semitism—he knew these people would never change, and it didn't hurt that the second he put that golden band on her finger, they deposited one hundred million dollars into a joint account.

When Susannah rushed to the door, wearing wide orange silk palazzo pants, a matching feather boa, and an ivory silk tank top, Phillip practically leapt into her arms.

"You're *soooo* wonderful to have us." He held her face in his hands and kissed her on the lips, ever so discreetly. Lips should be off-limits to people not married to each another. Again came the same old feeling of being excluded.

"Come in."

In the Grid, big-time hostesses throw dinner parties for a reason, never ever just to spend time with friends. They might toast a recently published author, give venue to a doctor who has just completed a report about eradicating malaria in southern Africa, or have just "discovered" a rising young black congressional candidate—a much more exotic and coveted guest than a well-known white Senator. When Susannah called to invite us to dinner, she always reviewed the guest list.

"You must come, Jamie, the Under-Secretary-General of the U.N. is coming *and* the editor of *Newsweek*. And Daniel Boulud is catering." Phillip and I came running every time Susannah invited us. Her parties were glamorous and fun and very good for my news networking.

To my left at dinner, I was seated next to the guest of honor, Yousseff Gholam, a prominent Jordanian professor from the Kennedy School of Government at Harvard and a perennial ornament on television news programs covering the Iraq War. Media experts like Mr. Gholam can't merely have written a dozen books and a hundred articles; in addition, they have to be television regulars (translation: *famous*) to hit the Grid dinner-party circuit. Mr. Gholam had just published a blockbuster book entitled *The Next 9/11: Why Homeland Security Is Doomed for Failure and Your City Might Be Next* that had hit the number one spot on the *New York Times* nonfiction best-seller list and had come out only three weeks before.

My dinner partners to the left and right were momentarily engaged, so I took a moment to survey the room. A high-gloss cantaloupe hue covered the walls of the dining room, enveloping us like a hermetically sealed cocoon. Matching tortoiseshell frames adorned twelve Hiroshi Sugimoto misty seascape photographs, four on each wall. The enormous round dining table had geometric triangle leaves that magically slid together and allowed sixteen to sit comfortably. I looked down at my perfect place setting, wondering how many man-hours were spent getting this table just right.

A small plate with painted birds in the center nested atop a larger plate with the same birds painted on its rims. Four crystal glasses stood to the right of my place mat: one for white wine, one for red wine, one for water, and a champagne flute to go with dessert. Miniature sterling silver apples held gold-rimmed place cards, written in calligraphy. Each guest also had individual cobalt-blue glass salt and pepper shakers from Cartier wrapped in silver lace next to their place cards. Susannah had placed flowers in a low silver trophy bowl—no doubt won by Theodore Briarcliff II in a sailing regatta at the turn of the century—so that the guests could talk across the table without visual obstruction. Golden pinecones, red and yellow fall leaves, and dried pomegranates were strewn across the table artistically. Dozens of small votive candles flickered in crystal holders, their reflections dancing on the ceiling. Suddenly a snapshot of Peter sitting here appeared in my mind. He would hate all this pomp.

Phillip, meanwhile, was fawning over Christina Patten on his left. She looked impossibly thin, her bony shoulders sticking out of a jeweled silk halter top. She pushed her food back and forth on her plate while Phillip was going on about the impossibility of securing the best cottages at Lyford Cay. Undoubtedly, like all socialites at dinners, she had claimed to Phillip that she had already eaten "with the kids." Susannah didn't much respect Christina, but knew she was a powerful player on the social circuit. And in this mercenary crowd, that's as good as a Nobel Prize in astrophysics.

Susannah had executed her guest formula with perfection once again this evening: a young clothing designer for Gucci who looked like Montgomery Clift and his partner, a director of a highly acclaimed repertory theater downtown, filled the gay and/or culture quota tonight; a young black lesbian modern artist from the Côte d'Ivoire (there was a two-year waiting list to get one of her paintings) took care of the minority presence; yours truly as well as the dashing editor of *Newsweek* filled the media slots. The two of us would be expected to weigh in on any and every current event topic. The Important Person in Public Service slot had been given to the Under-Secretary-General of the U.N. for Middle Eastern Affairs. The lead partner of a huge hedge fund filled the hundred-million-plus, wheels-up, fuck-you money allocation.

There was someone still missing in my mind: Peter. Then came a fantasy: me wearing a sexy wrap dress with all kinds of access points. Him wearing a thin black turtleneck under a tweed blazer. We were in Susannah's bright orange lacquered bar. He pushed the door slowly closed . . . and tilted up my chin . . .

Montgomery Clift, on my right, shifted toward me. "Fabulous earrings," he said.

I turned to my new best friend. "Really? You think so?"

"Stunning, especially with your dark hair."

"Tell my husband. He didn't think it was colorful enough."

"What does he know? That guy over there in the suit? What is he, a banker?"

"Lawyer."

"Look, baby, it's all the same to me. One of those money-making monkeys."

"So Susannah tells me you're a clothing designer?" There's nothing better than flirting with a gay man at a New York dinner. "Honestly tell me what you think of my outfit—fashion doesn't comes naturally to me."

"You want to know honestly?"

"Believe me, I'm interested." A few weeks before, I had strolled down the red carpet at nursery school drop-off in a fantastic new gray flannel suit with three-inch heels, thinking I had broken the code. Ingrid Harris had looked down at my legs and said, "Jamie, what the hell?"

I thought she was going to compliment me for once for reading the fashion memo correctly; my shoes were fabulous—even I understood that. "Where are you going? Doing your rounds?"

She must have seen the bewildered look on my face.

"The stockings. Puhhleeeese. You look like a nurse! Light-colored, sheer hose? What planet are you on?"

"I, uh . . ."

"Who dressed you this morning? Go home and change before you embarrass yourself any further." And so it goes in my stupid little insignificant quest to camouflage my middle-class suburban roots and play dress-up with the fanciest girls in the world.

Montgomery leaned his chair back on its two hind legs, looked me up and down, checking me out as if I were a racehorse, or an ox, depending on your point of view. Then, after twenty seconds, the verdict came in. "I agree with your husband."

"No!"

"Honey, yes! Let's start at the bottom. Good shoes." Pause. "But not for nighttime."

"How come? They're black leather Manolos. What could be wrong with them?"

"You're wearing velvet, which has a certain sheen. Your shoes are too matte for the sheen of your suit and the flash of your belt. Excellent bling-bling on the belt, by the way. And the earrings, the shells. Now that I see your whole outfit, they're all wrong." He shook his head and shook his finger in front of my nose. "Shells don't go with flashy gold. And don't wear a black top with a dark purple velvet suit. Too monotone."

"Okay. I'm not offended." I was totally hurt. "So my outfit's wrong for many reasons. Start listing."

"Fine, people pay lots of money for this, but you get it for free." He was actually adorable with his black, slicked-back hair and huge eyes. He smiled and squeezed the top of my shoulder. "The shoes: they should be black satin. A little bling on the shoes would be good—some chains, or sexy laces that tie up your leg, maybe a little rhinestone detail, just for evening. Evening shoes should be very slutty, no matter where you're going. If you can't find what you want at Manolo, go to Christian Louboutin. He's even more talented. Never ever wear plain black leather shoes at night."

He took a big, efficient gulp of wine; evidently this guy had much explaining to do and was just getting going.

"Your turtleneck: too dark. Something sexier; don't wear a business-suit-looking shell from the 1980s out for dinner. Anything bohemian to contrast the lines of your suit: you need a lacy, see-through silk blouse that hangs out of the sleeves of your jacket, a little messy-like. No bra, show a little hint of titty. Whatever you do, *don't* button the cuffs of the shirt."

I needed my reporter's notebook.

"The collar of the shirt should fall over the top of your lapels, but not too far. Your earrings: all wrong with the whole outfit. You can wear those shells only in the winter with a tight black turtleneck and black pants or jeans. Very hard in a fancy situation like this to pull those off at night. Shells are for summer; those are beach earrings, not city earrings. Put those babies in your L.L. Bean bag and take them in your big SUV to your beach house!" I had to laugh, because I would be doing just that.

"You should be wearing big gold hoops, maybe some big-time gems. You got some of those? You look like you might." I nodded. Phillip had bought me some sapphire drops encircled with small diamonds when Michael was born. "Okay, good. You're on Park Avenue, you gotta look extra hot and sexy, otherwise you look like a matron or, worse, a preppy matron. I'm telling you, big gold hoops to match your belt. Wear expensive fancy shell earrings like yours in the summer with a white T-shirt (make sure it's Petit Bateau) and white jeans. Get a rope belt for summer. And some cork platforms. It's all about the platforms."

I was about to crack the elusive fashion code. No one had ever explained clothes so clearly. With help from this Montgomery character, I'd be chic for once, the hens would covet *my* look, society photographers like Punch Parish would be following *me* around parties, I'd, I'd . . .

Clink. Clink. Susannah rapped a huge knife across her champagne flute. Amazingly, the crystal didn't shatter to pieces. "Excuse me, folks, quiet down."

Montgomery elbowed me. "Check out the knife. Pick yours up. See how heavy it is. Puiforcat sterling. Like six hundred and fifty dollars apiece."

"For a knife?"

"Yeah, and she's got three forks here per setting, two knives . . . must have full service for twenty-four, like times ten pieces per person. This woman is serious business."

Susannah smiled and rapped some more, obviously pleased with the lively, and therefore successful, conversation level. "I'd like to raise a toast to a dear friend of mine."

"Of yours? Who introduced you?" interrupted her husband, Tom, in a playful way. Everyone chuckled on cue.

"Okay, a friend of *both* of ours. Mr. Yousseff Gholam. Yousseff has briefed three consecutive presidential administrations on the turmoil in the Mideast. An author of nine, count them, *nine* books on the subject. Yousseff has also authored dozens of articles—one of which won the National Magazine Award for Public Interest, which officially means"—Susannah discreetly checked an index card underneath her dessert plate—"'the potential to affect national or local policy or lawmaking.' To you, my dear Youseff."

Youseff put down his wineglass. "People," he said gravely. He then looked down and decided to stand and begin his lecture. And then once again, "People. I don't see this as the death of dictators, but I think we have passed what I call the Autumn of Anxiety . . ."

More often than not, Park Avenue people drool over policy experts who make no sense; they all figure they're not intelligent enough to understand the gibberish, but pretend to nonetheless. I shot Phillip a look of exasperation, knowing the boring speech that would follow, but he returned a stern glance, as though I was being childish. I turned to Montgomery, my Peter stand-in, who winked at me. He too thought this Gholam guy was a pretentious windbag. I pulled my shell earrings off, placed my elbows on the table, rested my chin in my hands, and hunkered down for the long haul.

Phillip, who loved to show off in crowds, asked a question about Iran's uranium production. This new tangent only animated Youseff further, as it provided a new opportunity to show off his knowledge. "If you want to understand the future of Iran, I refer you to the events that took place in that region in the last quarter of the eighteenth century . . ."

Heaven help me. Sorry, Youseff, I was doing bong hits that day in the back row of history class. I needed a wine refill.

I'd been here before. With other Youseff-type bloviators of all shapes and sizes. There is a whole stash of writers, magazine editors, and foreign policy experts on a special list in the Grid. The experts get attention from and access to the city's most wealthy power brokers, and the hostesses get a dozen thank-you notes for the *fascinating* dinner conversation. But the experts also know they must perform like seals for their hostesses, like hired help. Name-dropping with governmental power figures is de rigueur.

". . . This came to mind when I happened to be in the Oval Office—a smaller room than you would think. While helping the President prepare his most recent State of the Union, what struck me is that he truly understands the subtlety of the Arab dilemma."

I tapped the top on my glass with my fingertips and whispered "Please" to one of the servers dressed in black silk Mao jackets who stood at strategic places around the table.

"And that reminds me of the concept of *virtu,* from Machiavelli's *Prince,* of course. Bush embodies *virtu,* Machiavelli's idea of human energy: that which shapes fate and fortune. He combined the subtlety of Cicero with the brutality of Caesar."

I had zero understanding of what this guy was talking about.

"Bush is not an intellectual, of course, but in a truly profound way, he has found genius. You really must think of the Medicis when you think of Bush."

Mr. *Newsweek* and the United Nations official sparred like Luke Skywalker and Darth Vader with their light sabers over the amount of dollars needed to secure American ports. Yousseff jumped in. The *Newsweek* editor wisely tried to bring the table talk down to planet Earth and steered Yousseff toward present dangers. "Let me all warn you of the peril of letting your guard down. Terrorists are very patient people . . ."

Yousseff went on with his scare tactics. I wanted more fashion tips from Montgomery—anything, anything not to hear this torturous talk about the danger headed toward my New York City family. Like every New York City mother, I had to fight hard not to let hideous, apocalyptic fantasies make me crazier about safety than I already was. I fantasized about a move back home, then I remembered Yousseff had specifically mentioned the Mall of America in Minneapolis as a potential target. Phillip stuck his neck out again with some smart-sounding questions that were pedestrian underneath his elaborate language. "If Bush the elder hadn't so brazenly abandoned the Shiites in the southern region of Iraq in '91, his son might have had part of the country on his side. Don't you agree, Yousseff?"

Christina Patten wisely refrained from venturing into the international affairs conversation. But apparently she had something so pressing on her mind that she couldn't stay silent any longer. "Mr. Gholam, do you think we still need plastic sheeting and duct tape? I mean, is that still necessary, living in this city with children? Or was that just the media going overboard? Also, my husband and I have been online and we couldn't figure out which gas masks to get."

George Patten, a man who retired fifteen years ago at thirty-five with a fifty-million-dollar inheritance, spent his days studying maps in his parlor. "Electrifying" would not be a term commonly used to describe him. He added, "We bought from the company in Israel that supplies the Israeli Army. They were a *fortune*."

Yousseff took a deep breath, trying to switch the conversation from highbrow geopolitics down to what the New Yorkers were interested in: namely, how it was going to affect *them*.

"Christina, we can cover that after dinner," Susannah interrupted, aggravated with Christina's line of questioning and trying to maintain the content at a high-level pitch.

Yousseff, catching on to Susannah's embarrassment, tried to bridge the gap. He turned to Christina. "Well, having fled Lebanon when the country first fractured, I do know a little something about feeling vulnerable to danger. It is difficult for me to gauge exactly when and where they will hit. And remember, anthrax dissipates once it is airborne, so unless you're in the subway car underground when it happens, the risk is remote. It's rather unlikely you would need a gas mask in your apartment. But I do know that the Israelis have the best-quality equipment. My own father bought the Israeli masks when the Intifada started and we were living outside Beirut."

"Okaaaaay," answered Christina. Then she made a sweeping gesture across the table. "Now I have a question for all the New Yorkers in the room!" I thought Susannah might put a napkin over her head to help deny the fact that Christina was ruining her dinner party. "So does this mean we all have to buy gas masks for the staff too?"

Stone-cold silence around the room. I looked at Yousseff; he closed his eyes, took a sip of wine, and coughed into his napkin. No one could come up with a response for that one. Even Christina's husband didn't try to save her.

At that Susannah stood up abruptly. "Why don't we retire to the living room for coffee, everyone?"

Where was Peter? I imagined him in some cool bar in Red Hook, surrounded by gorgeous, hip, younger women. I needed him to help me find the humor in this pathetic scene. But of course I was part of this pathetic scene. He was right about that.

And you want your kids growing up with these people's kids? Are you nuts?

I sat alone on the plush curved sofa in the living room and accepted an espresso with a lemon peel in a miniature china cup from a waiter. Venetian-lagoon-green taffeta curtains hung from antique wooden bars atop four large glass doors that opened onto Susannah's terrace. An eclectic array of thick brocade fabrics covered the furniture, some red backgrounds with embroidered flowers, some amber velvet, some green velvet. Two zebra throw rugs were placed in front of the fireplaces at each end of the room.

Mr. *Newsweek* came over and sat down next to me, interrupting my thoughts. He already knew Goodman had something big from the New York media grapevine, but he had no idea how big.

"Did you get Theresa? Does she actually sit down and talk to you? Does she admit anything? I mean, anything real on Hartley? Or will it be Kathy Seebright redux?"

"Not telling."

I knew what was coming next. "Jamie, think about it. I know your show airs on Wednesday. If you want, I could delay our close right now—actually anytime before midnight." He looked down at his watch. "Tell you what. Here's what I could do for you. I could put something in the magazine for this week that would create buzz."

"That's so considerate."

"Well, uh, no. I mean, we would credit NBS, of course. We would only build an audience for your show. Entice them, if you will. I would be sure to add something about your input."

"My input?"

"I mean, we could even mention that you had something to do with it."

"To do with the blockbuster that is about to befall the nation?"

Beads of sweat appeared around his sideburns. A few long seconds passed. "You've got an interview with some meat to it, don't you? Just tell me that, would ya? Put me out of my misery and tell me you have *the real deal*—a goddamn interview with Theresa Boudreaux."

I couldn't stop myself. "Let me tell you one thing, big guy: what I'm going to put on the air this week is going to leave your puny little magazine in the biggest cloud of dust this side of Kansas."

He threw a little velvet leopard pillow at my face and walked directly over to the crystal decanter of scotch.

After some small talk with the other guests, I went into the front hall to look for my husband, who had disappeared into the den some time ago. Montgomery, slipping into his heavy coat, put his arm around me. "And one more piece of advice, darling." He pulled me in close. "Keep your husband away from the hostess," he whispered, sashaying his cute little ass out the door.

23

Day of Reckoning

Phillip walked home from Susannah's with his nose in the air and his chest puffed out as if he'd just gotten laid. I ambled a few steps behind, trying to figure out if he indeed had. But when we came to the street corner, he reached for my hand, only just then noticing I wasn't by his side. I reluctantly gave it to him.

I was feeling queasy. I can handle two glasses of wine during dinner, but after three to four, as I had had this evening, my head spins.

"Hey, slowpoke, it's freezing out here," he said.

"Have you ever tried walking in three-inch heels?"

"What's with you? It's a beautiful night. We just spent a lovely evening at Susannah and Tom's. I feel wonderful. The company, the wine, the food. Man, that apartment is awesome." He breathed in the night air as he looked at the Briarcliff-Berger apartment in the distance. Susannah's landscaped terraces wrapped around the entire perimeter of both her penthouse floors. Little white lights hung from her spruce trees and shimmered in the cold winter night. "You know, that's the difference between money, our brand of money, and *real* money, real, fuck-you money."

"Tell me, Phillip," I said, disgusted. "What's the difference?"

"With real, fuck-you money, you get that staff in black coats, the caviar flowing like a waterfall, the '82 Latour. Plus the terrace. That wraparound terrace is a statement of serious wealth. I work like an animal and I can't even get a park view. I'd kill for that terrace." He shook his head and picked up his pace again, his arm tight around me. Then he pulled up short. "Can you imagine? One of those huge Williams-Sonoma outdoor grills in the city on a terrace? I could actually grill steaks on a fuckin' weeknight."

"Phillip, relax. We have a beautiful apartment. You have a grill in the country."

"It's a piece-of-shit three-hundred-dollar grill I bought five years ago at the hardware store, not even one of those Williams-Sonoma grills, you know, with the cooktop on the side for steaming mussels or boiling corn. I want one of those grills. Soon. And step on it." He chuckled. "Just kidding. I mean, I'll get it."

I wasn't amused. "We have a kitchen in the country which has plenty of burners for corn and mussels."

"That kitchen is small. I can't afford to renovate it. And the burners aren't *on* the grill," he griped. "We don't have any *outside* burners."

"Phillip! The kitchen is twenty feet from the patio with the grill! Listen to yourself. Whining about six-thousand-dollar grills."

"So I want to cook outside at night? That's all."

"You know what's really sick? Money depresses you more than it makes you happy."

"Stop with the clichés, please," he answered.

"It's true. You go to a bigger apartment and you get totally depressed the second you walk out the door. We have a great apartment. You love it, remember?"

"It's okay."

"Just for me, for twenty-four hours, let go of the trappings. How great would that feel? To be unencumbered."

He stared at me, considering that concept.

I thought I might be breaking through.

"Let me tell you something, baby, being encumbered with one of those big mother Williams-Sonoma grills *would* make me happier. I'm sure the corn tastes better if you cook it outside in the fresh country air. And man, those balconies in the city: imagine the freedom to cook whatever you want, whenever you want. You know, after a business trip, just grilling up a Lobel's strip steak . . ."

"Tell me that when you come home at nine-thirty from a trip to Pittsburgh, you're going to flip a steak like Fred Flintstone. You can grill on summer weekends."

"It's not that I'm actually going to *do* it, it's the freedom to do it if I *feel* like it. Even if it's only one night a year. Ever want that? Just to be able to have something available in case you *feel* like doing it, even though you know you won't actually go do it? I like the idea of having a full-time chef sit in the kitchen, with one of those white chef jackets with his name on it. And those ugly rubber clogs. He could have raw steaks ready for me all the time. The best part would be having him sit there doing nothing until eleven o'clock at night— even when we had dinner out. Just in case we *felt* like a cream puff when we got home. And, in a funny way, it would even be better if we didn't want a cream puff. Just that he's there if I want it. *That's* fuck-you money."

I wanted to divorce him right then and there.

"Jamie, make sure you send Susannah some gorgeous flowers on Monday. Go overboard. That was a spectacular evening." Then he shook his head and put his hands on his hips. "What a crowd. That *Newsweek* editor was sharp. Same thing with the U.N. guy. Impressive how they can just rattle off numbers and dates. But I think I played on their field quite well, if I may say so. May have even surpassed them. My point about the midterm elections and the current trade deficit got them thinking on a different plane. Don't you think?" He wasn't interested in my answer. "And God, that Middle Eastern Abdul guy was seriously smart."

"Yousseff, Phillip. Yousseff Gholam. He's a famous scholar. His name is not Abdul."

"He scared the shit out of me." Phillip shook his head again and scraped the toe of his loafer against the pavement. "Whatever the fuck his name was. Abdul, Abdullah, Mohammed, just another diaper head to me."

I stomped my foot. "Phillip. *Stop it.*"

"C'mon, lighten up, I just said that to get you going." He put his arm around me again, shepherding me forward, and I crossed my arms as tightly as I could. "Okay. Yousseff Gholam. Kennedy School of Government. Adviser to three presidents. Author of fifty books. Did I pay attention or what?"

I didn't know what exactly I was supposed to give him credit for. The bright streetlamps of Seventy-sixth Street illuminated the lime-stone and brick town houses with marble staircases and huge bay windows swathed in brocade and silk tasseled drapes. Behind every one of those doors were people who made the New York media, legal, and banking industries tick. They were the real players Phillip had tried so hard to become.

A few hundred feet short of our awning, he asked me, "One more thing: you didn't get gas masks for the staff, did you?"

When we arrived on our floor, I stepped out of the elevator before him and let the front door slam in his face. He deserved it. He was a pompous, spoiled, racist asshole.

He ran down the hall after me. "Hey, Jamie. What gives? One minute we're cuddling on the street and the next you slam a door in my face?"

I couldn't answer him.

"I'm sorry I called that writer guy a diaper head. Okay, that was immature, but I was just trying to bug you, maybe even get you to laugh a little."

"You can't be so racist, Phillip. I won't stand for it."

"C'mon! I was just joking. I already said the guy was a genius! What do you want from me?"

"I don't want you to talk about certain nationalities like they are dirty or beneath us, okay? I'm worried you're going to slip and do it in front of the kids sometime."

He put his head down. "I'm sorry, you're right, what else?"

"You're just so, so . . ."

"So what, Jamie?"

"You're so spoiled."

He looked at me blankly.

"You just *have* to listen to yourself sometimes, complaining about six-thousand-dollar barbecues. You make life so complicated when nothing is good enough."

"What the hell is your problem? Their apartment is a hundred times nicer than ours and I happened to mention that. I'm sorry I didn't grow up ice-fishing in Minnesota like you, Miss Low-Key Salt-of-the-Earth. I've seen lots of amazing apartments my whole life. I grew up in one, for God's sakes. I work like a fucking dog and can't afford the kind of home I'd like, okay? What is this sanctimonious tone anyway?"

"Susannah is my friend, not yours."

His eyes narrowed.

"What were you doing in the den with her? Why was the door closed?"

"Are you crazy?" He swallowed hard. "You think I've got something going with Susannah?"

"I didn't say that. You did."

"She was blowing me."

I shrugged. "C'mon, Phillip, even my dinner partner noticed."

"So, she showed me her new Diebenkorn drawing."

"I'd almost prefer you fucked Susannah. That would be more manly than whining about a grill."

"I wouldn't throw her out of bed."

With that obnoxious comment, I turned on my heels and stormed to our bedroom. I wasn't in the mood to get into an immature fight with my husband. Phillip was a spoiled brat, nothing new there. He did adore Susannah, so what? At the moment, I hated him too much to talk. Still, I wondered who besides Mr. Gay Clothing Designer noticed that they'd left the room for at least ten minutes during after-dinner drinks in the library.

In the master bath, I slammed the door shut. I was upset, and my anger was morphing into hurt—hurt that Phillip and my close friend had bonded over their snooty Eastern-establishment link, impenetrable to me. And I was too paralyzed to do anything at the moment but feel sorry for myself.

I sat on the edge of the bathtub and rested my head on my hands. So deeply confused. It was after midnight, and I was a little tipsy and nauseated by the grill-and-terrace conversation. Maybe I was taking out all my work tension and pressure on my husband. And then there was Peter.

I put my head in my hands and tried to come up with a happy Phillip/Jamie memory. I couldn't. All I could muster up were scenes of him screaming at me because I didn't supervise the placement of his nail scissors.

A knock on the bathroom door, then another.

"Phillip, I need some time in here to myself. I want to be alone."

"Jamie, this is ridiculous, we're fighting about nothing. Come out here, I want to make up with you. I didn't mean the Abdullah thing."

"It's not the Abdullah thing."

Pause. "I don't want Susannah to blow me. Nothing happened with Susannah. She's your friend. She promised to show me some additions to their art collection. Then we talked about her family. My mother rented her aunt's house in Plymouth one summer."

"Phillip, I want to be alone. It has nothing to do with you. I'm going to take a bath."

I pulled off my clothes and grabbed a terry-cloth robe from behind the door. When I did, Phillip's squash jacket, which also hung there, fell to the floor. I reached down to pick it up and decided to go through his pockets. I didn't trust him tonight. I don't think I'd ever seriously considered that he would cheat on me, but tonight I wondered.

There was something in the inside pocket of his jacket. A thick white envelope.

"Honey. Please. It was such a tacky thing to say about Susannah. I'm so sorry. I love you. Now let me in."

On the front of a thick white envelope, it read, "Subpoena for Laurie Petitt, Whitfield and Baker, From: United States District

Attorney, Southern District." Laurie Petitt was his assistant. The words blurred together. Something about patents . . . Reason to believe confidential patent information from Adaptco Systems was transferred . . . Adaptco Systems, a small Internet company and a client of Whitfield and Baker. Not a direct client of Phillip's.

Phillip's firm was being accused of passing top-secret information about that product to Hamiltech, Phillip's most important client, Hamiltech. Hamiltech. Phillip's bread and butter. I ran over to the toilet and threw up the caviar tart.

"Jamie, are you sick? Open the door so I can help!"

"Leave me alone."

An hour later, I emerged from the bathroom in my terry robe with wet hair and bloodshot eyes. The bedroom lights were on and the bed untouched. I put a kettle on for ginger tea to calm my stomach. Confronting Phillip tonight about the subpoena would be a dangerous distraction. I kept telling myself, *Don't talk to Phillip. Don't talk to Phillip. Save it for Thursday. After the show. Save it for Thursday.* I'd have to wait. I had fantastic willpower.

Phillip appeared in the kitchen in his pressed pajamas and red velvet slippers, one black Scottie dog embroidered on the left and a white Westie on the right.

"Was it the lobster?"

I stirred my tea in silence.

"Look, Jamie. I'm really sorry about the comment about Susannah. That was a really low-class move." He tried to snuggle me from behind, pressing his head into my hair and his pelvis into my back hip. His hard-on was beginning to blossom. "I only want *you* to blow me. There's nothing on earth like your special treats."

I turned around. "What the fuck is that subpoena in your squash jacket?"

"What subpoena?"

I looked down; his hard-on was lowering its mast before my eyes. "The subpoena from the U.S. Attorney's Office, who, from the best of my understanding as a layperson, is accusing someone at your firm of stealing trade secrets. Are you *that* desperate to hang on to the Hamiltech account? *What* is going on, Phillip? How could you not tell me?"

"Are you out of your mind? You think I would . . . You think I could . . ." He brushed the hair off my face. "Honey, it's nothing at all, a misunderstanding. It doesn't involve me."

"Are you sure?"

"The subpoena's for Laurie. She does the copying. Not me. I'm telling you, it's a misunderstanding."

"A *misunderstanding*? From the Feds?"

"They're always snooping around my business, or any firm that does corporate mergers and deals on the level we do."

"How do you know?"

"Honey." Boarding school headmaster tone. "Adaptco is a client, so is Hamiltech. I have tons of files on both companies."

"Adaptco isn't your client. Why would you have files on them?"

He shook his head dismissively. "You have no idea how a law firm works. I'm a partner. I am privy to information, okay? Doesn't mean anyone broke the law just because there is a complaint. And then, in turn, a subpoena."

"Are you sure?"

"Jamie, your worries are way out of proportion to what we are dealing with here. It's a small accounting matter, a misunderstanding involving my assistant and some of the paralegals. They mixed up some files; they didn't do it on purpose. You want to hear the whole story? Would that calm you down?"

"Yes, as a matter of fact, it would."

"Adaptco is a small company that's doing very well. It has a software application. That application may make them a lot of money. Hamiltech is a huge behemoth. They are onto the same application, but not quite there. Adaptco is desperately trying to stave them off and come up with a reason to squelch Hamiltech so they don't lose their market share to a bigger company. So Adaptco's coming up with bogus accusations. They're desperate, is all. Adaptco hasn't even got a case. You've got to trust me on this one. Lawyers get sued and investigated all the time and nothing comes of it. Now, there *was* a mix-up with the paralegals and Laurie over some files, but there wasn't anything real in those files. I'm taking care of it."

I retrieved the envelope from his squash jacket and for thirty minutes I grilled him on every detail of every page. He tried hard to minimize the significance, but it didn't work because his wife is not a dummy.

"Phillip, I really can't handle this amount of stress this week." And I left him in the kitchen. If I'd understood then the real trouble he was in, I'd have been terrified.

24

The Other Side of
the Tracks

Grid people don't go to Brooklyn. Ever. And if they ever had to go to the West Side, they'd deny it the next day. So it was no surprise that my husband didn't accompany Dylan and me to Peter's late-afternoon birthday party that Sunday. Not that I was really speaking to my husband. He was drinking a lime-infused Corona in front of a football game in his study as we were preparing to leave.

He yelled from his couch to the doorway, "You're actually going to a manny birthday party?"

"Yes, Phillip. Peter's invited us to come."

"Are the little ones okay?"

"They're playing Chutes and Ladders with the weekend sitter. They seem perfectly happy. You can take them for ice cream."

"What if they don't want to go?"

"Then you'll find something else. You're a wonderful father. Go get a lollypop with them instead. Dylan is excited to go meet Peter's friends, and I promised I'd take him."

"Jesus. Typical. Slow down. That's the last thing you need, with your piece airing."

"I'm fine. You're welcome to join us."

Phillip stood up. "No thanks. I've got some . . ."

"That was a joke, Phillip. Enjoy your game."

With the late-afternoon sun setting behind me, I drove over the Brooklyn Bridge to Red Hook with Dylan in the backseat. The criss-crossed cables on either side created a dizzying effect as we sped over the icy East River. I watched the white steam clouds pumping out of three red factory smokestacks on the shoreline. On the most bitter cold New York days like this one, the steam remained still and frozen in the air.

"Mom, stop hitting the wheel with your rings. It's bugging me."

Peter had given me clear directions to Tony's bar and explained them to me as if I were a total moron. He joked that I probably hadn't driven around Brooklyn by myself all that much and I should hire a car. So here I was, freaking out behind the wheel, praying I wouldn't get lost and have a *Bonfire of the Vanities* moment with a wrong turn, just to show him I was cool enough to drive a car to another borough. But I did find Tony's bar and even a parking spot, all without a single hit-and-run.

Tony's, an old steel diner from the thirties with its original neon sign, sat back on a street lined with friendly brick row houses. There were about fifteen people laughing and talking and smoking outside. Peter had told me that the owner, a pal, had agreed to close it to the public until six that night. Three adorable girls in their late twenties shared a smoke in casual clothes: army pants and jeans, oversized sweaters, and large scarves wrapped around their necks. A beautiful woman who looked a touch over forty leaned against the metal exterior of the pub wearing jeans and high boots, a thick white sweater under a silver down jacket, and exotic silver chandelier earrings. A turquoise Indian barrette held back a huge, curly nest of long dark hair. She was talking to two guys in their mid-thirties who were wearing baseball caps, expensive shades, and scruffy beards. They looked like the *South Park* writers.

A sexy sixtyish Marlboro Man sat in a chair with a worn sheepskin jacket. The last vestiges of winter sunlight haloed the edges of his brown, fraying cowboy hat. He half-smiled, watching my awkward gait in high-heeled boots as Dylan dragged me toward the entrance. There was no question he was checking me out—nothing subtle about the way he stared. I smiled back at him for the hell of it. I didn't want to look like an Upper East Side matron, so I'd worn a tight black scoop-neck sweater, large hoop earrings, a suede jacket, and my best jeans. It had only taken me about twenty outfit changes to decide on this one. I wanted Peter to think I might fit in with his friends, maybe even that I was a little bit hot. Dylan grabbed my hand, pulled open the door, and we were hit with a blast of music.

I'm all out of love, I'm so lost without you
I know you were right believing for so long

The front circular diner counters of the restaurant served as an open bar that linked to a large room with exposed brick walls. Peter—I spotted him instantly—hadn't seen us arrive. He stood in the corner with his elbow against the wall, talking spiritedly to a short, thin girl in a messy pixie haircut and white corduroys. She was wearing cowboy boots and a brown suede belt, a hippie, flowing pink blouse, unbuttoned low on her chest, and a cross, encrusted with pearls, hanging from a black velvet choker. She looked British hip, not just downtown hip, like she was best friends with Sienna Miller and Gwyneth Paltrow. It irritated me that her legs were much better than mine. When we were at Belvedere Castle, Peter had told me he hadn't found any interesting girls in New York, but he certainly seemed intrigued with this one. I felt like a nineteenth-century heroine who'd shown up at the ball only to discover the object of her desire enthralled with someone else.

"Mommy, there's Peter!" Dylan yelled, pulling me toward his manny.

"Sweetheart, let Peter talk to his friend. We'll find him later."

"Is that his *girlfriend*?" Dylan asked.

"I don't think he has one."

"Does too."

"What?"

"Chill, Mom. I said he has a girlfriend."

"Who is she?" I shot back.

"Don't know, but she doesn't love him back. I think that's her."

"Dylan, how do you know?"

"God, Mom, relax. Ask him! Okay?"

Pixie Girl looked like a real heartbreaker.

"Dylan!" Peter excused himself from his beauty and she turned to talk to some friends. I now saw that her butt was so teeny he could have practically cupped it in one hand.

"I can't believe you made it!" Peter high-fived Dylan and for the first time kissed my cheek and then rubbed my arm. "Really, it means so much you came." I noticed he let his hand linger on my arm. I felt heat. "The food's amazing—there's ribs, chicken, corn, corn bread. You hungry?"

I shook my head—suddenly it was tough to speak.

"I am!" said Dylan.

"Well then, let's get you some food, buddy. First I want to get your mom a drink and introduce her to my friends." He held my arm lightly in one hand and walked me around the room, where I met at least a dozen people. I noticed he had friends of varying ages, from the mid-twenties to sixties, and most of them looked like creative types to me. Definitely no suits in this room.

"There must be fifty people here. You've got a lot of friends for someone who just moved to New York a couple of years ago."

"Not really. Those two guys over there are my partners on the online program deal; about ten people live in other apartments in my building. We have a neighborhood here. And they love to drink and dance, especially on a Sunday afternoon. It's a little tradition with my friends, don't know when it started." He waved to the bartender and pushed a ten-dollar bill toward him. "Bobby! Get this woman a glass of chardonnay. A good one. She needs it!" He pulled out a chair for me and introduced me to two thirtyish-looking guys next to me at the bar. "Nick, Charlie, this is, finally, Jamie Whitfield. Take care of her, and don't embarrass me. Jamie, these are the roommates from hell I told you about. Except one thing: the fat guy here is the reason I met you. So I guess he's not so bad." He laughed, slapped Charlie on the back, and pulled Dylan over to the pool table.

I grilled the roommates nervously and asked them all kinds of questions. Does he get sick of Dylan? Is he working too hard? Does he have time for his software? Does he think we're crazy people? Does he know what a difference he is making? This wasn't going well. I know I sounded like a freaky, rich housewife. And to these people I was.

Charlie whispered something into Nick's ear and then said to me, "He, uh, thinks you're just fine."

Just fine?

Pixie Girl, having been abandoned, stood on the toe ledge of the bar just next to me. "Amstel Light, Bobby, please."

"Sure, angel."

She had the body of a dancer. Maybe even one of those girls who could make love in insane positions. Her elbow touched mine.

"Hi, I'm Jamie. Are you a friend of Peter's?"

"Yes. A very good friend. My name's Kyle." She looked me up and down. "How do you know Peter?"

"Uh, Peter works with us, in Manhattan."

"*That* Jamie?"

"Yep, that's me."

"Wow. You look so different than I'd imagined."

"How did you expect me to look?"

"I don't know, maybe not so down to earth. Not so . . . *normal*. He talks about you like you're a . . ."

"A what?"

"I don't know, like you wouldn't just be drinking on a Sunday afternoon in Red Hook."

I wasn't fond of the direction this conversation was taking. "Like I'm too . . . what?"

"Not *too* anything, just he really admires you, so I was thinking maybe more of a scary executive type or something, when actually you look like a college student."

I suddenly decided I *loved* Pixie Girl.

"Glad to know I fit in and you're sweet to say that, but I'm thirty-six."

"Wow. You don't look it."

"Thanks. How do you know Peter?"

"He lives downstairs. We hang out a lot at night. I go drinking with his roommates when he's working, which of course he usually is."

"Does he really work a lot?"

"Are you kidding? He's a workaholic! All the time. Obsessed."

"Do you work hard too?"

"Yeah, kind of. I'm the East Coast editor of *Wired* magazine. It's busy the week we close, but otherwise I'm pretty free nights."

"You must have a lot of guys fighting for your time." I was trying to be subtle, anything to get some information.

"Not the one I want."

I couldn't resist. "You can't possibly be single with that face."

"Thanks." She itched her hair so her perfectly coiffed mess was even more perfect. "I am. I wish I wasn't, but . . . it's just not happening, you know . . ." She looked down.

"Oh. I've been there." I took a sip of my wine. "It's tough."

She nodded with closed eyes.

"I'm sorry. Is the guy here?"

"Yes, he's here." She took a swig of her beer and paused for a while. "It's *his* party."

"Peter?"

"Yeah."

"And he doesn't reciprocate?"

She shook her head.

A tumult of emotions raced through me: relief that Peter wasn't in love with her and also an outpouring of female solidarity with this lovely little woman. "Does he know?"

"He knows. I've gotten drunk and told him. Fallen all over him. Doesn't work. Done everything I could except climb into his bed naked. May have even tried that—hate to admit. Didn't work either."

"Well, he's distracted. And working so hard to get his program funded."

"What are you talking about?" She looked perplexed.

I thought maybe I'd been imprudent, maybe he hadn't told her about his computer project. "Oh, I don't know, it's just a little thing he told me he's working on, you know, on the side."

"You mean Homework Helper?"

"So you know."

"Of course I do." She tried to gauge my level of awareness. "How could I not know?"

"Well, I just thought maybe he was keeping it private."

"Hello? How could he hide it?"

"What do you mean, how?"

"He's, like, famous now. Well, not quite, but he's going to be. They gave him all the money. He's got millions now to develop it."

"No."

"Yes. We keep telling him he's going to be like the YouTube guys."

"Uh-huh." I could barely speak.

"That is so weird." She tilted her head in Peter's direction. He was laughing with a group of people while holding Dylan piggyback. "Look at him. He's on cloud nine. Has been for two months now."

"You're telling me Peter's project has been funded for two solid months?"

"Uh, yee-ahhhh."

"And he didn't tell me?"

"I know. Honestly, we do ask him about that—'How come you're working at the house when you just hit payday on your project, man?'"

My throat was dry. "And what does he say?"

"He won't answer. We all think it's because he's just in love with your kid."

Someone tapped my shoulder. "Brown Eyed Girl" blasted from the jukebox.

Marlboro Man behind me, sans hat. "Seems like this is your song, darlin'. May I have this one?" His slight twang was sexy. His salt-and-pepper beard hid the lines in his face, which was worn by the sun. He had a belly, but somehow with his huge build, he didn't look fat, just large and strong. He wore jeans and a wrinkled white button-down shirt that pulled tight on his shoulders. He smelled so good and earthy. Then my mind raced to my husband in his pressed lavender striped shirt, watching football on his froufrou red paisley couch.

And then I looked way across the room at Peter, who was showing Dylan how to shoot pool, and my heart turned over. And he raised his head and looked at me.

"Uh . . ."

Twenty people were now on the dance floor. "Uh, sure." I finished off my wine before I stepped off my barstool. "Excuse me, Kyle."

Marlboro Man grabbed my waist and spun me around and right into Peter's arms.

"Sorry to cut in, man, but it is my birthday. I get this one." Peter held my hand, rubbing my palm with his thumb. I hadn't felt a jolt like that since the tenth grade.

Skipping and a jumping
In the misty morning fog with . . .
You, my brown eyed girl.

"You can dance, girl!" said Peter, laughing, as we steepled our arms and twirled underneath them.

Standing across from each other now, he kept my hands tight in his, caressing them with his thumbs and staring me down. All of a sudden, we stopped dancing. I pulled away, but he hung on tighter.

"Peter, what are you doing?"

"I'm looking at you."

I could not believe he said that.

"You look so good right now. *So good.*"

"Thanks." I had to downplay all this. "You're kind." He was surely a little loose from a couple of beers. That had to be it.

"Hey." He tilted my chin up with one finger. "Look at me. It's more than just being kind. You know that." He pulled me closer. I looked around nervously and couldn't believe he had the guts to keep holding me like this. Thankfully, people around us danced and shielded us in the middle of the floor. "It's all okay, Jamie."

"It is?" His friends were now watching us from the bar. Again I tried to pull away. One hand broke loose and as I pushed my hair back, I noticed my hand was shaking.

"Yeah."

I looked around us again; his friends at the bar were watching us, but no one else. Dylan was shooting pool with another kid his age.

"Do you understand what I'm saying, Jamie?"

Oh God. He called me Jamie again. "I'm not sure."

"You sure you're not sure?"

"Okay, well, maybe a little." I couldn't help but smile. He was beyond irresistible.

"Just checking."

My knees felt weak.

Kyle shot me a look of deep envy and left the bar.

I froze. Others would start noticing. I yanked my hands away from Peter.

"I can't . . . I don't know . . ." Dylan was now looking at me. "I just think I should leave. Right. Now."

I grabbed poor Dylan in the middle of his pool game and bolted for the door.

25

Clashing Cultures

What a weekend. On Saturday night after Susannah's party, images of handcuffed Phillips and "Park Avenue Perp Walk" headlines twirled around my head. But on Sunday night, all I could think about was Peter spinning me around his warm, sweaty body. Peter with all that funding. Peter and his secrets. Peter and his words. *It's all okay, Jamie.*

Monday morning, bright and early, I was sitting in my bathrobe at the kitchen table playing "the question game" with Gracie and Dylan when Peter bounded through the door.

I thought he'd come late. Or maybe wouldn't come at all. Too shocked to say anything for fear I'd totally misread him on the dance floor, I just nodded without looking him in the eye and focused on the children.

"Okay, Dylan, I have one for you. Name two things a lawyer would do."

"Divorces and gets robbers in court."

"Excellent! Gracie, I have a really hard one for you: name one thing a carpenter would make."

"Carpets!" she screamed.

Peter laughed. He was wearing his usual uniform of snowboard pants, running shoes, and a baggy sweater with an old T-shirt underneath. Before he got near me, I could tell he was all excited to be right in my face.

He bent down and put his head two inches in front of mine. "Helloooooo?" He wasn't big on cop-outs.

It's all okay, Jamie.

Do you understand what I'm saying, Jamie?

Did he mean me having a little crush was okay? Or did he simply mean our dancing was okay? Scratch that. I knew it wasn't just the dancing, but was he saying there was something going on between *both* of us, and that *that* was okay?

"Lean forward a bit," he ordered, and immediately began doing karate chops on my back as if I were a prizefighter on the side of the ring. "It's almost over. Wednesday at ten, it'll have aired. Three days and we can start celebrating." Then his thumbs probed deep into the tense muscles on my back. Too scared to surrender completely, too anxious about the piece, my back stiffened protectively. But he didn't stop. Slowly I felt myself give way a little under the pressure of his knowing hands. No wonder Pixie Girl was so heartbroken.

All night I'd been trying to figure out why he'd had funding for two months and hadn't said a word. Why he came on so strong, so suddenly, so physically on the dance floor. Was it just the power of the moment and he was giddy about it? Had he hidden deeper feelings like mine for a while? Either scenario was terrifying.

I felt his strong thumbs outlining my shoulder blades.

The phone rang.

I leapt up and grabbed the receiver. It was my mother. "Hello, Mom." I tried to focus on her rather than on Peter's hands still touching me.

And then something really bad happened: Phillip. Shell-shocked. Staring at me from the doorway in his bathrobe. I willed myself to ignore Peter's forward behavior and every thought I knew it had sparked in my husband's mind.

"Mom, let me take this in the other room. Hold on."

Unfortunately, my husband was not ignoring Peter's behavior.

"Young man, may I have a word with you?"

Omigod.

Peter winked at me. How could he wink? How could he possibly think this was funny?

"Mom, uh, maybe I need to call you back, I think."

Phillip held on to my shoulders and physically turned me toward the door. "I think not. I think you should take the call right now." Headmaster glare.

Husband and manny fireworks show. I couldn't miss this.

"Give me a minute." I put the phone on hold, hoping my husband would speak to Peter right there—and not feel a need to have a man-to-man talk in his study. Just real casual, "Massages aren't necessary, son." Something like that. No such luck. He directed Peter across the hall into his study like he was General Tojo.

Luckily, I could hear their study conversation from the hall. "Young man, what in God's name was that?"

"What, sir?"

"You know what I'm talking about."

I assumed he was wagging his finger in Peter's face at this point. "You don't come in here and give me that ski bum act like your head is in a gondola in some goddamn cloud of smoke."

"Interesting image, but I don't smoke. Never have."

Phillip then closed the door to his study and I couldn't hear another word. Fuck. I ran into my room to grab the phone, my heart beating dangerously fast.

"Your father's on the phone too."

"Hi, Dad."

"You sound out of breath."

"I'm just . . . in the kitchen . . . there was just a little altercation . . ." How was Peter reacting to Phillip's reprimanding him like a child? Like he reprimanded me?

"You don't sound haaaapy."

"Going through a stressful period here. I'm almost through it."

"Is it going to be okay, I mean, with the congressman and all?"

Tears welled up in my eyes, and though I tried to control them, I could never really hide my distress from my parents.

"Oh, honey." My dad always melted when I cried. "I know my little girl when she's having a tough time."

The dam broke and I tried again to suppress the tears.

"Catch your breath for a second. Where's your husband?"

"In his study." I pulled a tissue from the box and blew my nose.

"Why don't you get him in there to comfort you?"

"Because he's busy spanking the manny."

"What?"

"You don't want to know."

"It's the stress of the piece and your life and your kids and all you're juggling. When this piece is over, I want you to take some time. You and your mother can go to that inn we love in Albuquerque. What is it, dear? Pueblo . . ."

"Pueblo Cassito, dear. It's a middle-class hotel. She doesn't want to go there."

"Mom!"

"Sure she will, it's on me! A break is exactly what you need."

"Daddy . . ."

"And then ask Phillip to take you away."

I thought about the subpoena. I thought about him needing his pajamas pressed. I thought about him dry-humping my thigh. He wanted my Peter out of the house.

"Not doing that."

My father asked, "What does that mean?"

"Dad. Mom. I don't know what it means. I just can't talk about anything until after Wednesday. Please. Don't get me more depressed than I already am. I've got to go. I love you." I hung up.

I blew my nose again and returned to the kitchen, rubbing the tears off my cheeks with the back of my hand.

Peter, amazingly enough, was back at the table, looking like World War Three hadn't happened. "Peter, I'm beating Dylan, I'm beating Dylan!" screamed Gracie. They were playing checkers. "I got three kings so far, and Dylan only got one!"

Dylan asked me, "What did Dad say to Peter?"

"Nothing," Peter answered.

"Yes he did. He was mad."

I mouthed to Peter, *What* did *he say?* Peter just brushed me off like he didn't care one bit what Phillip *ever* said to him.

"I'm still beating Dylan," said Gracie.

"Hey, no fair! She went first, that's why she's winning." Dylan, instantly distracted like any nine-year-old, crossed his arms and slumped, trying to hide his watering eyes.

"Hey!" Peter whispered to Dylan. "What do I always tell you? Don't be a pussy just because you lose a game. It's not cool."

Dylan hit Peter in the face with another pillow. "No, *you're* a pussy!"

"That's right, good move. Anyone calls you a pussy, you fight back." They started wrestling on the banquette, with eight orange juice and water glasses placed precariously around the table in front of them.

Michael jumped up and down, "Me play too, me play!"

Carolina ran over. "Boys. *No!* Not at my table. No fighting!" An orange juice glass fell over, and when Peter tried to catch it, he knocked over a glass of water. Carolina threw her hands in the air cursing *Díos* and ran for a towel. I jumped up to avoid getting splashed.

In the midst of this early-morning testosterone display, Phillip appeared at the doorway again wearing a shirt and tie, boxers, and charcoal socks. I stood erect and still, like a sentry.

"Carolina, please bring me a cappuccino and fruit salad on a tray in my office; I've got a conference call before I leave. And make sure you use my special mug. Dash of cinnamon while you're at it." He checked out his watch and walked over to the table. "Jamie, could I talk to you?"

Once we were in our bedroom, he closed the door behind us and walked through to his dressing room. He quickly thrust his legs into his suit pants. "I know I'm on thin ice right now and I don't want to test my luck by skating out even farther, but I have to tell you something."

"What?"

"Don't let the help touch you."

"Excuse me?"

"I mean it. Do not let the help touch you."

"You aren't for real."

"To shake your hand, fine. You could even hug Carolina, and hell, even Peter when you give them their Christmas bonuses, but try not to instigate any other contact. It sends so many wrong messages, I don't know where to begin."

"Peter was just joking around. It was like a karate chop for a boxer."

"I don't know . . . what the . . . ugh . . . shit . . . hell it was." His voice was strained because he was now jamming each foot into his new loafers with a long tortoiseshell shoehorn attached to a leather stick with tassels on the top. "But it's not appropriate in front of the kids, or the other help. That's a big boundary. A *big* one. Once you break that down, then you no longer have a subordinate relationship."

"I don't really want to have a—"

"I know you don't want to listen to me right now, given the week-end events. But I'm going to tell you this anyway." He hit the floor hard three times with the tip of the shoehorn. "I have been a fucking prince and I want some credit for it."

"A fucking prince?"

"Yes."

"How so?"

"On your manny deal. On having a pothead ski bum in my home."

"He's got a successful software business that's about to hit big. It's going to help kids in schools all over the country. And he doesn't smoke pot."

"Maybe not on the job."

"And he's making a difference with your son."

"I know that. I can see that. That's why I've accepted this by default. Have I complained once since you refused to fire him?"

"Okay, Phillip, I'm not sure 'prince' is how I'd categorize it, but yes, you've been accepting of him. Not that you've ever said a word to him."

"Why do I have to talk to him? He works for me! That's what you don't get . . ."

"Stop. This is going to turn into an argument and I don't have steam for another one. I take your point that you have been accepting and I take your point that maybe a boxer massage around the breakfast table isn't appropriate. Are we done?"

He grabbed me and pecked me on the forehead. "Yes, we are."

Back in the breakfast room, Phillip politely asked the table, "How's everyone doing?" He was trying to get on my good side.

Gracie looked up at her father. She was wearing yellow corduroy pants and a yellow Fair Isle sweater with a light blue turtleneck underneath. She had two yellow bows pinned on either side of her head, with blond curls falling down behind them just below her ears. "Daddy?"

"Yes, my angel?" Phillip's little gem made him all soft and gushy.

"What's a pussy?"

Dylan coughed into his napkin, concealing a laugh. Phillip took a sharp breath through his nose. He looked at me, then back at his five-year-old daughter. "Ask your mother."

Taxi horns blared loudly around us as their drivers tried to get past the double-parked SUVs that crowded the street in front of the school's entrance. Chauffeurs who cared far more about their employers than the taxicab drivers behind them stopped their vehicles right smack in the middle of the block to ferry their precious cargo to the curb. I raced upstairs to Gracie's classroom to drop her off, then found Peter outside again. I couldn't wait to find out what happened behind that door.

"So *what did he say?*"

"Who?"

"My husband."

"Oh, him. Something about me being a stoner and then something about terminating my employment if I transgressed again."

"*How* did he say it? On a scale of one to ten, how mad?"

We were about twenty yards down the block from school, and he took a step closer. "I've got to ask you this question, Jamie." When he called me that, when he said it in his husky voice, it made me crazy. "It, in fact, is a very important question: Do you actually care what that man thinks at this point?"

At this point. I thought about that. What point were we at exactly? I didn't want to have to answer that, so I hit the ball back to his side of the court. "What are you really asking me, Peter?"

"Let me connect these very, very complicated dots for you: 'Do you actually care what that man thinks at this point?' is really code for 'Are you still in love with your husband?'"

Oh boy. "We're not having this conversation."

"Oh yes we are."

"I'm late for work."

"They'll wait."

"Luis is here."

"Luis has been down this road before with us. I'd love an answer."

I was totally nailed. All those mornings trying to make sure my ass looked good in my sweatpants, all those fantasies of him leaning on his elbow in bed next to me, the walks alone, those looks he gave me. That hand squeeze on the Central Park steps. That dance last night. His gentle way with Dylan. Peter's magic with my boy made me fall for him more than anything else. And now he was asking me to tell him about my feelings. Here we were. "I am not in love with my husband. But I do happen to be married to him."

"For how much longer?"

"You are crazy! You can't just be asking these kinds of life-altering, earth-shattering questions outside drop-off. There're people here!" Oh. My. God. How could he be doing this?

"Would you like to go somewhere more private? Happy to do that, that's why I came in this morning."

"No." Was Peter just propositioning me? Understandably, the first thought that came to my head was that I was overdue for a wax.

He continued. "Just so you know what kind of man I am, by

private I meant for a quiet coffee where we don't know people. Or to the park."

My adrenaline rush started to abate. He wasn't talking here and now. I felt relieved. I could not believe that we were actually putting sex on the table as a conversation topic. And the best part was, after all this buildup, for him, it seemed like the most effortless thing to discuss. That's precisely why this guy was so sexy. Nothing scared him.

"I'm not going to touch you for real unless, first of all, you tell me it's something you want for sure, and second, until you are no longer with him . . ."

I felt a blast of his heat.

"I just need to know if the no longer with him idea is something that's on your front burner or not even cooking."

He was making this easier for me. "It is cooking. And it's very hot." I smiled.

"Boiling over?"

"Simmering." He looked disappointed and drew back. So I added, "I mean, there's those little bubbles starting to rise up. And there's quite a few of them."

"Is there a timer?"

"Does there have to be one?"

"For me there does. It's getting tough to be around you like this."

Suddenly he yelled, *"Jesus!"*

A woman had tripped on the curb just in front of her fat Mercedes. "Damn it, Oscar!"

Peter ran to help her. Ingrid. And Ingrid and Peter. I hadn't confronted my crazy friend. Not yet. What a time for this.

I watched Peter pull her off the pavement before the chauffeur even got there.

"I'm fine. Just startled." She dusted off her skirt and knee with one hand. "And I already have a hurt elbow." She placed her left arm back into a Hermès scarf sling tied around her neck.

"Are you injured, Ingrid?" I asked.

"It's nothing—a little skinned knee." She adjusted her scarf. "And this? Just Birkin elbow. Doing some therapy." For once, she looked embarrassed.

I went in for the kill. "So, Ingrid, you know Peter, of course."

Peter blanched. "Yes, we know each other. And I have an appointment. So I can't linger." And he was off. And he didn't have any appointment. "I'll catch you later!" he yelled from halfway down the street. I was grateful to be let off the hook of that steamy conversation which made me weak with tension.

Ingrid and I stood there face-to-face. "Of course I know Peter," she answered. "What are you getting at?"

"Should I be getting at something?"

"No. It's drop-off. And I'm just trying to drop my kids off. And my arm is hurt, so be nice to me."

"I am being perfectly nice."

"*And* I have a hurt knee now."

"I just need—"

"No, you don't. It's on a need-to-know basis and you don't need to know."

"Yes, I do. I really do."

"It's private."

"I need to know."

She considered that quietly for a moment. "Are you going to fire him over it?"

"Of course not. His personal life is his business."

"You promise?"

"Yes. I promise. I just really need to know."

Long pause.

"He wasn't into it."

"He wasn't? Are you sure?"

"I am. And no. He wasn't." Ingrid started up the stairs with her kids, then turned back. "And don't look so happy about that, missy."

26

Epic Snowjob

My insides in knots, I dialed Kathryn. I craved her voice of reason.

"If it's only ten-thirty on Monday, and you've already cried, this isn't going to be a great week," said Kathryn.

"Why do you think I called you?"

"What can I do, Jamie? You want me to hang out with you the day it airs? Maybe I can come to the studio just that night?"

"No. It's work. I'll be in the control room with Erik. Not a place for girlfriends." I felt ill. It didn't help that I'd once again left the house after having dragged baby Michael halfway across the apartment by my right ankle. He'd hung on for dear life, sliding along on his stomach, pleading with me not to leave him. Yvette had to tear him off my body as I slunk out. Once I stepped off the elevator at work, I could barely breathe for fear my Theresa story was going to implode. Yoga breaths in my office didn't calm me down. A few sips of hot tea with too much sugar didn't soothe me. My cranberry scone tasted like sandy cornmeal in my mouth.

"Well then, what can I do?"

"I'm so upset."

"Why?"

I rattled out the litany. "Well, my husband may be indicted by the FBI and bringing me to the pokey along with him. He also may be sleeping with Susannah. I am about to air a show that may take down a high-ranking member of Congress. My children are psycho because I've been working so hard and they haven't seen me in a week and . . ."

"Let's take this piece by piece."

"Fine. My husband could go to jail. I'll be like Mrs. Milken."

Kathryn spoke slowly and deliberately. "We went over that Saturday night after your fight. I'm sure, like he says, they get investigated and watched over by the SEC and whomever all the time. Just because it's his assistant making a mistake doesn't mean he's broken any law. Don't go to the bad place so fast."

"And then my husband and Susannah?"

"They've always flirted. They've always been obnoxious together. It'd be good news he's screwing her, then you could kick him out for cause. And you have fifty lawyers all over your piece, Goodman wouldn't let you run it if there were real problems. So we've solved everything."

"There is one other thing."

"Tell me."

"I think Peter might be leaving."

"What? He adores you! Stop this negative thinking."

"It's not me, not Dylan, not us at all. It's his software company. He got funding."

"I thought he already had some funding, I thought he was test-marketing it."

"He got a big wad of funding, and an office, enough to quit his manny job."

"Ooooh. That's bad."

"But he isn't quitting. Not yet, I mean. He's had the money for two months and hasn't even told me. His friends did, at his party."

"He's in love with you. That's why he's not leaving yet. That's why he's not telling you."

It could be. No. "Must be Dylan and the satisfaction—"

"Satisfaction my ass. It's you. You're the reason he's staying."

I wanted her to be right. "We danced yesterday at his party." And I told her everything: how he held my hands, how he wouldn't let go.

And then I got nervous that I told her. "I mean, I couldn't believe I danced with the manny."

"He's more than a manny at this point, Jamie."

I sighed. "That's what he says."

"Hello? That's like a declaration!" Kathryn was yelling now. "When did he say that?"

"When I confronted him about Ingrid. And then he asked me if I was hurt."

"Because he screwed Ingrid?"

"He didn't."

"Fine, if that's what you want to believe."

"It was more than a kiss, but they didn't go all the way. He swore to me they didn't."

"That means she gave him one of her epic blowjobs."

"Probably."

"That's bad for you. Really bad."

"What do you mean?" I knew exactly what she meant.

"The comparisons . . ."

"I am not planning on giving my manny a blowjob!"

Charles walked by my office at this very moment, cupped his hands, and whispered, "Then let me do it!" I threw a rubber band ball at him. He ducked and kept walking.

"Okay," said Kathryn. "After he fessed, and he asked you if you were hurt, I hope you were honest and told him what he wanted to hear."

"No. I was really mean and told him that I couldn't possibly be hurt because he just worked for me."

"That is so tacky."

"I know."

"He was asking you if you had the same feelings he does."

"I'm married."

"That's why he has to talk in code."

"He only meant that he was more than my manny." I was smiling.

"I *know* you're smiling right now. You get paid lots of money to figure out people's motives and you're so clueless on this."

"Okay, fine. You win. I'm not clueless."

"Tell me."

I stalled. "I can't."

"Oh, please God, this is so good and Phillip can be *such* an asshole to you and just please you deserve a little flirtation now and then."

"All right."

"Tell me."

"It's a little more than a flirtation."

"Did you sleep with him?"

"Are you crazy?!"

"Did you?"

"I swear I did nothing. Nothing. Ever. Not even a kiss."

"Okay, so what's there to tell me?"

I decided against telling her about Peter wanting to touch me for real. "Just when we were dancing. The way we were looking at each other. The way he held my hands. He rubbed my palm with his thumb."

"That sounds sexy."

"It was. Very. For me, anyway."

"Did anyone notice?"

"Not Dylan definitely. But two or three friends at the bar saw the whole thing. Even some poor gorgeous girl with a perfect ass who's totally in love with him."

"How good is her ass?"

"Better than mine."

"That sucks too. Are you sure he's not doing anything with her?"

"I'm positive, not with her anyway. She's totally heartbroken. She told me so. And she watched us dance. I felt bad."

"So what are you going to do?"

"Try really hard to ignore it."

"Are you sure?"

"No. But you know what? I can't do this right now. I will admit my feelings for him are confusing. That's all you're going to get. At least until Wednesday at ten p.m. when this goddamn mother of all pieces will be over. Maybe we can have drinks on Thursday or something.

But even if I get drunk, the story is the same. I feel close to him, but I am very confused. And I am married, last I checked."

"I will remind you that you were planning on leaving Phillip this year sometime. You remember that, right? And this year's almost over."

"Yes, I know all of that, but it's not going to happen right now."

"You're going to need a major kick in the ass to leave. Just keep it all clear. Don't flirt with Peter just to get your mind off your husband. Then the break won't be clean if it ever happens. You'll always blame it on your crush on Peter when it's really all about what you want and need for yourself. Also, if Phillip finds out about you two, he'll never take responsibility for his—"

"There's nothing to find out about me and Peter." It was so much more than a crush.

"Would the weepy girl with the perfect ass in the bar agree with that?"

27

Wrong Week to Stop Sniffing Glue

Erik looked at me. "What is *with* you?"

"Nothing. Just nerves."

"I've been covering politics for twenty-five years. This woman is for *real,* okay? You can tell by the look in her eye."

Goodman tried to talk me off my cliff. "Look, Jamie, we've done all we can. We've got just about twenty-four hours to go. I'll take the heat on this—"

I broke in. "I've never done such a big political story before, and it's just so squirrelly down there. No one talks, no one knows her."

"Charles found two people who've seen her hanging with the Hartley camp," said Erik.

"But Hartley's camp is denying any relationship with her. They say she was a minor acquaintance of Hartley's, but that she knew some of his former aides quite well," I pleaded, not even sure where I was going with this. I wanted the piece to air, and I knew we had good grounding. I couldn't tell if it was justified nerves or if I was having a girlie moment in front of all the macho guys at work.

"You, as the producer, have done more of the research, more of the checking, more of the reporting. You know all this better than we do," said Erik. "Hell, Theresa agreed to do the interview with you before she even met Goodman."

"Hey!" Goodman interrupted. "I went down to Jackson once, just before she agreed."

"Okay," Maguire jumped in, sounding like the overpaid babysitter he was. "Okay, Goodman, you had a lot to do with it too."

"That's not the point I was making, just that I'd met her before."

"Drop it, Goodman." Maguire put his hand in the air.

Goodman went on. "Plus she's got a motive—he jilted her! Her feelings are hurt."

Erik turned to me. "If you were me, executive producer of the broadcast, would you kill the piece or not?"

"I, I . . ."

Maguire cut in. "Jamie, I may be top dog, but as far as I'm concerned, this is on *you*. Yeah, Goodman's got his hand in it, but as the lead producer, my eye is on you."

"I, I . . ."

"Tell you what I'm going to do," Erik said, leaning into the table. "I'm going to send Charles Worthington back down one more time to Jackson on the next flight. The piece is scheduled to air in"—he paused and looked at his watch—"thirty hours and—"

Maguire interrupted in a terrifyingly even tone. "Let me be crystal clear. Just let Mr. Worthington know that he'd better be pretty fucking on point if he sees fit to derail this broadcast. Unless one of you in this room comes into my office screaming that we're all going down if we air this, we're running the piece as planned. Wednesday, nine p.m." With that, Maguire put his hand on my shoulder like Rambo with a tattered white rag around his head and said, "Jamie, if there's a problem after this piece airs, I got your back. We're all in this and I'm a Marine . . . so I ain't gonna leave anyone behind. *Semper* gotdamn *Fi*." Ever goddamn Faithful.

The phone rang seven hours later, Tuesday evening. I picked it up before the first ring had finished. "Charles!"

"Hello, Jamie."

"What do you have? What exactly are you doing?"

"What do I have? Nothing. I'm picking up my rental car at the Jackson airport."

"Where are you going first?"

"To retrace our steps: the local newspaper, the cops, the funeral home guy. I'm going to have a drink with the manager of our affiliate down here; maybe he'll get some people talking in a bar."

"Charles, you've got to go somewhere we haven't been!"

"I'll do anything for you. Forever. You know that. It's just I don't know what else to check. We were here for three days and found two people who know they were together a lot, hanging with Hartley's political hacks. That was a good addition. But you have to manage your expectations. There is not going to be a Paris Hilton–type, doggy-style videotape. I promise. But I'll keep looking for someone who knows something about Boudreaux."

"It's not new people, I mean not new random people. Cabdrivers and bellhops aren't going to give us anything we don't already have. It's a whole new direction we need to take."

"Jamie, your piece is airing in twenty-three hours. It's cut and edited, audio-sweetened and color-corrected. The promos have been running for three days."

"Charles, pleeeeese."

"Don't pleeeeese me, I'm here to help you. I'm just a little out of options. When you say 'new direction,' what are you talking about? Like maybe morgues because of the funeral home guy who saw them together?"

"No. That funeral home closed years ago, remember?"

"Of course I remember."

"Okay." I felt bad pushing him so hard and a bit guilty he had to hightail it to Jackson and I was in New York. "Sorry. I don't know. How about finding more people who used to work in Mississippi politics?"

"We have done a database search on every staff member that ever worked for Hartley. We've reached almost all of them. There's no story. They're still loyal."

"Maybe you're right."

"I'll keep working on it meanwhile. Get a good night's sleep. Tomorrow's Wednesday. It's going to be a big day for you."

Charles called back at six the next morning. My husband was asleep, but clinging to me and practically edging me off the bed. "Who is calling so goddamn early?"

"I know it's for me." I tried to wiggle away, but he held me tighter.

"Don't answer it. I'm feeling horny."

I swatted him and broke free.

"Did you get anything? Please tell me you can confirm the whole Theresa side of things."

"I can't," answered Charles. "But there are some real rabid bloggers around here."

"And what did you find?"

"The guys in the bar told me they're outside Jackson, a whole community of them."

Phillip rolled over. "Honey, please. Take that somewhere else, I'm trying to get some sleep here. You've got to respect my needs. It's still dark out." Then something hard poked at my thigh. He pulled the underwear off my butt like the girl in the Coppertone ad. I punched his shoulder.

"Just so you know, some NASCAR freaks in a bar told me about the bloggers. Went to their sites and didn't see anything remarkable, hadn't heard of any of them. The guy said some of them worked in congressional offices down here and hung out at the hotel bar where I had a drink. Maybe nothing. Just congressional aides. But I couldn't put anything together."

"That's too bad."

"C'mon!" Phillip put a pillow on his head.

I put my hand on the speaker and said, "Phillip, I just . . . I can't. This is too important. Sorry!" I got back on the phone and tried to keep my voice down. "Keep trying to find someone who'll confirm they were romantic. And then I'll never worry. Ever."

"Jamie, remember, you've got to manage your expectations. This is a squirrely story."

"Try the state troopers again."

"Okay."

"Try the morgue thing too. I changed my mind. I like that."

"Okay, I'll try the morgue situation too."

"Excellent, Charles. We have to try everything. It's like twelve hours away."

"I know. Call you later."

"**S**traight Talk with Theresa Boudreaux! Finally! Exclusive Interview on Newsnight with Joe Goodman! Tonight at 9 p.m.!" Grease dripped on the newspaper ad spread in front of me from the cheese-omelet-on-bacon-on-buttery-bagel breakfast I'd made. Normally there's nothing as peaceful as the special time between six-thirty and seven a.m., when my husband and kids are still asleep and Carolina is just beginning to putter around her room. Only this morning, I was beyond belief on edge.

It would have been extremely difficult for the network to pull the piece at this point, with all the trumpets blaring. I put my hands over my eyes and tried to talk myself into a state of acceptance and resignation. *Okay, so be easy on yourself, girl. You've got a big mother story, you're playing in the big leagues, you've covered your bases, now just go with it.* Bill Maguire, speaking as president of the entire news division, had told me point-blank that he was standing by my side. Still, I wanted Charles to burrow his highly tuned investigative nose into every possible angle in Jackson one final time.

I heard the flow of the shower in the bathroom and prayed Phillip would take his time getting ready. I hoped he wasn't rushed, wasn't feeling needy and frantic, and would leave me alone this morning. Just this once. Gracie appeared at the doorway sucking her thumb and rubbing her bunny's neck ribbon between her fingers. She climbed up on the banquette and nestled the top of her head into my right thigh and lay still on her stomach, one thumb in her mouth and the other strangling her bunny. She didn't say a word. Maybe she just sensed my tension and understood how much her presence would comfort me. I rubbed her back in appreciation, marveling at her exquisite sixth sense.

Not surprisingly, Phillip did not display the same subtle comprehension of my vulnerable mood as my five-year-old. He marched into the kitchen in his boxers, charcoal socks, and white T-shirt.

"Where's Carolina?"

"She's in the laundry room."

"Does she know where my larger rolling bag is?"

"I don't know, you're going to have to ask her."

He didn't like that response; he hoped I'd fix everything for him so his morning was smooth and comfortable. He looked at my plate. "What are you doing, Jamie?"

"I'm eating breakfast, Phillip."

"What's with all the calories? I thought you were trying to firm up a bit."

He walked over to the fridge and poured himself a glass of fresh orange juice from the pitcher, then held the glass up to the light. At this inopportune moment, Carolina walked out of the laundry room with a small pile of neatly folded dishtowels.

"Carolina, how many times do we need to go over the orange juice rules?"

Carolina, as strong as she was, melted in fear when Phillip reprimanded her. She put the towels down, hung her head low, and let out a sigh.

"I don't like pulp, okay? Remember?"

Carolina had to remember his directive number 352, but Phillip couldn't even remember it was Theresa Boudreaux D-day for me. He picked out a small steel strainer from the utensil drawer and shook it at her face. "Before you put the orange juice in the pitcher, please please do me a simple favor. Strain it. Please. Very simple." He threw the strainer into the sink and walked back to his dressing room.

Michael toddled into the kitchen in his adorable miniature-man pajamas. Then he too climbed onto the banquette and quietly snuggled his head on my other thigh. I rubbed his back, trying to be thankful for my healthy, beautiful children.

Ten minutes later, now dressed in a dark suit and yellow polka dot tie, Phillip issued out new requests: "I've got a business trip this afternoon to Houston and then to Los Angeles. I won't be back until Saturday morning on the red-eye. So I'll be needing a few things."

"A few things?" I asked incredulously, trying to fathom how he still hadn't mentioned the interview.

"Yes, Jamie, a few things. Have you forgotten I'm gone from eight a.m. to eight p.m. every day? I have no time to take care of little things. And you look fantastic in your tight sweatpants. You're firming up, just a bit more to go." He grabbed a little pocket of fat on my upper thigh and pecked me on the forehead.

I couldn't respond. I despised him too much. It depressed me even more that I wouldn't be seeing Peter that morning. He said he'd be late because he had some meetings. He was probably waiting for the piece to air to give me the news about his backers. And I don't know what role our little "situation" played in his head in his decision to stay or leave. That only worried me more.

Now in came Dylan wearing his school tie and jacket with his usual wet clump of hair sticking out of the back of his head.

"So . . ." Phillip continued brazenly, "I'm really sorry to ask this, but I need you to get my squash racquet restrung . . ."

"You can't do it at the club?"

"I told you, I won't be there until Saturday, and my game is at four."

"You have ten squash racquets in your closet."

"But I only like the Harrow racquet. I left it on the chair in the bedroom. Also it's my mother's birthday next week. Can you pick up something? I never buy the right thing. Only girls can shop for each other." He walked into his office to get some papers and returned stuffing them into his briefcase.

"Did you forget anything, Phillip?" I was giving him one final chance before I throttled him.

"Hmmmm." He started checking his BlackBerry, rolling the dial up and down on the right side. Absentmindedly his voice trailed off: "I

don't think so . . . I think I'm set . . . the racquet, the gift for Mom . . .
please remind Carolina about the pulp problem we seem to be repeatedly having in this house . . ." More BlackBerry button punching.

"Dad," Dylan said as he looked up at his father pleadingly.

"Hold on, Dylan, I've just got to answer one thing here."

"Dad!" Dylan screamed.

Phillip looked up, agitated that his e-mail focus had been interrupted. "What, Dylan?"

"You did forget something." Darling Dylan.

Phillip looked at him blankly and started counting the items on his
fingers: racquet, present for his mother . . .

"Dad! Hello! Mom's interview."

Phillip was rightfully horrified. He swooped Michael off my thigh
and placed him gently on the other side of the banquette. Then he
squeezed in next to me and tried to nuzzle his nose into my neck. I
pulled away. He looked deep into my eyes and held my head steady in
front of him with both his hands. I tried to look down. "Jamie, you are
a wonder. I'm a self-centered little boy. I'm sorry. This interview is
going to be your golden shining moment. I know it's been a tough
road, but you're at the finish line and I'm proud of you. You're a sensa-
tion and deserve all the credit for pulling this off. Really, I'm astonish-
ingly proud."

"Hardly shows." I was feeling extremely alone in the world at this
moment.

"I'm just awful. I admit it, I completely forgot. What with the trip
and all, my deal is in disarray. I love you and it's going to be wonderful. Unfortunately, I will be on a plane tonight at nine, but I've asked
the company in Houston to record it for me." He kissed me on the
cheek. He was late. His phone rang. It was his secretary. "Hold on,
Laurie." He looked at his wife and three kids with a guilty expression.
"I love you all!" We all looked back at him in silence. The kids knew
he was in the doghouse with Mommy and they were taking my side.
They also hadn't seen him much for weeks, so they resented him.
Seconds later, I could hear his voice trailing out the front door,

"Laurie, make sure Hank e-mails me the updated spreadsheets and send flowers to Jamie's office with a card saying . . ." The door swung shut.

"Are you going to forgive him, Mom?"

At seven-thirty p.m., Abby came into my office with take-out sushi to pull me through the final ninety minutes of waiting until the piece aired. Even though this was supposedly the biggest day of my career, I didn't have much to do. Except to feel panicky, of course. The piece had been done for forty-eight hours. Charles hadn't called for at least five hours, and every time I tried to reach him, his cell phone went straight to voicemail.

As Abby unloaded the plastic containers, I dug into my purse to pull out some makeup and was surprised to find a small, baby-blue Tiffany box. It lay in the side pocket of my bag, where I kept my emergency chocolate. Peter knew I overdosed on Kit Kat bars whenever I got anxious.

Inside the felt box, a sterling stopwatch. With an engraving:

Time for another dance.

Not soon enough. When had he had time to put this in here? But wait, could this be a good-bye present?

"What'd he get you? I hope it was expensive," Abby said out of the side of her mouth as she ripped open a soy sauce packet with her teeth.

"It's not from my husband."

"Goodman actually spent some money?"

"No, it's nothing." I bit my lip.

"Whatever it is, I hope it makes you happy." Darling Abby: perfectly content to reorganize and replenish her index cards all day and never produce a piece. She knew the risks producing big controversial pieces could entail and chose not to. That Wednesday, I wondered why I'd chosen my route.

"Who're all the flowers from?"

"My husband and Goodman. Goodman sends them whenever we have a piece that has killed me, but Phillip sent his because he's in the doghouse."

"What'd he do this time?"

"He forgot my piece was airing tonight and instead instructed me to get his squash racquet restrung . . . Shit. I forgot to send the racquet to the shop."

"You're joking, right?"

"No, really. I did forget."

"Listen to yourself, girl! I was talking about the fact that he makes you get his racquet restrung on the biggest day of your life."

"So I'm a lost cause. We already knew that." I dunked a piece of tekka maki in the soy sauce.

"What did you do when he forgot about the show?"

"I didn't tell him. Dylan busted him, which was worse than if I had said something. And Dylan was so pissed at him for forgetting."

Abby scraped edamame beans into her mouth with ferocious speed. "Maybe I don't want a husband after all."

I threw a soy sauce packet at her. The phone rang.

I practically dove for it, knocking over my Diet Coke on my keyboard and the phone. I picked up the wet receiver. "Yes, Charles. Give me a second." I reached for paper napkins in my drawer, mopped up the spill, and tried to hold the receiver between my ear and shoulder, but it fell on my desk. I could hear Charles's tinny voice yelling "Jamie!" through the phone.

"You haven't called in five hours! Where in God's earth have you been? I've been—"

"Just shut up. Don't you dare put the phone down on me again with ninety minutes to air. I've been out of cell-phone range traipsing around the boonies."

"And? Anything?"

"Get the lawyers into Erik's office right now. Plus Bill Maguire."

"Why? Charles! Why?"

"Because you could be totally screwed."

28

Morse Code for Big Trouble

"What the fuck am I supposed to do, rerun the goddamn fuckin' Britney Spears hour?" Erik James was raging around his office like a bull; he knocked over his jelly bean jar on purpose—took a well-aimed whack at it. Goodman and I followed the trajectory silently as the candies flew across the room.

"What the fuck does Charles want to talk about?" Erik bellowed at me. He looked at his watch. "Eighty minutes to air. Forget that. I don't want to hear a word until the lawyers and Maguire get here." He paced some more and swept jelly beans off the corner of his desk.

I answered, mustering up the courage, "I don't even know what Charles has. Thank God . . ."

"Don't you 'thank God' me. My ass is on the line now, not yours. My name will be in the papers, not yours. They're not going to go after you if this goes south."

Goodman stood up. "Try to calm down, Erik, we don't even know if there's—"

Erik stood up and did his King Kong impersonation. "You want me to calm down? With three days' worth of promos in fifteen key markets? And we just ran the Britney Spears hour five months ago. I don't have enough pieces in the can to remake a new show in . . . now it's seventy-nine minutes! Hilda! Get me an intern!"

Within forty seconds, a sprightly young brunette ran into Erik's office. She was all excited to be called into the executive producer's office an hour before an airtime. "Yes, sir?"

"Popcorn. Now!"

"Excuse me? Any kind? Where?"

"What the fuck, are you, like, is this your first fuckin' day and they send you to me? I said *popcorn*. My fuckin' movie popcorn from the Sony IMAX down the street. Butter. Lots of it. Salt. That movie salt. Hurry!" And she ran out the door.

Next Erik dialed the director in the control room. "Cue up the goddamn fuckin' Britney Spears hour." Erik bobbed his head as he listened to the entreaties of his director. Then he took a deep breath and rolled his eyes. "You're acting like the fuckin' Morse code guy on the *Titanic*. Do not question the message I am delivering here." We could hear the director's scrambled voice in the receiver from across the room. "Doesn't mean we're running it over Theresa, but we might have to. Do not ever question my authority. Yes. Yes. Do it right now."

"*Lord* have mercy." Bill Maguire entered the room with the lawyers and listened to the tail end of Erik's phone call to the control room. "The ain't-shit Britney Spears hour? Do you have any idea what we've dropped on promoting Boudreaux?"

Erik pushed his intercom button. "Hilda, put Charles Worthington through immediately!"

"Line two!" she yelled from her desk and the phone rang inside the office. Bill Maguire jumped for the phone next to the sofa and Erik James grabbed the phone on his desk, then they both hung up, assuming the other would stay on and push the speaker button.

"Fuck me!" yelled Erik. "Hilda, get Worthington again!" He looked at Maguire. "Do me a favor, Bill. I know you're the boss, but let me answer my own goddamned phone."

Twenty interminable seconds passed. The phone rang again. Erik picked up the phone, dragged it over to the coffee table in the middle of all of us, and put it on speaker. "Okay, Charles, this is your moment of reckoning. Tell us what you got." He looked at his wall of clocks showing us the time in all four American time zones, London, Jerusalem, Moscow, and Hong Kong.

Charles began: "You know the RightIsMight.org bloggers? The farthest-right-wing, pro-life, pro–death-penalty, pro–prayer-in-schools people with a vendetta against NBS?"

"You think I'm a fuckin' dumb shit? Of course I do. They're idiots. No one respects them," Erik answered. He glared at his wall of clocks again.

"Well, a lot of people read them. And I think they're down here in Pearl."

I felt a sharp pain in my heart. I thought of Peter and his doubts. He didn't have any juice to back them up, but still he felt them, and I hadn't given him the time of day. I had been totally arrogant, and anyhow, desperate to put distance between us. Silence in the room. The lawyers looked at each other and put their palms in the air in confusion.

Bill Maguire leaned back on the sofa with his hands on his face. He put his mouth close to the phone again. "Damn it, Charles, you trying to raise my blood pressure over some bloggers? What's your point? Why do I give a shit if they're in Pearl?"

I butted in. "Because that's where Theresa lives."

Erik James's face turned red and he slammed his hand down hard on the coffee table, then he stood up and began pacing the room. "And do we have any proof that there's a connection between the woman and these people?"

My voice was shaking. "No. They post their blogs anonymously. We don't know their names."

Goodman had had enough. "So this floozy lives in the same Red State as some right-wing nuts. I'm not seeing how that affects my interview."

Charles spoke on from the speakerphone. "It's not just the same state. It's the same town. Listen. This is some of the best investigative work I've done in years. I called a hundred political sources and am pretty sure RightIsMight.org is here. That's a big story in itself."

Goodman was incredulous now. "Charles, you want me to give you credit because you are 'pretty sure' RightIsMight.org is based near Jackson?"

"A drunk guy in a bar last night told me there were bloggers in a small town outside Jackson. I put that together with my White House sources, one of whom swears RightIsMight.org is near here."

Bill Maguire cut in. "Let me get this straight. Some hopped-up low-life tells you bloggers are in town. Then some D.C. playah who doesn't know shit about the South tells you he thinks RightIsMight.org is near Pearl. You'd better have more than that before you come steppin' to me . . . like something showing the two, *and* that bitch, are linked."

Charles's voice was shaky now. "Well, I guess I don't know for sure they are linked to her."

"He's right. And even with five more trips there, we may never link them. But maybe . . ." I couldn't finish my sentence. Tears pooled in my eyes. For some reason, I could only think of Peter. I wanted him to comfort me. He wouldn't ever say he told me so, but he would know enough to talk me through this. Peter claimed I had a habit of kowtowing to the powerful men in my life. Just in case he was right, I had to tell myself *not* to appease them, *not* to silence myself just because that's what they wanted. But even factoring that in, I still didn't have enough conviction to stop the presses.

Erik picked up a coffee-table book, slammed it on the floor, and started pacing again. "Everyone is now going to shut the fuck up except for me," he said. "This is my reputation on the line here." He towered over all of us and stared us down. "Here's what I think. I think Jamie is so overtired she can't make a rational argument. I think Charles cannot close this loop. That's what I think."

Erik, Goodman, and Bill Maguire all looked back and forth at each other and nodded in secure male agreement.

Charles answered, "I don't know they are linked, no. Just a feeling this could eventually lead us somewhere."

Erik started pacing the room like a bull once again. "You mean to tell me you want me to pull the biggest interview of the year because of a *feeling* you have, Charles?" He continued sarcastically. "Do you think you could hire a shrink and discover your fuckin' feelings and figure out if they are real next time, say, twenty-four hours *before* my broadcast begins?"

Maguire looked at me. "Charles . . . I didn't send you down there for your feelings. Stand up for something! Be a man! Not a . . . !" He rolled his eyes at Erik. "Can we air this piece or not? Remember, this is all about her side. We're not pushing anything else."

I sighed. "I'm not telling you you can't air it after all we've been through, but I—"

Maguire screamed, "You *what*? You jumpin' like a jackrabbit tellin' me not to air this or not?"

I looked down. "I just don't know."

Maguire shook his head resolutely. "You don't know. You don't know. Is that your final answer?"

"I guess."

"Charles?" he yelled into the speakerphone.

"It's not my piece. I stated everything. It's a hunch, but I can't prove it."

"'Nuff said. I'm not pulling the piece at this late date, team. Not because of no feeling. We state very clearly that we cannot verify the relationship with Hartley. It's simply her side of the story."

Goodman pursed his lips, then said, "You two people are from a different generation—you haven't lived through the political storms Maguire, Erik, and I have. I have my own *feeling* that this woman is telling the truth. I also happen to have a *feeling* that when someone is rejected by a lover, and notified of this by state troopers, they like to take their sweet revenge. And conveniently for us in the news business"—he pointed to the executives around the room and continued—"those rejected, revenge-filled people with an axe to grind like to air their dirty laundry on national television."

News president Bill Maguire stood up like he was going to sing the national anthem. "That's right, Goodman. Especially when I send a sophisticated, intelligent producer down to Jackson ten times to convince her to talk. They feel *compelled* to tell it." He was trying to butter me up as he looked down at me. "And that's when they turn it loose . . . their whole gotdamn story. Shit . . . all networks, broadcast and cable, wanted her, why shouldn't she choose the best?" He looked around sanctimoniously and slapped his heart twice. "And we are the best network in the business. Theresa Boudreaux figured that out on her own . . . *after* getting with everyone's producers. And you can bet Leon Rosenberg told her that too. That's why she came to us, got her hair and nails done, and dogged out the congressman." Maguire pointed his finger in my face and squinted.

"People don't lie on network news. They come to give us their stories, to relieve their anger and pain. No one—especially no one tryin' to play herself off as some Southern belle with that big hair— goes on national TV to talk about getting tapped from behind. Not for no good reason." He put his hand down and started toward the door, but then turned back. "The piece airs in thirty-seven minutes. I am now, as is my habit, going to sit in my leather chair upstairs, pour myself a glass of Wild Turkey, and enjoy another fine, groundbreaking broadcast of *Newsnight with Joe Goodman*. Thank you, ladies and gentlemen." And with that, he marched out of the room.

29

Cool-Down Period

Message One. Beep.

Hi, honey. It's Christina Patten.

Two things. One small. One positively HUMONGOUS. First small. Before the Fabergé benefit on February first, we're going to have cocktails for the patrons on the benefit committee at the apartment, all of you generous souls who bought tickets. You'll need to be there, though I'll need to be in the receiving line. You won't—it's just that it's your first year and all and they will be a little surprised with a new face. Secondly, biggest news ever. WE MADE THE COVER OF MADISON AVENUE MAGAZINE! Yes, the photo of our table was chosen. I hear we look beautiful, pictures inside are said to be great. Can't wait. Kiss kiss.

Peter was going to kill me for that picture. He didn't even know I'd done it. Peter had become the baseline for me in every segment of my life—nothing happened without me daydreaming about how he would react, what he would say, how he would tease me. I'd kept the stopwatch in my pocket all night at the show, running my thumb along the engraving on the back.

Message Two. Beep. My darling bride. I am very proud of you and your blockbuster piece. I'm already getting breaking-news e-mails though I didn't actually see it. Will do tomorrow. You are the best producer in the business. I hope Goodman knows exactly how lucky he is to have you. I know I do. And I am so proud. And again, sorry about this morning. Beep.

Okay, maybe I wasn't going to divorce him or kill him. Sometimes he could actually be kind and touching. Maybe the Peter thing was just a dangerous distraction. Perhaps this marriage had a chance if I could figure out how to encourage Phillip's good parts.

Beep. One more thing. Don't forget about my squash racquet. Beep.

On second thought, perhaps it didn't.

But that night, I didn't have the energy to focus on marriage— neither fixing it nor ending it. Even though the Theresa piece had aired, I had to steel myself for the attacks that were sure to explode in every possible form of media in the days ahead. I knew the Theresa story wasn't over. Perhaps Erik and Goodman and Maguire were right; they were tougher, seasoned pros, after all, with far more political experience than me. They believed Theresa; I would try to do the same. Life moves on.

I crept down the hall to check on the children in their rooms. They were sprawled across their beds, feet and legs out of the covers. Placing the blankets back on them gingerly, I swept their hair off their faces and kissed them softly. Back in the kitchen, I shuffled through the mail and then found another huge bouquet from Phillip waiting for me on the counter. He had never sent me two bouquets in the same day before.

I grabbed a handful of cashews from the glass jar on the windowsill and poured myself a glass of white wine. Then, walking by the table in the hallway, I lit a small candle for my bedside table. I climbed onto my bed and started crunching on cashews and savoring every honey-laced sip of my favorite chardonnay. Then I just lay there for a long while, spread-eagled on the bed, staring at the ceiling. Heaven: no television, no music, no cell phone, no e-mail. I gave myself permission to put all my anxieties to the side: no NBS, no crumbling marriage, no second thoughts about raising my children in New York.

Instead, I thought about how Peter smelled: tangy, sweaty, active, muscle-y, like male nectar. I couldn't master my feelings and ignore him. He just made me happy. There was no denying that natural, evolving certainty.

I remembered how he curled his hair behind his ears just before he said something serious, the bounce in his walk, his thumb rubbing my palm. I closed my eyes and imagined him lying next to me, his head resting on his elbow and one of his knees holding my leg down firmly. Once, I'd seen him half naked when he'd changed out of a T-shirt in Dylan's room. He had a strong but medium build and a sexy little patch of blondish hair in the middle of his chest.

I took a sip of icy chardonnay to cool me down. It was awfully nice being in the bed alone. I laid my head back and closed my eyes.

And then I thought about Peter some more and decided I didn't want to cool down. So I had a nice evening with myself.

At dawn, the city still dark, I jumped. Woke up in a sweat and looked around the room. Then I remembered. It was all over. Kind of. I lay back down on my stomach. Put the pillow back on top of my head. But of course I couldn't resist. I reached for the TV clicker on the side table and aimed it back at the television to turn it on. I kept my eyes closed, my head covered, and listened to the audio.

"You saw it, everyone in this country saw it, did you think she was credible in her . . ."

Click.

"I'll tell you something, that network better watch its behind if it thinks that airing some salacious item like that is furthering the cause of . . ."

Click.

"Sure, Imus, I think they should have run it. There's enough evidence out there that they may have been together. If she's going to talk, they're not going to refuse . . ."

Sounded like the expected ranting of morning shows. I clicked the remote control off. I had to get to work. I had to make sure I was on call for everyone.

On the way to work, I made Luis stop at a newsstand so I could buy all the papers I hadn't already read. The *New York Times* had put its piece in its national section on page twelve. The headline ran "Allegations of an Extramarital Affair Involving Congressman Hugh Hartley Are Broadcast Before a National Audience." I was dying to know how the newspaper of record would handle the sex part. Paragraph 9 discussed his preferred intercourse style: "When pressed on the sexual details by Joe Goodman in an effort to ascertain the veracity of her recollections, Ms. Boudreaux responded that Congressman Hartley 'showed a preference for a particular brand of sex.' The accuser went on to imply that sodomy was the consistent and frequent act between the two." The *New York Post* ran the headline "Back Porch Romance for Huey." The *Daily News* tantalized readers with "Hartley Sez: I'll Take Door Number Two!" The late-night comedians were going to feed off this for years.

My cell phone rang. Charles.

"Where are you?"

"Just making a connection in Atlanta from Jackson. Be in the office around lunchtime."

"Good."

A few beats of silence. Then he said in a low voice, "How you feeling?"

I took a deep breath. "Fine. Relatively."

"Relatively?"

"Yeah, beaten up, but resolved, I think. We did all we could. Perhaps you and I were just too tough on ourselves. Maybe . . ."

"Maybe we should have told them to kill it."

"Charles, don't say that! I can't take it."

"It's just so weird. The whole thing. The story. The bloggers. Everything. Like a bad media acid trip."

"We tried our hardest."

"Listen, you did all you could, I'm just . . ."

"What?"

"I'm fine with our piece. I mean, kind of fine. But I don't like this Internet stuff, these guys are nuts! I was up all night reading their postings; could you believe the RightIsMight.org stuff?"

"Didn't see it yet."

"Would you *please* get hip to the blogger thing? How can you not have logged on? They're acting like fucking terrorists!"

"Charles, I'm in the car. I'll be at the office in fifteen minutes. Can I call you from there?"

"No, I'll be taking off. Just so you know, Abby just told me Maguire is freaking. The lawyers too, so get ready to deal with them."

Unlike the upper network brass, Erik and Goodman were in heaven. This morning, when I walked in, they were high-fiving each other like two football running backs in an end zone and saying, "Bring 'em on!" Based on the overnight ratings, *Newsnight* had a 47 share, almost as big as Monica Lewinsky with Barbara Walters. I slunk by them and into my office to get up to speed on the blogger reaction to my piece.

Congressman Hartley still had not spoken publicly to refute it. Perhaps, I reasoned, Theresa Boudreaux was telling the truth and he figured that if he went before the cameras à la Bill Clinton to say "I've never had sex with that woman, Miss Boudreaux," he might live to regret it. Especially if, like Bill Clinton, undeniable evidence surfaced. (And yes, of course I had asked Theresa if she had any stains on any of her dresses or sheets. She, appropriately disgusted, refused to supply my brazen request with a verbal response.)

Charles was right. Coordinated blogs denouncing NBS had appeared within minutes of our broadcast on dozens of right-wing websites, unusually unified in their message. Clearly these people had planned a campaign ahead of time to discredit Theresa the minute the interview aired. They called for the Federal Communications Commission to file complaints about our delving into the sodomy subject and urged their readers to boycott NBS local stations around the country as well as our advertisers.

A group of five right-wing bloggers, led by the RightIsMight.org people and backed up by their ToBlogIsToBeFree.org compatriots, offered up an Osama bin Laden warning: that our side, the evil liberal elite side, would suffer great consequences for our actions. The lawyers tried to prepare for the possibility that they would actually fire back with something more than criticism or incredulity, that they had something nuclear in their arsenal.

Maguire stood at his desk, sweating profusely, staring at his wall of seven screens—four networks and three twenty-four-hour cable stations. From a black dial at his desk, he switched the audio from station to station. He looked like the Chairman of the Joint Chiefs in his Pentagon bunker with blinking lights and maps all around him. You would have thought two SS-20s were headed straight toward the nation's capital by the terrified expression on his face. I kept thinking, This guy is an ex-Marine. He's supposed to be tough. I don't like that he's losing his cool like this. As I walked beside his desk around to the sitting area in his office, his right knee was bouncing a hundred miles an hour.

Erik, Goodman, Charles, and I entered his office in single file and snaked around his coffee table to the couches so we could watch. Just like the Monica era: it was all-Theresa-all-the-time. The ranting of the cable hosts and roundtables melded together in my head and I closed my eyes and put my head in my hands. I was just plain tired of it all. My Peter stopwatch was in my pocket. I massaged it for strength.

Issue Two: Cokie, did NBS prove anything?
Yes and no. It's her word against Hartley's. We have to wait for his response, but they did move the story forward: her travel receipts, the photos of them together all prove . . .

And now, for our midday roundup: our reporter is staked outside Huey Hartley's headquarters in Jackson, but so far his camp is mute on the lurid allegations . . .

Speaking for my party and my congressional colleague Huey Hartley, this nation is damned if the press continues to . . .

Maguire positioned himself before his troops. "Here's what I don't like. I don't like the coordination on the Internet. It's no good for us, for this piece, or the news business in general." He paced and paced. Then he clicked his computer mouse from site to site for a few long minutes. "And I don't like being called a liberal network, because it just isn't accurate. I have voted Republican down the line. I am *not* a gotdamn Hillary supporter. I can't stand her. Nor that pansy John Kerry on his windsurfer." He wiped his brow and then his entire head with a hankie. "I don't like these Internet small-town vigilante bloggers posting their views and people believing their crap. You've got to earn the public's trust. Pay your dues. Learn from your elders. Get your work fact-checked by researchers. Work for a trusted organization! You can't just buy a gotdamn computer and—presto!—become a journalist!"

Erik had had a powerful mood swing: he was decidedly melancholy. "You can now, Bill. And we'd all better realize that so we can hold our own with them. Know your enemy, man. I'm sure you learned that in basic training."

30

Hold On to Your Birthday Hats

My whole body itched: behind my ears, my scalp, deep inside my armpits. Sitting on the floor, I wriggled my backside into the satin rope fringe hanging from the sofa behind me and arched my spine slightly, aware that he was watching me. All the tension from the last two days was lodged in my neck; I cocked my head to one side to try to release it. It didn't work. Nothing worked.

Peter, sitting on an ottoman across the room, nodded with a poker face and kept his eyes focused on mine, targeting sexual energy my way from across a living room filled with forty people. I then concentrated my gaze downward, distractedly pulling the loose yarns of the enormous Aubusson carpet between my fingers. Even that felt sexual. I looked up again and he was gone.

In front of me, a sea of children, dressed like the opening scene in *The Nutcracker,* sat on the floor in the living room to celebrate Susannah and Tom's son Anthony's birthday—Michael and Gracie in the front row. A group of adults made up of mostly well-dressed mothers in slacks, cashmere sweaters wrapped casually around their shoulders, and short kitten heels lined one side of the room. All their nannies lined the other. Tom Berger sat on the floor near his son and a few other men were scattered around the room; I assumed they were uncles or second godfathers.

Silly Billy, wearing huge red glasses that matched his suspenders, swirled colorful silk scarves over the children's heads, whipping the little darlings into a frenzy. Suddenly, all of the children stretched their arms to the heavens: "Pick me, pick me, pleeeeese." The grown-ups chuckled, eyeing each other knowingly. Billy teased them further until the children could stand no more. He finally relented and allowed the birthday boy to help him pull a white dove out of his jacket pocket.

A maid in a black uniform with a starched white apron discreetly passed tomato and butter tea sandwiches on a silver tray with one hand, and offered linen cocktail napkins in the other. The men and women, bored to tears, politely discussed how quickly the children had sprouted up. They weren't toddlers anymore. Imagine that.

"Doesn't that lady passing the little tomato sandwiches with the nurse contraption on her head look exactly like the dog in *Peter Pan*?" whispered Peter, surprising me from behind on the couch. "She even has the same craggy, droopy face."

Dylan, standing next to him, cracked up.

"Stop it, you two."

"Chill, Mom. He's right. She totally does."

Silly Billy let a bucket of plastic snakes spring out of a basket. One of the little boys started sobbing and his mother rushed to him like he'd been hit by a car.

Dylan elbowed my hip. "Mom, can we go now? This is so babyish."

"Shush!"

"Can I go watch TV? Now?"

"Let me take you."

The Beethoven "Für Elise" muted tone rang from deep inside my purse. I reached in and saw Abby's number flashing on the screen—I didn't want to answer it. I'd gone through enough hell at the office trying to navigate my way through the reaction to the Theresa piece in the past two days. I put the phone on vibrate; they could wait for me to return their calls. I'd also given Charles and Erik Susannah's home number in case something large blew up.

With Dylan happily clicking away at the TV in the indigo-blue den, I sat back down on the floor. Again I felt Peter staring at me, his gaze an invisible wire vibrating between us. He was taunting me.

Susannah's Labradoodle barked loudly and tried to pull a young boy across the shiny floors by his suspenders. Another elderly woman passed a tray with large crystal goblets filled with Perrier, topped with round slivers of lime. I reached for one and willed myself not to look Peter's way.

I studied the orange and purple Mark Rothko masterpiece to my right above the sofa in an attempt to distract myself. For the first time I noticed that Susannah had actually trimmed her velvet sofa underneath in a satin eggplant cord that matched the painting.

Suddenly a hand grabbed the flesh on my hip and I jumped, thinking instantly that Peter had crossed an inappropriate line here, but so happy he had. "How's the star producer?"

I turned around. Phillip. "What . . . what are you doing here?"

"My Friday dinner got canceled so I caught the first flight out this morning." He kissed my cheek. "And I wanted to come to my godson's party." Translation: he wanted to kiss Susannah's Waspy ass.

"Honey," he continued, "how are you? I saw it."

"Fine. Actually bad. Exhausted. Scared," I responded, trying to focus on this conversation rather than Peter's presence somewhere across the room.

"You should be scared. You're taking on one of the most powerful men in Congress."

"You're just making me more nervous, Phillip."

"Everything's going to be fine, but I think this should be your last political story for a while. You can still be a winning journalist without getting into this messy political crap."

"I know. It's too much." For once, I agreed with him.

"Too much on you. On the kids. On me. And we need you and you need to enjoy your life again and get off this treadmill. You're like a hamster, running, running . . ."

"Phillip, I can't have this conversation now. I don't know what I'm doing next. I know you are right on some level." The stout old lady with the tomato sandwiches passed by and I grabbed three. Phillip looked furtively around us as if I'd swiped a china box off an end table and put it in my pocket. "I didn't have lunch, Phillip, okay? These things aren't filling and I'm feeling a bit shaky now."

"You don't need to calm yourself down by gorging on calories."

"Hello, you two!" Susannah. She was wearing a black crocheted Chanel sweater, a luxurious ruffled blouse, and a tight pencil skirt, whispering some directives to her housekeeper out of the side of her mouth. She rearranged her thick white coral choker. "Well, if it isn't Little Miss Firestorm Creator over here! Jamie, that was riveting." She gave me a hug and held my shoulders tight with her outstretched arms while she continued. "I can't believe the elephant balls on you, woman. Have you been watching the cable news shows? They can't talk about anything else."

"I know, it's, it's overwhelming." I started to feel a bit nauseated.

My cell phone began to buzz again. I looked at the number. Couldn't Goodman manage the backwash on his own? Couldn't Erik, "Mr. Experienced Political Story Journalist," handle everything for thirty minutes while I took my kids to a Friday afternoon birthday party?

"Won't those people leave you alone? You're at someone's house!" said Susannah, throwing up her hands. "Don't know how you manage."

She took off and Phillip followed her.

"Let me come kiss that birthday boy!" he yelled after her.

But now the buzzing was getting difficult to ignore; there must have been three calls in a row. I reached into the bottom of my bag and missed the last call by a nanosecond. When I checked the incoming number, it was Erik. Not Charles. Not Goodman. But Erik. This I couldn't ignore. Erik only called when he was "fuckin' pissed."

Three mothers were pointing me out to one of the elderly ladies in a black uniform and starched white apron, who then headed toward me. I knew instantly. Erik was calling with Charles on Susannah's landline.

There was a problem with the interview. That sinking feeling I had had about Theresa was about to materialize into one big disaster. I just knew it. My heart raced. I leapt to my feet and knocked over a Diet Coke in an eighty-dollar crystal goblet from the side table and it crashed into thousands of tiny slivers of glass on the mahogany floor. All the kids turned around. Silly Billy took his black hat off and watched me, stopping the show; I could almost hear the trombones petering out. I stood up and slipped backward on the spill like I'd stepped on a banana peel, but caught myself on the corner of the sofa, almost knocking over the antique vase lamp in the process. A mother grabbed the lamp to steady it.

Across the room, the parents looked at me with a "Calm down, lady" expression in their composed, well-dressed, genteel way. The Labradoodle ran over to the mess and tried to lap up the Diet Coke. I pulled its collar back harshly so it didn't cut its tongue.

"Phillip!" I yelled into the air like a lunatic.

He had disappeared. No one moved.

"Peter!"

Suddenly Peter came plowing through the crowd like Michael Jordan driving the lane and leapt over the zebra poof in a single bound to grab my arm. "Jamie, I'll handle the dog, go get your call." He looked deep into my eyes, concerned, as if the call were serious, as if maybe someone had died. It turned out to be worse than that.

I picked up the phone, closed my eyes, pressed the receiver against my chest, and prayed silently, *God, please save me on this one.* Then I took a deep breath and put it up to my ear.

"This is Jamie Whitfield."

"Are you watching?" Erik bellowed.

"Watching what?"

"The Theresa tape, it's airing at five p.m. on the Facts News Network."

"What do you mean, 'the Theresa tape'?" I tasted bile in the back of my throat.

"I don't know what I mean," answered Erik. "All I fuckin' know is Facts News just announced that they have a tape from Theresa Boudreaux. It came to them anonymously in an envelope marked 'RightIsMight.org.'" The Facts News Network anchors licked their chops every time the "mainstream media" or the "liberal media elite" tripped up. They had blasted us 24/7 for airing the Theresa Boudreaux tape, presenting her as a lying, vindictive, jilted nobody whom Huey Hartley barely knew.

"Where's Charles?" I asked, panicking.

"He's here with me." There was some muffled sound on the other end of the phone for a moment. "And, Jamie, you and I are in this together, don't forget that. We're a team and we're gonna handle this one as a team. We *both* are in this mess. I'm not going to let you fry." My tongue was so dry, it stuck to the roof of my mouth. I motioned for another server lady to please get me a ginger ale. She pretended not to understand me.

I opened the drawer next to the phone to search for some paper and a pen. No pen. No paper. Just clear Lucite boxes in thick, built-in compartments with P-touch labels over each section. I opened one, labeled "Entertaining Accessories: Hors d'Oeuvres," and picked up a small handful of shell-encrusted toothpicks. And though it was completely sick, considering my larger problems, I remember those damn toothpicks actually making me feel inadequate. In our house, we didn't even have birthday candles in the heat of the moment.

Someone tapped on my shoulder. "Everything okay?" Peter was standing behind me with a pile of wet linen cocktail napkins. He began shaking the shards of glass into the wastebasket.

I shook my head no. He came up behind me and tried to listen to the receiver over my shoulder. His chest touched my back.

"Put me on speaker, please, Erik," I said firmly, trying to sound like I could fix this.

"We're here, Jamie," said Charles into the speakerphone.

"What do you think, Charles?" I prayed again that he would say this was just a silly ploy to make us nervous.

But he didn't say that.

Instead he said, "I think we're totally fucked, that's what I think."

Erik interjected, "Now come on, everyone, let's take a breath here. She can't recant now. Forty-eight hours ago, she said her piece in front of twenty million Americans in prime time."

"Doesn't matter," said Charles.

"Why not, Charles? Why not? Maybe it's just . . ."

"Just because it doesn't." Charles paused. "This is going to be something unusually bad. The RightIsMight.org people are a venomous, dangerous bunch. Hell, they post their blogs anonymously so they can pull shit like this. And even though no one knows who they are, everyone in Red-State America loves 'em."

"What's on the tape?" I asked.

Erik jumped in. "All we have right now is that it was delivered with a RightIsMight.org logo on the envelope and those fuckers at Facts News Network have been promoting this for half an hour. It's airing in seven minutes, at five p.m. sharp. Just enough time to make it the lead story on the evening news broadcasts tonight." He paused. "Are you near a television, Jamie? In fact, where the hell are you?"

"I'm . . . I'm near the office. Something I had to do," I answered, trying to sound professional, but feeling like a wad of jelly. "I'll watch from here. I can't make it back in time. Obviously. I'm going to put you on hold for a minute and find a TV."

"I think there's one next door in Susannah's husband's office," whispered Peter. Was I going totally crazy, or did he just pull my hair up and let his lips touch my neck?

He guided me to a green velvet couch, then grabbed the remote and started switching the channels furiously.

"Facts News Network. Channel 53, Peter. It's cable! Hurry!" I sat down on the sofa and picked up the blinking telephone line.

"Okay, Erik, I'm back, I'm watching." I turned to Peter, miming that I needed to drink something; he nodded and ran out the door.

Bill O'Shaunessy here with the Facts News Network. We Give You the Facts, You Decide. We have just received a tape from a Miss Theresa Boudreaux exclusively. Unless you've been hiding in a cave with Osama, you know Miss Boudreaux went on the NBS television network to tell Joe Goodman that she had carried on an affair with the representative of the good people of Mississippi, the patriotic Mr. Huey Hartley. Now, Congressman Hartley hasn't bothered himself with what his chief of staff has labeled these "preposterous allegations," and rightly so, many believe. But somehow NBS saw it in the public interest, with the war on terror raging and the budget debate roiling Congress, to put this woman's rantings on prime-time network television.

So why are we doing the same? Well, good question. The cat is out of the bag now, and Theresa has some follow-up information we felt we couldn't ignore. Facts News will show you her follow-up to the NBS interview after this brief commercial break . . .

"Jamie, what on earth do you think she is doing? You know her best." Now there was Bill Maguire's voice on the speakerphone. I felt sick and dizzy, with my blood pressure rising by the second.

"I just don't know, Bill. Why wouldn't she send the tape to us? They said 'follow-up.' Maybe she's just clearing the air some more. Getting her story out there again on another network." My voice cracked. "Maybe she wants to apologize to Hartley, or give a better reason why she felt she needed to tell the truth?" Peter, sitting next to me and handing me a ginger ale, nodded yes. Surely that's all it was.

"No chance, Jamie," said Charles. "She sent it to the enemy. Or what she sees as our enemy. It came in the RightIsMight.org envelope. They told us they'd be throwing a firebomb our way, and my best guess is it's thirty seconds to D-day."

"Charles, enough!" yelled Goodman.

I closed my eyes. Could I have known better? I told myself I did the best I could, given the information I had. I was a professional. I made grown-up decisions. And I was going to live with them.

Charles continued. "This is exactly what I feared . . ."

"Shut up, Charles, you little—" Maguire stopped himself, then continued. " 'I told you so' is no gotdamn good to me now. The piece has aired! Thirty seconds to go. Quiet!" We all stared silently at the Billy Blanks Tae Bo videotape commercial. Then the beating of huge bass drums as the "Facts News Breaking News Exclusive Report" banner slid on the screen like a snake.

Good afternoon, I'm Bill O'Shaunessy with a breaking story from the Facts News Network. A shocking development in the Theresa Boudreaux story. A Facts News exclusive: Theresa Boudreaux has another story to tell. One that is far more ominous for the executives who make decisions at the NBS network than for Congressman Hartley. Let's roll the tape.

I put my head in my hands, balancing the silent receiver against one shoulder. I couldn't look. But then I peeked out with one eye between my fingers. Peter sat beside me with both his hands covering his mouth.

"Fuck me! Arghhhhhh!" That would be Erik. I heard the entire jar of jelly beans smash on the floor.

31

The Boudreaux Bombshell

Theresa looked beautiful, serene. And evil.

She stood in front of a generic tropical locale, much like Osama or al-Zawahiri would stand in front of a nondescript Afghan cave. There were palm trees swaying in the wind to her left and azure-blue water off in the distance. Her curly dirty-blond hair fell into her face as the breeze picked up. She pulled long strands behind her ears and the afternoon sunlight caught her green eyes and turned them into translucent pools. She could have been anywhere in the southern hemisphere.

She looked down to compose herself. Then she raised her head slowly and focused her glare purposefully into the camera lens. Then Theresa took a full, prideful breath, sticking her beautiful bosoms up toward the heavens, and began:

A few months ago, I hatched a plan. Along with someone I shall only identify as a close friend.

"That's RightIsMight.org! I know it is. I knew it!" yelled Charles from the speakerphone.

"Shut up, Charles!" screamed Bill Maguire.

It was kind of like conducting an experiment. An experiment with what my friends and I call the "Mainstream Media" . . .

"Holy fuck!" wailed Goodman.

"Whoaaa," said Peter quietly.

We wanted to see how easy it would be to go on a national news network, one that caters to liberals. So we found an eager producer, an eager anchor, ready to take down any upstanding Republican they could sink their claws into . . .

Tears sprang from my eyes, splashing off my knees like raindrops. I wanted to bury myself in Peter's arms, but I didn't. So I took it on my own, with the receiver pressed tightly against my ear, my chin on my hand.

. . . And we wanted to know how far the mainstream media would go to take down any patriotic, Republican leader—anyone with conserva-tive values, values that help keep America strong. We wanted to know if they'd even stoop to put tales of sodomy on the air. They didn't care. They just did it. Hired some poor audio experts, used a few receipts as proof—calling themselves careful journalists. . . . As my friends and I proved, those guys'll put anything on the air, as long as that "anything" is fodder against the right wing of this country.

"Cunt," said Charles.

. . . So, ladies and gentlemen, for the record, on the soul of my sweet departed mother, I swear I never had an affair with Congressman Huey Hartley. I never had sodomy with him . . .

After one more minute of sugary patriotic propaganda, the screen switched to black once again and faded up on a smug William O'Shaunessy, who somberly began to address the contents of the tape, with an ever-so-slight smile.

Someone's hand slammed down so hard on the table, I had to pull the receiver back from my ear.

Bill Maguire now addressed his team. "Jamie, Charles, Goodman,

Erik. We, my friends, have been bitch-slapped by a gotdamn waffle house ho. I want to see the mother of all press releases on my desk in thirty minutes. No, in twenty minutes. Listen to me: we are now at war. And we need to kick some serious vigilante blogger ass. And if we're going down, we're going to go down fighting with our swords ablaze and our heads strong. Good-bye." He slammed Erik's glass door behind him. I could see him in my mind's eye: striding across a newsroom of silent employees.

I was quietly sobbing, unable to speak. Finally a voice from the phone. It was Charles. "Jamie? Are you there?"

Somehow I managed an answer: "Yep." My life had turned into some kind of surreal horror show.

Now Erik. "Get yourself in front of a computer. We're going to have to draft this thing together right now. Then the lawyers will have a whack at it." He thought for a moment. "Jamie, I'm going to have to put your name on this as the lead producer. After Goodman, then me as the executive in charge. Charles can stay out of it. He went down to check, but it's not his baby, never was."

"I won't have it, Erik," said Charles. "I'm in this waist deep, I've been advising Jamie at the end here."

"Exactly. Just at the end. This isn't your baby. It's ours. We three gave birth to this monster, you just assisted. Your name's off the press release. We've got to save the careers we can." And thus, Charles was spared from the lions.

"Let's not get carried away, Erik," said Goodman. "I've been at this network for twenty-five years. I'm not gonna let this ruin a quarter century of good work."

"Goodman, sit down. This *is* going to ruin a quarter century of good work. Get used to it. The only solace is that Jamie and I are in this with you; that will soften—"

"Hey," responded Goodman in a crazed, high-pitched voice. "I only met her twice and I—"

"Don't you pull that fuckin' correspondent shit on any of us, Goodman. We've seen that one before, pretending like your producer did all the research and you were oblivious."

I fell on my sword. "I did do all the research."

"See, she said it herself," interjected Goodman. The slug. Ten years of loyalty to him, working my ass off to make him look better and smarter than he was. Never would I have seen that coming. Not from him. I felt sweat around my hairline. I tore off my sweater.

"Shut up, Goodman. We're in this together," said Erik. "The *three* of us are in this together."

Charles broke in. "I did the investigative checkup work, Erik. You really should make that four—"

"Charles, enough!" Erik was screaming now. "I want to keep anyone clean I can. This is going to be a fuckin' disaster in the coming days and I don't want to bring anyone down with us I don't have to."

Peter rubbed my back. I think I actually leaned into him. He didn't know what to say, or do, for that matter. So he started fanning me with a yellow satin throw pillow.

Erik started again. "Jamie, I'm sitting at my computer. I need you to go over, in chronological order, all your dealings with the Theresa monster from the very first time . . ."

I swallowed repeatedly to settle my stomach. Peter put the cold glass of ginger ale against my forehead and held the back of my neck.

"Jamie, what was the first—a call from her lawyer Leon Rosenberg telling us she was ready to talk, or did you go down to Pearl to try to get her to talk on your own? I forget. Did he solicit us with the interview or did I send you down there to sweet-talk . . ." Erik stopped. "Jamie? Are you still there?"

"I, I can't, Erik . . ."

"Jamie, stick with me, girl. We've got seventeen minutes to punch this sucker out. You have to remember, it can't be that hard . . ."

"Erik. It's not that." I was going to be sick, no question. "I'm . . . I'm . . . Excuse me . . ."

"Jamie!"

I stuffed a leopard pillow against my face and scrambled over the coffee table. I tripped on the other side, but regained my balance to keep from flying into the birthday party with another clumsy move. Peter scurried around the table and grabbed my elbow, but I smacked him away. Life was bad enough right now; I didn't want to puke all over him. I wanted to die. This whole thing was about to become front-page news for the next week, the network would be destroyed, Goodman's anchoring days were over, I would lose my job, my credibility. For the rest of my life, everyone would point to me and say, "That's the woman who fell for that waffle house wait-ress's story . . ."

I couldn't find the bathroom off Tom's office and almost ran head-first into a closet filled with his files when I swung open the door. I clutched the pillow tighter against my face.

"The kids' rooms are down that hall," Peter said, tugging at my arm. "I'm sure there's a bathroom off them."

I smacked his arm again, but he stayed close behind me. I ran down the hall, palming the walls to keep my balance. I tried another door. The linen closet. I started to taste the tomato tea sandwich in my mouth. There were only a few seconds left before I had a big accident on Susannah's beautiful hallway rug, in front of all the fancy Grid girls and their shell-encrusted toothpicks.

I made for the last door at the end of the hall. The doorknob was stuck, half locked, then Peter stepped in front of me and pushed it inward with brute force. A child's room at last. A bunny crib, a Peter Rabbit mobile, a cabinet filled with silver cups. I looked for a bath-room door. I looked right. Nothing. I looked left. Something. Some-thing horrible.

A woman lying on her back on the floor with her skirt pushed up around her belly and her beautiful legs pointing skyward in a perfect V punctuated on each end with her purple crocodile stilet-tos; her arms splayed on the floor at her sides. A man's head was buried between her legs. He was munching furiously on his prey, like an African lion with a freshly caught zebra. His butt in the air, clothed, thank God, in black pin-striped suit pants. His yellow striped starched shirt was untucked, his suit jacket crumpled in a pile next to him. The woman was moaning, "More, more." She suddenly grabbed the hair on the back of his head, pushed her pelvis into the air, and mashed his head farther against her. She slammed her right hand repeatedly against the floor. "Yes! Yes! Phillip! Yes!"

Phillip? *My* Phillip? And weren't those Susannah's favorite purple crocodile shoes?

32

Wild Life

Let's just say Phillip wasn't welcome in the house very much after that performance. And, a week later, I got fired.

My work, the pursuit that bound my self-esteem into a tight, sturdy package, gone in an instant. Those powers of regeneration and renewal and inspiration lost, when my judgment ever so briefly failed me.

Erik had tried so hard to save me, and all of us, but our vessel took on water too rapidly. For days after Theresa's bizarre testimonial aired, we all hung on, trying to come up with justifications that the public—and perhaps more important, our colleagues—could understand. We had checked her out: she had shown us receipts, the taped conversations sounded like Hartley. Three credible experts had confirmed his voice—how could we know they'd doctored the tapes so well?

But she had lied through her teeth. How could we have known? We didn't want people to commiserate with us, pity us; we wanted them to comprehend the context of our decisions. In the end, the public latched on to one thing: NBS investigators had fallen for a hoax, and Ms. Boudreaux had screwed us. She had even duped the savvy Leon Rosenberg. NBS being the most powerful network on television, people reveled in our undoing and danced on our graves. It was all so damn ugly.

When the vultures first started circling Bill Maguire, he fought back valiantly. For his own skin, that is. *Semper Fi,* my ass. He told the swarming media that he'd been at fault, that he'd made a mistake, blanketing the airwaves with his pleas of contrition. But he confessed to the wrong sin by telling them he'd taken a backseat to the production; that he'd been preoccupied with overall programming and left others to oversee the facts of the Theresa Boudreaux segment. Explaining that he asked us repeatedly to check our tracks and burrow into her background, he claimed ignorance and thus saved his job. His story seemed plausible to the public, at least to the media outsiders; he was the president of the news division, after all. Presidents didn't sully themselves with the dirty production details, did they? Insiders knew better.

And what was I supposed to do with that betrayal? Try to justify it? Try to understand? Acknowledge how far Maguire had come from the mean streets of Gary, Indiana, as though his hard-fought position excused him from loyalty to his colleagues? Was I supposed to be easy on him because he was black and grew up poor? I didn't give a hoot where he came from, whether he was black or white: he was a slime bucket who ducked for cover when he told me he'd stick with me. Rambo left us high and dry. He had been briefed on all the facts, and Maguire, the ex–Marine commander, on whose desk the buck stops, had decided to run the piece and pour himself a fucking glass of Wild Turkey.

When my fury subsided, my guilt seeped in and illuminated a more complex picture. I saw that Maguire didn't have to go down with us if he could articulate his supposed distance. My anger tortured me with its fuzzy, shifting rationales. In the end, Bill Maguire held on tight to his job, promising to keep closer track of his producers and to set up a team to reorganize the fact-checking process at the network.

And what of Goodman? The man I'd serviced for a decade? Helping him look more handsome and sound more intelligent than he could on his own? I'd fixed his scripts, sharpened his questions, powdered his shiny brow, and combed his wiry hair. He too claimed to be out of the loop when the daggers were drawn. Told everyone that news anchors travel so much, they can't keep track of all the stories they cover, can't possibly be responsible for all the investigative dirty work. That's what producers are for. Producers check the facts.

And so, Anchor Monster Joe Goodman was vanquished, but not destroyed. They reprimanded him publicly, removed him from *Newsnight,* but gave him his own unit for hour specials. That's exactly what he wanted anyway; he'd been lobbying for years to get off the *Newsnight* grind and have his own unit to cover "larger issues" in an hour-long, more in-depth manner. Some punishment.

And in the end, it was the producers who took the fall. Erik, true to form, stayed by my side to the bitter end. I'm not sure he had a choice. Erik and I were asked to resign, having betrayed the public trust. *Even though we couldn't have known. Never would have imagined.*

I waited outside Maguire's office one week after the interview aired. Ever since the Facts News revelations, he had been deliberating about my fate with *his* boss, the chairman of the parent company to NBS. Their board of directors was demanding heads, trying to save face, hoping not to lose customers in any of their publishing and cable divisions over the Theresa Boudreaux fiasco on the NBS network, their crown jewel.

Maguire welcomed me in and I knew instantly. "Jamie, I'm not going to play you, so let's get right down to it. I've met with the company's board. We're going to have to let you go, starting right now. Of course, the severance will be . . ."

I sat before him, speechless. I quickly scanned the room. He certainly didn't look like *he* was packing. I guess the little people lose their jobs while the chieftains remain safe. Not the first time this book has been written.

"The severance? That's it? A decade here and we're on to the severance in the second sentence?"

"Jamie, don't make this uglier than it is."

"Bill, I did nothing wrong. I've been here my whole life, or almost, my whole real career. This isn't . . . it's not fair. I couldn't ever have known I'd be intentionally duped by crazy people with a vendetta against the entire network! They were hitting *you,* not just a cog in the wheel like me."

Maguire shrugged.

I went on. "I checked everything out ten times. There's no way I could have known."

"You produced the piece that let us down."

"I voiced my doubts. *You,* who never leaves his troops behind, told me you'd covered campaigns, that you knew better, that the buck stopped with you."

"You are in no position to throw that back at me. And the buck damn well did stop here!"

"Then why am I losing my job? *You* are the president of the news division! You green-lit the piece!"

"This is the way it is."

"Why can't you save your men, isn't that what the Marines are all about, isn't that what *Semper Fi* means, didn't you learn anything in—?"

"Jamie, it's done. It's all over now."

"But I—"

"It's over."

There was nothing more I could say.

"Maybe I could take the fall with you. But I'm not going down over this. I've always been crystal clear that this was your baby." He leaned forward over the desk. "As I told you in Erik's office, ultimately you are the producer of the piece. And you are very wrong about those last points you just made. Very wrong. You raised doubts, you did not insist we kill the piece, and there's a very big difference."

I paused. The Marine had a point. And here was the odd thing: at this horrible moment when I was getting axed, all I could think about was Peter. Why I'd dismissed him. Why I'd had a tin ear to his views: all to keep my feelings for him at bay.

"We may have pushed you, but you're going to have to live with the fact that you allowed us to push you. I told you if you jumped up and down in my office, I wouldn't run the piece. You fought a bit, but not enough. You didn't punch hard, you just swatted the air and then withdrew. You were taking on one of the most important dogs in our government. This is grown-up time, not bitch and whine time. I didn't betray you, Jamie. You're the best I've got. You betrayed yourself. You didn't trust your judgment enough. You relented to three older, more experienced men. That's where you erred, and that, ironically and truthfully, is why you are losing your job."

Abby was distraught when I came back from the executive suite. "What am I going to do without you?" she howled through her tears.

"Well, what do you think I'm going to do without my job?"

"You'll find another, you're so good at what you do," she reasoned.

"I'm radioactive, Abby. No one is going to hire me, they can't. My name's been in every news outlet in the country, linked to this fiasco. Even if they want to, it will be in the papers that they hired me and it will reflect badly on them."

"No, it won't," she pleaded.

I raised my eyebrows.

She continued. "Okay, maybe it will, and maybe you are radioactive right now, but it will dissipate, like Chernobyl."

"Abby, no one has moved back within a twenty-mile radius of Chernobyl; it'll be radioactive through the next century."

"Oh."

"Uh . . . yeah. Not like you not to know that."

"All right, then you won't be like Chernobyl, you'll be like a nuclear reactor accident that almost happened, but didn't in the end."

"Abby, in this story the accident did happen."

Later that afternoon, I took Dylan for a walk in the park to tell him what went down at NBS. He needed to be anchored, he needed me to explain to him in simple terms exactly what had happened with Mommy's job. Theresa Boudreaux had lied to me, not to hurt me, but to hurt the whole television network. It had nothing to do with me. He was relieved I wasn't the target. After we talked, we went up to Belvedere Castle to have a look at the view and check out the wildlife. I was sitting ten feet behind my son, straddling the thick railing of the top balcony with my back against the castle tower. The wind picked up a little and I pulled my huge shearling coat tighter, the bitter cold alleviated by the strong afternoon sun shining down on us. The familiarity of that spot was comforting in a world that had otherwise fallen out from under me.

"The turtles keep moving around. I can't keep up and lose count."

"You do know you've been counting them down there for like ten minutes, Dylan."

Inside my pocket, I rubbed my fingers against the engraving on the back of the stopwatch Peter had given me—*Time for another dance.*

"There's one turtle that can't get up. He's like so close, but he can't get on the rocks. So he keeps paddling like crazy, then gives up and tries another spot that seems easier."

"I'm cold, we can watch the wildlife another time, sweetheart, we need to go soon."

"I'm sure he is too. Why can't they just give him a push with their heads? They're just watching him suffer."

"So are you, Dylan."

"Yeah, but I want him to get up. And I would help him. They're not. I want to stay."

"Fine. I know that this is your favorite spot. So take your time."

"Is that lady going to jail? Do you go to jail for lying on TV?"

"Unfortunately not. She's moved far away to some island, no one even knows where she is."

"That's weird. It's weird that Peter isn't here."

"He'd love to be here, sweetheart."

"What happened at Anthony's party?"

The sun moved behind the clouds. "That's when the lady went on TV. And Mommy and Daddy had a disagreement there. How's the turtle doing?"

"I think I'm over it," Dylan answered.

I put my arm around him. "You want to go home?"

"I want to ask some more questions."

"Shoot."

"Are you and Daddy ever going to love each other again?"

"I told you, honey. We will always love each other. We are just taking some time. This is a very confusing time for children. But it's not your fault."

"I know. Why does everyone keep saying that to me? I never said it was my fault."

"I don't know, honey. Grown-ups have crazy ideas in their heads."

33

A Funny Thing Called Fear

Six Weeks Later

February 1. The morning of the Hermitage benefit, I woke up late. A bit of insomnia exacerbated the headache that had greeted me most mornings ever since that ghastly afternoon at Susannah's apartment. With the covers over my head, burying my face under a pillow, I tried to will the pain away. Not a chance.

The phone rang. "I have an idea! Beyond genius. Oscar's on his way up."

"Ingrid, stop. I'm sleeping."

"Not anymore. It's nine o'clock. Get out of those pajamas and get dressed. He's probably got his hand on the knocker right now."

"Why on earth is he coming up here?"

"We're redoing your life. Time to get organized. I have a new line of work for you. I've got it all figured out. A new job. You're not good with the unemployment thing."

I managed to rouse myself into a sitting position. "Ingrid, you've been a wonderful friend. But—"

"I told Oscar, no matter what you did, he was to go straight into your closet. With a camera. Or else I'm going to fire him."

"What!"

"He's going to photograph your clothes. He's good with digital cameras. Then he's going to Bridgehampton to do the same."

"I don't have any clothes there."

"So he'll photograph your clothes there." She wasn't listening. She was on an Ingrid roll, all excited, like she'd stumbled on North Korea's nuclear code. "Then he's going to Kinko's to laminate the photos, totally neat and catalogued by color, and then by season, and then by dressiness factor, then by house, in a notebook. You're nonstop chic. That way you know where everything is. You're organized. You never look for anything. Then you match them. Like Garanimals. Of course, your book will be pathetic, but you'll get the concept better if you go through the steps with him. He did it for me. He's bringing mine. It's gorgeous. Yours will be hideous, but at least you'll have the skills."

"Are you out of your mind?"

"Everyone wants them, but they can't execute. There's only one Oscar."

"And . . ."

"You're going to produce these books! You'll direct the shoots, you'll organize the books. Now you're a producer *and* an author! Presto!"

Carolina stuck her head in the bedroom door. "Mrs. Harris's driver is here."

There was no stopping Oscar. Ingrid was so terrifying when she gave him an order, I let the poor guy do his thing. Now the Park Avenue ladies were trying to manage my career. Beyond depressing.

But I was used to being depressed those months. A plastic smile stretched across my face all the time as I tried valiantly to act happy in front of the kids. I still tried to go through the motions, to make an effort to spend some family time together and have dinners with Phillip. There were even days where I wanted to save my marriage—for me, for us, for the children especially.

Phillip, banished first to the couch in his study, tried to be contrite, but didn't succeed. Mostly he went to sleep in his mother's guest room. We had been to therapy a dozen times to discuss the reasons behind his actions—he felt distant from me, he didn't think I would care because I didn't seem to be attached to him anymore, he craved attention and love. All good reasons to stray, I assume, but while the therapy helped me see things clearer, it didn't change the empty-well reality in my heart.

As for Peter, at least he waited until the New Year.

It happened in the kitchen, after the kids were in bed: the first Friday night in January, when Carolina had gone for the weekend and Phillip at that very moment was boarding the red-eye from San Francisco.

The conversation on the sidewalk played in my head constantly. *I'm not going to touch you for real unless, first of all, you tell me it's something you want for sure, and second, until you are no longer with him.* He wanted me, he wanted us. And I wasn't ready to make that plunge for real. I couldn't just go sleep with him at the Carlyle Hotel one day and act normal the next. There didn't seem a way to go halfway with him; what were we going to do? Go to second base and stop there? And perhaps most important, even though Phillip had betrayed me, that didn't give me license to do the same.

That betrayal, while shocking, didn't push me over the edge immediately. I needed a few months to totter on that edge, just to see what the landscape beyond looked like before I let go. And Peter, sensing my hesitation, had been cooling. He said he was distracted with his program, but I knew better. Clearly he was waiting for me, wondering why I didn't leave my husband immediately after the betrayal. But I was paralyzed, still trying to keep the family together for the kids. To give it my best. And then, of course, there was that funny thing called fear.

I was stirring some chamomile tea by the counter when Peter walked in, around nine p.m., after he put Dylan down.

"So," he'd said, standing right in front of me. "Game over." He took my hands in his. No crazy turn-on massaging this time.

"Can you at least look at me?" he asked.

"I'm not sure." A wave of grief spread down my body.

"Well, then it's game over in a way I hadn't even imagined."

"What?" I looked up.

"I can't stay."

I closed my eyes. "You can't do this."

"You're right, J.W., I can't do this. So I'm leaving."

"What can't you do?"

"This game. This hide-and-seek, house-of-mirrors bullshit. Either you and I are doing something here or we're not. And you can't deal. And you won't move. And it's almost like you're enjoying feeling shitty all day."

"Can't you be patient? I've gone through hell here."

"I have been patient. And now, I'm saying it finally: I can't stay here when I feel the way I do about you."

"Really?"

"Grow the fuck up, would you? Of course I do. What kind of bizarre denial state are you in? I've tried so hard to lay back and be supportive. But it's too hard."

"I know."

"Not being able to hold you, to be with you, to show you how I feel, when you're all held back and cold and weird and not dealing. And what for? Because of him? That cheating prick? You waiting for his okay?"

"No. It's just so hard to make the break."

"What are you scared of? Scared you might even be happy?"

"That's not it." I don't think.

"Well then, what are you waiting for?"

"The kids, Phillip—I just can't move yet."

"You know what?" Peter looked wounded, frustrated, and resigned. "That's fine. That's just fucking A-OK, but I'm not waiting around here for you to decide to move."

"So what are you going to do?"

"I told Dylan just now."

I didn't like that one bit. "How could you?"

"He's fine. I've been coming less anyway. I'm going to take him to the Adventurers sports group every Monday still. I told him I had a lot of work. But that I'd still be hanging with him on Mondays."

"How'd he take it?"

"He was tired. He's a kid. He's in the present. I reminded him Monday is two days away. And he liked that part."

"Uh, so . . ."

"So I'll pick him up on Mondays, go with him, and leave him downstairs with the doorman and he can come up on his own."

"You mean like this is a divorce and you can't even come up?"

"Hey, that's your choice, baby."

And then he gently held my neck with one hand, kissed me softly on the lips, and walked out the door.

I was devastated. And his mouth was perfect.

That February night, Phillip and I, bravely pretending we were actually a happily married couple, walked out of the hired car and up the steps to the DuPont Museum. I didn't own a white fur shrug, or a floor-length white coat, so I'd wrapped a white cashmere shawl around my shoulders, which worked about as well as cheesecloth against the single-digit temperatures. Phillip put his arm around me to keep me warm. I let myself lean into him, trying to suck some warmth out of his body. As I walked up the dozens of marble steps, I thought about last night, why I had done what I had done. It had all started when he came into the bathroom, after he'd put the kids to bed.

He had said, "Jamie, if you'll still have me as your date as we had planned, I would very much like to take you to the benefit tomorrow night."

I splashed my face with water and looked at him. "I don't know," I answered in a neutral tone. I wasn't feeling particularly angry with him for a change, perhaps because I hadn't seen him for the past two days.

"Well, I was hoping for a little more information than that."

I held my wet toothbrush like a pointer. "How can you expect anything?"

"I know I'm hoping for too much, but I thought maybe since we hadn't fought for a while, I could sleep in our bed for the first time in seven weeks, as a special thing, tomorrow night after the benefit."

Making him suffer wasn't that much fun anymore. He just looked at me: no pleading, no begging, just direct in his Phillip way. He had betrayed me, yes, but he had explained why he did it and he had apologized. He didn't ever whimper or whine for forgiveness, which I appreciated and respected. I was trying to forgive him, trying to accept his apologies, trying to work things through.

"Jamie, so what do you think? Can I still take you to the benefit and can I then sleep in our bed?"

Dr. Rubenstein had said that sex might heal us, would break the wall of anger. How could I have sex with him when I endlessly fantasized about Peter?

"Jamie, I'm not going to ask every day, just every other day as I have since this tragedy started. Denying me sex is an effective weapon in your arsenal, and I understand that. We could give it a try. You're on the committee, you're going to be dressed in a beautiful gown, you'll want a man by your side." I didn't answer.

"Besides, if you won't do it for us, just do it for Gracie. If it's true the whole Pembroke board will be there, we should meet them together, arm in arm. Smiling." He put his fingers on either side of his mouth to make his smile bigger, faker.

I laughed. I felt kind of bad for him. He was trying so hard. "Okay, be my date. But I'm not sure about the sleeping arrangements."

Then he gave me a hug.

That took me by surprise; even more so when he clung to me like a huge brown bear. He rubbed his fingers deep into my spine and didn't let go. We stood there, not sure of the rules. He closed his eyes and kissed me. Softly at first, then with more passion. A tear rolled down my cheek. He kissed it away.

"Let's give it a try. I know what you like."

I told myself to let my inhibitions go like a college girl, the way you do when you sleep with a stranger. He led me to the bed. And I sat on the edge, stroking my forehead with my fingers.

"You have some matches, Jamie?"

"In the drawer."

He was getting all geared up with no return. Should I say no right now? Should I tell him I don't want him? Should I try?

Phillip lit two candles. Then he walked over to dim the lights and lock our bedroom door. "I have some plans for you."

I forced myself to lie down.

"I still love you, Jamie. You're a lovely woman."

Phillip climbed on the bed and started to kiss my forehead and then my mouth. I arched my back, trying to get comfortable. He pushed my nightgown up and laid his head on my stomach. Maybe I could do this.

"There's only you."

I was trying to think sexy thoughts, but instead I considered asking him if he went down on my former friend Susannah the same way he went down on me.

"You've deprived me. You're getting me so hot."

I closed my eyes again. This was going to take an immense amount of concentration. I willed myself to touch the familiar contours of his back, his arms, those slim legs, to try to focus on Phillip's body, not Phillip the man. It began to feel like home again.

When we were done, he said, "Don't forget how good we can be."

Tears streamed down my face. Phillip smiled tenderly; I knew he believed I was falling in love with him again. He grabbed my chin. "We're gonna make this work."

I pulled back.

"C'mon, Jamie, don't resist me just for the sake of resisting me."

Was I just resisting him for the sake of it? Maybe. Was it just lingering anger? Was Peter even real? I looked at my husband's face, seeing the little lines around his mouth and the freckles near his eyes. There was something . . . there. Between us. Some reason I stayed beyond the children and the creature comforts. Or was it just fear? Peter's voice rang in my head. *What are you scared of? Scared you might even be happy?*

The snapping of fingers in front of my face. "Jamie, snap out of it. Just let go and forgive and let's move on together."

"Phillip." I sighed. "I'm not ready to make a decision. And it's not just Susannah . . ."

"Haven't I taken good care of you and the children? We have a history, Jamie."

"I'm not giving up, I'm deciding what to do, what I want. There's a difference. A big one."

We lay there silently for a while. I started feeling restless and claustrophobic, like I'd led him on, and I didn't want that.

I sat up abruptly. "Phillip. This is all very fast. And completely unexpected. Please, I need you to go back into your study tonight to sleep. Or your mother's." To my surprise, he got up willingly. He knew he'd gotten farther than he'd imagined. He was smart enough not to push any further.

34

The Belle of the Ball

A sea of air kisses. Arms flying in the air. Women twirling their white gowns like five-year-olds playing princess dress-up. Exaggerated "Helloooooooo's," and "Look at yooooou's." Phillip and I stood in the huge museum entry foyer with marble vaulted ceilings that amplified the voices below, pinging them back and forth across the arches. Fluffy white Hollywood snow had been piled in the corners of each step on the majestic marble stairway, and holly and evergreen branches had been artfully laced through its bronze balusters. Enormous jeweled eggs, replicas of the original Fabergé masterpieces, hung unevenly from transparent wires all over the ceiling. White-gloved waiters in white tuxedos served Phillip and me champagne from silver trays and we searched for some people we actually liked while we nodded to the many others we knew from the Grid or school drop-offs.

"There's one, there." A young woman pointed to me, photographer Punch Parish at her side.

They were about twenty feet away, standing beside a white spray-painted palm tree dripping with golden eggs. Punch was too preoccupied with the social climbers in the room who were circling him like hyenas around a campfire. There were the unabashed ass-kissers, laughing at his every word, slapping his arm for his naughty remarks: "Oh, Punch! Stop! You're *too much*!" Then the too-cool-for-school girls who pretended not to care if he took their picture, but wanted to make sure they were on his radar. "Hi, Punch!" they yelled, waving their bejeweled little wrists and walking past him, knowing full well he wouldn't have enough time to get them in a shot just then. He would have to show an effort and find *them* in the room later on, or so they secretly prayed. And the real socialites, desperate for his attention, milling around the edge of his orbit with a studied nonchalance that could win Oscars. All this for a man they would never deign to acknowledge, save for the camera hanging around his neck.

The Verdura woman tugged at Punch's shirt. "Over there, we have to. She's wearing some nice items. Remember? We're your client? Verdura?"

Exasperated, Punch tried to get a better look at me. I pretended not to notice. "Who?" he asked her. "Why her?"

She pinched her earlobes, no doubt explaining to him that I had fifteen-thousand-dollar Verdura earrings dripping from my ears. She needed a shot of me for publicity pictures.

"She can wait. You'll find her later."

The woman ran up to me and introduced herself, Jennifer something, the PR girl from Verdura. "I forgot your name, but I know we gave you the earrings and we need some shots, please. Punch! Come here! I need one of this woman here! We might lose her later."

He ignored her.

She said, "By the way, we'll need the earrings back tonight, right after dinner. Our guy is waiting in a room just off the kitchen."

"I know. Someone explained everything—"

"We'll find you. What is your name again?" She took out a notebook. At first I had appreciated the idea of borrowing a gown and jewels: easy, not to mention free. Now I felt used, cheap, tacky, wearing product to hawk someone else's business.

"My name is Jamie Whitfield; this is my husband, Phillip."

"That's right, of course. Just stand together and lose the drinks behind your backs, please. Punch! I've got them set! Now please!" He aimed his camera toward us from fifteen feet away without even

looking through the viewfinder. Two flashes. He winked and continued his conversation.

"Good." She looked at her pad. "Just two more to go." She left
without saying thank you or good-bye.

"Tom!" Phillip grabbed the arm of one of his law partners.

Tom Preston turned around and faced us, whispered to his wife,
and we both caught his wife muttering to him. Obviously he wasn't
to linger with work colleagues when she could mingle with the
drop-off hens. While the two men talked, his wife kept rubbernecking at the crowd. So did Tom. I saved them both. "Phillip, excuse me,
but we need to find our hosts."

The wife smiled brightly for the first time. "Oh yes, Tom, let's not
hold them up."

The room was unbearably loud, I felt humiliated by the earring
moment, angry with Tom's bitchy wife, and I could sense Phillip's frustration. He was not in command of this situation. I wanted Peter to
surprise me and have his way with me behind a seven-foot-tall egg.

"Damn it, Jamie. Who are these people?"

"I don't know. They're Christina's crowd, I guess."

"You bring me here and you don't know anyone?"

"I do, they're just . . ." I started to feel rattled for a moment because
I needed to fix this.

"I'm not going to stand here like an idiot, let's move!" He grabbed
my hand and pulled me around the room, searching furiously for
some familiar faces.

Christina pinched my bottom and I jumped. "Hello, darling!" she
said. "You look very sexy from the back. I don't know how your
husband keeps his hands off you."

Phillip broke in. "It's almost impossible. Thank you for having us,
Christina." He put his arm around me and pulled me in close. No one
knew about him and Susannah. No one knew we as a couple were
ending.

"And, Jamie, I'm sooo sorry about the magazine. I can't believe John
Henry would cut *anyone* from my table off the cover," said Christina.

"It's fine. Really."

Christina, looking like a glorious social swan of yesteryear, wore a chiffon Carolina Herrera halter gown, with crystal beads holding the dress around her long neck and a short ruffled train flowing behind her. I air-kissed her very rich husband, George, who looked like the most asexual human being I had ever seen. He stood erect like a toy soldier with a little neat potbelly. Thick Brylcreem held back his black hair, accentuating his balding hairline and neat rows of hair replace-ment grafts.

"George, Christina, what an elegant crowd. We appreciate your having us at your table."

"Oh, Jamie. The pleasure is ours." George kissed my hand. "I can't wait to discuss the elections with you."

God help me.

An old, short man, looking like a waddling penguin in white tails, walked around the room ringing a little gong to announce dinner. We walked down a baronial hallway with the Pattens and two other couples from our table. The wives, Leelee and Fenoula, didn't even remember meeting me at the photo shoot.

The ceiling of the DuPont Museum had been covered entirely in white birch branches, forming a thick canopy. About fifty tables of ten, covered in blood-red cloths, filled the atrium room. White and red roses cascaded down the fountain-shaped centerpieces on each table. More windswept Hollywood snow was sprinkled in the corners of the room, crevices of the marble columns, and across the black marble dance floor. Our table was right near the stage.

Christina immediately introduced us to the president of the bene-fit committee, Patsy Cabot, a plump woman in her early sixties with a sensible haircut. She ran the board of the Pembroke School. Patsy stuck out her chubby hand and smiled efficiently to my husband and me—just the kind of no-nonsense *Mayflower* descendant who adored Phillip. I noticed she had a simple Timex watch with a tan leather band—perhaps the only woman in the room without a dress watch.

"It's wonderful to meet you, Patsy." He shook her hand like a Boy

Scout, just as his mother had taught him to do. "You have done a remarkable job for an important cultural and historic cause."

"I appreciate that. Thank you, Phillip. I am trying."

He continued. "After all, the Hermitage, after ninety years of Communist neglect, has finally regained its imperial stature. As it should."

Patsy batted her eyes at my husband, intrigued that someone seemed to care about the purpose of the event rather than what the women were wearing. "You know something about the Winter Palace?"

"Oh, yes." I looked at Phillip as if he had lost his mind.

"Really? Have you been to St. Petersburg?"

Phillip ignored her question and chuckled arrogantly. "Patsy. The Winter Palace holds the greatest collection of Fabergé eggs, most of them commissioned by Alexander III and Nicholas II for their spouses. My favorite, of course, being the Lily of the Valley egg. Crucial work you're doing to protect the heritage of these masterpieces." He had never once talked about saving a cultural institution or the mere existence of the Fabergé eggs.

"I adore that one. There's a model of it over there . . ." She pointed to the corner of the room.

"I know. With miniature portraits of Nicholas II and the Grand Duchesses Olga and Tatiana—for Empress Alexandra." He touched her shoulder.

"You, you know the eggs well?"

"Like my own children." Phillip looked down, feigning modesty. He'd won over juries, colleagues, and clients with this same magic. I stood there watching him hypnotize Patsy and felt a tug inside. He was so effective in situations like this.

"Really?"

"Yes. Really."

Patsy sucked in a deep breath and inflated her bosom. "Have you seen the Coronation egg with your own eyes?"

"I have. A religious experience. With its golden background of yellow starbursts and the Imperial Eagle at each trellised intersection with . . ."

She finished his sentence: "the miniature Nicholas and Alexandra coach inside! How do you know so much about . . ."

"There is no greater calling than preserving the masterpieces of our time," he said. I pinched his hip and he patted my shoulder, telling me to stay calm and shut up. "My father, Phillip Whitfield II, my namesake, had a phenomenal book collection that he and I would pore through during our summers in Plymouth. We'd sit under the willow tree in our hammock and study great works of art and where they were held. I know every room of the Hermitage by heart: the exact placement of da Vinci's *Madonna Litta,* of Rubens's *Bacchus,* of Picasso's *Three Women.*" He looked her deep in her eyes as if he were fucking her senseless, something I was absolutely positive she had never experienced.

"And all my favorite pieces are tightly locked in the Hermitage, in *your* museum, Patsy. I would love to get my hands on them." He breathed thickly through his flared nostrils.

"*My* favorite work, that has hung in the front room of the first floor for a century, is Titian's *Danae,*" said Patsy, dizzy now.

"A century minus four years during the Siege of Leningrad, when over a million Hermitage masterpieces were sent to the Urals, a safe distance from the Nazis."

"Touché!" moaned Patsy, as if he had just penetrated her.

My daughter was into Pembroke before we even applied.

Dinner was less successful. After a few introductory remarks by the heads of the DuPont Museum board and the Hermitage board, I couldn't wait to leave. Christina's painfully dull husband, George, wanted to talk about current events for the first time in his life with a real journalist. He asked inane, open-ended, sophomoric questions like "How long will the Iraqi insurgency last?" and "Why do you think Hillary is such a polarizing political figure?"

Phillip was seated next to the wife of a man he despised, Jack Avins, he of the Hadlow Holdings deal. Alexandra Avins, diamonds the size of headlights in her ears, droned on and on about how the architect and the contractor had been at each other's throats during the construction of their new Sun Valley home. Phillip had a sour expression on his face through the appetizer, which I knew would only get worse. I walked over to his seat and asked him to dance, anything to get away from the boring, self-indulgent, pretentious people at our table.

He held my back firmly, leading me with confidence as we glided by other couples. For a moment, I allowed myself to enjoy his strong touch, his handsome, tall frame.

The twenty-piece orchestra, all men in white tuxedos, played "In the Mood." Phillip twirled me around boldly, proud of himself, his cantankerous mood softening. As if on cue, they switched to our wedding song, "Fly Me to the Moon." First I'd had sex with my husband, now we were moving to a wrenching song under white birch branches and a thousand flickering candles. He pulled me in closer.

"Thank you for helping me escape Alexandra Avins. I can't even look at that presumptuous prick of a husband of hers."

I whispered into his ear, "You were unbelievable with Patsy Cabot."

"I know." He spun me around.

"How did you . . . ?"

"Just like closing arguments, with a little help from a research packet an associate prepared."

Maybe, maybe, maybe I could fall back into tune with him. He *was* a phenomenal dancer.

"You look gorgeous tonight. That dress, those earrings, and don't get me started on last night. I'm getting hard just thinking about it." He pushed against me. He wasn't joking about being turned on. I tried to convince myself that Peter didn't really love me the way a husband would, that it was just make-believe with him. I felt comfortable with Phillip for the first time in six weeks and remembered that the sex wasn't that bad last night. And Jesus, he was smooth on the dance floor. The kids needed us to be together; maybe I could close my eyes and jump back in . . .

He looked around the room. "There is some serious goddamn *cashish* in this room. Let's take George and Christina to dinner soon. I want you to have some more dinners." He kissed my forehead. I didn't want to have any dinners with the Pattens. "Let's just move in this direction . . . I see a client." He glided us closer to the front of the dance floor and waved to a man seated alone at a table. "Hey, Phillip!" the man said. Phillip leaned over and shook his hand, strongly gripping my back with the other. "That's exactly what I mean. More potential clients. Fewer journalists, more of this cultured set." He spun me around some more.

"These people are not cultured, Phillip. They are showy and vulgar. And unintellectual and boring."

"I disagree. I think you're rebelling again."

I stopped dancing. "I am not rebelling, Phillip. This is all about getting our daughter into Pembroke."

"Really?"

"Yes. I don't like these people."

"You're in a free dress and jewels, you're getting your picture taken, you seem to fit in just fine."

"I'm regretting that."

"It's the same thing over and over. You're not in Kansas anymore. Stop fighting it." He grabbed me in close. "Just go with it."

"It has nothing to do with whether I come from New York or not. I just don't like these people up close and personal."

"I remind you once again you got your picture taken, Miss Social Butterfly."

My back stiffened. He didn't notice.

"I don't even want that picture published. I don't feel like being a complicit cog in someone's marketing strategy . . ."

"Did I or did I not see a glossy spread of you posing in a white dress with the most fabulous socialites in New York? In front of eggs, no less?"

"That was a big mistake."

"You seemed pretty into it at the time. I know you hate to admit that." He patted my butt. By teasing me, he thought he'd broken through to normal times. His familiarity only infuriated me. I wasn't ready for him to lose his repentant tone.

"Well, I'm not excited anymore. Trust me."

"Fine. I do trust you. I just think it's great that you're cozying up to these people. It's good for us, as a couple. Once we're through this stage, I mean. I'm enjoying myself. Jack Avins aside."

"You didn't look like you were having fun at dinner, that's why we're dancing."

"Doesn't matter if I was having fun. Did some business. May have persuaded that guy at our table to hire us for a big transaction. I could make some serious dough-re-mi tonight."

Back at home, Phillip fiddled with his black tie studs. The White Nights' dramatic glamour that had momentarily lifted my husband's aspirational spirit now darkened his mood. "Jack Avins is an asshole." He stepped out of his tuxedo pants and carefully hung them on the hanger.

"You need to move on from that one deal."

"And his wife had bad crabcake breath. Help me with this." I untied his bow tie like any wife would do.

"I do appreciate your efforts with Patsy Cabot."

"Thanks." He looked very grumpy.

"I'm sorry you didn't have fun at dinner, Phillip. We weren't planning on having—"

"Can't stand Jack Avins."

"That's come through loud and clear."

"Can't believe I worked on the same deal with him and that dickhead has his own plane."

"Jack Avins runs a big fund. His father—"

"What do I get? Just fuckin' lawyer fees." Phillip shook his head. "It's not right. I made that Hadlow Holdings deal happen for him."

"Phillip, we've got plenty of—"

"We don't, Jamie."

"Yes, we do."

"I was the poorest guy in the room. I'm swimming against the tide." He was pissed at me for suggesting anything to the contrary. "You don't get it, do you?"

I got it all too well.

"Can't you see?" He pulled off his socks and wrapped them in a little ball that he shook in my face. "I'm working hard as an ox and still I've got limits all around me. Limits everywhere. I can't even—"

"No, you don't."

"Yes. I do. I want to be *limitless,* like the guys at our table, around that whole room." He tore his shirt off and threw it forcefully into the hamper in his closet.

"Phillip, what are you saying? We've got plenty of—"

"Here's what I'm saying: I want a plane. I want it to take off." He outstretched his arms and ran around in little circles in his boxers, as if he were flying through the clouds. "I want the pilot to say to me, 'Where are we going, sir?' I want to tell him back, 'I don't know, I'll tell you when I fucking feel like it.'"

I scratched my head. He looked at me blankly.

"Sleep on the couch, Phillip" was all I could muster.

35

Grown-up Time-out

"How come Daddy isn't coming to Aspen with us, Mommy?" asked Gracie. Her car seat was wedged between two huge duffel bags. Ski bags protruded from the trunk, past the third row, into the middle row. It was a little after dawn on the Friday before Presidents' Day weekend, and the kids, Yvette, and I were heading to Kennedy Airport in the SUV.

"Because Mommy doesn't like him anymore," answered Dylan matter-of-factly. "That's why he's been sleeping in his study or Nana's apartment and that's why they trade off weekends."

"Dylan!" I snapped. "You know that's not true. I have enormous admiration for your father. And he loves you very much, no matter whether we are having some disagreements." I gave him a dirty look. "And you are not being helpful to the little ones."

"Are you divorced now?" Gracie piped in.

"Honey, that's a big word for a little girl. All you need to know is Daddy and I are very good friends and we will always be your parents and we will always love you. In order to be the best parents we can, we need a little time out from each other."

Dylan continued defiantly. "She doesn't like Daddy anymore. The same way she doesn't like Anthony's mom, Mrs. Briarcliff, anymore."

He was right about that. I'd ignored Susannah at the school scene, making it impossible for her to give me a sorry-assed explanation in person. "Dylan, you are completely off base and out of line. You and I have talked a lot about this. We all have as a family. If you have any more questions about what is going on, we can talk about them tonight before bedtime. Now is not the right moment."

"Well, then how come you don't talk to her at pickup if she's supposed to be your best friend?"

"She was never my best friend. Kathryn is my best friend."

"Okay, a *close* friend, excuuuuse me!" He humphed and stared out the window.

Two hours later, the lumbering 737 roared its engines and bounced over the cracks in the runway. As it gained speed, I held Gracie's hand tightly and leaned my head against the hard clear plastic window. Two months had gone by since the "incident."

Phillip's pleading to come with us to Aspen played in my head for a brief moment as we took off, but then drifted away with the clouds that rushed past the window. We'd planned this trip together six months ago. Everything was nonrefundable. Left to my own devices, I would have chosen a more low-key, un-Grid locale. Regardless, I reasoned, the mountains would have curative powers. My stomach fell to my feet as we made the sharp initial ascent. Gracie looked up at me and smiled with droopy eyes. I placed her bunny in the crook of her neck and helped her lay her head on my lap, and she drifted off. And so did I.

When I woke up, we were flying over the Rockies. The mountains and sky filled the entire frame of the window and the world seemed like a very big place. I don't know whether it was the beauty of the rocky cliffs jutting up above the clouds, or the rush of independence I felt at taking my kids on our first trip together without Phillip. Or the simple knowledge that having them on my own as a permanent concept didn't faze me at all. In fact, what a relief not to be hauling along a fourth child in the form of a six-foot-tall whining preppy. So, looking down at the Colorado River cutting through the rock face, I felt happy. Content. Resolved. I wanted a divorce. I even had started to say the word. Ingrid had come down last night for a glass of wine and noticed that we weren't packing bags for my husband. When I explained that he wouldn't be coming on a lot of vacations, she got the drift. ("Honey, I have some videos that will get you through this period," she offered.) And I'd tell Phillip when we returned from the long weekend.

And that meant I was ready to talk to Peter for real. Ready to tell him what he'd been waiting for. He'd been pulling away steadily since our big conversation in the kitchen. When I'd met him down in the lobby the last few Mondays, he'd said he was too rushed to talk. He canceled on Dylan because of some work in Silicon Valley. Then he didn't return two phone calls. I began to worry about that skinny, beautiful Pixie Girl at the bar in Red Hook. I bet he didn't say no when she climbed into his bed naked these days. Had I lost him? The uncertainty gnawed at me. Deep down I knew he'd listen when I called, and that he'd welcome the news. I had to tell myself that. I closed my eyes and repeated it to myself: *He'll be there. He'll be there.*

Someone was jerking me awake. "Jamie? Good God! Is that you? In coach? Why?"

I flickered my eyes open. Then two toothpick legs right in front of my eyes. Alligator cowboy boots. A kagillion-dollar turquoise and sterling belt with matching earrings. Tan suede chaps with fringe over the jeans. A chinchilla vest. And, worst of all, a black cowboy hat. Christina Patten. Fuck me.

"Are you, like, dying back here?"

"We're managing." I looked over her shoulder for her lasso.

"There's so many people. In so many nylon warm-up suits. Oh God." Then she knelt down and whispered, "And they all look like Joey Buttafuoco." I wanted to tell her it was preferable to looking like Dale Evans, but I didn't have the nerve.

Grid people like Christina bring new meaning to the term "fashion victim." For example, they get on the plane to Aspen in New York looking like East Coast royalty in their khakis and luxurious, sherbet-colored, cashmere cable knits. But then, somewhere over the midwestern plains, they sneak into the bathroom with their carry-on bags and they emerge as cowboys and cowgirls. They *have* to nail the cowboy chic look the minute they enter Colorado airspace. Just in case Ralph Lauren shows up and invites them to ride bareback on a palomino once they touch ground.

Just across the aisle, Yvette shot me a look.

"Didn't know you were coming." Christina surveyed our row. "Phillip's not with you?"

"Nope."

"Well then, let's get together! How fun! Let's have dinner Saturday, the kids will love it. Does your house come with a chef?"

"Amazingly enough, it doesn't. And we need some family time. So, I'm sorry, I just can't do it."

"Are you sure?"

"Thank you, but we can't."

"I see." Her eyes swept across the poverty-stricken landscape of steerage. "Well then. Can I at least bring you back a mimosa?"

"I'm going back to sleep now, Christina."

We landed in Aspen at about three in the afternoon after a two-hour layover and connection in Denver. Five juice-and-Sbarro-pizza-stained beings trudging through the aisle, pulling wheelie bags filled with sippy cups, cards, markers, portable DVD players, trailing sweaters and snow jackets. Yvette, wearing a tight maroon warm-up suit that only made her large frame look heavier, carried in her arms a screaming Michael, who, minutes ago, had been rudely awakened from his slumber. I, from the rear, tried valiantly to get Gracie and Dylan to steer their own little wheelies up the aisle, picking up markers and clothing as my little disheveled team edged on along in a slow line as if we were trekking across a ridge in Patagonia.

A fleet of private jets stood on the runway against the backdrop of crisp white mountains and indigo-blue sky. Here were dozens and dozens of jets signifying the affluence and power of Aspen's elite. I figured it being a holiday weekend, at least a fifth of those shiny steel capitalist monstrosities belonged to members of the Grid. They stood wing to wing, their noses lined up like F-14s on an aircraft carrier.

Then an enormous jet, larger than most of the others, taxied to the small terminal. I counted about nine windows and saw the *G-V* emblazoned on the tail. A black Suburban SUV with darkened windows and an oversized golf cart pulling a metal luggage trailer drove right up to the arriving plane. *People* magazine Aspen images shuffled through my head. Jack Nicholson? David Beckham and Posh? The door opened and the stairway began to lower in one smooth hydraulic move. The porters, lined up at the ready, straightened their shoulders and stared up into the cabin at the Hollywood royalty inside.

The staircase touched the tarmac. I shielded my eyes from the blinding late-afternoon mountain sun. A passenger appeared at the door of the plane.

Susannah. Frozen on the steps. Right in front of me. We'd spot each other at drop-off and pickup, then I'd walk in the opposite direction. She'd written me a terse note:

Jamie:
It had nothing to do with you. How low I fell. It was short. And it never should have begun. It is over. No one will ever know. I am so sorry.
                                                                Susannah.

I hadn't responded. Now I had no choice. She was walking quickly down the steps. I couldn't have her running after me on a tarmac with Yvette and the kids inside. The face-to-face confrontation would have to take place. Here and now.

I put my sunglasses on my head and looked her in the eye.

"Hello, Susannah."

She stepped off the staircase onto the shiny black asphalt and took off her glasses as well.

"Jamie." She pursed her lips. This elegant woman had nothing elegant to say.

I broke the ice for her. "You here with the whole family?"

"They got here yesterday. I had a board meeting. And you?"

"With the kids."

"Oh. Good." Long, uncomfortable silence.

"One thing, Susannah: when you told me it was all about blowing your husband, I wasn't aware that included your friends' husbands as well."

"It wasn't meant—"

"You might have warned me of that little detail, because that part definitely wasn't clear."

"It happened just once."

"You sure?" Phillip had told me in therapy that they had gone to the Plaza Athénée twice in the afternoons.

"Don't tell Tom. Please don't tell him. He has no idea."

"Are you sure he has no idea?"

"Positive. It would destroy him."

"Are you sure it was just that once?"

"Okay, maybe one more time. But it had nothing to do with you."

"How could it not?"

"Because. It was just a thing, a flirtation between us. Tom has been working so hard for months . . . he's never home . . ."

"Susannah. It has everything to do with me. I was your friend."

"I don't know, Jamie, he's so . . . and you were so uninterested . . ."

"If you mean that he's attractive, I know that. It's one reason I married him."

"Well, I'm . . ."

"You're what? Sorry you slept with my husband?"

"Well, yes, of course. I feel awful. But I get so lonely. You must be so devastated."

"I was devastated. Now I'm not."

She took a step closer. "Jamie. I'm so sorry."

I stepped back. "I'm sorry for *you,* Susannah."

She looked shocked. "You are?"

"Sleeping with your friend's husband isn't something a happy person does."

Entr'acte II

The silver Mercedes S600 slowly made its way along the small side street in Red Hook, then pulled to a stop beside a well-used, dust-covered Subaru wagon. Just outside the corner café, two elderly Cuban gentlemen in warm winter coats sat in white plastic chairs at a small table playing dominoes. They watched the swanky, completely out-of-place automobile and knew instantly that it wasn't a drug dealer car. Though the rapidly gentrifying neighborhood had driven most of the criminals to nearby towns, the bad guys drove by once in a while. Still, the old Cubans were sure this definitely wasn't one of them.

"¿Quien es eso?"

The other shrugged.

A chauffeur in a bowler hat sat erect in the front seat while the dark black window rolled down in the back. A hand, weighted down with heavy gold bracelets, pointed urgently to number 63. "Oscar! Stop the car! It's right here, next to these tenements."

The wise, older Cuban man ashed his cigar and chuckled.

She yanked off her Verdura earrings. "Put these in the glove compartment."

A crocodile boot stretched out of the car, then a very shapely thigh, then a very, very rich woman, incredulous, surveyed the block.

"Oscar! Guard me! Guard the car! If I see a fucking rat and it bites me, you call the goddamn Platinum desk at Amex and get their helicopter to medevac me out of this shithole! You have that number?"

"It's on the dashboard, where it always is, madam."

"And you push that Onstar button right next to it on the dashboard. I don't know who answers that button, but you push it a hundred times."

Oscar ran around the car and gently cradled her elbow, which hung in an Hermès scarf sling. "Whatever you do, I don't care if fifteen cops tell you to move the car and circle the block, *you wait. You say no. You resist arrest. You go to jail maybe eventually, but you do not leave me.* If I come down here and you are not here, a gang member is going to jump me and steal my favorite boots."

"This neighborhood is perfectly safe, madam," said Oscar as he walked her to the front door of a brown-shingled town house. "But I will be here. There's nothing to worry about."

"Nothing to worry about? Hello? It's like *Mad Max* around here!"

The very rich woman buzzed apartment number 5, Bailey.

"Yeah?"

"Is that you, Peter?"

"Yeah."

"It's Ingrid Harris."

"Oh Jesus."

"I heard that."

"Uh, I, um, am pretty busy right now."

"I don't care. I need to talk to you."

"You do?"

"Yes! No, actually, I was visiting some really dear friends in that lovely housing project next door and I thought I would drop by. Listen, it's not, you know, like before. What you might think. I mean, I'll keep my paws off this time."

One Cuban man elbowed the other.

"Uh, yeah, um, thanks. That would be good."

"Yes. I promise. Open the door."

He buzzed her in.

The woman clacked her heels up five flights of steep, rickety stairs. She thanked God for that sexy Panamanian trainer who'd made her use that step machine. Someone unbolted three locks as she neared the third floor, then a door swung open.

A nicely dressed black teenager in a ski hat and down vest appeared on the landing and ran down the stairs two by two, and then stopped and looked at her.

She froze, eyes wide, clutching the stair rail and pressing her body into the wall and as far away from him as possible.

"How's it going?" he asked politely.

She tried to answer, but words wouldn't come. He shook his head and bounded down the stairs.

She then sprinted up the remaining two flights faster than the Road Runner. Peter Bailey was waiting with the door open and she practically knocked him over as she ran inside. A bicycle rested against the wall just inside, next to a coat stand with ski jackets and hooded sweatshirts hanging off it.

"Are you okay? Should I get you some water, a cool cloth, or maybe some oxygen? I mean, for you to come out here . . ."

She looked over her shoulder to see if any other very scary people were on the stairs. "Peter, I swear, if someone kills me, I'll come back and haunt you forever."

"You already are," he said. She walked past a small kitchen with a tiny stove and refrigerator and mismatched plates lined up in an old rubber dish rack. In the front hall stood a lonely oak table and three different chairs. Books, newspapers, and magazines stacked haphazardly in shelves covered all the walls in the living room. She stepped over a maze of Internet and TV cords and finally reached an old green canvas sofa, sagging in the middle.

"Do you have a towel or something?"

"For what?"

"To sit on."

"The couch is clean, Ingrid."

"I can see it is, the apartment is actually kind of neat. But I was worried about germs, from bugs or something."

"Good thinking. I found a scorpion under the cushion there just this morning."

He handed her a blanket that hung from the oversized armchair and she gingerly placed it under her bottom. She was on a very serious errand.

"I didn't come here to, you know, rekindle anything."

"Good to hear." He sat down in the oversized armchair next to her. "So. What's the urgency?"

She crossed her fingers under her thigh and then said to him dramatically, "I'm only here because I can't stand to see him so down."

"Who? Phillip?"

"No! You think I'd risk my life to come all the way here for that loser?"

"Then who?"

More drama. "It's Dylan."

"What about Dylan? He's in Aspen. He should be having a great time." Peter plucked a dried leaf from a sad-looking plant on the side table and then finally said, "I haven't been able to take him to sports for a few weeks."

Ingrid, for whom manipulation was second nature, suddenly felt bad about what she was about to do. She felt bad about lying, especially about Dylan. But Jamie was a mess, and Ingrid figured she owed her. "Tell me about it. He's, like, *catatonic.*"

"Oh God. I have to call him right away." He leapt up from the chair and grabbed the phone.

"Wait! Can I propose something better?"

"You promised! And we don't even have a linen closet."

"God. And Jamie told me you were really smart. Not me and you. Not ever. Not that I didn't like it!" She snorted. "And you certainly seemed to enjoy yourself."

"I did, Ingrid. Thank you. Very much. But what does this have to do with Dylan?"

"We need to get you to Aspen. On my plane, with us. It's wheels-up in three hours."

"You're nuts."

"That has often been said."

"No."

"I hear the snow is amazing. I hear you like to ski."

"I've got work. I have to fix my program this week. And next."

"Honey, you've got to fix him first. He's got a broken heart. And she's, well, she's leaving Phillip for good, not that that's a factor."

36

Return Engagement

When you look around the Caribou Club, the hottest place in Aspen, you see the exact same people you see in the Grid. You know maybe half the people. Everyone looks just like they do at home. Only colder. They mix fur with the cowboy thing. Fur boots that make them look like Sasquatch, fur neck scarves, fur earmuffs, fur trim on the leather coats, fur everything. And it isn't mink. It's more expensive than mink. It's sable or chinchilla.

I opened the huge mahogany and brass door and walked down the dark staircase into the foyer of the club. A woman who looked like a Dallas Cowboys cheerleader took my coat. I'd come into town for a late-night girls' dinner with Kathryn. We'd have fun. We'd share a bottle of good wine. Then I'd call Peter and tell him what I'd decided.

I searched the crowd for her curly long mane, knowing Kathryn wouldn't have arrived. She's always late. A waitress took my drink order and found a place on the edge of a large sofa covered in Western-style Pendleton blankets.

"You on your own?" A good-looking, dark-haired man in a checked flannel shirt moved a little closer.

"My girlfriend is coming, actually. But she's not here yet."

"Are you two on your own?"

"We're having dinner. The two of us, and we're both married."

"I don't remember asking."

"It's just that there's a lucky girl somewhere in here and I wouldn't want you to miss out.

"Can I buy you a drink just because you're so pretty?"

"Thank you. That's very kind of you. But no." He couldn't stop looking down at my legs—I was wearing a worn-out pair of Levi's 501s that I hadn't been able to wear since before I'd had children.

"Then I'll just sit here and smell your perfume."

After a few excellent celebrity sightings, someone tapped me on my shoulder. I pulled my coat off the couch in back of me, ready to stand, thinking it was Kathryn.

Christina Patten. Again. Dead center in my field of vision. Complete buzz kill. Kiss kiss. She put her hand on my knee. "I am so happy to see you. Can we get the girls together? You could come for dinner? Or if you don't want to move the troops, we could come to your house. Whatever you want."

I smiled politely, or tried to, and looked over her shoulder to see if Kathryn by any chance was about to rescue me.

She pushed. "We've all got the kids, and mine are looking for some friends at night." Christina looked at me with her big, brown, puppy-dog eyes. "Please? How about tomorrow? We could do it at either house. You want to use your chef or mine?" She laughed and snorted.

Aspen has got to be one of the only places on the planet where a woman whose husband draws in one and a half million dollars a year is made to feel down and out.

"Christina, to be totally honest with you, I just need quiet time with my kids. Sorry. But I'm just not up for dinners this trip."

She leaned over and placed both of her hands on my knees. A sweet expression warmed her face, one that I'd never seen before. "I saw you in the park."

"Excuse me?"

"I mean I *saw* you in the park." I thought about Peter behind me, grabbing my hand as I slipped up the rocks to the castle.

"I . . ."

"You looked happy, Jamie."

"I . . ."

"And I know you think I'm a flake, you're not alone—everyone does—but I want to tell you something really serious."

"You do?"

"Do exactly what you need in life to make yourself happy. Don't for a minute think all of this is easy for any of us. Be wise to yourself and whatever it is you want in this life." She clinked her wineglass against mine and walked away.

I was still reeling from that encounter when Kathryn strolled in five minutes later and untangled me from Joe Venture Capitalist Man from Seattle.

While we waited to be seated, she said, "You are so bad."

"What?"

"Look at you! Hot tamale time."

"You're late. I should be giving *you* hell. Some guy was hitting on me, I couldn't get rid of him."

"Well, you're formally separating. You must be screaming available or something."

"Stop picking on me. I just wanted to feel good for myself and nobody else."

"Sure."

The energy was palpable in the dining room. Handsome men of all ages in dark turtlenecks and suede blazers were laughing loudly, arms around women on either side. Grid people looking like total fools in ten-gallon hats were scattered among them. Tall blondes with wild Texas curls in high cowboy boots, tight jeans, and twenty-thousand-dollar salt-and-pepper chinchilla vests were table-hopping all over the restaurant. People everywhere were letting off some steam; their sexual energy was contagious.

A drop-dead gorgeous waiter came up to our table. He had a dark tan around the lines where his goggles fit that made him look like a panda bear. He handed us two menus and told us he would person-ally make sure we were very happy with our evening.

"You could make things simple and do *him*. He just offered," Kathryn suggested.

"No. I'm not going for the waiter."

"Then just save yourself for Peter. Does Phillip sense anything at all?"

"He barely knows his last name. Still calls him the coach guy."

"What is the Phillip thing exactly as of today? Have you called that lawyer yet?"

"I'm thinking mediator. And I'm telling him it's official when we get back. Maybe even Monday night."

"I've heard that before. You sure?"

"I know so. He won't even be shocked. He has some young girl he's seeing, I hear. We're just stalling for the final conversation."

Kathryn polished off her glass of wine. "And when you're freaking, as you will, don't forget Peter's in love with you. Even if he isn't calling."

"I'm worried he's moved on."

"No way. He's just making his own chess moves."

"Well, even if he does call, I don't know how everything will play out between Peter and me, in terms of 'us.'" Kathryn shook her head vehemently while I said this. "I wouldn't want to confuse him as a father replacement for my kids or . . ."

"Why does it have to be like that? Stop. Why isn't it okay for you to fall for Peter just because of the man he is? Why does it have to be some pathological Phillip-replacement theory? Can't we keep it simple? He's fantastic. He adores your kids. He adores you. Period."

"You know very well that it doesn't work that way, but I sure like the sound of it."

"So get down to business when you get back. And get down to professional business too. It will make you feel better."

She was referring to the documentary project Erik and I had begun to develop over the past two weeks. He'd called me out of the blue and asked me for lunch. The minute we sat down, he put a folder with a proposal in front of me—a documentary project for feature release telling our side of the Theresa story, in his words, "not the fuckin' candy-assed version the NBS lawyers vetted," and advancing the story on the bloggers who set us up.

I knew Kathryn was right about jumping back into work once we returned to New York.

★   ★   ★

Our condo sat by a little creek a few miles from the base of Aspen Mountain. It had four bedrooms and a little sleeping alcove above the garage. Tan plaid sectional couches filled the living room and a clean Formica kitchen with functional appliances opened up to a small dining area. My sanctuary of a room, with a fireplace, faced the creek and the pine forest beyond it. Kathryn dropped me off right out front a little before eleven. I was happily tipsy. After her Jeep sped away, I leaned against the railing of the porch and stared at the billions of stars lighting up the sky. In New York, the nighttime reflections of the skyscrapers prevent us from seeing the constellations. I sat on a lone Adirondack chair on the porch and pulled a gray wool blanket around my knees.

Leaning back, I scrunched my hands together between my legs. The center seam of my jeans rubbed against me and sent a sexual tingle straight to my core. I was antsy. I wanted to party like I used to: to smoke some pot (which I hadn't done in years) or have a glass of red wine that would warm my insides in the cool night air. Still restless, I stood up against the railing and tried to make smoke rings with my breath.

I leaned over the railing to catch a glimpse of the creek and saw a red glow coming from the living room window. Could the house be on fire? No. It had to be the fireplace. It wasn't like Yvette to start a fire this late at night, or ever. I ran inside.

And there he was, standing behind the couch, the glowing orange light making dramatic, wavelike reflections on the walls. He looked like a creature standing in hell. I laughed.

"What's so funny?" he whispered.

"Your silhouette, with the flames behind you, you look like the devil."

"You look beautiful."

I didn't move. I couldn't.

"When did you get here?" God, it was so good to see him.

"This evening. Don't ask how, because I'll never tell you. Yvette let

me in. I got to see Dylan before he went to sleep. I was really concerned about him."

"Why?"

"Because he's been so down. Like before I came."

"He has?"

"Uh, yeah. That's why I'm here."

"Did he seem down to you?"

"Honestly, not really."

"Well then, what are you talking about?"

"I said I came here because I heard Dylan was in really bad shape."

"Who told you that?"

"I can't tell you that either."

"Well, it's bullshit. He's been doing fine. He doesn't like it that
you've been in Silicon Valley, but he understands."

"He does? Interesting." He looked like some lightbulb had just
turned on above his head.

"So. How are you, Peter? Thanks for returning my messages."

"All that matters now is I'm here. And happy to be."

"Me too."

He turned around and grabbed two empty wineglasses from the
coffee table, and then a bottle of red wine, already opened but
untouched. I stood in the hallway frozen. Holy moly, holy moly, holy
moly. I couldn't believe it might actually be happening.

He grabbed my hand, squeezing it for an instant like he had in the
park, and led me to my bedroom.

"I'm thirsty" was all I could say. And it wasn't the altitude that
parched my throat just then.

He poured some water into one of the glasses and handed it to me,
his finger resting a second too long on my hand. I thought I was
going to die.

"Drink this." He smiled like this was no big deal. Like I should just
relax.

I took a sip while he walked over to the bedroom fireplace in the
dark room. Light from the hallway lamp helped him navigate his way.
He built up the logs, stuffed some tight bundles of newspaper

between them, and threw a little piece of fire starter underneath the andirons. He stood there, in his white T-shirt and jeans draping like velvet over that body, hand on hip, watching the fire catch. He was such an insane turn-on.

He walked toward the door. For a brief second, I thought, with disappointment, that he was going to leave, but he was just flipping the lock. Then he came back to me, smiling that killer smile. I looked down and waited. He was running this show.

He bent his knees slightly and looked up at me, then he took my face in his hands and said, "You are so beautiful it makes me ache." He kissed me softly. He put his arms around the back of my shoulders to steady me and stepped in closer with his knee between my legs in a Fred Astaire dance move that placed me up against the side of the bed. Then he was kissing me like a crazy man, urging my body down to the bed. I couldn't believe how much I wanted him. He then grabbed my legs and pulled them on the bed so I was lying next to him. One of his knees held my leg down. Even that turned me on. He tasted delicious, sweet like honey. He was kissing my shoulder and tracing a line with his finger down from my ear, to my neck, to my stomach. Placing his hand on my belly beneath my shirt, he rested his head just above my shoulder and circled my belly button with his index finger, grazing the top of my pants. Oh. My. God. I prayed Gracie wouldn't be all thirsty and headache-y from the altitude and want to come in.

The fire crackled loudly and an ember popped against the screen. "You okay?"

I closed my eyes. "I'm freaking just a little. But it's okay." I nudged myself an inch toward the side table and away from him.

"You want to resist me?" he asked.

"I'm trying not to."

He smiled, clinked my glass, and took a sip of wine. *It's all okay, Jamie.*

"How come now?" I had to ask.

"Let's just say the circumstances surrounding this trip worked in my favor. And a little bird gave me news about the status of you and

Phillip. Besides, my patience was all dried up." He tapped my nose with his finger. "And I wanted to make you happy. And, for me anyway, it's way overdue."

"Like since when?"

"Like since the first day at your office."

"That long?"

"Yeah. You were so funny. And pretty. And brave, trying to manage work and the kids and all that."

"Really then?"

"Yeah. Like big-time. Right away. And the whole time, you're too busy to even see it, or notice."

"I didn't want to see it."

"I'm aware of that. Believe me. It was torture."

"I'm sorry." I kissed his sweet mouth.

"You should be. This guy isn't waiting any longer."

A little drop of wine fell down my chin to my neck. He licked it off. Then he rested his head on his elbow and started unbuttoning my shirt.

Again he asked, "You okay?"

"Hmm-mmm."

He pulled my arms in the air and peeled off my shirt. The crisp air felt fresh against my skin. It was never like this with anyone. Not even in college. I couldn't believe I was thirty-six and getting to feel this way. I wanted to consume all of him. He lay on top of me now, and then, straddling me, tore off his shirt. Oh my God, that chest.

He looked so happy, like he was having a really, really good time. Finally. "You still okay?"

"Hmm-mmm."

"So."

"Yeah?"

"You sure you want to do the manny?"

I burst out laughing. "Positive."

37

Rude Awakening

It was eight-thirty the next morning when Peter and Dylan's wrestling in the living room woke me up. I rolled over and remembered that Peter had left my room only two hours before. We had gone on all night, like two teenagers starved for stolen moments, until dawn came and he moved to the small studio apartment above the garage. I was amazed he was standing. My body felt like spaghetti. My bed looked like a pack of wild dogs attacked it. I cracked open the door to hear them.

"On the mountains where I grew up, you little shrimp, I am going to kick your behind on my new Arbor Element snowboard."

"No fair! I only snowboarded last spring for a week!" wailed Dylan, half laughing, half whining.

"And with any luck, we'll be surfin' some nar-nar pow-pow."

"What's nar-nar pow-pow?" said Dylan.

Peter leaned forward some more. "Chill, Dylan. If you're gonna snowboard with me, you gotta know the lingo. 'Surfin' the nar-nar pow-pow' means boarding on a powder day. Like when it's snowed overnight, and there's tons of gnarly fresh powder, so you feel like you're gliding on feathers the whole way down. And when you're doing great turns, I'm going to say to you, 'That was a sick line, Doctor.'"

"What's a 'sick line'?"

"It's a nice path through the snow."

"Why 'Doctor'?"

"I don't know, it's just a dumb thing boarders call each other."

"Wow. Cool."

"And when I'm done with you, you're gonna be twistin' and turnin' and shreddin' up those trails just like me."

"You think?"

"I don't think. I *know.*"

We spent all day Saturday on the slopes, Peter and I so worn out, it was a miracle we didn't hit any trees and die. In the afternoon, we dropped the kids into ski school and skied on our own. We kissed on the ski lift with reckless abandon; he wrapped his arms around my stomach as he skied right behind me, yelling instructions at me, laughing at my clumsiness when I conquered some Volkswagen-size moguls for the first time. It was sublime, supremely so, because of the potential for danger and heartbreak.

Saturday night, after the kids were sound asleep, there was more of the same otherworldly lovemaking. We laughed. We watched some TV. We ate cookies and drank wine. Then we went at it again, back and forth, inside and out, until we could take no more.

Someone pounding on the front door of the condo woke me. Seven-thirty Sunday morning. It must have been a mistake. Loud bashing of a gloved hand hitting the door with a dull thud. I put a pillow on my head, hoping the creep at my door had realized his mistake. He didn't. The banging continued, now with knocks on the windowpanes next to the door.

"Shit!" I got out of bed, threw on a robe, and surveyed the half-empty glasses, finished bottle of wine, and my clothes strewn across the floor. I reeked of sex. I was furious, and so exhausted, and so angry that this loser had gotten the wrong condo. I peeked through one of the stained-glass windows that framed the door. Oh. My. God.

Phillip. Here. In Aspen.

I ran back into my room to put the second wineglass in my bathroom and to make sure Peter had taken his boxers with him. I flipped over the covers but couldn't tell for sure. I put some cream on my hands to hide the scent of sex that was all over my body, my hands, my mouth. I didn't have time to wash my face either, so I patted my cheeks with lotion. For the first time in ten years of marriage, I had spent two nights with another man.

And when I thought about that, I decided I definitely didn't regret it *or* feel guilty.

Then I steeled myself and unlatched the door. "Hello, Phillip."

"Hello, Jamie."

"Come in." He kissed my cheek lightly and walked into the front hall pulling a small carry-on wheelie bag. Phillip threw his coat on the couch. He looked like hell. His hair stuck out sideways like Einstein's. He smelled of airplane.

"Well, Phillip, would you like some coffee?"

"I've had four cups. I've been up all night. Took a dawn connection through Houston. Slept in the airport Hilton there for five hours."

"You didn't bring your ski equipment. What's the urgency?"

But I knew he was coming to beg. He jumped in quickly. "I also didn't come because of us. I mean, I didn't come here to try to patch things up or anything. I'm in trouble, Jamie."

So *that's* why he looked like the Fugitive.

"Take me to your bedroom. We have to talk privately."

I contemplated this turn of events, a lot to digest this early in the day. The poor guy needed a drink of something. I opened the fridge and reached for the "Lots of Pulp" orange juice, but I opted for a bottle of Evian instead. We walked quickly down the hall to my bedroom.

Motioning for him to sit on the armchair next to the fireplace, I threw the comforter on the bed, praying a pair of boxers wouldn't fall out. Then I locked the door and pulled the desk chair in front of my husband.

"Okay. Tell me everything."

"I can't tell you everything, I don't want you to know everything because I want to protect you."

I threw my hands in the air. "Phillip, is this big-time trouble like Dennis Kozlowski and prison, or is this little-time trouble like a slap on the hand? Are you talking about losing your job and disbarment?"

"It's potentially big-time, but not necessarily."

"Okay." I straightened my back. "But you can't tell me what it is?"

"Not entirely."

"Soooooo, what would you like me to do here? Why are you here?"

He took a deep breath and looked down, ashamed. "I need you to forget some things."

"What things?"

"Certain things."

"Is the trade-secret subpoena for Laurie that you told me was a little routine problem now a little bigger problem?"

He nodded.

"And the time I caught you and Alan in the study?"

He nodded.

"And the time you called from work asking me to hide the contents of the Ridgefield file?"

He nodded again and then added, "And if you get subpoenaed . . ."

"Phillip, I have spousal privilege. They can't subpoena me as long as we're married." Suddenly I saw what he was getting at. If I divorced him for *cause,* for his adultery, then they might question me. Or, more precisely, if I hated him enough, I might sing like a canary. He was worried I would turn him in. "You want me to forget the papers in that file."

He leaned in with evil eyes. "Did you read them before you put them away?"

I leaned right back at him. "I'm not going to answer that."

There was a knock on the door, a light one. I felt like I might throw up. I poked my nose out the crack. Thank *God* it wasn't Peter. "Yes, Yvette?"

"Gracie wants to get in your bed."

Yvette was holding a sleepyhead Gracie in her arms. "Not now, Yvette." I reached out my hand and rubbed Gracie's cheek. "Mommy is busy. Just snuggle with Yvette." I closed the door. Gracie screamed like a hyena and Michael started wailing three minutes later. Two screaming kids meant that Peter and Dylan would emerge from the cocoon above the garage. Now I worried that Peter would come back into my room at this horrible moment.

We went over the details for fifteen minutes. Phillip's subpoena, the subpoena for his assistant Laurie, his lawyers, his job, the allegations, the repercussions. He seemed to be clear on the charge of stealing trade secrets, but that Ridgefield file could change things for him. I had to make some decisions, and fast.

Phillip stood up and whacked the air with a flat swat of his hand when I again refused to discuss the contents of that file I supposedly had hidden. He inadvertently hit a huge stand-up lamp, which crashed to the floor. I heard heavy footsteps running down the hall. Like those of a hunky manny.

A loud knock on the door. Peter yelled, "You okay?"

"Fine," I yelled back from the chair.

"Can I—"

"No!"

He started pushing in on the door and the flimsy panels started to give with his weight. He thought I was playing games with him.

"What is that guy's problem?" Phillip walked over and opened the door. "Yes?"

"I thought she might have gotten hurt."

"She's fine. Just fine."

I had to say something. I could not have this fantastic man wondering anything. But I couldn't leave to go to him, which is all I wanted to do. So I just tried to explain the best I could. "Peter! As you see, Phillip has some important business that couldn't wait. Everything's okay. I promise you." Kind of. And he closed the door.

My soon-to-be-ex-husband and I sat down again, both of us extremely tense. "Yes, Phillip, we have some business. A few items, in fact." His eyes widened.

"About your sex life." I tried to look really scary.

No response.

"You been busy with a young blond woman in the past few months?"

"I don't see how that is relevant to our current discussion."

"Phillip. A few minutes ago, I thought to myself, I've got you in a vise."

"I beg to differ, but you can see it any way you like."

"So I want to take advantage of the position I'm in to get some more answers from you."

He cleared his throat.

"Don't lie to me, Phillip. After all, you don't know that I didn't make a copy of the contents of those files before I . . ."

He lunged at me and, for the first time in my life, I actually thought a man was going to punch me. I was terrified I was in over my head. The imploding marriage was enough to handle, but now with the subpoena, and Peter last night.

"God help you, Phillip, if you ever, *ever* lay a hand on me!"

He sat back down. "I wouldn't."

"You looked like you might." My eyes welled with tears.

"I wouldn't. Ever. You know that, Jamie. I'm sorry I frightened you."

"Okay. Let's bring the temperature down. And if you think this relationship has any chance of surviving, even as an amicable partnership as parents of those three precious children, you'd better be honest with me right now."

He looked up at me; the venom had gone, momentarily at least. I could see he felt guilty about it. He softened. "I will."

"All right. Who was the young blond woman whose ear you were biting at Caprizio's two weeks ago?"

"How do you know about her?"

"I know. People talk."

He shrugged his shoulders. "You kicked me out of the bedroom two months ago, then into my parents' apartment. You never said I couldn't see other women."

"You're right, Phillip. I only said I wouldn't share a bed with you again, but I need to know what's going on with you. It will help me deal with everything if I know that you are being truthful." I was hoping to find some peace, trying to speak to him rationally and constructively.

He sighed. "She's a paralegal. Her name is Sarah Tobin. She's not very smart, but she likes to take care of me. You haven't exactly been willing to spend quality time with me."

"Does Susannah know about Sarah?"

"Susannah dumped me back in December, you know that. She just wanted to flirt. When it became a bit more . . ."

"Seemed like a lot more to me, Phillip. Of course, with her legs in the sky like—"

"That lasted a week."

"And the Plaza Athénée?"

"All in the same week. I was lonely in our marriage."

"Uh-huh," I answered with sarcasm.

"Uh-huh? You think you understand my motives better than I do?"

"I do, actually."

"Really?" he answered sarcastically. "Let's hear it. This should be interesting."

"Fine. Here's what I think: and, by the way, it's totally obvious. I think fucking her on her soil meant you could own those master-pieces, even for ten minutes. Fucking her made *you* rich."

Silence.

Then: "You're way off base."

"Phillip. If you can't be honest with me, at least be straight with yourself. I repeat: *fucking her made you rich*. Not rich like us. Rich like you want to be rich. Wheels-up rich."

"I can't even respond to that."

"Fine."

"A mistake. That's all it was. I'm not a bad guy. You weren't crazy to marry me, you know."

I could hear the kids playing in the other room.

"I know that. I do."

"You sure?"

"Yes, I'm sure."

He tried again. "Did you read the folder or not? I need to know. Now I need *you* to be truthful with me."

"Phillip, I'm not going to tell you that."

He began pacing around the room, and started doing his old Madrid bull breathing. "Damn it, Jamie! You may hate me for all I've done. Believe me, I know I'm not easy. But you owe it to me, to the children, to protect me."

"Copies of the Ridgefield file are in a safe-deposit box."

"You're fucking joking." He slapped his thigh and let out a forced laugh. "Tell me, Jamie, you are fucking joking!"

"I'm not."

"Why would you do a thing like that? It's so reckless!"

"I thought it prudent."

"Did you or did you not read them?"

"Immaterial." What did he think, that I was an idiot and wouldn't?

He paced around the room in more little circles. "Okay. What do you want?"

"I want you to find a young girl whose mission in life is to take care of you. Someone who is wowed by your breeding, your passion for life, your financial and professional success."

He looked confused, but hopeful. "Is that all?"

"Nope."

"I didn't think so." He sat back down.

"I want to make some changes. I want to move downtown."

"Have you lost your mind? Who in God's earth with any money would want to go down there with all those disgusting factories, and no doormen . . ."

"Phillip, I don't want to live in the cloistered environment of Park Avenue with all those provincial wealthy families anymore. And I don't want our children there either."

"If you're going to knock the way I—"

"This is not directed at you. In fact, it's not about you. It's about me. And my happiness, and the ultimate well-being of our children. I want to live in a different community. A less judgmental community."

"You're not going to find it in Manhattan. Or Brooklyn. There's nothing snobbier than downtown artists who think they're so cool."

"I'd like to give it a try. Dylan will make the commute uptown for two more years and then he can transfer downtown to another school in seventh grade. And we applied to St. Anthony's Church school for Gracie anyway. It did seem crazy at the time, but now it's suddenly making more sense."

"That's great. You've been planning to move since last fall when the applications were sent and you never told me?"

"St. Anthony's was a fallback in case Gracie didn't get into Pembroke then. Anyway, I'd like you to sell our big apartment and buy two smaller ones: one for you, and one for me. I want all my reasonable expenses paid until I can get back on my feet professionally. Then we can figure out a reasonable percentage that I will contribute based on my salary. Just like we did before. I will give you a budget when we return."

"Do you have any idea how much that will cost? Running two apartments?"

"I know, Phillip. I handle the family finances and bills, remember? That's why I know exactly what you can afford. And I don't want any lawyers screwing this up. I want a mediator, not a corporate lawyer with fangs, to handle this divorce." Saying that made me shudder, but once I uttered the word "divorce," it emboldened me. When he heard that term, he didn't flinch. I didn't know if it was the lawyer in him or whether he had indeed moved on as well.

I continued. "This is my final and only offer. I want a new apartment. I want enough cash to pay all the bills for the children, which I will. And I want you to take care of my own expenses as long as I need you to. I want friendly, joint custody so you can come and go as you please. I want as little tension as possible. And I want you to give me everything I am asking for in return for . . ."

"In return for what?"

"In return for my hiding that safe-deposit key."

"Jamie. I need to know where it is."

"Nope. I swear on the life of my beautiful children that I will bring it out of hiding only if you renege on my offer."

"Pleeeese, Jamie. Tell me what you know."

"I know that I care about you. That I want you to find someone more suited to you who makes you happy. I want you to see your children often and have a healthy relationship with their mother. And if you consider dicking around with me on the finances, remember I have extremely dangerous information."

"But you wouldn't destroy me. You would never."

"You don't know what I would and wouldn't do. You do know that I have the information. And you do know that the money doesn't really matter to me as much as it does to you. Not even close. So if you push me hard enough . . ."

"Okay, okay. Let me consider this a few days. Let me take this in."

"Take your time, Phillip. But remember, no lawyer negotiations."

"Can I spend time now with my kids?"

"Of course you can. Would you like me to leave or stay?"

"You can stay. In case I need help," he answered.

"I understand."

"I have a flight back tonight."

"Fine."

It took ten years to have that conversation and it was finally behind me. Before I could absorb that, I had to move straight into facing Peter and reassuring him.

"Daddy!" yelled Gracie from the living room. "I can ski! Are you going to see me?"

Dylan chimed in. "Are you skiing with us, Dad? Will you?"

"Kids, I can't. I didn't come here planning to ski." Peter had disappeared to his small bedroom above the garage. What could he possibly have been thinking? I promised him last night it was going to be over *for real* with Phillip and then, presto, Phillip shows up four hours later, like we're a happy little nuclear family?

With Dylan now going full speed into a depression spiral because his father wouldn't ski with him, Phillip felt awful. He looked at me just like he always did when we were officially married—*Jamie, rescue me here. Do something.* This whole coparenting-the-kids-while-getting-a-divorce thing was going to be a nightmare. No way around it. Then Phillip's face brightened.

"Peter! Peter!" he yelled up the back staircase. "Come here, please!"

Omigod. *Now* what could Peter be thinking? He shuffled down the stairs in his adorable army pants that hung low on his perfect, beyond perfect, ass. "Yes?"

"Can you do me a favor?"

"Honey, it's *so* not okay to ask Peter to do anything right now. He's busy with his other projects. Very, very, very, very busy. Yvette or I can do whatever you need."

"Hell, he's in the house, isn't he?" bellowed Phillip, all confident that he was in charge of everything and everyone. I swear I saw a bulge growing in his pants. *Put the young man to work, it's good for him!* How could I possibly explain Peter was just visiting?

"Peter. Do me a favor. Call one of those places that rents ski equipment: skis, boots, poles, and clothes. Gloves. What have you. I want to see these kids ski. Would you mind coming with me? Mrs. Whitfield could use some time to herself. Might as well make myself useful while I'm here. You and I can take Dylan up, and then when I have to leave, he'll just stay with you."

"Honey . . ." I said, regretting it. Peter instantly shot me a look. *You called the guy "honey"?* "Phillip. Stop with the General MacArthur behavior. Please. Peter is *not* coming skiing with us."

"Mom!" screamed Dylan. "Come on! Peter flew all the way out here. Peter *has* to ski with us another day."

"I agree with Dylan! You're right, son! If Dylan wants Peter to come, I say bring him on!" And Phillip ruffled Dylan's hair and patted Peter's back hard like he was a good old fraternity brother.

"Sounds great!" agreed Peter, and he goosed me on his way down the hall.

Next thing I knew, I was on a quad chairlift with Peter, my husband, and my son, thinking *I am going to go into severe cardiac arrest.* Phillip, at his end of the chair, was acting like Fred MacMurray in *My Three Sons*: all chipper and moving forward. That's what WASPs do with adversity, they pull up their damn bootstraps and they forge ahead, men! Dylan, next to him, was over the moon with delight. And then came Peter, thrilled at how much I was going to owe him. While Dylan and Phillip planned their ski runs on the map and the chairlift machinery squeaked, I whispered into Peter's ear: "I *so* know you hate me. And I know you came skiing for Dylan. Not me. And I so know how you think—you're going to give me all this hell that now I'm going to owe you. Well, how's this: I just told him that we were getting a divorce." He kept facing forward but discreetly rubbed my shoulder with his.

At the top of the mountain, Peter knelt down to Dylan. "Show your dad. Show him your new moves. I promised I'd watch you do this run, Doctor. But I'm only staying for a minute to see that, then I'm going to go. I have some friends to see."

And Dylan was off doing his new turns. Which left me, Phillip, and Peter standing side by side, with our skis hanging off the edge of a cliff, watching Dylan become smaller and smaller. Phillip asked, "Honey, you going to ski with us, or you want Peter to stay?" I could not believe he was thinking Peter was still the help.

"Peter is leaving. He just said that," I explained. "Why don't you have some quality time with Dylan. I'll just go off on my own and ski by myself."

"I need you," Phillip answered. "In case I'm ready to get off the slopes. I can't keep up with Dylan all day when I'm this tired."

"You can call me. I'm going back to the condo."

"He's right." Peter was actually agreeing with Phillip for some insane reason. I assumed he was just trying to drive me crazy. Or was he hurt that Phillip and I were acting as if we were normal? "Go with your son and your *husband*. Dylan's like the Energizer Bunny, he'll want to ski till the very last lift closes. Maybe I'll catch up with you Monday before you go." And he looked at me over the top of his sunglasses, his expression unreadable, then sped away.

"You know what, Jamie?" Phillip asked. "Hate to say it, but I like that guy. How much we still paying him?"

38

Resolution

Peter traced the outlines of my mouth at two in the morning, our last night in Aspen. He called around eleven Sunday night to say he'd finished dinner with friends and wanted to come by now that Phillip had left. I tried to apologize about Phillip's surprise raid, and he said, simply, "Can we move on, please?"

We lay still. He let his fingertips glide over my chest, just like in my sexual fantasy from months back. Only we'd already made love, so this moment's caress was familiar, not a step into some unknown place.

He spoke first. "So I've been thinking that when I said 'It's time,' I was wrong."

"Actually, you didn't say 'It's time,' you said 'It's overdue.' "

"You're not ready, Jamie."

"Why is it up to you to tell me if I'm ready?" This is exactly what I was afraid of. That Phillip's arrival would derail us. It was all Phillip's damn fault: Peter now feeling I wasn't ready. Then I got all fidgety inside because part of me knew he was right. But I pushed that out of my mind. I had fallen big-time for this incredible man and it was so much easier to be romantic and daring. His mouth tasted so sweet, his neck smelled so delicious. All I wanted just then was to dive into a frenzied make-out session that tangled us up in the sheets and made us fall off the bed. I couldn't handle a dollop of reality at a time like this.

"Don't go there. Our time together has been amazing. I'm really, really sorry Phillip showed up. It was awful timing. But he's got a business problem. It had nothing to do with me."

"My issue isn't about him showing up. You guys aren't done yet. You just fall right back into place with him. I saw it today."

"Today on the slopes was for Dylan. You know that. And what more can I do? I told him I wanted a divorce, is that not enough?"

"You need breathing room."

"Who says I want breathing room? I've been waiting around in this loveless marriage for years trying to justify it. I'm done with that and I feel great. I don't want to wait. I've waited too long already."

"Trust me. I know what I'm talking about."

"You're being arrogant again. Why are you voting my vote?"

"Because I care about you and I care about us. This is so obvious: if you don't take this time, we'll never be good."

I liked that he was talking about us as a full-fledged entity, but I didn't like the mandatory waiting period. And then again, deep down I knew even a fourth grader could see he was making perfect sense. But I still wasn't ready to admit that.

"There's something else: I've gotten a commitment. My backers came through."

"I know. Your friends told me at the party."

"They did?" He was amazed. "Why didn't you tell me you knew?"

"The funding was too good a reason for you to leave. And I wanted you to stay with me and the kids."

"Well, I couldn't bring it up either," he answered matter-of-factly. "Because then the question would have come up. And I would have lied." He kissed me. "I was still in a painful holding pattern." He kissed me again. And then he stopped abruptly. "So, this program could be a big thing."

"Great."

"So, over the next few months, my time's going to be tied up with perfecting the program and marketing it."

"I see." Was this code for he wasn't sure? Was that whole breathing-room time a ploy to get me used to the idea this really wasn't going to work? Couldn't be. I leaned over the bed and slipped on my white tank top. I wanted to be dressed, half dressed anyway, to have this conversation. We'd be returning to New York in the morning, though I knew our stolen nights in Aspen might get damaged in transport. My brain went to hash for a moment, like static on a TV screen. Then my head cleared, at least enough to recognize that Peter didn't play games. If he didn't want to be with me, he would tell me straight out. Okay. So did I need time? Was I really ready to transplant Peter into my New York life tomorrow starting at four p.m. when the plane touched down at Kennedy? Just mention to Yvette and Carolina that he'd be sleeping in my bed from now on but that he didn't need to have pajamas pressed?

"Okay," I said rationally. "You need to focus on your work."

"It's not just that. Being out here feels so good. I'm going to stay a few days with my old friends. I'm mostly in California anyway until the financing happens in a few months. Then I'll be home."

My heart sank. No way were we going down this road.

"Why? At least come home with us. You have a ticket on our flight."

"There's a whole long path you two have to go through. You've got to work out the divorce details, shore up the kids, find new apartments. Almost as important, you've got to start working again. You need space for all that."

"Do you have any doubts about me and Phillip?"

"Besides the fact that you still call him 'honey,' no. But he's not the issue, you are. And when you're not settled, or you're in transition, you pull back. Do you have any idea how icy you were in New York?"

"I wasn't icy! I was traumatized."

"You ready to tell me you want to jump in now? For real?"

"I, uh, I think."

"See? Right there you said it all. You can't say for sure, because you're *not* sure. I know you care for me. I know we connect. And I've got this deal I've got to make work. Now. Full focus. And though you hate hearing this, you don't even know what you want, when it really comes down to it."

"Stop going down this road. Think about the last few days. We're good. We are really, really good."

"I'm trying to do the right thing here." He looked too serious. "You're not ready to run off with me. And I'm not setting myself up for that kind of crash."

We kept talking in circles. I felt tired. Doing the right thing was overrated. Independence was overrated. I'd had months of hell and all I wanted was to devour this man all the time. Finally, I lay back down on the bed and stared at the ceiling, thinking about what months without Peter would be like. It seemed I wasn't winning this argument. "When did you become Mr. Rational?"

"Only when it counts," he said.

"But Dylan . . ."

"I'll stay in touch with Dylan. You deal with your husband. You figure out what you want. Our time here was amazing. And maybe, in a few months' time, once you get everything settled, it will be amazing again. But I'm going to stay away."

The kids, unusually calm and well behaved, were waiting for Peter to make his famous blueberry pancakes, their favorite breakfast. A sense of eeriness pervaded the room. All the games on the living room coffee table had been cleaned up and put away: Scrabble Kids' Version, Boggle, and Chinese checkers. In the hallway, the kids' Magic Markers and drawing paper were neatly stowed in separate plastic Ziploc bags next to their backpacks. I checked Michael's diaper bag for the flight; it was properly stuffed full with diapers, wipes, some thick Bob the Builder picture books, his sippy cups, and a change of clothes. On the deck outside the front door lay three enormous L.L. Bean duffel bags, the zippers closed snugly. As I walked back down the hall to the kitchen, Peter met me halfway and handed me a glass of orange juice.

He announced, "Your skis are on the ski rack of the car." Poker face, no hint of emotion.

The kids went crazy when Peter missed catching a few pancakes on their way down and they splattered on the floor; I knew he'd moved the skillet on purpose. I maneuvered around him as I poured myself a bowl of granola. He didn't smile at me, he didn't brush alongside me, he didn't let his finger caress my palm as he handed me the cup of coffee. He just kept entertaining the kids as if nothing at all had happened between us.

We all sat together around the table: me, the kids, Peter, and Yvette. Halfway through the meal, Peter clapped his hands loudly. "Okay, guys, I have an announcement."

The three kids looked at him wide-eyed. Yvette, who in spite of herself had grown fond of him, listened carefully.

"I need to do some big-deal work. You remember the software I showed you?" The kids nodded. "Well, the people that paid me to do that want me to do a lot more work so I can help more children in schools." Tears pooled in Dylan's eyes. He understood before the little ones.

Peter noticed, but didn't stop to handle it. So unlike him, I thought. "So I need to be in California a lot."

Gracie began to understand. "For how long? A whole day?"

"Well, it's going to be a bit longer than that, but I do one hundred percent promise I will call you as soon as I know." Yvette sucked in air and put her hand to her mouth. A rainfall of tears dropped down Dylan's cheeks.

"Why is Dylan crying?" asked Gracie.

Now Peter's eyes welled up, too, and that put me over the top. I pulled my chair out and went into the kitchen. I leaned over the kitchen sink with my arms stiff, closing my eyes. I felt unbearably defeated.

As I returned to the hall, I remembered one particular scene last night in my bedroom on the floor before the fire. I lay with my back arched with a pillow over my eyes, slightly self-conscious of my intense pleasure. At one point, I peeked at his chest rising and falling above my eyes and soaked in the smooth motion of his body. If I continued to let the memory play, I would have walked into the wall.

The mournful scene around the breakfast table hadn't changed:

Michael oblivious, Yvette wiping crumbs off the table, Gracie putting her chubby fingers through her Barbie's hair, trying to get out the knots. I noticed her top lip curling, like it always did before she cried. Suddenly, Peter picked up Dylan in his arms, something he had never done because of Dylan's size and weight, and cradled him on his lap on the couch. He hugged him tight. Dylan, in a fetal position, sobbed like a baby. Peter rocked him back and forth.

"There, there, buddy. It's not going to be forever, just a little time away. Remember that airport control tower we built? It took four days, I think, and I didn't think you could be that patient. Hell, I couldn't wait any longer to be done. But you told me how Patience Is King. Remember that? Patience Is King? And that tower was so friggin' . . ."

Dylan just sobbed harder. He didn't give a damn about Lego towers. My son's heart was breaking in two.

"You can't just leave! It's not right. It's not fair!"

"Dylan, buddy, I'm not walking out on you."

"You are." Then between gagging sobs and breaths of air, "First Dad, now you, it's all the same!"

"Dylan, cut it out." He turned Dylan's cheek to face him directly while he cradled his head in his arms like an infant. "Cut it out, Dylan. It's not like your dad. Your dad's not leaving you. Your dad loves you to death. I love you to death."

"You're not even going to be in the same state!"

Now Gracie crawled over to Peter and snuggled against him. "Are you going to come back to see us?"

"Yes. Of course. Just not right now, cutie." She just sniffled and stared out in front of herself in a daze with her thumb in her mouth, not sure why Dylan was crying so hard and not able to comprehend how Peter could remove himself from her little life as she knew it.

An hour later, Peter had stuffed the last bag into the Expedition. I left the condo key on the front hall table, locked the door behind me, and walked out toward the car. Peter slipped in behind the wheel and I got into the passenger seat. The kids, in the back, were perfectly silent. I was jumpy. I started plotting. My ears popped as we snaked down the mountain toward the small local airport.

I hated that he was right, but I couldn't just cut-and-paste him into my life right now. Being on my own might just be okay. He was also right about my work; diving into the documentary with Erik would be healing and energizing. I needed work to channel my drive. And once I remembered that I'd have that soon again, I didn't feel so jumpy anymore.

We passed through security in silence. Peter walked us to the gate piggybacking a despondent Dylan, whose head lay on his shoulder. He said his good-byes to the children when we got to the gate and they moped forward with Yvette, who practically smothered Peter to death with her enormous breasts as she hugged him for the first time. Then she ushered the kids onto the plane.

Peter pulled me over to the wall away from the passengers and the commotion. "You are so damn beautiful. You are so strong and resilient. You are the most unbelievably sexual and sensual being I have ever been with. All the stumbling blocks that have fallen in your path in the past year will crumble beneath you; you're almost over them already. You are so much more together than when I first met you: so much smarter, so much more aware."

He walked with me to the glass doors. I looked out and saw the last of the passengers boarding the plane. He kissed me furiously. I wanted my body to melt into his. He'd done a pretty damn good job of handling us.

The airline lady made the final boarding call into her microphone. He pulled his head back. "You know everything's fine."

"I do?"

"Yeah. You do."

I pulled my body close. "I need you to be with me. You need to be with me."

"Yes. And I will." He held my face in his hands. "Just not now. I know this is a funny thing to say right now, because I should have told you last night, but I really do love you. I love you. Now go."

I needed another minute to get up my nerve. "I just need to know when we're going to be together."

He looked at the date on his watch and thought about that for a moment. "August eighteenth. Nine a.m. Belvedere Castle."

"How'd you come up with that?"

"Six months from this moment. Feels right."

Then I got up the nerve. "Look at me. I love you back. I should have told you in the park."

I yelled as the gate door closed, "You'll be there?"

"Of course I will."

And so he was.

Acknowledgments

I would like to thank my very patient husband, Rick Kimball, who has graciously allowed me to write a book about an insufferable husband, knowing people might wonder if that husband resembles my own. For the record: not in any shape, way, or manner (except when he shops with me). My love, passion, and devotion to my Rick are infinite and he knows that.

I am most indebted to my editor at The Dial Press—the inimitable Susan Kamil. As I reviewed her edits, I was reminded of a plastic surgeon's delicate and precise hand. To Nita Taublib and Irwyn Applebaum at Bantam Dell, my utmost gratitude for believing in this project. Barb Burg and Theresa Zoro have been instrumental in the publicity, and Noah Eaker pulled me down from the cliff numerous times.

Kim Witherspoon at Inkwell Management has been my most trusted advisor from the beginning. I am also indebted to Inkwell's David Forrer for his spot-on comments and to Alexis Hurley for her rights acumen. My stepfather Michael Carlisle, also a partner at Inkwell, introduced me to Kim and counseled me ever wisely.

I am very grateful to the people who gave so much of their time to help with pre-publication reads and factual points of reference, chief among them Peter Manning, with his hilarious take on life. Kyle Gibson guided me, Darren Walker and Heather Vincent answered my queries, and Josh Steiner and Neal Shapiro saved me at the eleventh hour. And without Ashley McDermott, I wouldn't even know what a manny was.

I am indebted to: Lynne Greenberg, Juju Chang, Eric Avram, Amy Rosenberg, Ali Wentworth, Andrea Wong, Electra Toub, Andrew Wylie, Jeffrey Leeds, Susannah Aaron and Gary Ginsberg, Jay and Alice Peterson, Peter Meryash, the very naughty Joel Schumacher, Barbara Walters, Susan Mercandetti, Harvey Weinstein and Jonathan Burnham for their early inspirations, Danielle Mattoon, Charles Fagan, Tom Watson, Martha Pomerantz, Alex and Eliza Bolen, Jen Gasperini, Jody Friedman, Brenda Breslauer, Wilkie McCoy Cook, Betsy West, Barbara Kantrowitz, Carole Radziwill, Holly Parmelee, Cynthia McFadden, Fareed and Paula Zakaria, Keith Meacham, Kathy O'Hearn, Suzanne Goodson, Jeff Greenfield, Paul Hurley, Jess Cagle, David and Sarah Holbrooke, Rob and Vanessa Enserro, Ann "wheels up" Coley, Anastasia Vournas and Bill Uhrig, Joe Caldwell's writing class at the 92nd St. Y, Alannah Weston, Daniel Romualdez, and Steven Shanstrom.

Thank you to those who assisted in the delivery room in various forms and reincarnations of this whole concept, including Tina Brown, Esther Newberg, Liz Smith, Pamela Gross, Plum Sykes, Lisa and Richard Plepler, Joe Armstong, Silvia Guadalupe, Andre Bishop, Lisa Frelinghuysen, Muffie Potter Aston, Jeanne Greenberg, Marie Brenner, Marc Burstein, Dr. Wilbert Sykes, Brooke Garber Neidich, Peggy Noonan, Mike Nichols, Diane Sawyer, Leslie Singer, Christine and Ella Studdiford, Bobby Harling, Jill Gordon, John Margaritis, Carolyn Strauss, Sarah Condon, Kathy Deveny, Susannah Meadows, Trent Gegax, David Patrick Columbia, Patrick McMullen, Trampas Matney at mimeo.com, Jane Rosenthal, Jennifer Maguire, Perri Peltz, Alice Tisch, Sloan Lindemann Barnett, Beverly Grayson, Digna King, Celeste Ferreira and of course David Enteles.

Those who helped in a professional manner, though friends as well, include my bosses at *Newsweek*, Mark Whitaker, Jon Meacham, and Alexis Gelber, who agreed to let me hold on to my job by my fingertips during the editing process. Bob Levine, Conrad Rippy, and Kim Schefler handled the legal aspects with grace.

My thanks to Michael Lynton, Doug Wick, Lucy Fisher, and Burr Steers for trusting this material to film.

And finally, I would never have been able to even consider writing a book without my loving, supportive, teasing, bundle of immediate family: my parents, Sally Peterson and Pete Peterson, my stepparents Joan Ganz Cooney and Michael Carlisle, my in-laws Anne and Dick Kimball, and Johnny, Jim and Patti, David and Wendy, Michael, and beloved Meredith, who will always be with us.

And last but not least, to Chloe, Jack and Eliza, who make me so very happy and so very proud. My favorite moment of every day is waking up and remembering I get to be their mom.

About the Author

HOLLY PETERSON spent a decade as an Emmy Award–winning producer at ABC News. Her work has been published in the *New York Times, Harper's Bazaar, Talk,* and *Newsweek,* where she is now a contributing editor. She lives in New York City with her family and is working on her next novel.